MW00332736

BENEATH THE KUDZU

BENEATH THE KUDZU

Stephanie G. Sewell

Email: info@sgsewell.com
www.sgsewell.com

Cover design by Lydia Morris
Photography © Lydia Sewell Photography

FIRST EDITION

ISBN 978-1-7378190-0-4 (eBook)
ISBN 978-1-7378190-1-1 (paperback)
ISBN 978-1-7378190-2-8 (hard cover)

Library of Congress Control Number: 2021917191

Printed in the United States of America

To my husband and children

You are adored.
Never stop pursuing your dreams.

# PROLOGUE

THROUGH NO SINS of the father, a universal curse falls upon the youngest of a much older, extended family—Death's constant promise of depleting one of kinsmen throughout a lifetime—sometimes expected and sometimes not.

No words resonate louder than when reared in the South where large families with their histories and mysteries are as implanted into the landscape as kudzu's veil inching its way across every holler and telephone pole along the roadside. In other words, they come with the territory.

Although some might debate its origins, a valued trait, not inherited through one's DNA but taught from the moment life's sweet oxygen enters into a baby's lungs, is understanding your family's history is just as important as your future existence on this earth. It is the foundation upon which each builds his or her life whether good or bad. Like every generation before, one has the luxury of learning from the family's past; thus, allowing each the ability to add or take away when shaping his or her own destiny for the next generation's lesson. Nothing shines truer than when living in a small community where anyone knows everyone and their relations. Mysteries, on the other hand, are another matter entirely.

On the rarest of occasions, do you find one so young haunted by both.

# CHAPTER 1

KNEELING IN THE darkness, a small voice whispered, "Make him stop... I promise to be good, God. Please just make him stop."

Screams echoed from her parents' bedroom and down the long corridor. She heard a slap against flesh, causing yet another painful cry to boom within innocent ears. A door slammed, trapping the agony and suffering inside as her mother's cries turned into muffled sobs.

Pools of water flowed from the corners of her stark blue eyes, and her stomach ached. She thought she might vomit at a moment's notice, yet from the shadows, she continued her heavenly plea.

"Please... it's my fault. It's all my fault..."

The louvre doors created a gated sanctuary from the evil lurking beyond their hinges. With the hall light flooding through wooden slats, her limited line of vision was weak at best. She scooted back into the closet, pulling down whatever clothes hanging above would camouflage and cover, but she needed more.

The quilt gifted on her ninth birthday and folded on the shelf overhead found her stretching on tiptoes to reach, pulling it down atop her. Covering herself, she scrunched into the corner and drew her knees tight against her chest as she hugged them beneath the multitude of fabrics.

Her body shook as if possessed by some unknown entity caused by her adrenaline's constant pumping of its drug. Its creation of ringing within her ears made it difficult to concentrate, much less hear with every beat of her heart's never-ending pounding. Within seconds, shallow breaths quickened as though trapped in the bottom of a sinking boat with the water rising too fast. She panicked thinking she would suffocate. Lifting the material, she sucked in the fresh air blowing against her face, expanding her lungs to capacity.

Her thoughts soon mimicked the hums of an eastern monk chanting a mantra. *Focus on her words… focus on her words… focus on her words.* Her hands clasped over her ears as she screamed in silence. *What words? What words!*

Recalled whispers encircled her mind.

"Stay quiet, honey, and do not let him find you. No matter what you hear or see, cover your ears or close your eyes, but above all, stay hidden. Do not forget."

She nodded in response.

The roof popped and creaked from the cooling of the evening's temperatures. She strained to hear, but their hushed voices left an eerie silence within the shadows. From her fleeting haven, she grew faint from the not knowing. She bit her lower lip. With her arms wrapped around herself, she rocked back and forth, attempting a song to comfort. She whimpered a shaky pitch only she could hear.

"Jesus loves me, this I know…"

Exhausted, her mind surrendered to the rhythm and her head dipped, drifting like a bobber floating across wrinkles of water until she nodded off to sleep.

Her body jerked itself awake to the clock's subtle tempo as it grew louder with each movement. Remembering where she was sitting, her body continued its trembling. She shook her head from side to side to remove the drowsiness from her mind.

Abandoned in the closet for hours, she needed to pee.

Standing as she clutched herself with both hands, she shifted her weight from one foot to the other in her weak attempt to battle the pressure mounting within. Her body could restrain no longer. Much to her horror, a warm, yellow stream pushed between her fingers and ran down her legs forming a puddle surrounding her feet and spreading beyond.

She fell to the floor grabbing the quilt to absorb as much liquid as possible, but the thick material would not reach beneath the doors. She shoved her hand inside a thin t-shirt. With extended fingers stretched beyond the closet's imaginary borders to remove the final traces, her bare knuckles scraped against the bottom of the door's rough edge, tearing her thin skin. She jerked back from the pain, making the weak doors rattle.

She heard familiar footsteps. Her father called out, "Katydid?"

Frightened, her lips moved, but no words escaped.

Sounds of scuffling and angry shouts poured into her room, but from where she did not know. A loud crash followed. Her mother screamed her father's name when a loud pop echoed. And then another and another. She held her breath and listened—nothing.

She flinched when a joyful yelp shattered the quietness.

"Oh, yeah! I showed you, didn't I? I surely did! Who's stupid now?"

Staring through the lower slats of the bifold door, she saw a pair of tennis shoes stop in the doorway of her bedroom as if waiting but vanished as fast as they had appeared.

The kitchen's screened door banged shut, causing her to jump yet again. She pulled the quilt to her chin, but the odor of urine made her wince. Although all was silent, her feet refused to run as though cast in concrete.

The screened door creaked open, followed by a loud grunt. Metal scraped across the linoleum floor with sounds of splashes hitting against hard and soft. He seemed cheerful humming a familiar tune, repeating the stanza over and over as though not remembering the song in its entirety.

A toxic odor filled the air causing her to cough. She slapped her mouth closed with both hands to muffle the unexpected noise. The shoes ran into her room and paused. Her eyes bulged as she drew in her breath and pushed to hold the air within her lungs as smoke continued to creep through the doorway.

All was lost. As if maniacal priests were exorcising demons from tortured souls, her lungs blasted the smoke from their chambers, creating a loud racket as she gasped for air.

The bi-fold doors jerked open, and he yanked her from the makeshift fortress. Her screams permeated the house as she scratched at his crazed eyes.

Grabbing a fist full of black hair, he slammed her head against the doorframe, and she dropped to the floor like a rag doll. He kicked with an insane rage as if controlled by the devil himself. Her small frame snapped backward with each blow, shattering her ribcage within.

Pain ricocheted like a rogue pinball bouncing throughout her body as he used his feet to roll her back into the closet. He grabbed a coat hanger before slamming the doors shut. She watched through her sobs as he struggled to wrap the wire around the tiny knobs locking her inside.

The blaze rolled across the ceiling causing bits to fall the same as if a meteor shower had pierced the heavens. She saw him glance back toward her prison as he reached the door, and then he paused. Resembling a cock crowing at dawn's first light, he bellowed with great fervor, "Old man, old man, oh, don't you cry for me!" He jumped into the hallway.

Something wet dripped from her face as her cough worsened. Despite the pain, self-preservation arose within. She screamed when she kicked at the doors, popping the handles from their tiny holes. The slightest movement caused her to shriek in agony as she pulled herself across the floor. Rolling over onto her back, she tried to shout, but only a raspy whisper revealed itself.

"Help me... please..."

Despite a final effort, her body inhaled the inescapable fumes. Her lungs collapsed as the smoke intensified, and her responses weakened as the unbearable pain escalated within her chest and head.

While flames leapt a never-ending dance of wild merriment, Death's determined grip continued to strangle as she gasped for air. A rafter engulfed in boiling redness disintegrated and struck what appeared to be the final blow. As her eyes closed, she watched his silhouette recede into a crimson haze, devouring him within the foggy abyss forever gone.

 CHAPTER 2

THE WARM KITCHEN offered solace in the nostalgia of the aromas of home. Catriona combed the pantry for the chamomile tea and placed the teapot atop the gas grate. With the turning of a knob, a quick hiss was released. A blue flame erupted into an explosive dance, flickering back and forth across the eye while heating the contents of whatever sat above.

She leaned back against the island and tightened the sash of her robe. Rubbing her face to remove the fuzzy memories floating through her sleep-deprived mind, her eyes landed on the number "30" written in bold print across the top of Cookie's kitchen calendar. There was a question mark scribbled next to it. She thought it odd since her birthday was not until the following summer. Knowing Cookie and Lillian, they would plan a large party, and it was never too early to start. The corner of her lips turned slightly upward but fell back into place. Her brow wrinkled as she stared blankly at the number—another reminder of nearly twenty years passing since the fire. She shuttered.

"No party."

Catriona was an oddity in her own right and a sharp contrast to the "everything goes" standards of today's sidewalk runway. Not that she knew, but she turned every curious eye in a room as did her birth mother before her. It was not so much her physicality grabbing one's attention, although that alone would have been enough. She appeared to have miraculously transported to the present from another era—a throw-back classic Hollywood icon, mimicking Audrey or Katharine Hepburn as her iconic fashion plate. Despite the once rambunctious spirit of her youth, she reflected a tranquil air of subtle graces rendering her likable, and although she never thought of herself as pretty, her humbleness simply added to her charm.

She had departed Charlottesville only yesterday, but not before dropping the top on the old convertible to take advantage of the cornflower blue sky. Sunshine strobed through the trees, and the brisk air released unaware the choking grips of an imaginary garden spider's tangled web constricting her body and soul. Her silk scarf trailed behind her as she cruised through the maze of roads northward. Adjusting her sunglasses as she glanced into the rearview mirror, an unexpected ease descended knowing the two people who loved her most were awaiting her arrival.

Back in the kitchen and waiting for the water to boil, she sat at the long table staring into the shadows of the dimly lit room. Her mind began playing its relentless tricks again. It deceived her into believing she was attending Sunday dinner surrounded by familiar faces of old and young alike.

"Who are you?" she asked aloud.

The German short-haired pointer dropped his head onto her lap.

She looked down at her intruder and glanced back up. The images faded as though a droplet of water had fallen into a quiet pool rippling over their reflections.

She looked down at his sweet face again.

"Well, hello, Patches." Taking his head into her hands, she spoke as if expecting a reply. "When did they allow you to stay in the house? Huh? I have no food. Besides, it might upset your momma if I give you anything."

The old dog cocked his head sideways listening to every word and did not seem to mind the absence of treats as she rubbed his face. She was thankful for his company. Staring into his sable mink eyes, she said, "If you could talk, I bet you would help me remember."

The shriek of the teakettle's whistle startled her back to the task at hand. When she stood to pour the tea, a long shadow stretched across the kitchen floor and landed at her feet. She glanced over and smiled.

He said, "There's the smile I remember the first time I saw you. Your mother held you in her lap while sitting on the porch swing at Grandmother Dunne's. Do you remember?"

"No, I can't say I do. Did I wake you or can you not sleep either?"

"Maybe a little of both. I was reading when I heard someone... I thought it might be you."

"Would you care for a cup of tea?"

"If you're pouring... sure." Scott dragged a barstool beneath him and placed his book on the island beside him. "Why are you awake at this ungodly hour, Katydid?"

She was not one to speak without quiet reservation, but with her father, Catriona withheld nothing. Gathering saucers from the cabinet, she hesitated before answering as if searching for the right words. "Are you prepared to hear me complain?"

"You never complain without good cause. What's wrong?"

"Things have turned upside down it seems. I mean business is good, but..." She paused.

"... but what?"

"I'm not sure I can explain, but I have detected a mental breakthrough."

"And what would that be?" He reached for a spoon unaffected by her words.

She clutched her robe at the neckline as if addressing a room of imaginary medical colleagues. "I've discovered an unknown pathway in experiencing a new euphoric psychosis. Me and me alone."

He frowned looking over his reading glasses. "What are you talking about?"

"It's true. Not euphoric, but I tremble for no reason. I have random thoughts going through my head, and then without warning, these unknown images appear taking me to another place and time. Sometimes, I'm unsure if they are people or places I've known or figments of my imagination."

"Well, that's not good."

"You think? My emotions are raw. I feel as though I'm wobbling on a tightrope strung across a bottomless pit." She dropped her eyes as she poured the liquid into their cups.

He remained silent.

She recognized his slow response time orchestrated from years of experience in dissecting truth from fiction benefited them both to quiet reaction—most of the time.

He reached for a cheese straw stirring his tea with the tip of his spoon. "You know I can still read you the same as any witness in a courtroom. Let's be honest… this negativity isn't like you."

"I'm always honest."

"You know what I mean."

Staring into her cup, she watched the teabag seep its flavors into a dark brew before pulling it from its liquid bath. She considered her therapist's words warning of her unhealthy drive toward perfectionism as they searched for a cause. She knew the irony of its pursuit had helped her to become successful in the business world—rare, considering her condition.

"Hello? Sweetheart? Where did you go?"

"I'm sorry." She stretched backward and readjusted her shoulders. "As I said… it's… it's weird. Distracted appears to be my norm. What did you ask again?"

"I didn't, but how is work?"

She continued to stare into the cup. "I'm unsure of myself for the first time in a while. Maybe it is the workload… self-inflicted, of course. Are you aware I'm considering opening another store or maybe even branching out full scale via the Internet?"

"No, but good for you. I didn't know business had grown to the point of…" He paused, then his tone changed. "Sweet girl, are you sleeping at all? The doctors have warned of over-indulgence."

She rubbed the lines forming across her forehead hoping to ease the tension. "I can't recall the last time I slept… well, a doctor's definition of sleep anyway. Tonight, I had another terrific nightmare. I remember none of the details, except I awoke shaking and could smell smoke. That's kind of weird… don't you think… and my headaches have returned too."

She had convinced herself the phantom smoke still lingered, taunting her of memories surely not her own.

"Not to hurt your feelings, darling, but you look exhausted and it appears you have lost more weight. Cookie will have something to say about it, I'm sure. Here… eat another cheese straw." He smiled when handing her the plate; however, they both watched her thin fingers take one.

"I know you're worried, but Dr. Stark convinced me to visit home for a few days or possibly a couple of weeks, if needed. A little downtime is all I need, and besides, I've missed you and Lillian."

"So, you think about us every once in a while, do you?"

"You know I do."

Scott chuckled. "I've looked forward to your visit from the moment you phoned."

"Me too."

"So… how's the car?"

She knew he would approach the subject sooner than later and laughed. "The car is great, and I drive her only when the weather is perfect. I thought to catch the train but decided the drive would be more fun. Besides, I thought you would want to give her a good going-over. Am I wrong?"

"No. I'll ask Mitch to give her a checkup in the next day or two."

"I guess I've inherited your intuition as well or is it a 'Scott McKenna' thing you do?"

"I think you've missed out on a viable law career. You should trust your instincts more often."

Catriona chuckled recognizing his smooth tactic of diverting the conversation. "Yes, sir, the car is perfect. Funny how many people compliment her… especially the color."

"Everyone loves a vintage Jaguar, honey. Do you tell them I chose the paint color to match your eyes?"

"No. I would never. Besides, it's your eye color too."

"Well, there is that. Isn't there?" He grinned from ear to ear. "I did a good job restoring her too."

"For the millionth time, you did, and thank you again for the present."

"You're welcome."

She frowned. "You don't seek out compliments. Are you okay?"

"I'm becoming sentimental and desperate in my old age."

"You are far from old or desperate. Besides, sixty is not old."

"I won't be sixty for a while. Am I sixty? Really? I don't feel sixty." His white teeth shown beneath his grin.

"We know how old you are. Still."

"Thank you, doll. Everything we do is for you... we could not be prouder. You have overcome hurdles... no... mountains to be where you are. You have this cool, but friendly demeanor, which everyone finds appealing. More importantly, you are a powerful force in your profession. You are self-motivated. You show excellence in your abilities, and all the while you are making consistent monetary gains. I would say that is something."

"Thank you." Her cheeks flushed red. "You are prejudiced."

"You bet I am with anything relating to you. It's true though. I wish I could go back when my days in D.C. weren't so tedious. Dealing with senators and representatives continuously gets old. Everyone is on a mission or fighting a noble cause. Albeit most of them are good. Makes me miss traveling with you even more collecting our car projects. I miss going with Lillian on her treks buying horses too."

"Maybe you should allow the other partners to take more responsibility."

Scott took a sip of tea. "Not ready to pass the gavel yet, darling. Maybe a new partner or two. While we're at it, I want to hear about this new venture with your business since you have my undivided attention. Who knows? Maybe together we can sort things to relieve some stress and help you fall back to sleep."

Catriona left no detail unturned. Plans were to open a series of stationery bookstores in the state, but still researching to find the most lucrative locations and not give up the intimacy of the small-to-medium-sized town ambiance she valued. She did not want to lose the one-on-one interaction confirming her successes—her most revered selling point professed by her company's customers who kept in contact once their business transactions were complete.

She confessed, in jest, if only her personal life could be as open to relationships, she might be happier. Catriona admitted in a defeatist fashion she never took time for herself nor had she enjoyed life of late as an incurable workaholic.

"Sweetheart, I think we both know trusting others on a more intimate basis is your most difficult hurdle… it's understandable."

Her lips flattened. "Deep down, I know several factors are causing my recent headaches and flashbacks. However, it's impossible to run away from my genetic inheritance, isn't it?" Her lips formed a grin. "Those McKennas with their 'Cats in the Cradle' work ethic."

"Touché."

They laughed in the comfort of knowing each other's idiosyncrasies were their own.

"Regardless, Katydid, I don't want you to worry about the legalities. I'll handle them. Promise you will do nothing without consulting my legal advice first. It's smart to have a fresh pair of eyes overlooking the fine print of any lease or purchase."

She half-frowned. "Okay."

"I'll ask Gloria at the office to research the logistics of any real estate deal; that is if you want me in your business. It's up to you."

"Thank you. Fresh eyes are a good idea." She sighed, then laughed under her breath. "I guess I'll need to file away another tidbit of wisdom learned from you. Right?"

"If you say so, darling… if you say so." Scott relaxed into the back of the barstool. "If you are visiting for a while, then who's minding the storefront?"

"Tia Douglass. You met her a few years ago."

Scott stared without blinking.

"Good grief, Scott. Tia visited here when we were in school. Don't you remember? I never bring people home with me. You know, maybe you are growing old." She grinned wide.

"You need to remember it's been a year or two since you were in college."

"I won't argue that point." Catriona thought back to school. Lost in a memory of long ago, she took another sip of tea.

"Please continue," he said.

"What?"

"Tia?"

"Oh. Sorry. If you must know, we ran into each other months ago. As soon as we talked, I knew she would be an integral part of my company and I hired her on the spot."

"Wow… that's not like you. How is she doing?"

"She's the best decision I've made in the past year. Tia tackles problems or welcomes new experiences head-on, and she is brilliant. Her business perspective differs from mine, yet we are the culmination of an old soul and a contemporary one. Everyone loves her outgoing personality too. She loves anything high-tech and modern, which is the opposite of me. So, in layperson's terms, I guess we complement each other… sort of like… like… peanut butter and jelly or biscuits and gravy." She bent over her cup and slapped the counter as she laughed.

"Please tell me you are not planning to be a comedienne. It isn't your strongest attribute, sweetheart." His eyes danced when he handed her another cheese straw.

"I cannot wait for you and Lillian to become reacquainted with her. Tia is teaching me to laugh more. I am trying. Besides, this move has been a long time coming. Maybe you should follow my lead."

"In what way?"

"Before the possibility of losing my mind with the overwhelming success of trying to keep up, I realized I should share more of my everyday operations. I promoted her to store manager within her second month. Her advertising knowledge of understanding marketing across multiple social media platforms is incredible and is another reason my business growth has exploded over the past few months. She is more than qualified to oversee the business and the staff in my absence. Besides… I trust her." She turned away from him, then sighed. "At the same time, it has become oxymoronic. As the growth rate has increased, so have my stress levels."

"Do you need more staff?"

"I've hired two additional full-time press operators bringing the total staff to fourteen including three part-time college students. My printing business has increased to where we've moved the commercial division upstairs and it's booming." She stopped talking and her eyes widened. "Oh, my word... I have divisions now."

"You've confused me. Are you operating out of the second floor?"

"No... and yes. The main level remains retail... rare books and what-not, but now, it includes a bridal section and it's gorgeous. I needed privacy for my consults, so I took a few warehouse windows purchased at a demolition auction, and I built a separate room on the main level. They look fabulous and original to the building. I might have pictures on my phone." She shuffled through her phone's gallery. "Here... see? I threw in a few overstuffed chairs for my clients and completed the workspace with my drawing board, invitation samples, and studio supplies. Although it's detached, it's not isolated, and I can see the entire shop from my little piece of heaven. I could pinch myself. You and Lillian should visit, and the best part is... pardon the cliché... I'm making money hand over fist while doing what I love."

"I'll be the first to admit when I'm wrong because I had my doubts when you wanted to purchase that old two-story. I thought it was too big."

"It's amazing. Now you can understand why I needed this break, and it could not have come at a better time. I miss the stables and the horses, and anything reminding me of fall. You know how much I love being outdoors with the leaves changing and Virginia Cavalier football too. I haven't been to a home game this season."

"Welcome to the world of being a small business owner."

"I guess so. There is never enough time. Do you want a refill?" She walked to the stove to pour another cup.

"No darling, I'm fine. Maybe the stress is on the downswing. Taking time off will be good for you without carrying the full weight of the shop. How is Charlottesville?"

"Grace Meade will always be home, but I connect with the intimacy of the rolling hillsides there. I love Monticello with its sophisticated simple design and vision. I use it as my escape from reality. Believe it or not, I enjoy volunteering with tours when time permits, especially with the recent historical discoveries, and for me, the impressive President's gardens still housing the same plants from over two hundred and fifty years ago."

"We slipped down a rabbit hole, didn't we?"

She sat at the island again. "I caught that… but I do miss the gardens. Again, my personal time is non-existent. It's still incomprehensible how this trip pulled together. It was as if all the stars and planets in the heavens aligned themselves and directed me home to Grace Meade."

"Please tell me you don't believe in that hullabaloo nonsense."

"I don't, but there are too many coincidences all occurring at the same time. First, the Cavaliers are away for at least three more weekends, so the store will be a little quieter without all the Hoos' fans pouring in, and there are my brides. Their orders are complete or in process, and it's still too early for the holiday craziness. Oh, and there's Grace Meade's annual horse auction scheduled next week and the International Gold Cup Races next month. But most of all, you and Lillian are both available. Rather good odds if you ask me."

"Sounds like it. Maybe we should drive to Glenwood Park in the morning and place a few bets." Another grin crossed his face.

"Don't think I don't see you trying to be funny too; however, I'm serious. After handing over a few last-minute instructions to Tia, I left without a hitch. Her instructions for me are to disregard phone calls, texts, or emails, and should a problem present itself she cannot handle, she'll reach me on the landline. To be transparent, I'm thankful I don't have to worry about it for a while."

"What about your cell phone?"

Catriona's cheeks grew red as she grinned. "Didn't you tell me that Grandmother Dunne used to say, 'An idle mind is the devil's workshop?' I thought if I read through a few emails or phone messages, I could fall back to sleep. My phone is my lifeline to everything and…" She paused.

"… and what?"

"Oh, my word. I sound pathetic." Catriona's shoulders dropped as she reached for her teacup.

"Put the phone away. You could hand it over and I'll put it in the top drawer of my desk."

"Here. It's yours." She slid it across the counter.

"You need to relax. What about a ride in the morning? I'll call Declan, and besides, Lillian has purchased a new filly I want you to ride."

Catriona glanced up from her cup. "Who is Declan and what's happened to Samuel? Is he all right?"

"Samuel retired. Did you know he is eighty-five? His retirement was long overdue."

"I should have called home more often. I'm not sure what to say."

"Me neither. He continues to pop in at the stables, but on his terms. There is no reason to worry; he's alive and kicking and still sharp-witted as ever. We invited him to stay at Grace Meade as this has been his home for nearly forty years. Besides, this place wouldn't be the same without him. However, he surprised us by making one big change. He moved to the cottage near the springhouse in the upper eighty. Said it made him feel independent and not in the way."

"He could never be in the way."

"Try telling him… stubborn old mule." Scott took a long sip from his cup.

"Oh, that is funny coming from you. It's the Irish in him, and we all inherited that trait, didn't we?"

They both laughed.

Scott said, "I guess we did, and so you're aware, we hired a new stable master to take his place. His name is Declan O'Connell, Samuel's grandson."

"His grandson?"

"Yes, believe it or not. When we started the hiring process, Samuel threw in Declan's name amongst several others. He's been working in Kentucky for the past several years, so Lillian placed a few calls."

"Is he any good?"

"He is. He came with outstanding recommendations from a few reputable buyers in Louisville, and I like him. There is a steadiness about him, and for someone his age, a great understanding and knowledge of the horses. He's a natural with the animals, but people too. You won't believe this, but Lillian calls him her 'godsend.'"

"You're kidding. Where have I been while the world continued turning at home? Well, now that I'm up to date... yes, I'll try your filly. Will you ride with me?"

"I can, but must we invite Lillian?"

"Yes!" Catriona laughed, startling Patches beneath her feet. She corrected herself. "I wouldn't want it any other way." The tension began to release from her shoulders as she stretched her neck to each side. "So far this conversation has been only about me. Why are you up at this hour?" Propping her elbow up on the island, she yawned as she dropped her chin against her fist.

Scott yawned in unison as he rubbed his eyes. "A big case has been building for months. It involves the coal mining industry, but I don't want to talk about it or I won't sleep at all. I'll save it for another day. Besides, your tea is doing the trick. Come on, Patches. Let's go to bed. Love you, darling."

"Love you too. I'll clean up."

He hugged her before leaving the room.

As she cleared the dishes, a frightened young woman's reflection stared back from the kitchen sink window.

"He's right. You don't look well. Who's the funny one now?"

Only hours before, her day's journey had ended at the large wrought-iron gates engraved with the property's crest. As she buzzed inside, her spirits lifted as the car followed the winding lane between the stone walls leading to the historic nineteenth-century home. Without realizing it, she prayed silently. *God, thank you. I'm not alone.*

She recalled the words of her now gone mother.

My sweet Katydid, always be thankful for what the good Lord has given you.

She whispered, "I am, Momma. I am."

CHAPTER 3

FOLLOWING A QUICK shower, Catriona slipped into a robe and wrapped her hair into a towel as she walked to the window. The morning sun enlightened the room. Frost glistened on the pane and she blew her warm breath against the cold glass forming its own frozen mist. She traced her initials, but wiped them away with the tip of the towel and smiled. She noticed her car was missing.

"Thank you, Scott," she whispered. "Forever looking out for me."

She turned back into the bedroom and caught a glimpse of the scars covering her upper thighs as their reflection glared back from the full-length mirror.

"Not you, though. Always there to remind me of death, aren't you?" She traced the rippled ridges with her fingers. "What did Dr. Stark say?"

"*Stay positive. You've got this.*"

She folded her robe across the quilt chest and chose her favorite riding ensemble—a white silk blouse, red woolen vest, gray breeches, and polished, tall field boots. Pulling her hair into a ponytail, she chose not to wear make-up but applied blush and lipstick. Samuel remarked once that even a barn looked better with a little red paint. She smacked her lips together, then tied a plaid silk scarf into an ascot and squeezed the ends behind her blouse's neckline before adding the single pearl stud earrings. She heard Lillian's voice resounding within her mind.

"*Darling, pearls go with everything,*" and Lillian was rarely wrong.

Catriona allowed herself a smile when glancing into the mirror at her finished image. Grabbing her tweed jacket with its black velvet lapels and matching leather gloves, she descended the stairs as if in school again, running late for competition.

Entering the kitchen, Cookie embraced her in a big bear hug. Angelica "Cookie" Johnson, a sweet, robust woman, treated Catriona as a princess. She reminded Catriona of her Grandmother Dunne—the sweetest woman who had ever lived. Cookie continued her questioning as if she were a bee buzzing around newly bloomed flowers, knowing the answers before Catriona could reply.

"So, how long has it been? Christmas last? You need to move back home! There is more than enough room in this big old house. I promise we will leave you alone. Let me take a good look at you. You've lost weight and your face is much too thin. Are you sleeping?"

"Yes, ma'am, I'm sleeping."

"I don't believe you."

"Okay, maybe not."

Cookie hugged her again. "Don't you worry none, hon. It's good to have you home. We've missed you. You can plan on putting weight on those bones while you're here and not so far away. Your parents are in the breakfast room waiting. Hurry… I've fixed your favorites and take a mimosa with you."

"Yes, ma'am."

Although Catriona had long been an adult, her parents expected good manners when addressing anyone, including the estate's employees—most of whom were more her own family than if they were blood-related—a trait ingrained into the McKennas from every generation before.

Already a self-made man, Scott came into more money when he married his true love, Miss Lillian Rose Pruett, an Alexandria Southern belle from a prestigious, aristocrat family. Although a refined, beautiful woman owning a gentle and loving nature, she could be a force one did not cross if caught being untruthful or unfair. Others had compared her to their native Live Oak—graceful, yet strong. Others in the business considered her one of the finest horsewomen and breeders in Virginia, Kentucky, and most of the Northeast. She knew her business frontward and backward and everywhere in between. The equestrian world trusted her expertise and admired her strong work ethic, but other social circles held her in high esteem as well.

Lillian's generous spirit reached throughout the Virginia Commonwealth with her charitable efforts and genuine kind-heartedness. She and Scott met at a political gala held at the Kennedy Center where she later invited him to her family's much-anticipated horse sale conducted each fall at Grace Meade. They complemented one another in every way a couple could.

"Good morning." Catriona leaned in, kissing Lillian and Scott one-by-one on the cheek, and placed her riding jacket on an empty chair. Patches lay at Scott's feet waiting in anticipation of a morsel dropping from the table, but not before Lillian's two Pembroke Welsh corgis, Samson and Delilah, approached with wagging tails and begging eyes.

Touching Catriona's earlobe, Lillian smiled. "Well, don't you look dapper this morning? Don't feed those two, they know better. Did you sleep well?"

"Thank you… I won't… and yes, I did."

"Really?" Lillian asked.

Recognizing her mother's infamous I-can-see-into-your-soul glance when she knew someone was not telling the complete truth, she said, "No, ma'am, I did not sleep well. Scott and I had a cup of tea in the wee hours of the morning. By the way, Scott, thank you for moving my car."

"My pleasure. I moved it to the carriage house out of the way of the trailers."

Lillian frowned. "Scott, love, why didn't you wake me?"

"Hey, don't look at me. Our conversation was nothing… a case of catching up. Right, Katydid?"

"Yes, sir." She took a sip of the citrus concoction from the champagne flute.

Cookie walked in carrying a platter of her infamous eggs Benedict. With English muffins used as the base, her poached eggs sat atop mouthwatering crab cakes drizzled in a creamy hollandaise sauce. As for sides, she served the end-of-season sliced tomatoes, oven-roasted asparagus sprinkled in olive oil, and a bowl of raspberries and blueberries topped with a dollop of cream. She finished the meal by serving Catriona's favorite Earl Grey breakfast tea, along with Scott and Lillian's standard of black coffee.

"Goodness, Cookie. You have outdone yourself." Scott smiled ear-to-ear. "Our girl coming home is always a special occasion."

"Yes, it is," she replied.

Catriona grinned. "You are too good to me. Thank you for remembering."

"I love you too, Katydid. Now eat. You need it."

Unexpectedly, Scott asked if he could say grace and Lillian nodded. Catriona lowered her food-filled fork from her lips as this was not their normal practice, except maybe at Easter, Thanksgiving, or Christmas.

"Dearest Father. Thank you for bringing Katydid home. You have blessed us beyond measure, and we are thankful. Thank you for the food Cookie has prepared. And Father, if it's your will, provide the peace and answers Katydid needs to revitalize her mind and body while here. Allow us to be ever mindful of your grace. In Jesus's most holy name. Amen."

"Amen!" Lillian and Catriona spoke in unison with Cookie chiming in a half-second later from the kitchen. The three looked at each other and laughed.

Lillian said, "We've made a few changes around here. Did Scott tell you about the new filly?"

"Yes, he did."

"Well, you need to ride her this morning. Scott, are you going to the stables with Katydid?"

"I am."

"And did he tell you about Declan?"

"Yes, ma'am."

"Well, I guess we have nothing further to discuss, do we?"

Catriona touched her mother's sleeve. "Don't be jealous. We have plenty of time to talk."

"I'm never jealous, darling. I blame my behavior on missing you so much."

Catriona laughed. "Thank you."

Scott's eyebrows burrowed deep as he glanced at his daughter. "Katydid, I'm unsure if or when another chance will present itself, so I'm just going to dive in. May I ask you a question?"

"I guess." She frowned, knowing from the tone of his voice a dissertation was forthcoming. She watched Lillian's eyes dart toward him.

"Not now, love."

"Lillian, she needs to hear this."

Catriona watched as he laid his fork on his plate. He sat with shoulders back against his chair.

"Since you touched on the subject last night, don't you think it's time to find a new doctor?"

She became irritated at once. "Do we have to do this again? Why a new doctor?"

"You have been seeing Dr. Stark far too long. Money has never been an issue for us, but I become more frustrated with each invoice I receive as there appears to be no improvement... just money gone."

"Scott, don't be so vulgar. Money is not a topic for the breakfast table." Lillian laid her spoon on the saucer in front of her.

"Please allow me to finish."

Lillian raised her eyebrows. "As long as you promise to keep the conversation short."

"I promise. Now, Katydid, we don't give a hoot about the costs... you know that, and I would give everything I own to help you as long as you are receiving help. Please know I'm not suggesting you take over any financial obligations."

"Then why bring it up? I can take care of myself."

"That was not our agreement. And for mercy's sake, money is not the purpose of this conversation. You are! It's obvious you're not better. He is your fourth psychiatrist, and it's been three years since you became his patient. Is he helping you progress at this point?"

Catriona paused for what seemed a lifetime. The all too familiar argument had grown old. One could blame the blind-sided attack, but an unnatural calm through clinched teeth caused her to wait before answering. With a tone of dryness that could choke a thirsty horse in the middle of a cold stream, her frustration grew as she answered.

"Wow. No one can ever accuse you of not being direct, can they?"

Scott interrupted. "Catriona…"

"No. My turn to speak." Her eyes darkened. "I'm not sure what has prompted this critique of my doctor when you know so little of him. This is not the place nor the hour. I didn't realize you were burdened to the point where we could not discuss this at another time. How did you think I would react?" She tossed her napkin onto the table.

"I'm not sure, and that is why I'm asking. I guess my timing is off, but I want you to take time to consider your physical and mental well-being while you're here and not interrupted with job responsibilities. You know me… if something appears askew, then I attack it head-on. Sweetheart, you do not have more weight to lose. I should have called before now with my concerns, but the timing has never seemed right."

"Why are you attacking me?"

"I'm worried and frustrated!"

"Well, it may surprise you, but guess what? I'm frustrated too. Do you not trust me to decide who my doctor should be? Goodness, I am almost thirty and no longer the little girl who needs your protection or money. You do not attend my sessions, so how would you know what I need?"

Leaning forward on his elbows, he replied, "We trust you, yet sometimes a fresh perspective can be helpful too. Have you become complacent about not wanting positive change? It frightens me because you continue to shut out everyone in your personal life. You admitted you are on the edge of falling, and we have been here before, haven't we?"

"Too bad."

Lillian interrupted. "Okay. Let's stop before someone says something they regret."

"Lillian, darling, do not think I am condescending. You and I have discussed this too many times and now is the time to complete it." He looked back at his daughter. "My sweet girl, we are proud of you, yet I don't want you to look back with regrets of living a life alone… regardless of how financially successful you may be. Success has become your sole focus. Having a partner to share all aspects of your life is important. It might be the answer to helping you discover who you are. There's so much more to life than work. I cannot bear the thought of you remaining in this state of influx and continuing a life alone. I can't. Of all the people I've known, you deserve the greatest happiness life has to offer."

Lillian said, "It's true. Your happiness and well-being are all we care about."

Catriona sighed and looked down at Patches. "I know, but it's hard to believe we are discussing this again and for the four hundredth time. This is exactly why I do not visit more often."

Scott continued. "Please do not close yourself off. I know I'm talking to my own stubborn reflection, but I want you to consider it. With Lillian working on the hospital board, she has learned of a new psychiatric team. Haven't you, sweetheart?"

"I have. Their practice has received rave reviews with techniques helping their patients in a positive, progressive rate of recovery. Each person is different… we are aware. We want you to consider it, and even more so now that we know you're experiencing difficulties again."

"I should not have confessed my problems. I wasn't expecting this harsh reaction from either of you."

"Don't do that," Scott said.

Catriona fired back. "Do what?"

"Turn your frustrations on us."

"You have turned your frustrations on me. What's the difference? Not playing the victim here, but truly you cannot believe I do not want to remember anything about my biological parents other than what you have told me. I'm terrified I will never recall my past life leaving this large gaping hole that only remembering can fill." Catriona's eyes shimmered with tears.

Scott sat back in his chair. Everyone knew her tears were his downfall. "Honey, I'm sorry. I'm treating you as if you're a hostile witness. Of course, you want to remember. I apologize to you both. I have been consumed with worry, and you are here to escape your everyday stresses. As parents, we are allowed to worry, aren't we?" He reached across the table and placed his hand on hers. "Consider it. No more lectures, I promise. I am insensitive and coming across somewhat passive-aggressive too."

She removed her hand from his. "Passive-aggressive? Try just plain aggressive."

Total silence loomed again.

Lillian said, "Sweetheart, we want what is best for you. Nothing more."

Catriona released a heavier sigh. "I guess I'll think about it; however, I don't want to discuss it any further today."

Lillian turned toward Scott. "It's settled then. No need to spoil a good breakfast. Besides… this cannot be good for our digestive systems. Right, love?"

Scott took Catriona's hand again. "I'm sorry."

She squeezed his fingers. "I know you're an excellent attorney, but you need to turn down the courtroom drama at home."

Lillian said, "Hear! Hear!"

Scott chuckled.

Catriona grinned. "I accept your apology, and I promise to think about your suggestions, but next time, let's discuss this before dinner or with a warning at least. That is if it's okay with you?"

"You have my word."

Lillian said, "Mine too, darling. We are behaving as though we have no manners whatsoever. Enough is enough."

"I love being home, regardless." Catriona returned her napkin to her lap.

Scott waved his fork in the air, encircling the room. "You can move back at a moment's notice as Grace Meade will be yours one day."

"Stop."

"You can be so morbid sometimes." Lillian shook her head at her husband. "We would love for you to move home, Katydid; however, not until you are ready. First things first. Let's eat our breakfast without further arguments. Okay?"

They both nodded.

Catriona ate in silence. She knew he was right. However, finding a new doctor was terrifying enough, much less becoming involved with someone long-term—an impossibility. She had accepted that fate long ago.

Turning heads was easy; however, turning them away became her norm—her self-protection. Most men were manipulated by a pretty face, and it irritated her. She was no more in control of her physical person than the male species proved regarding his visual compass. Pushing men in the opposite direction helped maintain her focus on her business goals. She did keep one secret to herself—the true reason for her physical difficulties of late—the deep-seated fear of discovering the truth. Who would she become once the memories buried in the dark corners of her soul become unearthed for all to see? At least for the moment, her mind's secrets were its to keep.

Lillian said, "My darlings, the morning is wasting. You two go ahead to the stables, and I'll join you in a bit. I have a phone call to make regarding the auction. Are we good, Katydid?"

"Of course, we are. Speaking of auctions, I'm planning to attend an estate auction while I'm here."

"Oh? Well, that sounds interesting. Are you planning to buy something or is it for fun?"

"Both. I signed up to receive emails from a private management firm out of Alexandria. They are known for liquidating on-site estate sales. I received their advertisement and online catalog regarding an auction this coming weekend, and in their words, 'in the heart of Virginia Hunt Country.' It's a few short miles from here. The ad also stated the items were owned by a prominent, pre-Civil War family, and you know how I couldn't resist such a temptation. I have been looking for a specific piece of furniture to place at the shop's entrance, and they have a writing desk I think will work. I know you are crazy busy, but would you like to join me?"

"Me?" Lillian asked.

"Yes, you."

Lillian's eyes danced. "What a fun idea. Better yet, let's make a day or two of it. I am unaware of any guests arriving this weekend. Do you know of anyone, darling?" She looked at Scott.

"I know of no one."

Lillian's smile grew wider. "Declan has a handle on everything, and it has been a while since I've taken any time for myself. If you purchase the desk, we will ship it here, freeing us wherever we wish to go. What do you say?"

Catriona beamed. "I say, 'Yes!' It's been too long since I've had a little spontaneity in my life too. You can count me in."

"It's decided then. I'll make the arrangements. You enjoy your ride this morning. I have asked Cookie to prepare a late lunch on the terrace around one o'clock, and don't dare be late. You know how she is about everyone eating on time."

Scott said, "Well, girls, do you want to take the convertible? If you do, then I'll make sure it's checked today."

Catriona nodded with her mouth full. "That would be perfect. Thank you, and I hope you do not feel left out."

His laughter filled the room. "Don't be ridiculous. I have business in the city and will stay in town if you're not here. To be frank, this plan works better with my schedule."

Lillian left to complete her tasks. They thanked Cookie again, and Catriona threw on her blazer and gloves as she and Scott headed outside with Patches following at his heels.

It was good to be home.

# CHAPTER 4

Her Childhood Hometown

FORTY OR FIFTY years ago, give or take a few, Sageville stood as a modest, one-red-light community in the northern part of the county. Sheltered in a lush deep-green valley with rolling hills, quiet farms, and a small river meandering between two mountains of the Appalachians, its borders lay at the headwaters of the Tennessee River watershed in Southwest Virginia.

In its heyday, it housed one of the largest coal mines in the Buchanan and Pocahontas coalfields wandering through Russell, Buchanan, and Tazewell counties. The once-bustling township accommodated the only live theatre in their remote part of the state, and the mining of coal had brought other booming businesses into the mountainous region. The coal trains and trucks hauling high-quality coal outranking its northern coal counterparts used to run in and out of town for more than one hundred years.

Death was as common as rain when working in the dangerous occupation of going underground to dig coal for one's income. No one thought about moving elsewhere or changing careers as generation after generation was born into it, especially in an area where jobs were scarce and one could support their family while digging for the black, deadly ore.

As a child, Catriona adored her large extended family. She recognized them in her own identity through their love and the stories of the rural community of Sageville where she lived. Like most in her town, her family taught her reverence for God, love of family, respect for others, and loyalty to country.

Reared as a child of the Bible Belt, they also taught Catriona from the scriptures to honor her mother and father, and with that commandment came a promise from God, "… that one's days will be long upon the earth."

Darwin's theory contradicted in arguing the one who is fittest proves to compete, survive and reproduce. He proposed later as further proof, animal and human emotional expressions are learned and culturally transmitted as well.

She was a culmination of both understandings.

Her family lived on the upper side of town in a white house built by the previous titleholder who owned the town's hardware store. The property included a couple of acres where their neighbors envied her father's meticulous garden planted next to the barn. Their small farm included a mule, a few chickens, several hunting beagles, two ponies, and an ever-expanding colony of rabbits.

Catriona lived a simple life. She and her cousins entertained themselves for hours in a playhouse made from an outbuilding near the barn. Each spring, they anxiously awaited the appearance of the first butterfly proclaiming the ground's temperatures warm enough for shoeless feet. Her father frequently provided her with a tin can and hoe to dig for worms in the dark, rich garden's soil before heading to the river to cut their bamboo rods growing alongside the river's edge. After tying a string and meaty hook to the pole, she dipped the line into the slow-paced movement of water as strider bugs skated on tiny feet across the wet surface, feasting on larvae floating below.

When early summer reached their mountains, her mother would cut a piece of thread so Catriona could tie June bugs to a string. She would hold tight as the bugs darted back and forth, mimicking ace fighter pilots dive-bombing the enemy below. They would fly away to lay their eggs, soon to hatch into white grubs with their voracious appetites wreaking havoc on the local gardens and lawns.

Running through patches of clover, she dodged honeybees as their wings carried them from bud to bud, filling their stomachs with nectar to be carried back to the square box hives sitting along the fence row.

Soon the cool shades of evening caused lightning bugs to take flight, rising beneath the tree limbs above. Catriona would catch and place them in a jar with holes punched into the lid by a heavy hammer and a rusty nail.

When the night's moon shone as bright as midday, hide-n-seek became the game of choice, making for more fun before retiring to the mosquito net-covered beds on their summer porch. Staying cool by wearing one of her father's thin tees, her legs, pink from the day's sunlight, stretched beneath the lightweight sheets. Listening to the song of crickets and tree frogs crying for rain, their common lullabies lulled her to sleep. There was nothing to fear other than the mines in the quiet town where life was idyllic for any young child.

Later, the world changed for their hometown when a massive fire caused by a methane explosion destroyed Mine No. 11. Men were dead. The flames engulfed the mining camp and part of the town, leaving nothing but blackened ashes and ruin in its tracks. Everyone knew at least one name immortalized on the large marble stone in the town's center square.

With the coal industry regulators making expensive demands and the town forever changed, their small mine closed for all of eternity. Once where the town's primary source of livelihood prospered, now lingered fragments of charred, caved-in buildings and vacated steel and crossties. Most sorrowful were the repetitive, ghostly images floating across old men's memories of a by-gone era, and the kudzu-covered, dirt roads whispering of where coal mines once thrived.

Money had become scarce in Sageville. Just because one was poor, did not mean one was dishonest. An occasional loaf of bread or pie taken from a window to feed one's family maybe, but murder? Never.

CHAPTER 5

THE MCKENNAS LIVED near The Plains in the northern horse country of Virginia at the Grace Meade homestead, a large equestrian estate Lillian inherited upon her late father's death—a historic property with over three hundred and fifty acres of prime real estate. Built following the Civil War, the house remained glorious with its gray and ivory stone façade. Its arched trusses welcomed guests as they entered the magnificent foyer, transporting them to a European country house with its high beams looming overhead. There were seven bedrooms, multiple fireplaces, and large rooms for entertaining many guests at one time. Along with the pool and manicured gardens, there were the carriage house and a few cottages and tenant houses—home to many of their employees. Past the gardens and gracing the landscape below, the storage barns sat alongside the large stable, donning traditional gabled rooftops. The expansive facility contained eighty stalls, tack room, and spaces for washing, healthcare, the farrier, trainers and riders, the business office, and the indoor and outdoor riding arenas, including more than enough pasture for riding and grazing, which made for happier horses. Lillian ran the thriving full livery and breeding business with a reputation for meeting most equestrian needs.

Besides the daily in-and-out of horse trailers and vehicles arriving and leaving, there were always houseguests present—business associates regarding the horses or a few dignitaries from Washington to discuss private matters with Scott. One would arrive as another was leaving.

Walking to the stables after Cookie's breakfast, Catriona breathed in the brisk morning air as the warm sun beamed onto her face. Dew glistened from the spider webs. Most of the summer flowers had faded to nonexistent, except for a few morning glories and honeysuckle running along the fence row here and there. The earth's fragrance filled the senses as fall made its full dissension upon the land, lifting the aroma of decaying leaves and soft moss beneath her feet as they moved through the flower garden next to the orchard.

"Oh, my goodness. Look at the apples and pears this year. Do you think Cookie would make apple butter and pear preserves while I'm here?"

Scott made his way beneath their branches. "I'm sure she will... you need only ask. I remember when you and Henry planted them."

"They make me happy." She looked upward through the branches and whispered, "What a weird thought... but they do make me happy."

He picked a few apples from the ground. Examining for yellow jackets before placing them in his pocket, Scott headed toward the stables. Several horses greeted them at the fence, and he released a deep laugh as their heads bobbled back and forth, nickering for his attention.

"Now, now... who will be first?"

Catriona watched as he patted each muzzle. She admired him for his toughness and his ability to be gentle. She thought him handsome with his salt and pepper hair. Wrapping her arm inside his elbow, she laid her head on his shoulder. He started to speak when someone interrupted.

"Excuse me... Scott?"

"Yes?" Scott turned. "Oh, good morning, Declan. I'm sorry we're running a little late."

"No problem, sir."

"Catriona, allow me to introduce you to the man in charge of our barn equine management and sales. This is Mr. Declan O'Connell. Declan, this is my daughter, Ms. Catriona Harrington-McKenna."

"It's nice to meet you, Mr. O'Connell." She held out her hand and he shook it. Smiling up at his face, she noticed his kind eyes.

"The pleasure is mine, but please, call me Declan. Would you like to meet your horse for today's ride?"

"Yes, I would." Her eyes danced the same as her father's.

Declan walked into the stable, and as he passed, he strummed his fingers down the back of the calico, Miss Peaches, who was sunning herself on the stone wall perched out of reach of the dogs. It surprised her to find Declan younger than she expected. He appeared to be in his mid-thirties. He was tall, but there was an odd familiarity to his gait.

Catriona held onto Scott's arm as they walked in silence. He pulled her close. Catriona knew it was his way of reassuring her, ever mindful of providing his protection.

The barn was her fortress with the aroma of fresh hay, the soft snorting of horses, and the warm scent of leather bridles and saddles. As they crossed the threshold, Catriona confessed, "I love this old place. I love how the horses' hoofs and the sound of my boots against the brick pavers echo off the rafters... it's one of my favorites places in the world."

"Mine too, honey. Mine too."

Samson and Delilah bounced into the stable along with Lillian, who had appeared at the side door. "Have you shown her?"

"Not yet." Declan stepped inside the stall.

"What are you up to, Lillian?" Catriona asked.

Declan pulled the filly into full view. "Miss McKenna, it is with great honor I introduce the newest member of the family and your new horse. Meet 'Katydid's Black Irish Angel.' We call her 'Angel' for short."

Catriona stepped back and looked at the dark beauty paused in front of her. "Is she really mine?" Her voice cracked.

"Yes!" Scott and Lillian chimed together.

Lillian said, "Since Chief passed away last year, we have searched for a horse. Declan has spent the last three months looking for the perfect girl. We were thinking she would be a Christmas present, but now that you're here, we couldn't wait to show you. Well... what do you think?"

"She... is... beautiful." She looked at Declan with an inquisitive eye. "Mr. O'Connell... I'm sorry. I mean, Declan. I wasn't expecting to be impressed today. You know a splendid horse when you see one. Thank you... thank you so much!" She laughed as the tears fell from her cheeks.

His face reddened. "You're welcome."

"Why 'Black Irish'?" she asked.

Scott said, "In the old country, our ancestors would have called us 'Black Irish' because of our physical features and not because of the family's poor economic status."

"What physical features?"

"I thought you knew this."

She shook her head.

"Well, darling, you and I share the same physical traits inherited through the Gallagher-Dunne bloodline. We do not have what others consider a typical Irish appearance because we are unique with our icy-blue eyes and pale skin that never tans." He laughed. "And like Angel, we both have black-blue hair shining like the coal buried deep in the mountains back home."

"Black Irish. I like it."

Declan said, "Angel is a Friesian... one of Europe's oldest breeds and a warhorse dating back centuries from the Netherlands. She is a true black with a coat shimmering like onyx. As you can see, there are no areas of reddish or brownish hair to be found."

"She is lovely. You have certainly done your homework. Should I know more?" Catriona wiped the tears from her face.

"Well, the breed is known for their exceptional long lines, heavy curly mane, long tail, and feathering on the lower legs. Her chest is muscular too. She's magnificent with a height of almost seventeen hands."

"She is a tall girl, isn't she? There are no words... I am in shock... truly." She hugged Scott and Lillian and then hugged Declan, causing them all to laugh.

Declan said, "Miss McKenna, you know what you're doing so I'll leave you to it."

"Thank you, again, Declan. She is incredible, and please, call me Catriona."

"Yes, ma'am. After your ride, bring her through the eastern doors and I'll have her brushed down. Will you excuse me?" He turned and walked toward the other end of the stable.

Catriona called after him, "Thank you!"

He glanced back, then tapping the brim of his suede high country hat, he nodded his head and grinned.

Without warning, everything turned black. Her eyes burned with pain, and she sensed herself falling as she stumbled sideways. Her mind plummeted backward to a small white house where she sat on the porch swing and recalled her father's face and voice.

"Daddy, may I go?"

"Not this time, darlin'."

"So, where are you goin'?"

He walked across the porch toward the old truck. He answered with a question with no expectation of a reply. "Are you writin' a book?"

Not wanting to be left behind, she answered, "I am."

"Well, honey..."

"Yes, sir?"

"...you can just leave this chapter out." He laughed hard, but then reprimanded her. "And you know better. There's no need to be gettin' too big for your britches, little missy. Never talk back."

She stared at him in disbelief as he pulled from the driveway. He glanced back, raised his hand, and tapped the brim of his cap. Nodding his head out of the pickup's window, he grinned as if sugar dripped from his lips. Some would have accredited him a varmint by his words, but she knew his true heart and couldn't help but laugh.

"Catriona? Catriona! Sweetheart, are you all right?" Scott braced her from hitting the brick pavers.

"Yes... yes, I'm fine. Of course, I'm fine."

She noticed Scott and Lillian's worried glances.

Catriona regained control as she reached out to touch Angel's neck. "Will you look at this gorgeous horse? How could I not stumble? She is fantastic. Can't I be a little overwhelmed without you two worrying so much? I only tripped… it's no big deal."

Hoping to dodge more questions, Catriona straightened herself as she stepped to the opposite side of the horse. She shuttered, afraid to tell anyone about the returning blackouts.

The horse snorted. Her attention diverted back to Angel. "What a beautiful horse."

Scott said, "She may be large and powerful, but has the sweetest disposition and will join up with you untethered… she's smart."

Catriona replied, "I'm dumbfounded. Let's take her for a spin. Shall we?" She laughed aloud with delight.

"Are you sure you're up to it?" Lillian frowned.

"Of course, I am. I'm fine… I promise. You are such the worrier, and I love you for it."

Catriona led Angel outside, and Scott helped place her foot into the stirrup as she mounted the incredible creature. "Please hurry. She is ready and so am I."

Declan brought out Scott's thoroughbred stallion, Maximillian.

Catriona looked away so as not to catch Declan's eye.

Lillian chatted on about something, but Catriona no longer listened. Scott mounted. Soon, they were in a soft trot through the gate and into the pasture beyond.

Catriona heard Lillian call after them, "Remember to be back before one."

Both turned and waved, watching her walk back toward the house with all three dogs in tow.

***

Declan returned to his office. He knew of Catriona through his grandfather and thought her an illusion Samuel had created. She had been a constant topic of conversation since the old man had learned of her impending arrival. Surprised, she was not the young girl he assumed her to be. Instead, she proved to be everything Samuel had described and more. His cheeks flushed red again.

Declan spoke aloud. "Come on, old boy. What's wrong with you? I know it's been a while since you've dated but still." He could hear her laughter ringing in his ears.

Samuel walked into his office. "What are you running on about?"

"Nothing, Grandpops. Nothing." Declan's cheeks reflected a deep, ruddy complexion.

"Did she see the horse?"

"Yes, sir, she did. Her words were 'incredible' and 'beautiful.'"

"If you can believe it, Catriona is sweeter than she is beautiful... don't you think?"

"I guess... I just met her." Declan remembered the happy tears cascading down her face and he smiled.

"Well, she is," he said. "I love that girl. Did I ever tell you how she came to live at Grace Meade?"

"No, sir, you did not."

"Well, where do I begin?" Samuel sat in the chair opposite his grandson, and Declan knew he would be sitting for a while.

"Let's see... oh, I know. According to Lillian and unknown to Catriona until much later, Scott and her birth mother... who, by the way, was Scott's aunt... were nearer in age and were close companions when they were kids. Everyone assumed they were cousins instead of aunt and nephew. Catriona's momma was much younger than the rest of her large family. When Catriona was born, her parents asked Scott to prepare their wills listing Scott as her guardian should anything happen to them, and he confessed to me no one had made him happier. He wanted to be a father more than anything, and he had the means to take care of her too."

"Wow. That's a hefty responsibility."

"Yes, it is, but it's what good families do. I remember when the police called the night of her parents' deaths. Scott instructed them to air-lift her to Inova Fairfax Hospital in Falls Church. She was unconscious when they pulled her from the burning house, and she had multiple first, second, and third-degree burns on her upper thighs, along with third-degree burns covering her torso. Not only that, but she had multiple broken ribs and internal damage to boot. She also received a hard blow to her skull after a large beam fell."

Declan's eyes darted away, and he looked down at the papers in front of him.

"Are you listening, Grandson?"

"Of course, I am. You have shocked me, that's all. I can't imagine anything worse than someone suffering from severe burns. You might have prepared me a little."

"I guess I should have, but how could I?"

"I am not sure, but does this story get worse?"

"It does... much worse."

Declan grimaced. "Okay."

"She is a walking miracle, but do you know what I think?"

"No, sir. I wouldn't attempt to know what you are thinking." Declan's sheepish grin received no reaction.

"She lost her memory."

"Are you serious?"

"I am. She can't remember anything about the fire and very little before."

"That's terrible." Declan's brows turned in toward his nose.

"I think the shock of what happened to her is why she can't remember. Her hospital stays lasted for more than seven months, and the hyperbaric oxygen chamber treatments helped heal her wounds well enough so she could mend at home."

Declan pictured a young girl suffering through intense pain and sympathy swelled within him. He swallowed hard. "How old was she?"

"Bless her heart, only nine, and it gets worse. While she was in the hospital, she couldn't attend her parents' funeral services. My sweet girl has had a tough run... you can be sure of it. Lillian never left Catriona's side, but still carried on the estate business from that baby's hospital room. By the way, I may be a bit prejudiced here, but I'll say it a thousand times and will fight anyone who says otherwise, but there is no one finer than Lillian Rose McKenna."

"She is a wonderful boss."

"Both she and Scott are good people and they love that girl. Once the hospital stays ended, Catriona carried the one thing left from her childhood… a quilt scorched in the fire. But do you know what that sweet Lillian did?"

Declan grinned at his grandfather's love for Lillian—maybe the daughter he never had. "What, Grandpops?"

"That sweet lady had an expert quilter make repairs, and Catriona has it on display in her bedroom to this day."

"That's all she had left?"

"Yep. It was a sad sight to behold, but Lillian has made sure Catriona has never wanted for anything since. Lillian is one of God's angels sent to live on earth for the rest of us."

"Seven months? Incredible."

"Catriona is damaged not only physically but also mentally. You see… her emotional health is fragmented. No one understands to what extent her mental state balances between knowing and forgetting. Poor thing. Lillian says that Catriona changed into this fragile shell of who she had once been… no longer the carefree girl they had known when visiting their family back in southern Virginia. They provided her with the best reconstructive surgeon in the state and her psychiatric care has been superb. They have spared no expenses to help with her losses. Who truly knows what damage happens within the minds of children when such tragedy strikes?"

"You would never realize their pain, would you? They appear to be the ideal, happy family."

"Every family, no matter how happy they may look from the outside, has their secrets and heartaches. You never know what battles they have faced or are facing. You can either be happy or wallow in self-pity, and the McKennas are not the wallowing kind… regardless of their money."

"Has she recovered?"

"To look at her, you would think so. She pretends to be strong, but she is not wholly healed, and her wounds were not mere scratches. She has plenty of scars on the outside she hides pretty well, but if you could see what's on the inside, that's where you would see the actual damage. Once her nightmares subsided a few months later, Catriona came out of her shell. The horses helped her most. She was in the stables every day. Scott told me her headaches and memory issues remain because of what her physicians believe to be her body's protection in suppressing the details of what happened. She may never recover completely. No one saw or heard anything."

"Nothing?"

"Nope. There was a big firework display that night and some thought firecrackers or some falling debris might've caused the fire. Makes sense, doesn't it? According to the newspapers and what little information Cookie discovered, they stated 'a lack of mitigating circumstances resulting in an undetermined cause' in the fire investigator's report. They declared it an open-and-shut case. Catriona told me she doesn't recall much of her homeplace either… bless her heart. The saddest part is she doesn't remember most of her family members. Scott told me they were all dead or have moved on and out of touch."

"How terrible for her."

"Oh, and to make matters worse, she lost both of her maternal grandparents just a couple of months before the fire. It's funny how that works… large families go their separate ways after the grandparents pass away. Too much loss in too little time. You can understand how easy it would be for an adult to shut themselves off from the world after such a tragedy, much less a kid and her fragile emotions."

Declan frowned. "What a nightmare. How do you live through something so horrible and not come out on the other side a different person?"

"Exactly, and so we're clear, Catriona's grandparents were Scott's grandparents too. Not only is Scott her eldest first cousin, but she is his adopted daughter. So… to say he is overprotective is an understatement."

"I can imagine."

"Scott is a good man. Although he may not have realized, he needed a child to balance his life. Lillian could never carry full-term, and left a terrible hole; that is until they rescued our sweet darling after a tragedy no child should have survived. She does no wrong in Scott's eyes—his weakness, you could say, and Lillian could not love her more than if she were her birth mother. Not until Catriona understood they loved her beyond a promise kept, did she agree to the adoption. In memory of her parents, her last name remains, but they added theirs as well; she is the first and only of the Harrington-McKenna bloodline."

"I had wondered why Scott introduced her the way he did."

"Who cares that it happened almost two decades ago? You cannot put time on grief knowing neither has allowed themselves to grieve properly. Scott has never taken her back to the area either. I think he's afraid of what it will do to her and maybe to him too. There are secrets there, I can feel it in my bones, and Catriona holds the missing pieces to the puzzle."

"Twenty years ago, and she still can't remember?"

"No. I wish she could at least remember more of her momma and daddy. All I can say is my baby girl has been through hell and back, and no one…" his voice cracked as he shook his head, "… and I mean no one had better hurt her again. She's a wounded soldier. I don't care if she is a grown woman. Every time I look at her precious face, I see the hurt girl I came to love and still do, as much as anyone, and I dare anyone to say different. I will say my prayer life has improved since she came into our lives. God has His arms around her… of that, I'm certain." His sigh weighed heavily over them. "And there you have it. Now, you know as much as I do."

"Wow, it's hard to comprehend so much trauma. I didn't know."

"Well, why would you? No one ever talks about it," Samuel said.

"You would never realize she has suffered so much. There is a sweetness about her." Declan shuffled the papers on his desk. "Is she married?"

"No one will ever be good enough for her if you ask me. But no, she isn't. There never has been a fella, but that's none of our business. Is it, Grandson?"

"If you say so, Grandpops." Declan laughed because his grandfather knew everyone's business.

"Behave yourself. C'mon. Let's grab a cup of coffee in town."

"Give me a second." Declan called out, "Hey, Brad?"

"Yes, sir?"

"I'm not sure how long we'll be. I need to buy feed and will grab lunch while we are out. Please watch for Scott and Catriona to return before one o'clock if I'm not back before then."

"Yes, sir."

"Ready, Grandpops? Let's go."

Declan grabbed his hat and keys. He was uncomfortable with Samuel's continued knowing glances. As he walked toward his truck, Declan thought how incredible she was—unafraid to show genuine emotion, yet a total stranger and proven survivor. He was awestruck. Although his grandfather was growing older and his memory and eyesight were not as acute as they once were, he was right about one thing—Catriona McKenna was beautiful—breathtakingly beautiful.

 CHAPTER 6

"WOULD YOU JUST look at the trees? Aren't they spectacular?"

Driving amidst the falling leaves, Catriona chuckled under her breath as Lillian chattered on about every hill and curve as their car meandered through the countryside. She felt a contentment missing for months.

"Katydid, honey, are you planning to buy this desk today?"

"I hope so. If not, I'm sure there will be another calling my name."

As she pulled into the estate's entrance, she hoped to be the first to review the furniture before the sale, but many dealers were already in pursuit.

Lillian removed her sunglasses. "Oh my, they have stables. I think I have been here as a child with my father. I'm sure of it. Who did you say lived here?"

"I didn't. They will tell us once the auction begins."

Moving into a vacant spot and grabbing their belongings and folding chairs, the two walked toward the large lawn leading to the front façade of the beautiful home where the auctioneer's lectern stood facing his audience.

"Look, darling. Susannah is here… what fun! I forgot to tell you she has opened an antique shop in Alexandria and doing well. I'm happy for her, but talking to some people is like trying to fold a fitted sheet."

"What in heaven's name does that mean?" Catriona frowned at her mother.

"You know. It's a case of no matter how hard you try, the conversation never turns out just right, and if you're not careful, it could end up a little messy."

"I cannot believe you. She is a sweet person."

"Yes, she is genuine too, and one of my oldest friends, but she can be a little gossipy. I'm not being mean. I know what I can and cannot say around her... most of the time. As I said, she is a fitted sheet."

"Lillian Rose, I'm surprised. Maybe, even a little disappointed. I have never known you to be hypocritical or mean, especially about Susannah Moore."

"No, darling. I'm sure she hides things from me too. No one tells everything they know... at least, we don't. It's an unspoken code between old friends, but I guard my words with anything regarding you and Scott."

Lillian called over, "Hey, Susannah! How are you, honey?"

"I'm fine, Lillian. Oh! Well, hello, Catriona. What a pleasant surprise. You look as if you have stepped out of a dream, honey, and I'm so jealous."

Catriona blushed. "Thank you. You are sweet to notice."

Susannah grinned. "Sweetheart, you are the total package. I can never tell if it's your makeup or clothing or simply you because you never fail to look radiant. You need to bottle those secrets and share them with the rest of us. Forget the paper business, honey. You could make a fortune and I would be your first customer." She laughed at herself. "What are you girls doing here today?"

"Oh, Catriona is looking at a few things. We thought we would spend a couple of days enjoying the weather and doing nothing too stressful. We are enjoying some much-needed girl time," Lillian said.

Catriona removed the scarf from her neck. "It's good to see you again, Susannah. I hate to be rude, but excuse me for a moment while I register with the auction company."

"Yes, yes... the registration table is over by the front steps." Susannah waved her hand in the direction Catriona should go.

"Thank you." She slipped away, leaving both ladies clamoring on about nothing.

Although she was not an antique expert per se, Catriona saw beauty in most items. She appreciated the old and unique, especially those pieces reflecting an artisan's attention to detail while revealing their expertise and fine quality of their time-earned skills. She never missed an opportunity to add to her shop's inventory.

After registering with the auction house, they handed Catriona a printed card with the number '312' printed in large letters to do her bidding. She made her way to the mixed array of items scattered around the lawn.

She loved the graceful, yet understated, furniture displayed from the eighteenth and nineteenth centuries. As she was studying a petite dresser, she glanced over and saw the small secretary sitting next to a sofa on the sidewalk. The carved front was exquisite and in mint condition. Cautious not to show too much interest, she sauntered over and opened a small drawer behind the upper cabinet doors still containing the original hand-blown glass. The dovetail joints were original and showed the desk's true age. She was deep in thought when a voice interrupted.

"Do you like the desk?"

Startled, she turned. "Well, yes. Yes, I do," she snapped. Her eyes widened. "Oh, my word. Please excuse my abruptness, you caught me off-guard. I'm embarrassed."

Standing behind her was an attractive man with sparkling dark brown eyes peering beneath an ivy-style suede riding hat as if he knew a secret waiting to be told. He had a warm smile showing through the short stubble of his well-groomed beard.

"Don't be. I should be the one apologizing. Allow me to introduce myself. My name is Peter Tramwell."

"Catriona McKenna. It is my pleasure. Are you interested in the desk?"

"Not really. Are you a dealer?"

Careful not to give herself away, she said, "No, I'm here of my own volition. Just looking. Besides, it's a fun way to spend a beautiful fall day. Don't you think? And you? Are you a dealer?"

"Not quite. However, I appreciate things of beauty with intriguing histories," he said, directing the comment her way.

Unnoticed, she said, "Me too. So… what are you looking to buy today?"

"Oh, I don't know." He looked around at the objects on the lawn. "Did you see the cello by the front door?"

"No, I didn't. Do you play?"

"A little, but nothing to get excited about, and when you think about it, who has the patience to sit for lesson after lesson? However, I believe the piece is old and played by one of the owner's ancestors. In all seriousness and to quote you, if I may, this is 'a fun way to spend a beautiful fall day' or at least it is now."

Cocking her head to one side, Catriona paused and stared. "Are you mocking me, sir?"

His gaze appeared even softer. "Not at all."

"So, you are comfortable speaking to strangers and making them feel ill-at-ease? Is that it?" Her tone was stern trying not to show her slight interest in him as well.

"Again, not at all. Far from it as a matter-of-fact; I'm taking too much pleasure in teasing you, I'm afraid. You must accept my apology."

"Must I?" She smiled.

"To be truthful, this is my desk or I should say one of my grandmother's desks. It sat in her bedroom for as long as I can remember, and I'm here out of courtesy to my family overseeing the business of the day."

"Oh. This is your family's property. We were wondering who owned this beautiful place." She hesitated, then with a sadness falling across her face, she said, "I'm sorry. How difficult this must be, watching everything your family owns auctioned away."

He shifted his feet while pulling back his wool blazer with one hand, resting it at the waist of his tweed trousers. "Well… yes and no. In fact, they have sent most of the heirloom pieces with an emotional attachment to family members. These are the items remaining, but they are still high-quality and desirable. I must admit I dreaded today, but this experience has not been as bad as I'd imagined. Thank you for recognizing the connection… and your kind words."

"You are welcome."

An announcement came from the direction of the stage's lectern. "Please, everyone, find your seat as the bidding will begin in five minutes."

"Please excuse me. It was nice meeting you, Peter."

"You too, Miss McKenna. May I escort you back to your seat?"

"No. I can find it, but thank you."

"I hope you enjoy your fall day."

"Thank you, I will." She smiled, then looked toward Lillian, but returned her gaze to meet his. "I must go."

"Of course."

When she approached her chair, Lillian handed her a glass of the complimentary Chardonnay.

"Who is that fine-looking man, Katydid? A friend of yours?"

"No, precious lady, I regret to inform you he is not. We just met. This is his family's property… the Tramwells. Does the name sound familiar?" She took a long sip of wine.

"Tramwell? Tramwell. Hmm… I must call Samuel. He will know, but I swear it's familiar. I wonder if they have sold their horses or gear. I need to ask Declan to get in touch with the auction house for contact numbers or maybe I'll talk to your new, handsome friend? How about it?"

"You are something else sometimes. He was making small talk. Nothing more." Catriona laughed as she rolled her eyes.

Lillian patted Catriona's arm. "If we don't leave here with a desk, maybe we can package that dream of a man instead."

Both laughed. Lillian could always say something to lighten the mood. It was one of many traits Catriona admired about her.

Most of the day had been filled with excitement and laughter as each item was purchased. The auctioneer told fascinating stories about each, and Catriona, engrossed in his words, allowed her mind to escape to another era. Toward the end of the day, they presented her piece next for auction. They carried the desk to the front of the makeshift stage.

"The next item is number sixteen fifty-two on page ninety-three of your brochure. It is a Regency-style mahogany writing desk, circa seventeen fifty to seventeen sixty, with a beautiful inlay and rope pattern carved on the cabinet doors and the drawers below. Originating from the United Kingdom, it traveled by sea to the new world where a bright future awaited the Tramwell family. The owners have in their possession many letters of correspondence written from this beautiful desk between the Lady Tramwell and the First Lady following the Revolutionary War. No restorations have been made as it is in pristine condition. We will begin the bidding at two hundred and fifty dollars. Two hundred and fifty dollars? Do I hear two hundred and fifty dollars?"

The numbers rolled over the lips of the auctioneer as the numbers climbed from two hundred and fifty dollars to three and four hundred and then reached five. Not to appear too anxious, Catriona raised her number at five hundred dollars.

"Five hundred dollars to number three twelve!" the auctioneer bellowed.

She listened as the bid climbed to five hundred and fifty, then six hundred, six fifty and seven hundred dollars. Before the bidding became too frenzied, Catriona spoke, "One thousand dollars."

"You heard the little lady. One thousand dollars to number three twelve!"

Everyone quieted, turning to look to where she was sitting.

"Do I hear twelve hundred? Twelve hundred dollars?"

An older gentleman sitting across from her winked in her direction and said, "I'll go twelve hundred dollars. Why not?"

The auctioneer continued, "There you have it, folks; number sixty-two challenging at twelve hundred dollars! Do I hear thirteen? Thirteen hundred?"

"Two thousand dollars!" Catriona called out. One could hear only the harsh chirping of a mockingbird in a distant tree.

"I have a bid of two thousand dollars from the lady in blue. Do I have a bid for twenty-one hundred? Twenty-one hundred? Sir? Last time at twenty-one hundred dollars. No? Sold! To number three twelve for an absolute steal at two thousand dollars!" The auctioneer slammed his gavel as it resonated across the lawn. "Congratulations!"

There was soft applause as most attendees had left because of the late hour, and it thrilled Catriona to have purchased the desk for such a great price.

"Well, darling, it looks like the desk is yours. Good for you."

"Yes, ma'am, it is. It was meant to be, and it's gorgeous. I don't think I could be happier. I thought it would pull in at least seven thousand or more. Fortunate for me that most bidders have left for the day. You have always said patience is the key to getting what you want, right?"

"You are so right, darling. Go get your prize."

Catriona made her way to the cashier's table and made payment.

"I'm glad she will live with you."

The voice came from behind her. She turned and Peter was smiling.

Catriona could not contain her smile. "Well, thank you. I'm thrilled to have the pleasure of owning such a beautiful piece of history. I mean... well, I guess it's your history."

He laughed. "I guess it is. Do you need help taking it to your van or truck or how were you planning to take it home?"

"Oh, I'm having it shipped to my home. It's not too far away, but I thank you for the offer."

"No problem."

"Catriona, aren't you going to introduce me?" Lillian appeared without notice.

"Lillian, this is Peter Tramwell, a family member of this estate. Peter, please allow me to introduce you to one of my priceless treasures, my mother, Mrs. Lillian Rose McKenna."

Lillian held out her hand to shake his. "It is my pleasure, Mr. Tramwell. What a fun day this has been. Thank you for allowing us to come to your family's homestead instead of some stuffy old auction house. It has been the perfect fall day of complete leisure, superb wine, and great conversation."

Peter took her hand. "You are most welcome, Mrs. McKenna... wait. Lillian McKenna? Are you by chance related to Scott McKenna?"

"Yes, I am. Scott is my husband... now, how do you know him?" she asked, still holding his hand.

"I have the pleasure of working with him on a case, and I believe I recall him mentioning his wife, Lillian. I can't believe I didn't make the connection. You are in the horse business, right?"

"Yes, I am. I cannot believe this, Catriona. Can you?"

"No, I can't." She glanced away as they continued to talk. She couldn't believe that out of all the men in the world, he would know Scott.

"So, I'm assuming you are an attorney too?" Lillian grinned.

"Yes, I am." He laughed.

"Well, what a small world this is... right, Catriona?" Both Peter and Lillian looked in her direction. Lillian released his hand.

"Yes, ma'am, it is." She almost blushed while shaking her head.

"Mr. Tramwell, we're staying at 'The One-Eared Rabbit Inn' near Old Town Alexandria over the next couple of days. Would you like to join the two of us, as well as Scott, for dinner on Monday evening?"

Catriona interrupted with great hesitation. "Oh, Lillian, I'm sure Scott is too busy. Besides, we're not sure of his schedule, are we?" Her eyes pleaded with Lillian to not know Scott's appointments.

"It's not a problem, honey. Scott and I have already discussed dinner, and he wants to take you to a new restaurant in the city. Well, Mr. Peter Tramwell, of the pre-Civil War Tramwell family, what do you say? Would you want to join our small party for dinner?"

He laughed. "It would be my honor." Taking out his wallet, he presented her with his business card. "You can leave a message at this number with the place and time... that is, if it's okay with you, Miss McKenna?" He directed his question toward Catriona.

It was obvious he had sensed her reluctance. Appearing more awkward and in an attempt to not appear rude, she said, "Of course,

Peter. You can tell me more about my new desk. Lillian is in control of my calendar over the next few days, but please, call me Catriona."

Lillian said, "Great. It's a date. You can expect to hear from us."

"I'm glad this is not a permanent goodbye. Have a safe journey, Mrs. McKenna and Catriona." He reached to shake her hand, and when she reciprocated, he squeezed her fingers as his eyes held a steady gaze. Surprised, she pulled away without Lillian's notice.

"Goodbye, Peter."

"Yes. Goodbye, Peter," Lillian echoed.

Catriona turned in disbelief as she started toward the car. Her mother's actions proved she was determined to make a match, and it caused her to laugh. "You are something else. Truly, you are."

"Well, honey, not only did you win your beautiful desk, but it's not every day we find a good-looking attorney who comes along with it. He's a dandy."

"You are impossible."

"And aren't I the lucky duck? I have his business card and will have Declan call about the items in those stables. I scored a 'two for the price of one!'"

Lillian continued to laugh as Susannah came from behind her van interrupting them. "Girls, I would love for you to see my shop while in Old Town Alexandria. Come by and I'll give you a tour."

"That would be fun. What about tomorrow?" Lillian asked. "We would love to see your shop in person."

"Alrighty then, I'll count on seeing you there, and, if possible, maybe we could grab a late Sunday brunch too."

"Even better," Lillian cooed.

"Great. Be careful, ladies, and try to stay out of trouble."

Catriona replied, "I would say under normal circumstances, there would be no cause for concern. However, when you travel with Lillian, you never know what might happen."

All continued laughing as the ladies departed each to their own cars. After Catriona fastened her seat belt, panic arose the same as floodwaters cresting the banks of a river. She found it hard to swallow and her palms were sweating.

"Lillian…"

"Yes, doll?"

"I think…" Her mouth turned dry, making it difficult to speak. "I think… what I need is one-on-one time with you… I… I enjoy spontaneity but without the stress." She swallowed hard. "No schedule… just you."

Lillian noticed Catriona's hands were shaking as she pulled on her driving gloves.

"Of course, darling. Susannah will not mind us changing our plans. You have nothing to worry about."

"Thank you… that would help."

"Are you okay?"

"Yes… just tired. Before we go any further… and, in all sincerity… thank you for today; it was an enjoyable break."

"Oh, darling girl, there is no place I would rather be. You're my top priority always."

"I love you." Catriona's voice cracked as she spoke.

"Well, honey, I love you too. Are you sure you are okay to drive?" Lillian's eyebrows turned downward.

"Yes, ma'am. I believe my body is winding down from work overload."

"Let's blame the Chardonnay, shall we?" Lillian smiled and patted her on the arm.

"I only had one glass or I wouldn't be driving."

"Of course, darling. I was just trying to… oh, never mind. All is good?"

"Yes, ma'am. All is good."

As Catriona drove through the pasture's parking lot, she noticed in her rearview mirror Peter watching her. He waved. She waved backward over her head; however, Lillian turned and waved as well.

"Interesting."

"Lillian, stop. He is only being nice."

"If you say so, sweetie. I do wish you would consider dating someone, and he appears to be a good someone."

Catriona's lips curled into a half-smile as she shook her head. "Let it go, Lillian. Between you and Scott, I would be an old married woman before the new year. I wish you could be happy with me just doing me."

"Oh, fiddlesticks, Katydid. No one is happy just 'doing me' forever. Give love a chance. It might surprise you where it leads."

"We'll see." She pulled her car onto the two-lane highway and headed toward Alexandria for the evening.

***

Peter looked to where she had been sitting. Catriona had rattled him. He watched as she outbid her opposition with such ease and quick confidence—a cat waiting to pick the perfect time to pounce. She was worthy of pursuit, and not only intelligent but thoughtful without an ulterior motive—not to mention beautiful. Different from any woman he had met of late around the D.C. area, he wanted to know more. Most women within his limited social circle were seeking as much attention as possible from powerful men in high places. He noticed her sweater matched her penetrating eyes and her mannerisms were subtle and elegant. He envied Scott. Lillian had the same subtle, confident air as Catriona, and her smile had been warm and welcoming. He thought her eyes shone like one who had been happy most of her life.

When the convertible passed, he saw Catriona's reflection in the rearview mirror and waved. They both had returned the gesture. After watching the car disappear, Peter made his way to the auctioneer's table to inquire about the desk and shipping arrangements. He requested they move the piece of furniture into the house.

"I'll take care of all shipping regarding the desk."

"Of course, Mr. Tramwell. Do we need to contact the buyer?"

"No, I will. Thank you."

"Do you want to ship the cello or are you delivering it as well?"

"No, the cello is mine. You can ship it to my home in Georgetown. Here is the address. Bill it to the estate sale's proceedings."

"Yes, sir."

He searched his phone's contact list and dialed a number.

"Good afternoon. I want to place a rush flower order to be delivered this evening. The card is to read… 'Here's to a beautiful fall day.'"

# CHAPTER 7

"I LOVE OLD Town Alexandria. Don't you?" Lillian was in rare form as they strolled together.

Catriona replied, "You know I do. You don't have to sell this town to me. It is intoxicating when I think of the men and women who have walked these streets."

"You should have gone into politics or majored in history, darling. Oh, look. Here we are."

Lillian and Catriona entered the large double doors and stepped inside.

Susannah greeted them at the door. "Hey, girls! I've been looking forward to your visit. Come in… come in."

Lillian said, "Susannah, you have outdone yourself. This must be one of the prettiest antique galleries I have seen."

"Well, thank you, sweet friend. I've tried to make it beautiful. I have worked hard to provide quality pieces covering a variety of price ranges and incomes for all of my customers because I do not want to exclude anyone. However, I must confess, the overall design is not original. I copied the layout from a shop I toured in the French Quarter of New Orleans and gathered a few ideas from another store in Atlanta, yet we're here in Virginia, so I think I'm not a complete copycat, would you say?" The telephone's ring interrupted her. "Oh, excuse me. I'm here alone. Jocelyn has stepped out to run an errand for me. Make yourselves at home, and I'll be with you in a moment."

"Take your time, Susannah. No need to rush."

Catriona meandered through the aisles when spying a framed newspaper article regarding the closing of a mine in southern Virginia. She saw the name "Sageville" and started to read.

Lillian called out, "Sweetheart, did you see this desk?"

Catriona joined her. "It's pretty, but I'm happy with the one I have."

"Only making sure." Lillian could be childlike with her mind darting back and forth. "Oh my, look at these large urns. Do you think they would work in my garden?"

Before she could reply, Susannah called to them from the mezzanine level. "Ladies, come upstairs. I want to show you something."

Catriona and Lillian met her at the top of the landing. Displayed before them were a Louis XVI table and its two accompanying chairs.

"Aren't they to die for? I'm so proud of them. They shipped in from Paris last week, and on the phone was a potential buyer. He's coming by this afternoon, so I'm afraid I cannot join you for brunch. I hate to cancel like this, but I hope you understand."

"It's no problem. We needed to change our plans too, so this may have worked for the best." Lillian smiled at Catriona.

"Maybe we could have dinner tomorrow night instead?" Suzannah asked.

"I'm sorry but we have plans for the rest of our trip. We are meeting Scott and one of his colleagues for dinner."

"I hate this as I never see you. Next time then. Promise me," Susannah pleaded.

"I promise."

"Good. Well, ladies, I was planning to suggest this at the restaurant, but now is as good a time as any. Catriona, Lillian told me yesterday you were considering opening a second store and in our area. Is this true?"

"Well, yes. I am considering it." She looked at Lillian somewhat surprised.

Lillian shrugged her shoulders. "Sweetheart, Susannah asked about your business. That is all."

"I want to help. You must contact my realtor. There are several old buildings nearby that may meet your needs. It would be lovely to have you as a neighbor. Do you think you would be interested?"

"Maybe. It doesn't hurt to look, but do you think your realtor is available today? It is Sunday, and I'm sure his afternoon calendar is full."

"Let me find his card. I'm sure he can assist you, and if not today, maybe tomorrow morning. The retail space in this area is gobbled up as soon as it hits the market."

"That would be helpful. Thank you." Catriona dropped her head and closed her eyes.

Susannah disappeared into her office and within seconds called out, "Found it. Come on in. You can use this phone as it is a private line and no one will interrupt you."

"Thank you. You are most kind."

Susannah asked, "Lillian, why don't we go downstairs? I have some tea brewing if you want a cup."

"A cup of tea sounds perfect."

The two women disappeared leaving Catriona alone. Looking at the card, she hesitated. She had not considered working again so soon, but she also did not want to miss out on a great property either. She dialed the number.

***

Monday evening, Scott sent a limo to escort the women to dinner.

Catriona leaned forward as she glanced out the window. "Lillian, look. There's Scott. Driver, please stop here."

He pulled to the curbside.

"Thank you." Catriona reached for her purse.

Scott and Peter were waiting outside when the long sedan arrived at the hotel in Georgetown. Taking Scott's hand, she was assisted from the car. Catriona wore a silk embroidered wrap draped around her shoulders, flattering her long silhouette. Her black hair contrasted against the cream-colored fabric, and her pleated skirt moved as she walked.

"Katydid, I cannot remember a time when you looked more stunning."

"Thank you, Scott. Lillian treated me to an afternoon of shopping. I'm excited to be here." She stepped out of the way.

Scott reached for Lillian's hand as she emerged from the car's rear seat. She looked flawless in her emerald green dress, coordinated coat, matching clutch, and shoes. Lillian could be counted on to make an entrance.

"You look beautiful."

"Thank you, love. You do too." She glanced over at Peter. "And my, oh my, Mr. Tramwell. Aren't you dashing this evening?"

"Mrs. McKenna, you will turn every eye in this town."

"I did not know you were such a sweet talker, but I thank you."

Peter said, "You both look beautiful."

Although the five-star restaurant was filled to capacity, they were seated immediately.

"Before I forget, thank you for the flowers, Peter. They were incredible. I have never seen an arrangement quite like it before, and it was most unexpected," Catriona said.

"My pleasure. I wanted to make a good impression."

"Well, you did. I loved them too." Lillian smiled ear-to-ear.

Scott asked, "How was your day with the realtor, Katydid? Did you see anything promising?"

"I did, but I'm sure Peter has no desire to hear about my latest real estate venture. We can discuss it later."

The server interrupted, "Please excuse me. Mr. McKenna?"

"Yes?" Scott turned toward him.

"Sir, the gentleman in the gray suit sitting across the room has asked I deliver this bottle of 2012 Château Laffite Rothchild to you and your guests. May I pour it for you?"

Catriona could see her father frown as he looked over.

Scott said, "No, thank you. Please send my thanks and apologies to Mr. Franks. He'll understand."

The waiter looked surprised. "If that is what you prefer, sir."

"It is."

He walked away.

"What is wrong with you, Scott?" Lillian whispered.

"There is nothing wrong with me, sweetheart. That gentleman is Thaddeus Franks, a wealthy businessman who owns several coal mines in Virginia and West Virginia. We filed a complaint against his company regarding unsafe labor practices, and earlier this morning, I have started an inquiry into a recent increase in black lung disease diagnoses for many of his employees."

Franks lifted his glass and toasted a silent gesture toward their table.

Peter interrupted, "If I may? Under the request of the current administration, Senator Williams has asked us to research illegal practices in the coal mining industry. Mr. Franks is our primary target of the listed defendants in our complaint. He has probably received his summons by now. If Scott agrees to take any gift from him, especially a bottle of wine costing in the neighborhood of a few hundred dollars, it could be viewed as accepting a bribe. He is a crude person... smart and dangerous based on reports we have received."

Catriona watched the gentleman approach their table carrying the bottle with him.

With a greasy smile, he said, "Good evening, folks. Pardon me, but I do not believe I've had the privilege of meeting the renowned Mr. Scott McKenna, Esquire. I am Thaddeus Franks. Aren't you going to introduce me to your beautiful guests?"

Scott stood. "Good evening, Mr. Franks. This is my wife, Lillian Rose, and my daughter, Catriona. I believe you have met my colleague, Mr. Tramwell. Ladies, this is Mr. Thaddeus Franks."

"It's my pleasure, but please, call me Thad."

"Is there something I can help you with, Mr. Franks?"

"I want you to accept this gift as a token of my mutual respect as we approach our future battle together."

"You know I cannot accept gifts."

"Why not? Are you afraid of me?"

"Not at all. Why would I be afraid of you? Although your gesture is appreciated, it is not appropriate and you know it."

"Appropriate? It's nothing but a glass of wine before dinner."

"Sir, I believe we both know the bribery laws in this state. You may call my office tomorrow if you have questions regarding this suit, and we can discuss it then… or better yet, you can call your attorneys, and we can agree to meet at another time and place."

A quick frown replaced the fake smile and with a grittiness to his voice, Thaddeus said, "What do you know about coal mining, anyway? You… sitting in your Washington office with all your pretentious senator friends, presuming you know what you're talking about, and all the while hiding behind some lawbook because of your obvious lack of experience. You wouldn't know a piece of coal if it bit you on the ass. You are an arrogant bastard, aren't you?"

"We both know your gift could be perceived as a well-played hand, and while we're at it, you can save your tactics for the courtroom. I find your language offensive, so if you would return to your table, I'm sure the patrons of this restaurant would appreciate it, including my family and myself. You do not want to turn this into an ugly scene. Do you?"

He leaned forward. "I don't make scenes. You don't know who you're dealing with, McKenna."

"I know exactly who I'm dealing with, and I expect you to be respectful of my guests. This conversation is over. If not…"

"If not, what? What are you going to do about it? All I've done is show a little courtesy between business acquaintances, so take the blasted wine. No hidden agenda and no bribe. You have no reason to get so high and mighty. Some might consider not accepting my gift as a personal insult."

"Again, thank you, but no."

"Your reputation precedes you… a true, hard ass. You and your little colleague had better steer clear of me if you know what's good for you. And if you are not careful, it could include your pretty little family."

Scott stepped forward and Lillian touched him on the arm. He replied, "You are out of line. I would suggest you leave before I ask management to call the police."

The restaurant patrons grew quiet.

The owner and maître d' approached their table. "Sir, please leave before I have no choice but to call the police."

"McKenna, you stay away from me with your preconceived notions of how I run my companies. If not, you might live to regret it."

"I believe that is your second threat this evening. Peter, did you hear another threat?"

The restaurant's owner asked again, "Sir... please. I'm asking you to leave."

Slamming the bottle onto the table, Franks remarked, "You can call it whatever you wish. I've warned you." He turned and stormed out of the restaurant.

The owner said, "Sir, please accept our deepest apologies. Tonight's dinner is on the house."

"Thank you, but that is unnecessary."

"I insist. Do you want me to call the police?"

"No. He was just blowing smoke. Please... accept my apology for the disruption to your patrons, and you may take this bottle back to the cellar."

The owner departed, taking the wine with him.

"Scott, what have you gotten yourself into?" Lillian looked distraught.

"Nothing, darling. Nothing. I want neither of you to worry. He's a hothead, but I'll contact his attorneys in the morning... and if necessary, I'll take out a restraining order."

Peter said, "Allow me to handle this. I recorded everything as he was speaking."

"You did what?"

"I used my cell phone to record his conversation. Let me handle it. I will not use it in court, but I will play it for his legal team."

"All right, but you let me know how they plan to handle their client who is obviously out of control."

"Of course."

Catriona sat silent.

Peter touched her hand. "Please don't worry. He is who Scott says he is… a hothead. Everything will be fine."

Peter's cell phone buzzed. He looked down at the caller ID and excused himself. "I apologize, but a family matter has come to light. Excuse me."

As soon as he was out of hearing distance, Lillian said, "Oh, Katydid, I hope this has not ruined your evening. Peter is wonderful. I hope you will consider seeing more of him."

"I don't know. Maybe." Catriona shifted in her chair.

"Maybe?" Scott smiled. "We need a reason to invite him to Grace Meade."

Lillian said, "Leave that to me."

"I can handle my own relationships. Thank you." Catriona laughed.

Peter returned to the table. Dinner arrived, but the conversation remained light. No one spoke again of Mr. Franks.

While waiting for their dessert and cognac, Peter asked, "Before we leave, I want to extend an invitation to join me at the Kennedy Center next Sunday evening. It's opening night for one of my favorite cellists performing with the National Symphony Orchestra. Tickets are orchestra level, ten rows back on the side… supposedly, the best seats in the house. I hope you will join me."

Lillian said, "What a wonderful idea. However, I cannot attend as I will be finishing the horse auction details on Sunday. I don't know about Scott. However, Catriona, dear, why don't you go?"

Scott nodded. "I'm sorry we can't be there, but I agree. Katydid, you should go."

Catriona shifted in her chair. "Oh, my word; three against one. I guess I don't have a choice, do I?"

"You always have a choice," Peter reassured her.

"Okay, Mr. Tramwell. I would love to join you. Weird thought, however."

"And what that be?"

"You dislike the cello."

"Why would you think I dislike the cello?"

"Oh, I don't know. Maybe when I was at your auction, you asked if I wanted to purchase an old cello near the doorway."

"You have caught me at my own game. Now, I'm embarrassed. It was my great-grandfather's cello with no plans of selling it. Someone had placed it outside without my knowledge, but no worries. It's now safe at my home here in the city."

Scott said, "Katydid, I've heard a rumor that Peter is an excellent musician."

"Really?" Catriona looked at him amused.

Lillian said, "How ironic. Peter, did you know Catriona plays the cello as well?"

"No, I didn't. Now, who's been caught?"

"What do you mean?" Catriona frowned.

"I believe someone else said she did not play. Am I right?"

"No, you're wrong. I said nothing. You asked if I wanted to purchase the cello, but you didn't allow me to reply. I own one, so there was no need for a second." She laughed.

"I stand corrected. We have found a common interest, haven't we?"

"Yes, I guess we have." Catriona found him more intriguing as the evening progressed. She turned toward her father. "May I stay with you next week while I'm in Washington?"

"Remind me for a key when I'm back at Grace Meade."

Lillian said, "Peter, may I assume you like horses?"

"I do. I play at the Virginia International Polo Club when time allows... although it is rare."

"Wonderful! I assume you learned at your grandparents' home?"

"Yes, I did. My grandfather insisted we all learn to ride, and borrowing his words, 'and learn to ride well.'"

"Great! Now that I know you will not be bored, we host a horse sale and auction each year encompassing an entire weekend of events. At the end of the auction on Saturday, we top the day with a casual dinner and dancing. Scott and I want to extend an invitation asking you to stay at Grace Meade as we have plenty of room. You can plan to arrive Friday evening if your schedule permits, all day Saturday, and you will have time to return to Washington on Sunday after brunch and arrive before the concert."

"I'm not sure I can refuse. Thank you. Would that be acceptable to you, Catriona?"

She smiled. "If Lillian Rose invites you, then you don't have a choice. Besides, the more the merrier. Right, Scott?"

"Always."

Lillian winked at Catriona causing her to blush. She couldn't help but think her mother should add professional matchmaker to her long line of skills. However, Catriona did not know how to play games nor was it her desire to do so.

Finishing the meal and gathering their coats, they exited the restaurant. Despite their earlier interruption, the evening had proved to be most enjoyable. None noticed a hooded man in a dark jacket approach the group from behind. He placed the barrel of the revolver into Scott's side and spoke in a low voice.

"McKenna, consider this official notice. You need to be careful who you offend. Next time, you won't be so lucky."

Lillian screamed as the assailant sprinted into the darkness.

At the sound of the high-pitched scream, Catriona's vision became blurred. She could not see but heard her mother's voice.

"Shh… you must be quiet, sweetie. Don't cry. Whatever happens, do not open this door. I'll come back for you."

Katie Jo closed the bi-fold door. A few moments later, the man slapped Katie Jo across the face causing her to fall across the bed as she let out a terrible scream. Catriona covered her ears, blocking her mother's cries.

"Catriona!"

Unaware, Catriona was falling backward into the street. Peter jerked her toward him just as their limousine swerved to miss. She sank to the sidewalk as he struggled to help her.

"Catriona…" Peter held her as he brushed the hair away from her face. "Can you hear me?"

She collapsed into his arms as all turned black.

CHAPTER 8

Her Birth Parents

ALTHOUGH LANKY AND awkward as a young girl, Catriona Elizabeth Harrington had grown into the mirror image of her mother—a misfortune in itself. Upon the day of her birth, her proud daddy described her in his unique manner to anyone who would listen.

"It's a girl, and she is somethin' I tell you. When God created my baby, He fired her hair from the blackest of coal and rendered her skin paler and creamier than any of the finest buttermilk ever churned, and that's no lie. He even painted her eyes a blue-green makin' the Caribbean Sea jealous with envy. Oo-eee, she is the most beautiful baby in the world. Here… have a cigar!"

Much to their surprise and deepest happiness, she came late into the seventeen-year marriage of William C. and Katherine Josephine Dunne Harrington (known to all as Bill and Katie Jo)—an only child born to them on the hottest day of the year where the hills of Virginia and Tennessee merge upon one another. They had a rare, loyal kind of love, and through it all, sickness and health, prince and pauper, the truly better and horribly worse, the couple made their marriage work.

According to Bill (and in no particular order), the following were of equal importance depending on the day or conversation; one's faith in God above, one's political affiliation, and college football, along with a little fishing and hunting on the side. Catriona's daddy, who had a monstrous heart and genetically could not help but be kind, was loved by all who knew him. He had the renowned Harrington irresistible persona and never missed an opportunity to use his quick wit and sharp sense of humor alongside a subtle one-liner come-back to make his point. Bill was a good and honest man who had strong, deep-rooted opinions—respected by all, whether they agreed or not.

Catriona was far from spoiled and was expected to complete her assigned chores without questioning her parents. She lived in a household where they treasured the beauty of a simple life, and all the while understanding hard work was part of living. Catriona was the recipient of many of Bill's favorite sayings and she could recite them verbatim. When he shared his financial wisdom, he would always end her lesson with these words: "You don't want to be so broke you can't afford to pay attention."

Katie Jo was a happy person who had a genuine, contagious laugh, filling an entire room with reciprocated laughter. She was a natural beauty and earned a good income as the best seamstress in three counties, always taking exceptional care with her appearance. One would never find her without hair or clothing in place, no matter the time of day. With her limited income, she sewed Catriona's dresses with beautiful details—always pressed for any outing. She was a master of her craft—a gift passed down from her mother.

Being a true daughter of the region, Katie Jo knew her colloquialisms too. There was never an occasion that did not call for one. Throughout her childhood, Catriona learned the expressive wisdom of the locals, but none more than those from her mother.

One could not find another more devoted to the church, except maybe for the pastor, and even then, some would have argued on her behalf. She and Bill had charitable spirits and would give every possession if a need arose. Her generosity was not one of boast and mostly unknown to others, except for those who were recipients of her kindness. Whether it be providing money for an unpaid bill, giving away fresh eggs or produce from the garden, repairing clothing, or delivering a meal to a sick neighbor, it was Katie Jo's way of helping whenever possible. However, she could spot a fake anywhere and be blatant with those who used their children as an excuse to beg for money, specifically those parents spending money on other vices instead of essentials for basic care. When those same kids arrived at school or the ball field with dirty faces and filthy clothing asking for a handout, she would give whatever loose change she had. Afterward, Catriona would always hear the same lecture.

"Bless their hearts. If I ever hear you're being mean to anyone for any reason, much less how they look or smell, I'll jerk a knot in your tail, Katydid. Ugly is ugly. It doesn't matter who's doing it. Do you hear me?"

"Yes, ma'am."

"You show kindness to everyone regardless of where they come from. It's not a child's fault. Not everyone can provide for their family's needs depending on their circumstances, but if their parents can afford a cigarette or can belly up to a bar for a drink, then don't tell me they can't afford a bar of soap to wash their child's face."

"Yes, ma'am." Catriona turned to look out of the window.

"Are you listening to me?"

"Yes, ma'am."

"I mean every word. We are all the same in God's eyes. It doesn't amount to a hill of beans who you think you are because we do not have the luxury of choosing how we are born into this world... the color of our skin, rich or poor, healthy or weak... that's God's doing, but we do have the luxury of choosing how we go out. Always do the right thing, Katydid. Your reputation is everything."

"Yes, ma'am."

Theirs was a life filled with laughter—a safe place for their daughter, or so it would appear. Why would Bill and Katie Jo ever imagine Catriona's life turning upside down by evil lurking so close?

***

A deep voice asked, "Where have you been, boy?"

"Nowhere."

He back-handed the lad across his face. "Don't be a smart-ass!"

The teenager licked at the blood oozing from the corner of his mouth and wiped it with the back of his hand. "I was at the ballpark."

"Yeah?"

"Yeah."

"Was that pretty Katie Jo Harrington flittin' around like always?"

"Yeah," he said, as he gritted his teeth. He did not know what he hated more—his father's treatment of his mother or his father's obsession with Katie Jo.

"Now, that's a real woman. I like the way she moves. Your maw could learn a thing or two from her."

"You leave her out of this!"

"Shut up, you little bastard." His father knocked him into the side of the garage, causing him to fall to the ground. "Do you want to die today?"

The boy shook his head no.

"Then watch your mouth. You should feel lucky I married your maw and gave you a last name." He pulled up his pants by the belt loops where they had fallen beneath his large gut. "You understand or are you stupid?"

"I understand, but I'm not stupid."

The old man kicked him in the thigh. The boy let out a loud grunt.

"You are what I say you are, boy, and don't you be forgettin' it."

The boy's eyes narrowed as his father continued. "One day, Katie Jo will see how little of a man Bill can be." Stretching back his shoulders, he lifted his chest, looking more like an old rooster too old to crow.

The boy stood limping, trying to dust the grass stain from his jeans. "What do you mean?"

"Mind your own business. Now, go see if that worthless maw of yours has my dinner ready."

The boy pushed open the screened door and looked back at his father. There stood evil growing darker than the coal emerging daily from the town's epicenter.

# CHAPTER 9

"CATRIONA HARRINGTON-MCKENNA?"

"Yes?"

"Dr. Pendergrass will see you now."

Lillian touched her arm. "Don't worry. I'll be here when you finish."

Catriona nodded and took a deep breath as she followed the nurse. She hated beginning again with a new group of doctors. The nurse directed her to an office where Dr. Pendergrass greeted her. She was a small woman, maybe forty to forty-five years of age, and wore a kind smile. Her office décor was intentional in creating a comfortable atmosphere with its overstuffed furniture, dim lighting, and soft music playing in the background. Catriona relaxed straightaway.

"Would you like something to drink before we begin... tea or coffee?"

"No, thank you."

"Are you comfortable in this chair or would you prefer to sit on the sofa?"

"I think I will move to the sofa."

Once they were comfortable, Dr. Pendergrass said, "Let's start at the beginning, Miss McKenna."

"Please... call me Catriona."

"Yes, of course... whatever makes you most comfortable. First, let me say thank you for permitting me to speak to your parents before our visit so I have a clearer understanding of your history. Your previous doctors forwarded their records; however, I wanted to meet with you before I reviewed their notes. I need to understand where your memories begin and end, and much later, we will explore the impact of your physical injuries. When I ask a question, answer with as much detail as possible, and if there are cloudy areas, tell me those too.

You will experience no pressure from me, but if you do, tell me, and we will proceed to another subject. Do you have any questions?"

"No, I'm familiar with the routine."

"Questions will regard basic information for today, and I will record every session. Are you ready?"

"Yes, I am."

"Close your eyes and forget about your day. Take a few deep breaths and let's begin in a safe place with something easy. What do you remember about your hometown?"

Catriona shifted on the sofa somewhat, closed her eyes, and slowed her breathing as Sageville came into focus.

"I remember some details from my own memories, but I can tell you more of its history from research I conducted in college. I was curious, but not enough to visit. Scott has asked me not to go there without him so I have honored his request."

"Let's start there."

Catriona told the doctor what little she knew of coal mining in the area. She recalled seeing miners after their shifts at Pritchett's or Smalley's Grocery wearing their helmets with tarnished brass lights, and their midnight black, soot-covered faces portraying a perfect impression of a Cheshire cat's grinning white teeth. She admitted she could not recall details of other businesses in town. She shared of the mines closing because of a ceiling collapse when she was a young girl.

"This is a good start, Catriona... excellent, in fact. What do you remember about your parents?"

"Scott told me they adored one another." Unaware, her eyes widened.

"Go on."

"According to him, I was a surprise pregnancy, but my parents were excited regardless." She fidgeted, crossing her legs at the knees.

"We can discuss something else if you prefer."

"No." She uncrossed her legs. "It's okay. I had a large family, but I do not recognize them in photographs. I want to remember. I'm uncertain why, but I have a strong desire to put others before myself.

That doesn't just happen, does it? I either learned by example or was taught. I yearn to know why I am the way I am. Scott and Lillian are an enormous part of my upbringing, but how did I get here through my other family?"

"You are right. All of us need to know who we are. What about your activities? Anything you did daily or can remember doing at all?"

"I'm not sure where to begin. We could be here a while."

"Start anywhere."

"We attended church every week. God and music must have been important because I remember lyrics of hymns when they are being played having never studied them. I feel a deep peace when we attend church with Samuel, although my attendance is sporadic or not at all. Someone taught me how to garden because I know how to cultivate and harvest plants without having studied horticulture. I love Monticello's gardens and can describe in detail how each plant is bedded and grafted. I have a small garden at my home in Charlottesville as well. It's unnerving to have worked alongside the gardeners at Grace Meade, and with no instruction, I can plant and prune the fruit trees. Someone taught me, but who? It may sound odd, but the aromas of tilled soil and mown grass comfort me."

"Aromas are powerful and can trigger previous memories you may have forgotten."

"I remember bits and pieces of my mother and a few conversations. She wore a yellow dress with pleating from the lower torso to the hem. I own a similar dress. I think in a feeble attempt, I emulate her. At least, Scott seems to think I do." She released a deep sigh. "My mother had a delightful smile. Lillian and Scott loved my parents too, and from what little they have told me, Scott and my mother were close."

"Do you feel Scott and Lillian knowing your past has helped you?"

"Yes and no. I try to remember what they are describing or stories shared, and yet, I cannot relate most of the time. I realize I'm more fortunate than most who have lost parents at an early age and have no one to tell of their history. It's frustrating. Why can't I remember those details without depending upon their memories and stories?"

"Do not worry so much. Let's concentrate on what you do know... whether told or remembered."

"When discussing family history, my mother said she and I were named after some great-great somewhere in the family's ancestral tree, although her name, Katherine, is the American derivative of Catriona. Mine is an old-world name, but she loved it all the same. And as far back as I can remember, my family has called me 'Katydid.' I'm unsure why."

"Anything else?"

"She... my mother would say the funniest things. On more than one occasion, I remember hearing her frustration when having to dress in the morning. She would yell from behind the closed door, 'I tell you what, Bill. We need to do something about this bathroom. It's so small in here, you couldn't cuss out a cat without getting hair in your mouth.'"

They both laughed.

"Every time I walk into a small room, I think of cussing cats."

"You are a rare patient. Most of my patients are seeking love from anyone in some form or another, but you were and are loved."

"I know. Is it selfish to want to remember my family?" Her voice cracked with emotion.

"Not at all. Everyone wants to know to whom they belong, whether good or bad. Let's go to a memory less emotional. You spoke of playtime. What did you play?"

"My mother transformed a storage shed into a playhouse. It held the few toys I owned. She had sewn café curtains to hang in the window and painted the walls a pale blue to match the sky. My daddy found a linoleum remnant at a flooring store near Hattiesburg to add the final piece to the renovation. It was my sanctuary. I owned a small play kitchen and a table with chairs for my favorite doll, Miss Olivia, and my stuffed animals. I would pretend to cook with the pulled privet hedge leaves surrounding the garden, imagining the finest meal being prepared by the best cooker-upper in town." Startled, she leaned forward. "Oh, my word, I don't remember having mentioned this before. Oh, my word!"

"That's great, Catriona, but slow down and take a deep breath. Do you remember anything else no one has told you?"

"There are some things. My mother had a lengthy repertoire of 'wisdoms' she would share, and one sticks with me more than the others. I'm not sure if these are her words or something she read elsewhere, but understand too, I was only nine when she passed away. She told me something along these lines... 'Honey, I want you to grow up to be a woman who is independent and free-spirited. I also want you to be the woman who can survive on her own without a man, but when you find a guy who won't let you, then that's when you marry him. You catch my meaning?'"

"I think I would have liked your mother."

"Dr. Pendergrass?"

"Yes?"

"My head is throbbing. I'm unsure I can do this any longer today. May we continue at another time?"

"Yes. It is more than enough. It should please you to have remembered so much, including something as simple as your childhood playtime. You should share today's session with your family. It may trigger more memories. I will ask my assistant to make an early appointment next week. I don't want to push too hard, but we need to head this off before there is another blackout causing you more harm by falling or worse. You should not drive for a few days."

"Not drive? I had not considered it. Thank you."

"Do you have headaches often?"

"When do I not have headaches? I have many physical issues, but who knows why? The fire changed my life forever." She raised her hands to cover her face. "I am done for today."

"I will review your medications and call in a new prescription if needed. I don't want to add to a mixture of medication causing more headaches or risk co-dependency. You may not need as many."

"I'll do whatever you ask."

"Thank you, Catriona. I will see you next week."

As promised, Lillian was waiting in the lobby when Catriona returned.

"I made an appointment for nine next Tuesday."

"We will make sure you are here. Did you like her?" Lillian asked.

"Very much."

"Good. What should we do? Lunch? We could walk uptown to eat. There is a new sandwich shop where they have great chicken salad."

"Sounds good because I have a terrible headache. A short walk and something to eat is what I need."

"Mrs. McKenna?"

"Yes?" Both Lillian and Catriona asked simultaneously, then laughed.

"Ms. or Mrs.?" Lillian asked.

"Mrs. McKenna, Dr. Pendergrass wants to know if you and your husband can attend next Tuesday as well."

"I can, but I will check Scott's schedule. May I call you tomorrow?"

"Yes. You may call the number on her printout. I hope you ladies have a great day."

"Thank you."

They left the office arm-in-arm, laughing as they walked.

Lillian asked, "Well, are you going to keep me in suspense?"

"It was the strangest thing..." Catriona wavered momentarily in sharing specific details not knowing how Lillian would react. "We discussed my mother. I hope you understand how much I need to remember her."

"Sweetheart. Of course, I do. You should never worry about discussing Katie Jo with me." She patted Catriona on the arm. "Your mother was a precious person who we all adored and who loved you more than life itself."

"Dr. Pendergrass asked me a simple question about my childhood and without hesitation, I remembered my playhouse and my toys. It was exciting but overwhelming too."

"How wonderful! I'm so pleased for you, darling."

Catriona grinned. "Me too. Let's talk about something else if you don't mind."

"Okay. Well, I have everything in order for the horse auction this Saturday. I have three short days to fine-tune everything and then the party begins."

"Are you sure you can do next Tuesday with Dr. Pendergrass? You will want to sleep for days following the auction."

"I wouldn't miss it for the world. You come first... always. Never forget, my darling, you come first. This is what mommas do. Katie Jo taught me through her example. It doesn't matter when you turn fifty and I'm... I'm... well, up there. You will always come first." Lillian stroked the side of her daughter's cheek with the back of her hand.

"I love you so much, Lillian. I'm overwhelmed with everything. I am confused, anxious, and yet happy to be home. I think my mind is too crowded, and I'm worried about Scott too."

"You are to worry about no one but yourself. Other than a good lunch, I know what clears my mind... a horse ride. When we return to Grace Meade, take Angel out for a long stroll around the property. I will ask Samuel to go along as I do not want you to be alone."

"What a great idea."

"Oh, look! One of our pickup trucks is at the sandwich shop. I wonder if Scott is here."

Catriona stopped walking.

"What's wrong?"

"I hate that Scott is working from home instead of his office. What an interruption I am. Both of you need to proceed with business as usual. I'm a big girl and will ask for help should I need you."

"Katydid, that is enough. You talk big, but you are coming across as poor-pitiful-me. We are doing what families do. Besides, Scott's team of attorneys is taking care of any slack... if any. No worries."

Lillian wrapped her arm around Catriona's waist and hugged her. They stood in silence, and Catriona dropped her head against the top of her mother's.

"Thank you, Lillian."

"You are my girl."

When they walked into the shop, the bell above the door rang and several turned their way. It was a quaint shop, and as the hostess moved toward them, Lillian greeted her. "Hello, Rena. We will eat on the garden patio if it is open today."

"Yes, Mrs. McKenna. Help yourself, and I'll make sure someone takes your order."

"Lillian Rose McKenna! As I live and breathe! It does my heart good to see you. Are you ready for the weekend?" The loud voice boomed from across the room.

"Hey, George! As ready as I'll ever be." Lillian approached his table. "Are you and Margaret coming to the dance Saturday night?"

"My dancing shoes are polished and ready to go. If it's okay with you, we want to come in the afternoon to watch the festivities."

"You are welcome anytime. Why don't you two make a day of it and come as early as you wish? I'll make sure Cookie has breakfast ready."

As Lillian continued to talk, Catriona made her way to the patio. There was a cool breeze, but the sun was beaming. She sat next to a small fountain tucked into the corner of the courtyard and closed her eyes beneath her sunglasses hoping the warmth upon her face would ease her headache.

"Hello there. Are you alone or would you like some company?"

Startled, she jumped. "Declan! I didn't see you.... what a nice surprise. Please join Lillian and me. She is inside chatting up the room as usual."

He was not in his normal work attire. Instead, he was wearing a white shirt with the sleeves rolled to his forearms, blue jeans with chestnut-colored boots, and a cowboy hat worn right above his eyebrows.

"Why are you in town today? Have I forgotten something for the auction?" He removed his hat as he spoke, revealing his dark auburn hair. He brushed it back with his hand.

As if from another world, she said aloud, "Your eyes are a crazy green."

She caught him off-guard, and he laughed hard. "Yes, they are. What are we talking about?"

"Did I say that out loud? Forgive me." Her cheeks blushed red.

"Don't be. It has been a while since anyone commented on my eye color. Do you blurt out whatever you are thinking?" He outlined his mouth with his fingertips as he yawned and laughed again.

"No, I do not. Let's start over... you have forgotten nothing. I had a date with my doctor, and now, we are eating lunch with you."

"Well, aren't I the lucky one?" He smiled with great ease.

"Are you headed back to Grace Meade? If you are, would you see if Angel is available this afternoon?"

"Sure. I'll call Brad on the way home."

"Do you know if Samuel is around? Lillian and Scott are uncomfortable with me riding alone at the moment."

"We can check. I'm headed back, but I need to stop at Burge's Feed and Seed before I'm finished with errands in town. Why don't you ride to Grace Meade with me?"

"We would need to drop by the drugstore first."

He smiled. "Shouldn't be a problem."

"Then I accept your offer. Thank you. Lillian plans to go by the florist and the caterer before heading back, and I do not want to tag along. However, I do not want to hurt her feelings. Are you sure you do not mind?"

"No, I would enjoy the company."

Lillian interrupted, "Well, hello, Declan. I wondered who was driving the truck. Are you joining us?"

"Yes... with your permission."

"Don't be silly. You are part of the Grace Meade family and never need my permission. Actually, you being here works better with my plans as they have changed. I was talking to George Franklin inside, and he has asked me to look at a horse he is considering selling. If it's not too much trouble, could Catriona ride back to Grace Meade with you? I will grab a sandwich and follow him."

"Sure. Not a problem."

Without missing a beat, she turned to Catriona. "Do you mind or have I made you feel as though I have dropped you off like a bag of feed?" She laughed.

"Not at all." Catriona propped her elbows on the tabletop and rested her chin on her fists. She was amazed at Lillian's skillful ability to give orders without anyone being offended.

"Great. It's settled. You two stay here and enjoy your lunch, and I will see you at Grace Meade." She hurried inside.

Declan said, "And there you go... no hurt feelings after all." They both laughed.

"She runs nonstop. I don't know how she does it."

"Oh, I had forgotten. Grandpops is visiting his sister in Williamsburg and is not returning until the auction on Saturday. However, knowing him, he'll be back sooner than later."

Sitting back, she puckered her lips, then sighed. "That's too bad. I guess I'll ride another time."

"Hey, I have an idea. I'll ride with you and Angel. Two more errands and my afternoon is free. Believe it or not, I'm ahead of schedule with the auction plans. We can ask Rena to pack our sandwiches here and take them with us. Are you game or am I being too bold?"

"You are not bold at all. You have rescued me, Mr. O'Connell. I'll call Cookie and have her prepare a basket for us. An impromptu picnic would be the perfect remedy to rid me of this headache and focus on the outdoors instead..." She paused. "Oh, my word. I'm having a pity party, aren't I? I promise there will be no more complaining today."

"Ha! Complain all you want if it makes you feel better. Let's go. I recommend the chicken salad... it's their specialty."

"That's what I've heard." She chuckled as they walked inside.

CHAPTER 10

BRAD LED THE black beauty out of the stall. "Hold on, Angel. Good girl," he said. "Miss McKenna, do you need help reaching the stirrup?"

"Yes. Thank you, Brad. Will you do me a favor?"

"Sure… anything."

"Please call me Catriona. Agreed?"

"Agreed, ma'am."

They both laughed as he helped her mount the horse. Declan came trotting alongside on a painted stallion.

"Wow. He's gorgeous," she said.

"That he is. He hasn't been out of his stall today and exercise is needed."

Cookie stopped them at the side gate with a basket filled with fruit, bottled water, and their pre-made sandwiches.

"I brought a couple of blankets to take along. You should go to the lake near the springhouse. It's a great spot to rest in the afternoon sun before it turns cool."

"Thank you for going to this extra trouble." Catriona squeezed her hand.

"You are most welcome, hon."

"Are you ready, Declan?" she asked.

"Ready when you are."

He suggested a slow pace so as not to cause her further harm. After a long trot, they arrived at the rise overlooking the lake. He helped her from her saddle, but Catriona's face flushed pink as she brushed against his jacket.

"Are you sure you're okay?"

Catriona dusted herself off. "Yes, I'm hungry. That's all."

"So am I." He roped off the horses, allowing them to graze as she arranged the quilt and the food to take advantage of the water view.

"Come." She patted the quilt. "Sit… please." She took a large bite out of her sandwich. "This is good." Her eyes widened.

"Their chicken salad is the best."

A long, awkward pause followed as they continued to eat in silence.

Declan said, "I hope you do not feel uncomfortable around me."

"Of course not. Would you like dessert? I'm sure Cookie added something sweet to this basket." She removed the napkins from the bottom and found the buried treasure. "Oh, look… lemon squares. Do you want one? They are one of my favorites."

"Sure… I'll take one."

She handed over the delicacy wrapped in wax paper as she devoured another tiny dessert in one bite. He covered his mouth with the back of his hand to hide his wide grin.

"What?" she asked.

"You would never know you liked them."

"Funny," she said with her mouth full.

"Here. Let me help you." Powdered sugar covered the bottom of her chin. He took his napkin and removed the white sweetness from her face.

"Oh, thank you." She laughed, licking her fingertips. "Cookie can make anything taste ten times better than it should. I will gain forty pounds if I'm not careful… oh, my… I have shown you my greatest sin and bad side. You didn't know I was a glutton, did you?"

"If this is your bad side, then I have nothing to fear." He smiled at her.

"You know, we haven't talked one-on-one since I've been home. I know about your professional background through Scott, but where are you from… what are your interests… how did you get into the horse business?"

"Wow… so many questions. Okay… let's make this a quick run-through. I'm thirty-six years old. Never married… never had time. My parents live on a large farm outside of Knoxville, Tennessee, in a small place called Strawberry Plains at the foot of the Smoky Mountains."

"Oh, a country boy?" She grinned, causing her eyes to dance.

"Yes, and proud of it. Since my childhood, I've known I wanted to work with horses. So, I did what any person of East Tennessee would do given the chance."

"And what pray-tell would that be?"

"Attend the University of Tennessee. Where else? Just made sense… I graduated with a masters in animal science."

"This conversation is beginning to resemble a job interview."

"Do you want me to continue or not?" His lips turned into a silly grin.

She laughed and scoffed down another bite-size lemon bar.

"Following school, I landed my first job at Churchill Downs. They pushed me to learn as much as possible about this business, and I did. Now, through some odd circumstance of my grandfather retiring, I'm here. I will confess I'm surprised how much I've enjoyed the short time I've lived in Virginia."

"Virginia is a beautiful state."

"Yes, it is. Running the stables for your parents appears to agree with me. Grace Meade is a remarkable place too. The hills remind me a little of home, but enough about me. What about you?"

"What about me?" She took a swallow from her bottle of water.

"Well, what do you do? Where do you live when you are not here? You know. What about you?" He leaned backward, bracing himself on his elbows as he stretched his legs out in front of him.

"Well, let's see. I've known your grandfather most of my life, and although I love Samuel, I know he has told you more about me than I would care to know. That being said, and with the morning being filled with conversations about my past, I rather not discuss old memories, if you don't mind."

"Whatever makes you comfortable."

"I'm not hiding anything. Okay?"

She watched as he removed his coat and created a make-shift pillow. He propped his head on the messy lump and stared into the blue sky. Bending one knee, he stretched out the other leg in front of him.

"Are you comfortable? I mean, do you want to hear this or not?" She thought him far cuter than he should be.

"Pardon me. Yes. Please… continue." His genuine laugh caused her to confess more than normal.

"Well, if you must know, I saw a new psychiatrist today. I'm not crazy… confused, maybe. I'm still reeling in from my appointment, so let's discuss my other life. The one I remember would be my preference."

"Whatever works."

He shaded his eyes with his hat, listening as she spoke. He exuded a quiet calm unknown to either of them, allowing her to relax in his presence.

Lying backward on the quilt with her arms by her sides, she rested her hands across her stomach. Watching the clouds overhead, she described her home on the outskirts of Charlottesville—a two-bedroom cottage with a small garden, yet close enough to fine dining, a few art galleries, and the performing arts, including the place where she spent most of her time—her shop.

She explained why her college selection had been an easy one with the mountains reminding her of a place in her dreams. She grew secure in the familiarity of the not-so-large city of Charlottesville containing the University of Virginia with its unsurpassed beauty, secret societies, and undeniable educational excellence. Proudly, she graduated from the McIntire School of Commerce with a concentration in finance and a double minor in art and architectural history—her true passions.

She discussed her business plans and the incident at the restaurant. She left nothing out but kept it to a somewhat *Readers Digest* version so as not to bore too much.

"… and there you have it, sir. My current life as I know it."

She rolled onto her side and propped her head upon her bent elbow. "Hello? Are you under there or are you sleeping?"

He removed his hat and laughed. "I'm awake. How is your headache... gone?" He raised upright.

Her hair had fallen upon the blanket, spiraling around her head and under her shoulder.

"It is. Well, what do you know? The food must have satisfied my hunger or better yet, the enjoyment of quiet company." She covered her eyes with her hand. "Oh, no... I have treated you as if you were my doctor. I'm embarrassed again. Please forgive me."

"There's nothing to forgive. You need to stop apologizing all the time. It's tough to offend me. Besides, there's nothing pending this afternoon... only preparing for the biggest auction of my life... nothing too important." He laughed again.

"Please do not make me feel more guilty than I already do."

"I'm kidding. I needed downtime before the chaos so this has worked in my favor too. I've enjoyed your company and trust me... you are far from boring. I will say you have blown me away. I'm not sure what I expected."

"You impress easily, don't you?"

"Not at all. In fact, quite the opposite. You are one of those remarkable people one reads about who has risen above it all. You exhibit incredible strength to succeed regardless of any circumstances you have had to overcome. To be more accurate, you, Miss McKenna, you fascinate me."

She blushed. "You must know very few people."

"I know more than a few."

She chuckled under her breath. "Thank you. It is my normal custom to save these conversations for Scott at three in the morning." She grinned, but acting out of character, she flirted with him. She nudged his elbow. "I'm glad I do not bore you to tears, Mr... Mr. Volun-TEER." She rolled onto her back, laughing at her little jab.

He laughed too. "You cannot be serious. Mr. Volunteer? Really? You need to hone in on your comedic skills."

"Funny. Scott said the same thing."

He laughed again. "I will not allow you to make fun of my school, Miss Hoity-Toity Cavalier. This man's blood runs deep orange, but not Virginia's orange and blue. Reminds me too much of the Gators for my taste."

She sat upright. "If you go to a ballgame with me, you must wear my school colors. It's a prerequisite."

He paused for a moment and looked at her with a half-grin. "Are you inviting me to a football game, Miss Wahoo?"

"Hmm… I guess I am. Can you handle a little football, sir, or do you know anything about the game?"

"I can hold my own."

"Oh, is that right?"

"Yes, ma'am."

The wind blew hard, making the air cooler.

Declan frowned. "That's not good. We should return before the sun sets. Everyone will wonder where we are, and the last thing I want or need is for someone to send a search party looking for their missing daughter."

"Do we have to go? I'm sure they haven't missed either of us. Everyone is too busy with last-minute planning." A strong, colder breeze blew her hair across her face. "On second thought, Mr. O'Connell, we should go."

He pulled her to her feet. They brushed off their clothing and gathered everything into the basket.

"I'm cold," she said.

"Where is your coat?"

"I didn't bring one. How stupid of me."

"Take mine."

"No, I couldn't."

"You must wear something."

Looking around, she answered, "I know, I'll use the quilt."

"Stubborn, aren't we?"

"I am sometimes."

As he wrapped the quilt around her shoulders, she lost her footing and fell hard against his chest. He caught her to keep from falling backward into the lake and could not help but laugh as he tried to balance them both.

She laughed. "Excuse me, sir! What do we do now?"

"Stop moving or we are both going to tumble."

They both laughed harder.

"Did you say, 'tumble?' Who says, "Tumble?'" She laughed until she no longer made any sound except for the occasional gasp for air.

"I do. What's wrong with the word 'tumble?' Stop laughing or we will be swimming." He laughed too, but finally caught his balance. He continued to hold her tight. She looked up into his eyes and both grew quiet. It was obvious he wanted more, but he refrained. When he released her, the quilt fell to the ground.

"I'm sorry. Please forgive me, Catriona. I... I... don't do that."

"Do what?"

"I'm not the type who takes someone out for an afternoon's ride with expectations of taking advantage. I am not that man."

"The thought never crossed my mind or I would not have come. The ride was my idea, remember?" She shaded her eyes from the sun with her hand as she looked up at him.

He nodded his head and began wrapping the quilt around her a second time to shelter her from the cool breeze drifting off the water.

"Thank you for today, Declan."

"Of course."

"Truly. I can't remember the last time I had a more relaxing afternoon. I am unused to someone listening without judging or wanting further information from me." With no motive, she leaned up and kissed him lightly on the cheek.

He said nothing, but this time, he did not hesitate. Pulling the blanket snug around her, he drew her in close, kissing her fully, but softly, on the lips. Surprising herself, she did not resist him. As he released her, she allowed the quilt to drop a second time as she wrapped her arms around his neck. He encased her with his firm embrace, and with total wantonness, they kissed slow and deep. It was the kind of kiss only true lovers were accustomed with its arousing allure. Glancing down and while still holding her, he brushed the hair away from her temple. He kissed her on the forehead, and she closed her eyes, soaking in the strength of him holding her. Resting her head against his chest, she wholly resigned and enfolded into his arms. His heart pounded hard against her cheek.

"Declan…"

"Please stop talking."

Wrapping the fallen strands of her hair into his palm, he raised her head and pressed her mouth against his with an even stronger passion than either of them thought possible. Taking her into his arms, she welcomed his tight grasp, yielding to his every move.

The painted horse snorted and stomped his hoof. A gray fox had crept to the water's edge for an evening's drink, startling the horse and interrupting the intensity of the moment. The couple turned their heads toward the mare, then toward the fox, and then back toward each other, and both laughed, causing the intruder to run away.

He whispered, "I do not want to go, but we must. It's growing darker by the minute, and we are at least an hour or more from the house. I'm risking injuring the horses and you could fall again. We must leave."

"Are you sure?"

"Catriona, if you think this is easy, it's taking all the strength I can muster to not take you right here, but I would want to continue making love to you until morning… not hurrying away as if ashamed of what we have done. I don't want to look back on any time spent with you with regret. Do you understand?"

She nodded and hugged him one last time. "Thank you for allowing me to feel safe, if but for a moment."

He wrapped the blanket around her shoulders and lifted her onto Angel. He squeezed her ankle as he placed her foot into the stirrup and she leaned from her high seat, kissing him one last time.

"We must go, Catriona."

He pulled on his jacket, tied the picnic basket to the side of his saddle, and mounted his horse. They rode side-by-side with no words spoken between them.

The outside lights were coming into view as they entered the clearing. She realized the moment he climbed onto his horse something had changed.

She broke the silence. "What's wrong?"

He took a long pause, then said, "I'm not sure where to begin as I'm jumping ahead in assuming more than I should. First, I apologize for placing you in an awkward situation. Kissing you… it was…"

"It was… wasn't it?" She smiled.

He returned the smile. "Please do not say anything or I won't be able to finish. Okay?"

She nodded.

"I know who I am. I'm not one to dance around any subject. Instead, I try to face everything in my life head-on. I'm not an over-thinker and trusting my instincts has proven successful… thus far. For some unknown reason, I have this uncanny ability to read people. I know you well enough to assume neither of us would jump into a quick in-and-out relationship or a one-night stand. Am I correct?"

Unmoved, she nodded her head in agreement.

"I know we are successful and have established ourselves in our careers. We can do what we want; we have earned the right or so it would seem. However, life is complicated with its rules and regulations. In the time it has taken us to ride back, this incredible afternoon has turned into a dreary reality."

"What do you mean?" Her heart skipped a beat.

"We both know any romantic relationship between us would be a mistake. I'm not calling you a mistake… far from it. Under ordinary circumstances, there would be no hesitation on my part in pursuing a closer relationship with you, but only if you wanted one."

"I'm in… so what's the problem?" She had said nothing similar before.

"The underlying reality is if I go another step closer, it could cost me my job... a job I love and have worked almost fifteen years to attain. I would destroy my career and reputation I've worked hard to earn within this competitive industry. With your family and my grandfather, I'm not willing to lose their respect and trust. It's a bad idea."

"Bad?" She frowned.

"Logistics alone prove it impossible at best. You live two hours away. I cannot be involved in a long-distance relationship because this job demands one hundred percent of my time... in this place... at Grace Meade. Even here, it would be difficult. You know firsthand the demands of my job as well as your own. One would be sacrificed, and I will not ask either of us to sacrifice anything. I must step back before I am incapable of walking away. You... Catriona Harrington-McKenna... you are the kind of woman wherein a man would lose his soul for all eternity and never recover if you were to move in the opposite direction. That is the undeniable, cruel reality where we find ourselves. I won't do that to you... or me." His voice trailed off into silence.

"Are you afraid?"

"No. I'm a realist."

She remained quiet as the horses sauntered near to the end of the railed fence. He had been direct to a fault, yet she admired his candor. Like Samuel, the Tennesseans were famous for their straightforwardness. His definition of their reality was true. It was unknown to him, but his words resounded truer than he realized. Halting her mare, she turned toward him.

"Declan, wait."

He pulled on the reins and leaned back in the saddle.

With quiet reasoning, she said, "You say you are not an over-thinker, but you are... you and Scott are a lot alike. I agree with you. I do not throw myself at men... ever. To be frank, I'm rather shocked I acted the way I did. Trust me, it is not my norm. Do you believe me?"

"I do."

"Okay. So… we can agree we lacked judgment." She smiled. "I'm overwhelmed by your compliments as I do not see myself in such a grand way, but thank you. When we started out this afternoon, I wasn't looking for a romantic relationship or friendship… no offense. I only wanted a little fresh air. This may surprise you, but I understand your reasoning better than you realize."

"In what way?" His horse flipped its tail to bat away a fly, and Declan adjusted his saddle.

"Are you listening?" she asked.

"Of course, I am."

"Would I ever allow a relationship to cost me my job? No. I have worked hard to build my business into a success. I choose not to have many friends so I can concentrate on my career, and I like my life as it is. Besides, maintaining friendships is hard work… at least it is for me. I hired a brilliant manager to work beside me who takes care of my social media needs and my outside activities because I struggle in those departments. I've told you most of my life's story, so you might as well know the rest. Promise me this conversation will go no further than this fence row."

"You have my word."

"I go out occasionally, but I never commit to more than two or three dates. I don't allow the relationship to go any further. It is a rule whereby I have safeguarded my heart my entire life. No man has been allowed to become anything more than a friend for reasons having nothing to do with him. I have unknown, hidden secrets no one has unlocked, and I will not place my burden on anyone other than myself. I'm as surprised as you about what happened earlier, but there was no hesitation on my part. You see, I can read people too. You did not act alone this afternoon… I think I prompted it. We succumbed to our own sexual tensions left unguarded for a moment."

"I guess… I would define it as something else." He shifted in his saddle again.

"Okay. I'll admit I won't be forgetting it anytime soon. I do not regret a single moment… not one. Maybe I'm lying to myself, and you are right to have read more into it because I felt it too. It was sensual and emotional. If we lived in a different place and time, this afternoon would have been a beautiful start to who knows where."

"True."

"We shared a great kiss… so what? Neither of us dates much. We've known each other a little more than a week, and if you want to blame someone, then blame Cookie and those irresistible lemon squares. I cannot believe I'm saying this out loud, but she must have added oyster seasoning into the batter." They laughed. "Scott and Lillian desperately want me to find someone, but I'm not ready. It was only a kiss… albeit a great one."

"I'm not sure whether to credit the lemon squares or the powdered sugar on your chin."

"We'll call it a draw."

They laughed, but she could see he remained on edge.

"Where do we go from here, Catriona? I cannot take back my actions, and I do not want any awkwardness between us. I hope to remain at Grace Meade; however, it's your decision, isn't it?"

She sat tall in the saddle. "They were my actions too, but I have a solution. May I suggest a business proposition?"

"I'm listening."

She said, "Would you be open to a proposal of becoming my friend without added pressure from either of us? Nothing more, nothing less."

"It's possible."

"It is as simple as that. I need a colleague here at Grace Meade who isn't related or thinks they are. At some faraway point in time, the responsibility of running this estate falls to me. I know our business relationship will be long-term if you're anything like Samuel, and you are a man of integrity. Trust is one hurdle where I have the most difficulty; however, from somewhere deep within me, I know I can trust you. So… Mr. O'Connell, how about it? Can we be friends and consider the last few hours a complete wash, or better yet, a lesson learned to put behind us? Is it possible to begin again?"

He was quiet. He removed his hat and rubbed the back of his neck. "Am I still invited to a football game or is that no longer on the table?"

"After everything I've said, you choose to focus on football?" She laughed. "That, sir, is an added benefit to this deal. I prefer to attend games with at least one person; it might as well be you. I will share my tickets for the next home game, but I can't promise I won't pressure you into cheering for Virginia."

"You can try... okay, friend. I'll take you up on your offer for your home game; however, I'll buy the next round of tickets if we go to Tennessee. Deal?"

"Deal... as friends. Let's shake on it."

She held out her hand. When his fingers wrapped around hers, she remembered his hand touching her face and she trembled. They held hands for a long moment without speaking, staring at one another in agreement and complete understanding. Everything would change to where they had first started once descending their saddles. He removed her glove and kissed the back of her hand. Holding it against his chest for a moment, he slowly let go.

"It was a good day, Miss McKenna."

She smiled. "Yes... a good day."

They proceeded through the gate leading to the stable. He dismounted and helped her from the high Friesian. As she stood beside him, she smelled the musky aroma of his jacket, the same as when he had held her.

"Catriona?"

"Yes?"

"Don't forget the picnic basket."

"Oh, yes. Thank you." She frowned as she untied it.

"Oh, and one more thing..."

"What?" she asked. It irritated her with the whole scenario in which she found herself.

"I was wondering. Please, this is serious. Will you look at me?"

Turning toward him, she asked, "Yes?"

His smile covered his face. "May I have the first dance on Saturday night or is your so-called cotillion card full? Nothing slow or romantic. It will be a little fun between future employer and employee. Might we negotiate a dance into this deal too?"

"You think you're funny, don't you?" Her eyes twinkled.

"I am funny."

"Okay, Mr. O'Connell. You drive a hard bargain, but yes, I can pencil you in as my card is not full... not yet anyway." She pretended to write his name with her finger on her palm. "There. Written as if in blood. The first dance is yours, and I will request the band to make it a lively one. We would not want to give Samuel or Scott any wrong ideas, would we?"

"No, we would not." He chuckled.

"I'll see you tomorrow, Declan. Sleep well."

"You too."

Making her way toward the house, she could feel his arms wrapped around her. Closing her eyes, she remembered the touch of his lips against hers and almost stumbled. Drinking in the moment, she shuttered. *Lord, have mercy on my soul.*

As if her mind were a separate entity, she debated with herself, hoping she would find some sense of rationality in their agreement.

Friends? Are you kidding yourself? What man tells you what he is thinking without holding something back? Why now and why him and why at Grace Meade?

Think, girl. What good will come of this? You know he's right. It's wrong to pursue a deeper relationship for many reasons. Besides, you can relax now that you won't have to tell him the rest of the story.

And what is the rest of the story?

You steer clear of men and why? The unknown secrets?

Yes.

What else? You need to admit your greatest fear... the ultimate secret.

And what is my greatest fear?

You know... the scars.

Oh, yes... how could I forget? No man, not even the best ones, will want me once they have seen those scars.

You're so good at covering them with your tailored clothing. What will happen when you're wearing nothing? Why would you put either of you through such humiliation? You're damaged goods inside and out. You have too many demons. Stick to your business ventures where safety reigns and successes follow.

You're right. I have never had a guy before so this should not prove too difficult. Besides, my business relationship with him is for the greater good. Grace Meade needs him.

And as quick as the flicker of a lit wick, the debate had resolved within her, and as further proof, a peace settled upon her once a final decision was made. Grace Meade needed Declan O'Connell more than she. She glanced back and saw the tall outline of his frame in the darkness and waved. He nodded his head and tipped his hat in her direction as she proceeded through the doorway. Shutting the door behind her, she closed him out of her mind forever.

***

He watched as she strolled the lane toward the garden and into the kitchen. Her words of understanding and laughter created an even stronger aphrodisiac, encircling his mind like a drug engulfing his every thought. Turning his face away, he whispered into the air, "Damn."

He led the horses toward the barn's opening. This was not the day he had envisioned when he awoke. He assumed during their time together, she would have revealed in some small way a spoiled personality who had lived a life with no monetary obstacles in her way. Nothing could be further from the truth. She had been a complete surprise. Her candidness surprised him. She spoke her mind, and it was refreshing to know she did not play games either. All the while, with her every word, he was attracted all the more wishing to hold her again.

"What are you up to, boy?" Samuel stepped out of the darkness and into the dim glow shining from the stable's floodlight.

He had not called Declan 'boy' since he had wrecked his grandfather's truck when he was a kid.

"Nothing, Grandpops. Nothing."

"It didn't look like nothing."

"Why are you here and not in Williamsburg?"

"I came back early because Lillian always needs an extra set of hands this week of the year. Brad told me you were out riding with Catriona. It was dark, and I was worried you might have had some trouble. I was heading toward the truck when I saw you two coming through the clearing. Looks like you were having a serious conversation. Anything I should be concerned about?"

"Not at all. It's business as usual. You don't have to worry about me because I know what lines I can and cannot cross, sir."

"You better be careful or she will get under your skin. She is the boss's daughter, you know."

"Yes, she is, and you need not remind me of the fact. By the way, I would appreciate it if you would not refer to me as 'boy' again. I'm not sure I deserved such a reprimand."

"Sorry, I thought…"

"You know better. Catriona and I have agreed to keep our relationship professional, but friendly, and that is all you saw."

"I'm sorry, Grandson. I'm an old man with old ways. I saw how you two were looking at each other, and that handshake… well, that was not nothing."

"I appreciate you looking out for me, but there is no cause for concern. Excuse me, sir. I need to put these horses away so I can head home. I'm hungry and tired."

"Sure. I'll see you tomorrow."

Declan walked into the stables leading the horses behind him. His mind would not rest.

She is intelligent… but even more vulnerable. She is funny too and likes football. What is that about?

Closing his eyes for a moment, he remembered her raven hair falling over her shoulders as she had turned to face him. He spoke aloud, "Yeah, Declan, old boy, this will be hard."

He had not seen Brad walking out of the stall toward him. "Don't worry, Mr. O'Connell, it won't be too hard. I'll take the horses so you can head to the house. You've had a long day."

"Oh, thanks, but I wasn't talking…"

"Sir?"

"Never mind. Thanks. I appreciate it." He handed Brad the reins. "See you in the morning. Be sure to brush them and toss in a little extra feed. Don't worry about coming in early. Eight o'clock should be fine."

"Yes, sir."

Driving back to his place, he reasoned their relationship would remain as friends only. She would return to her business in a couple of weeks, and his life would settle back to normal. Reassured, he said, "Come on, Declan, you've got this, old man. It takes a little focus."

Taking long strides into the house, he argued, "No harm done."

As he removed his shirt, he caught the light fragrance of her perfume lingering where she laid against him. He breathed in the sweet aroma. It was intoxicating as he remembered her kiss. Lost to her now, he relinquished with a defeated sigh.

"God help me. What have I done?"

 CHAPTER 11

Her Daddy's People

BILL HARRINGTON WAS blessed with a close, large family on both sides of his parents' family tree. His people were of Welsh origin and well respected for their noble character and inner strength. They had been miners for generations and the back-breaking work was all they had known. At one time, Bill drove a dump truck contracted by various mining companies to haul the coal to the prep plants but later surveyed roads and highways for the Commonwealth of Virginia.

Most of the Harrington family and distant relatives never missed church on Sunday mornings. Her people were not religious, fanatical zealots, but men and women who loved God and lived a life reflecting their faith. It was a lifestyle passed down through the generations, but faith with choices—God's creation of man's free will. Their faith was the foundation whereupon they built their lives, and God, nor his church, were mocked in any way. They overflowed with grateful hearts. They thanked God daily for His sharing of His unearned goodness in the ultimate sacrifice of His Holy Son.

James Clarence Harrington, Bill's daddy and Catriona's grandfather, was a sweet man with an enormous love for his family. He was the eldest son of six children and just a young boy of nine years when his father died from the black lung caused by inhaling the inescapable dust. Like those before him, he also became a miner but later drove a coal truck with his eldest son.

The music director at church would call upon James Clarence to sing his favorite hymn, "I'll Fly Away," and would render it acapella at that. He could pray down the Holy Spirit like no other in town. According to Katie Jo, her father-in-law's prayers were so sweet that heaven's angels would gather around to catch a whiff of the pleasing aroma as they ascended to God's nostrils. Catriona's grandfather would rise from the end of the pew and step into the aisle. Kneeling, he would begin his prayers with these words, *"Dear Jesus, I come to you on bended knee before your throne of mercy and grace, with a humble heart and a contrite spirit, asking you to bless us and forgive us of our sins and shortcomings..."*

In the coal mining community, funerals were more common than births. It was customary for a family member or friend to stay with the deceased body from the moment of death until the burial. It was a demonstration of love and respect not shown toward the departed alone but the family as well.

James Clarence died when Catriona was a small girl. Her daddy made sure, although young, she attended the wake held for her grandfather at her grandparents' home. They removed the furniture from the small living room to make space for his coffin. When Bill lifted his daughter to view James Clarence lying beneath a thin sheer veil, she recalled her Aunt Pamela placing her hand beneath the netting to touch his chest one last time as tears streamed down her own daddy's face as he looked on.

Frances Elizabeth Rathburn–Harrington was the wife of James Clarence. She was Bill's mother and grandmother to Catriona, who bore her middle name's sake. Frances was a hard-working, raven-haired woman, who had two children by her first husband. She lost him in a dynamite explosion when creating a new tunnel in the deepest part of the mine shaft. His passing left the young widow to do what she could for her little family, and all the while remaining faithful to her heavenly father. God revealed himself through one man in the hardest of her circumstances, and she married James Clarence. He loved Frances and her girls and treated them as his own. It was natural since both had come from large households, their family would grow to eight boys and girls—four of each.

When recalling her Granny Frances, Catriona always found reasons to smile. Their family had strong political views and loyalties. They were "yellow dog" voters; meaning if a yellow dog had been running on their party's ticket, they would have voted for him. They were respected for their deep convictions, although others might have disagreed with their choices.

Not yet old enough to cook around a hot stove, Catriona's grandmother taught her many household tasks and talents a small child could learn, such as the art of crochet where she created objects using a hook and yarn. She also taught her how to imitate the whistle of a bobwhite and wait for him to return the call just as the sunlight was hitting the dew-covered grass of the early morning hours.

Her grandmother was a talented gardener and a frugal housekeeper. Catriona would tag alongside as her Granny Frances planted, learning secrets under the tutelage of a seasoned master. Frances made her sausage and ground meat and grew the biggest "beefsteak" tomatoes behind her house but close to the kitchen door.

While dragging the garden hose behind them and toting a shaker of salt, Catriona, along with her cousins, would hide in the furrowed aisles to swipe a tomato or two. Warmed by the morning sun and hanging from their vines, the red fruit was picked, rinsed, and seasoned with salt. They would bite into the juicy sweetness—there was nothing better, except maybe consuming them with her granny's homemade mayonnaise on fresh slices of white bread. They devoured the lifted delicacies while staying hidden in their garden fortress, surrounded by the tall plants tied to the stakes with pantyhose dotting the garden row. For those unfamiliar with the ways of country-folk with a limited means of income, a child first learns to appreciate their ingenuity. In her granny's case, she was remarkable in her capacity to stretch a dollar. She threw nothing away if it had another use, including tattered pantyhose no longer worn because of the runners or pulls covering them. As a grower of tomato plants, pantyhose made the best rope to tie tender vines. According to Granny Francis, twine bruised them, but the old nylons did not.

Her garden included a few peach trees draped with fuzz-covered fruit each summer. When picking one from its lofty branches after climbing into the tree, the golden sap oozed like jelly at every knot covering Catriona's hands and clothes.

Frances was happiest when working in the kitchen. At the end of each harvest, she canned vegetables and fruit to last throughout the winter months. After collecting green beans from the garden in baskets, a family impromptu get-together of men and women would pull the ladder back, cane-stitched chairs into a circle beneath the cool evening shade of day's end. Gathering a handful, they would break the beans. First, stripping them of the strings lining each side and snapping each pod section apart, causing a popping, rhythmic sound. They would toss the green pieces into one or two metal dishpans seated in the center on the grass, waiting to hold their yield. The beans' delightful aroma of sweet cleanliness would fill the air with each snap, as everyone would laugh and talk about the local happenings of their day or share stories from their past. An unknown dance step subtly taught, Granny Frances would break one open now and then and run her fingernail down the hull beneath each bean, shelling them into her apron, and tossing them into the mess of pods. The green and white delicacy cooked in fatback would be the perfect accompaniment at Sunday suppers. There was no finer treasure, except for the childhood memory of the family's voices and laughter lingering beneath the branches of the old trees.

Frances was a Sunday School teacher and taught Catriona, along with her other grandchildren, to memorize scripture and the importance of tithing and charity work. Although a devout Christian and comfortable entering the hereafter, her granny didn't go to funerals. James Clarence would say, *"Frances, get on up and let's go or we're gonna hav'ta hire mourners when you die."*

Frances's siblings were lovely people who lived nearby. Her twin sisters contracted scarlet fever as girls, rendering one deaf and the other dead. Her great Aunt Leslie persevered and became proficient in sign language, allowing her to communicate; she later married and had a family of her own. Like so many in their community, she too lost her husband to the dark cavernous hole. The mine always seemed to win.

Catriona visited her often and her great Aunt Leslie would write everything on her notepad so Catriona could understand. She taught Catriona how to spell her own name, molding her fingers to form the letters. Despite her disabilities, Aunt Leslie's spirit remained one of sweetness and joy.

Another sister lived down the street whose husband was blind and difficult at times because of his physical handicap, but a kinder and gentler soul in a woman you would never find. Her great Aunt Ruth welcomed Catriona with a sweet spirit anytime she dropped in. She taught her life can be unfair, but *"... you, Katydid. You have a holy fire burning inside that can never be put out. The Holy Spirit will give you strength in times of trouble. You must always remember, honey. Always remember."*

Granny Frances taught Catriona life lessons through her stories while working in the kitchen preparing a meal. Catriona remembered one in particular.

"When your Aunt Pamela was little, she pretended to be me in all I did around the house. She couldn't have been more than three or four years old and had gone onto the back porch where our orange cat had delivered a new litter of kittens. She loved each one. Pammy had been quiet on the porch for a few minutes when she came inside and turned her attention elsewhere. Later, as she was helping me place my canned pickles in the root cellar, she told me about her busy morning and the canning she had done. Much to my horror, I ran onto the back porch. Lined in a straight row and sitting on the sill of the screened windows were several tiny containers. Innocence lost. Katydid, you must always remember you can't keep any animal or anything living closed or shut up because they'll choke. Whether it be in a jar, a bad courtship, or a coal mine with black dust a-blowing, make sure the living has room to breathe."

Granny Frances became quiet as she turned to look out the window and into the fields beyond. Even at her young age, Catriona knew there was a deeper meaning, but for her, it would wait until another day.

Her grandmother's beautiful, aged face continued to reflect the love she had for her family, although achieved through suffering the loss of two husbands, three sons, and a grandson because of the black ore's continuous crying for souls from somewhere deep underground. Well-earned lines graced her upper lip as if plowed rows in a garden, vanishing when she smiled. Her grandmother suffered a sunstroke one summer day in her garden and never recovered. Surrounded by her children and grandchildren, she passed away in her late eighties when one last stroke promoted her home to heaven, joining her Savior and family members forevermore.

Most of the town's populace, including her daddy's people (the Harrington and Rathburn kinfolk), made their living elsewhere. They scattered like the seeds of a dandelion into a far-reaching breeze, similar to the people mentioned in the Book of Zechariah, "… for I have spread you abroad as the four winds of the heavens." Their closeness of family reigned no more.

Nevertheless, Bill and Katie Jo remained in Sageville to raise Catriona in this protected sanctuary where family generations were buried before them—the only place they would ever call home.

# CHAPTER 12

THE BUZZER RANG from the front gate entrance.

Catriona answered the intercom. "May I help you?"

"Yes. I have a delivery for Miss Catriona McKenna."

Spying the car and trailer through the gate's security camera, she said, "You may bring it to the front door. I will meet you."

Before opening the door, she viewed herself one last time in the foyer mirror. She wore high-waisted, pleated wool cuffed slacks, a long-sleeved, cream silk blouse, and two-toned brown oxford shoes. A paisley-printed scarf was tied around her high ponytail. It appeared as if the 1940s were calling her home.

She walked outside as Peter drove toward her. She waved as he pulled the Cadillac SUV into park.

"Peter... I wasn't expecting you until later."

Opening the door, he said, "Good morning. How are you?"

"Again, I'm fine. You have been so attentive with the phone calls and texts. I'm not sure of the appropriate response any longer. Everyone is aware how sweet you have been."

"You have consumed my thoughts all week, and I have a special delivery for you today."

"You do?" She walked toward the back of the trailer. "What's this?"

"I believe you purchased an old desk belonging to my grandmother."

"I thought the auction house was planning the delivery. In fact, I paid them, didn't I? Oh, my goodness, did I forget to pay?"

"No. After you purchased the desk, I did not want to take the chance of never seeing you again. I told the auction house I would make the delivery myself, and they refunded you all shipping charges. Please consider this a gift."

"So, you wanted to see me again, huh?"

"Yes, I did." Peter smiled.

"Well, I don't know what to say, but thank you."

"I had hoped my delivery would be a welcomed surprise, but I realize now I wasn't thinking, was I? With all today's activities, my bright idea might not have been so bright after all."

"Don't be silly. It is a kind gesture, and I'm glad you're here." She smiled at him with a gaze that came as natural as if he were looking into a child's face who had received a gift on Christmas morning.

"I almost forgot. I have something else for you."

"More?"

She followed him to the passenger door where two large green cardboard boxes tied with white ribbon were propped on the front floorboard.

"One is for you and the other is for Lillian. I wanted to thank her for inviting me for the weekend."

"Peter, you shouldn't have, but thank you. The bouquet you sent earlier this week still looks beautiful." Catriona liked that he thought of her mother.

"Well, I couldn't come to a horse event and not bring roses. My grandfather would roll over in his grave if I had not."

Taking the boxes, she said, "Grab your luggage and follow me. Lillian and Scott are in the stables and should be back in a little while, but I can show you to your room and you can freshen up. How does that sound?"

"Perfect."

"Good. Cookie is preparing lunch for us to eat on the veranda, and I'll make sure she sets another place at the table."

"I should have called in advance."

"No reason to worry. Cookie always prepares extra... just in case. We have guests popping in all the time. It's not a problem, and besides, I never have guests. It will delight them to no end. Trust me."

Walking into the foyer, Cookie and Samuel were walking down the hallway toward them.

Catriona said, "Your timing is perfect. Samuel and Cookie, I want you to meet one of Scott's colleagues and my friend, Peter Tramwell. Peter, this is Samuel O'Connell, one of our dearest and most cherished friends. He taught me how to ride. He used to be in charge of our equine business on-site; however, he is now retired. And this is Cookie Johnson, my precious, pretend grandmother who is the best cook on the planet and all-around incredible caregiver of this house and all who dwell within it. I would be lost without either of them, and they know it."

Cookie said, "Mr. Tramwell, it is nice to meet you. I hope you have not eaten and will join us for lunch."

Catriona said, "I've invited him already, Cookie. I apologize. I should have told you Peter was coming earlier, but I did prepare the blue bedroom for his stay. You have enough to worry about, so I thought I would lend a hand."

"Thank you, hon."

"Peter has brought flowers for Lillian and me, and we are heading to the kitchen for vases."

"Don't be silly. Hand those to me and I'll take care of it. You can show Mr. Tramwell to his room."

Peter said, "It is nice to meet you both. Please call me Peter."

Catriona smiled. He was genuine in his response to them.

Samuel reached out and shook his hand. "Welcome to Grace Meade, Peter. No reason for Catriona to escort you to your room. I will take your suitcase, and I'm sure she would rather show you the grounds before everyone gets here."

Catriona hugged Samuel. "Thank you. You are too good to me."

Samuel grinned. "Oh, honey, it's always my pleasure. You two get out of here and have some fun."

Catriona said, "Oh, my word. I almost forgot about the trailer. Samuel, would you ask a couple of the guys to carry in a piece of furniture Peter has delivered for me? It's a small desk, and for the moment, you can place it against the vacant wall in Scott's study."

Peter said, "I can help unload the desk."

"Well, there's no time like the present. Let's see what we've got." Samuel placed the luggage in the foyer and followed them outside as Cookie took the boxes into the kitchen. When Peter opened the trailer's doors, Samuel looked it over. "This should be no problem at all. I think the two of us can handle it, don't you?"

Peter replied, "I think so too. Which way to the study?"

"Follow me." Catriona held the door open and led them through the hallway. After setting it in place, Samuel left to take Peter's luggage to his room.

Catriona stroked the carved wood circling the edge of the desk. "It's more beautiful than I remember. This desk could not be more perfect. Thank you for allowing me to purchase it."

"Grandmother's desk is the best thing that has happened to me. I would never have met you otherwise."

Catriona reached for his hand. "Come. Let me give you the grand tour, and then we can move your car to the carriage house."

"Lead the way."

***

Samuel joined Cookie in the kitchen as she was arranging the flowers, and they could see the couple through the kitchen's window walking into the garden.

Cookie spoke first. "That is a sight I have prayed for years. She looks happy and who would not be with a man as nice as him? Lillian was not wrong."

"Not wrong about what?" Samuel asked, never taking his eyes off of them.

"Lillian said Peter comes from an important family and is working with Scott. He seems to be captivated by Catriona too. She also mentioned Catriona would never want for anything if she marries him. I hope it works out for her."

"Catriona doesn't need to worry about money. She has her own and Lillian and Scott have made sure they set her for life… I wonder if he's a gold digger."

"You are too old, Samuel. Don't you want our girl to be happy? She deserves to be happy."

"She sure does, but she already has everything. Catriona doesn't need a man to give her things."

"Oh, shush, and hand me those scissors." Cookie turned back toward the island to finish arranging the roses.

Samuel remained quiet. It was uncommon to see her with a man. He continued to stare as if portraying a terrible spy in a movie. "How long did she say he's planning on staying?"

"The entire weekend, and then they are driving to Washington for a couple of days together. Sounds romantic, doesn't it? Why?"

"Oh, no reason. No reason at all." Samuel thought of Declan.

"Here… help me with these vases. Take this one into the foyer, and I'll take this one into the living room."

***

When Samuel and Cookie returned to the kitchen, Catriona and Peter were sitting at the island.

"Are Lillian and Scott here?" Catriona asked.

Samuel said, "I think I saw them heading into the garage."

"Thanks, Samuel. I think we will go look for them." Smiling, Catriona looked at Peter and asked, "Ready?"

"I am. Show me the way."

Making their way toward the front door, Lillian and Scott were in the foyer admiring the flowers.

"Peter, how good it is to see you. Welcome to Grace Meade." Lillian was all smiles and hugged Peter as if he had always been a part of the family. "I hope Catriona has shown you the accommodations while you are here, and let me say the flowers are gorgeous. You shouldn't have, but thank you."

"It's good to see you again, Lillian, and you're most welcome. Grace Meade is more than I imagined. It's an incredible place."

Scott shook Peter's hand. "Thank you, Peter. My Lillian Rose has lived nowhere but here, except when she attended William and Mary."

"Oh, my love, that was long ago." Lillian laughed. "We want you to feel at ease while you are here… please make yourself at home. Again, thank you for your quick actions on Monday night. If you had not been there to pull Catriona from the street… well, I can't think about it without crying."

"There is no reason to thank me, Lillian. I'm glad Catriona is better."

Scott patted him on the shoulder. "Spoken like a true hero if you ask me."

Cookie interrupted, announcing their lunch was ready.

Lillian said, "Thank you, Cookie. We will be right there. Catriona, after lunch, you and Peter should go for a ride and you can show him the rest of the property. We are setting up a casual dinner by the stables tonight so everyone can come and go as they please."

"What a great idea. Would you like to join me for a ride this afternoon?" Catriona asked.

"Sounds great."

"Let's not leave Cookie waiting. Shall we?" Scott led the way onto the veranda.

Following their lunch, Brad greeted them at the stable doors. "Catriona, Angel is ready, and Mr. McKenna has offered Maximillian to Mr. Tramwell for the afternoon."

"Thank you, Brad. Is Declan here? I want to introduce him to Mr. Tramwell."

"No, ma'am. He is prepping the staging area for the auction. Do you want me to find him for you?"

"No, thank you. I thought if he were close, then I would. Don't mention it as I will see him again sometime this weekend."

"Yes, ma'am."

Catriona turned toward Peter. "Declan O'Connell is our new equine manager for the estate. He is Samuel's grandson and has taken over his position. I had hoped to introduce you."

"Another time. I'm looking forward to our ride. It has been a while since I have spent an afternoon riding for pleasure."

Catriona agreed. "Well, what are we waiting for?"

Soon they were trotting into the meadows and on toward the lake and the springhouse.

***

Declan walked into the stables. He yelled out to anyone within listening distance, "Does anyone know why Angel and Maximillian are not in their stalls?"

Brad replied, "Catriona and one of her friends are out riding this afternoon. She told me she wanted to show him the property."

"When did they leave?"

"I'm not sure. I guess it has been close to a couple of hours."

"Thanks." Declan walked toward the stable entrance and glanced out into the meadow. He didn't see her.

"Who are you looking for?" Samuel asked as he walked toward Declan.

"No one, Grandpops. Why do you ask?"

"No reason. I met Catriona's friend. He arrived from Washington earlier today. He is a good-looking man... some attorney Scott's working with. She is excited he's here or seems to be, and he brought her two dozen roses and delivered a desk. Nice fella. Peter Tramwell is his name. They make a fine-looking couple too. I'd say he's in his mid-thirties... about the same age as you if I had to guess."

"Grandpops, what are you doing? What does her friend mean to me?"

"Nothing. Carrying on a little conversation, that's all."

"Thanks, but I can name twenty other things I need to be concerned with at the moment. Are you available to help me for a few minutes?"

"I am."

Declan and Samuel headed to the paddock. When he returned, Brad was brushing down Angel.

"Is Catriona here?"

"No, sir. You missed her, but she asked about you. I think she wanted to introduce her friend. She and Mr. Tramwell have headed back to the main house. They left only moments ago. You can probably catch them if you try."

Declan stepped outside and saw them as they entered the garden. He walked toward them as Catriona laughed, and then Peter kissed her. Declan stopped in his tracks as he overheard their conversation.

"A kiss, Peter? Who gave you the impression a kiss would be okay?"

"You are incredible, Catriona. It seemed only the natural thing to do. I hope I did not make you feel uncomfortable."

"I'm surprised. Nothing more."

"I hope it won't be the last." Peter held the kitchen door open as she passed.

Glancing up at him, she said, "Let's make sure it isn't."

Her response caused him to laugh.

"Yes, ma'am," he said, and followed her inside.

Caught off-guard, Declan backed into the stables. His stomach ached as if he had been gut-punched and his lips tightened knowing he had only himself to blame.

***

With the afternoon's auction completed, Declan stepped inside the party tent. Samuel had described to him how the Saturday night gala is planned with a different theme to be seen and experienced throughout the evening—always casual and fun for all. Café lights swaggered back and forth over the long farm tables and rustic chairs beneath the clear tent canopy. The latest rockabilly band on the verge of breaking onto the Nashville music scene was playing in the background as their three hundred plus guests were seated inside the outdoor pavilion.

Declan walked over to Cookie standing by the buffet tables.

"You have outdone yourself, sweet lady."

"Not this time. Lillian and I selected the menu, and we are allowing the caterers to handle it. This year we chose grilled steaks and fried chicken, served with sides of corn on the cob, fried pickles, Southern collard greens and kale, smoked sweet potato salad, fried okra, yellow squash casserole, bacon cheddar biscuits, and cornbread pudding. For the grand finale, I gave them my prized bourbon pecan pie recipe, but I made the special whipped cream."

"I have gained ten pounds just looking at this spread."

Cookie laughed. "You make sure to try a little of everything, Declan."

"Just for you, I will, but first, I need something to drink."

"The bar is in the corner over there. Beverages range from non-alcoholic lemonade and sweet tea to a variety of beers and wines of any choosing. Lillian would not have settled for anything less. This event is always her crowning touch on the day's events."

The auction had been an enormous success, and buyers and sellers alike were all in the mix, alongside the night's political guests for the lengthy night celebration. None would have left before partaking in Lillian's party of good food, drinks-a-flowing, and dancing into the wee hours of the morning. There wasn't a hotel within miles not booked months in advance.

Samuel motioned Declan over to a table near the back entrance.

"Wow, Grandpops. This is something, isn't it? I had not taken the time to come by earlier to check it out. I had no idea."

"Lillian knows how to throw a party. Shush. Lillian is getting ready to kick off the evening. Here… sit down."

Declan pulled out a chair. He watched as Lillian took the mic in hand. Scott and Catriona were standing on the stage behind her.

Lillian said, "May I have your attention, please?"

Everyone quieted as heads turned toward her.

"We want to thank everyone for being with us this evening as we celebrate another successful horse auction here at Grace Meade."

There was a round of applause and a few yelps from the guests.

"As always, ten percent of our total profit from today's efforts will go toward our charity hunger fund for feeding Virginia's needy children."

There was even louder applause. Declan whistled, along with a few others from the floor.

"Before we proceed, I want to introduce a few special people who have joined us this evening. We have our dear friends, the Honorable Governor Anthony Hughes and his lovely wife and Virginia's first lady, Mrs. Vivian Hughes, along with Senator and Mrs. Nathan and Sarah Williams. We welcome you as our honorary guests."

They stood and nodded to the crowd. There was a thunderous standing ovation. Declan watched Catriona as she beamed watching her mother.

"Thank you, everyone. Thank you. Please… be seated. Governor and Senator, I believe we have a majority in the house tonight."

There was laughter and more applause.

Someone yelled out, "There are a few of us here still representing the minority!"

All laughed and the applause was louder than before. Drinks were flowing, and most had not been shy in partaking of their hosts' hospitality of spirits.

Lillian continued, "My husband, Scott, our daughter, Catriona, and I, along with the staff here at Grace Meade, welcome and invite you to enjoy your evening as we eat, drink, converse and dance the night away, and might I add… regardless of your voting party preferences!"

Everyone laughed.

"The buffet line and bar are open, but I think most of you are already aware by the smiles I see on your faces."

"Yes, ma'am!" someone yelled from the crowd. More laughter resounded.

"First, we believe in honoring family here at Grace Meade. In keeping with this evening's long-revered tradition, we invite our guests of honor to join Scott, Catriona, and me on the dance floor as we begin this evening's festivities. Immediately following, I ask you to join in or if you prefer, grab a plate and drink. Our home is your home! Let's have fun, shall we?"

Lillian handed the mic back to the lead singer and Scott escorted her onto the floor along with the Governor, Senator, and their spouses joining them. Catriona looked back at Peter, but someone tapped her on the shoulder. She turned and Declan was standing behind her with an extended hand. "I believe you promised this first dance to me."

"Why, yes... good evening, Mr. O'Connell." Catriona turned to Peter and said, "I promised a dance. I'll be right back."

Declan smiled as he took her onto the floor. "You are gorgeous, Miss McKenna."

"Thank you, Mr. O'Connell. You don't look too shabby yourself." She laughed and then confessed, "No matter how many times I do this, I'll admit I'm not very good at the two-step."

"Let me take it from here. I'm supposed to lead, remember?"

A boyish smile crossed his face as they twirled around on the dance floor. The evening's attire was casual, and despite the important guests, Catriona was the center of every eye as Declan moved her about the floor. Her hair was styled to the side in a soft braid falling across her shoulder as it lay against the front of her floral form-fitting tee with its three-quarter length sleeves. She wore a Navajo Squash Blossom necklace and matching belt topping her multilayered skirt and cowboy boots, all the same turquoise color. She was perfection in his eyes.

Soon the dance floor was full as everyone poured onto it. They continued dancing as the next song turned into a line dance with both young and old alike enjoying the moment as the two relished in the fun. When the music dropped to a slower pace, Declan asked if Catriona would dance one more; however, she hesitated.

"I shouldn't, but thank you for helping me not look too awkward on the dance floor. There are plenty of wallflowers here who would be excited to have you ask them." She curtsied and then laughed. "I bid you a good night, kind sir, and have resigned my dance card to someone else for the rest of the evening. Thank you, again."

She then hugged him and return to the head table where Peter was waiting. Declan moved over to the drink station and then sat at Samuel's table.

"You two looked darn good out there. She is a pretty thing, isn't she?" Samuel was drinking a hard lemonade while his elbows rested on the table.

"You won't catch me arguing with you, Grandpops." He took a swig from the longneck beer bottle. The liquid ran cold against the back of his throat.

"Declan, I was wrong to confront you about Catriona. I apologize. I'm too old to be telling anyone how to run their personal affairs, but I will say this..."

"Of course, you will." Declan laughed, interrupting him.

"You go after her."

"I'm sorry?" His grandfather's words shocked him.

"You heard me. I could not dream of a better girl for my grandson. Although I kind of think of her as my granddaughter already, but you know what I mean."

"Wow. I can't believe it, and here I have worried about my job and upsetting everyone. Do you think she would go for someone like me?" Declan looked in her direction. She was laughing as she talked to Peter and Scott. He loved the way she appeared to enjoy every waking minute. He thought it odd he could fall so hard having known her for such a short time. She felt like home when he held her.

"Grandson, you are worthy of anyone in my book. The O'Connell family has no reason to sell themselves short either. They may not know it, but we do okay too, so what's with the less-than attitude, huh?"

"It has nothing to do with money, Grandpops. Grandfather Pierce made sure there was plenty, and I'll always be grateful I can do what I love."

"Then tell me... what is it?" Samuel asked.

"I don't know. It's a feeling I have. Scott's houseguest appears to have her full attention at the moment. Besides, she isn't interested in me anymore… I made sure."

"Oh, hogwash. Catriona is her own person and as down-to-earth as they come. She might look all gussied up and too good for anyone, but she could not be further from it. She's a rare diamond, and if you want her, then you don't stop until you get her."

Declan glanced over toward her again. He watched as Peter took her hand and led her onto the dance floor. They embraced when the tempo dropped to a slow melody. He could not help but notice she appeared to enjoy the way Peter held her. Declan's jaw tightened.

"You know, Grandpops, I think I might sit out the rest of the evening. She promised one dance and I got two. I should consider myself pretty lucky."

"Don't be dragging your feet because she won't last long, I'm afraid. She and Peter are leaving for Washington tomorrow."

"For how long?" Declan continued to watch as they danced. His lips formed a hard, straight line.

"Not sure. Cookie said something about a concert, and I think she is staying overnight at Scott's for a couple of days. That's all I know."

Declan thought himself a fool to have placed his job above her. He watched as they held each other swaying to the music, and he didn't like the view. "Grandpops, I think I'll call it a night."

"You haven't eaten."

"I'll get something to go. Truth be told, I'm pretty exhausted. Today was tough, but it was good too." Declan stood to leave.

"Yes, it was. Everyone helped make a ton of money today and it helps the kids too." Samuel paused and smiled. He touched Declan on the sleeve. "You did good, Grandson, taking over for this old man. I'm proud of you."

"Thank you, Grandpops, I appreciate you saying so." Declan patted his grandfather on the shoulder. "I'll catch you sometime tomorrow."

"You bet."

Declan walked over to the buffet and asked for two plates to go. Glancing back, they were still dancing. Declan watched as Peter kissed her. Turning to the catering staff, he asked, "Hey… will you throw in a six-pack while you're at it?"

"Sure, sir. Whatever you want."

Walking to the stables, he placed one of the to-go plates and a couple of beers in the fridge in his office. He checked on Angel. A horse could not have been more beautiful, except its owner. He then remembered Catriona's face when he had placed her foot into the stirrup. He petted the horse on her snout as she nuzzled against him nickering for a treat.

"Rest good, girl."

As he pulled into his drive, Declan could hear the music in the distance as it echoed across the fields. He sat outside on the deck and ate in silence. At that moment, he took Samuel's advice.

"A new business partnership can wait," he said aloud.

Creatures within hearing distance were reverberating their evensong as they cried for rain. He downed another bottle, attempting to quench the thirst growing within him. The next opportunity regarding her would not be wasted. He would make sure.

# CHAPTER 13

PETER PULLED THE black Mercedes against the curb in front of the stately three-story Georgetown home. Ringing the bell, he adjusted his coat as the housekeeper answered the door.

"Good evening. May I help you?"

"Good evening. I'm here to see Miss Catriona McKenna."

"Yes, sir. May I tell her who's calling?"

"Peter Tramwell."

"Please come in. She is expecting you."

He stepped into the dramatic two-story atrium with its winding staircase leading to the rooms above.

"I will let her know you are here. Do you want me to place the flowers in a vase for you?"

"No, I would prefer to present them myself, but thank you."

"Of course. You may wait in the living room."

"Thank you." Peter walked into the room.

The tan federal brownstone was elegant and tastefully decorated. He could see into the garden patio through the French doors located on each side of the fireplace. Hearing footsteps, he walked back into the foyer. Catriona descended the staircase. Her hair was wrapped into a French twist and diamond teardrop earrings fell below her lobes. She was wearing silver gloves stretched above her elbows, and her sleeveless, full-length, high neck gown made of red satin taffeta rustled as she moved. It included a full overskirt attached at the hips trailing behind her, revealing the pencil column fitted gown beneath.

"You look amazing."

"Thank you... so do you."

"I'm not sure a tux can compare to your gown."

"Oh, I don't know. I guess it all depends on your perspective."

He laughed. "I guess it does."

"By the way, you had me at the white scarf and the long dress overcoat."

"Did I?" He laughed again.

"I love a man in a long dress coat."

"I'll have to remember, won't I?" Peter's eyes danced when he spoke.

"Are those for me?"

"Yes. I forgot the flowers were in my hand. You have distracted me."

"They are beautiful. Thank you."

Rosemary approached the two standing in the hallway. She was carrying Catriona's hooded full-length red cape lined in the same silver satin as her gloves. Peter draped it around her shoulders.

"May I put those in a vase, Catriona?"

"Yes, thank you. Would you also place them in the living room?"

Rosemary nodded. "May I say you both look handsome tonight? I hope you have a wonderful evening."

"Thank you. I promise to have her home before dawn... don't wait up for us." All laughed as the two headed out the door.

They had not driven far when Peter noticed in the rearview mirror a black sedan following them. As he turned into the valet parking at the restaurant, the car continued driving past, but he could not read the license plate before it disappeared around the corner.

"What's wrong?" Catriona touched his arm.

"Nothing. Nothing at all. I'm starving. How about you?"

"Yes, I guess I am."

As they made their way through the restaurant, Peter recognized Senator Williams as they passed his table.

"Good evening, Senator."

The senator stood when seeing Catriona, and replied, "Good evening. What a coincidence. Didn't we see each other only last night?"

"Yes, sir," Peter said.

"Catriona, you look lovelier every time I see you."

Mrs. Williams echoed in agreement. "You do look beautiful, my dear."

She blushed. "Thank you. You're most kind."

Senator Williams continued, "We had a wonderful time last night. Please thank your parents again for their gracious hospitality."

"I will."

Senator Williams said, "Peter, I want you to call me over the next day or two. We should have lunch."

"I will. Thank you, sir. It would be my honor."

Mrs. Williams said, "Darling, let them enjoy their dinner. You can talk another time."

When seated, Catriona placed the napkin in her lap. "This is a beautiful restaurant. I don't believe I've dined here before."

"A good friend recommended it. This is my first time too."

"Let's hope the food is as good as its surroundings."

Peter said, "There appear to be several politicians here. I see the Speaker of the House and Senator Joseph from Tennessee sitting next to the window."

"You know how to pick the right places, don't you?" Catriona laughed because politics did not interest her, but Scott's and Lillian's social circles included politicians at all levels making her aware of the "Who's Who" in Washington.

They continued to discuss their likes and dislikes about the capital city and both enjoyed one another's company throughout dinner. As they were leaving, someone called out.

"Hey, Pete! How the hell are you?" He stood to greet Peter as they passed.

"Chad? It's been a long time. It's good to see you, man." The two men shook hands. "Please, may I introduce you to Catriona McKenna, my date for this evening?"

"It's my pleasure. I can't believe it. The one and only Pete Tramwell... you haven't changed a bit."

"Catriona, this is Chad Parks, one of my old fraternity brothers."

"It's my pleasure, Miss McKenna." He nodded as he shook her hand.

"Do me a favor, Chad. There is no reason to fill her head about our old, glory days."

"Those were crazy days, weren't they? Georgetown was too long ago, wasn't it?"

"Sometimes it feels like yesterday, but yes, it's been a few years. What are you doing now?"

Chad said, "Same as you is what I'm hearing. I'm working in Washington at the moment on a case for one of my clients. I believe you are one of the prosecuting attorneys in this mining lawsuit."

Peter looked surprised. "I wasn't aware you were on their team. You're in the mix of attorneys, are you?"

"Yes, but as one of the firm's associate lawyers. Our office is in Richmond, but I'm in town over the next few days. We should get together."

"Sure, why not?" Peter reached into his wallet. "Here is my card. Give me a call and I'll see if I'm available to grab lunch."

"Sounds good."

"Good night."

"Good night to you too. I'll call you sometime tomorrow. It was a pleasure meeting you, Miss McKenna."

"Likewise, I'm sure." Catriona smiled at him.

"Wait a moment. McKenna? Are you part of the McKenna Law Firm?"

She laughed. "No. I chose a different vocational path from my father."

"Oh, your father... that's interesting," Chad replied with a smirk as he nodded toward Peter.

"Oh?" she asked.

"I meant... never mind what I meant. Pete, you always were a lucky man."

"In what way?" Peter's sudden icy stare became obvious to everyone.

"Beautiful woman on your arm, along with her daddy owning the firm. You are working your way up pretty fast, aren't you?"

"I could always count on you to bring the conversation to a much lower level, Chad. I let my guard down again, didn't I? We'll see you in court. Let's go, Catriona. I do not want to spoil this remarkable evening surrounded by poor company."

"Go to hell, Pete. I had forgotten what an arrogant piece of work you could be. Always working on the next comeuppance scheme. I'd be careful, Miss McKenna."

Peter did not acknowledge him and took Catriona by the arm and escorted her out.

When they exited into the restaurant's portico waiting for the valet to bring their car, she asked, "What happened back there?"

"It's not worth discussing. Sometimes college days should remain in the past. You want to remember the good, but the bad can sometimes raise its ugly reminders of past truths. Let's not waste any more time discussing old friends."

She squeezed his hand. "You will not hear any complaints from me. Let's start over. Where now?"

He kissed the back of her gloved hand and placed it inside the crook of his elbow. "I believe I invited you to an evening of cello music."

"Yes, sir, I believe you did."

Upon entering the Kennedy Center, a crowd had already gathered, excited about the evening's concert; however, several people were whispering and looking in their direction.

Catriona asked, "Do you know these people?"

"No, I can't say I do. Why do you ask?"

"They appear to be talking about us."

"Not us... you." He found it refreshing she would not consider herself worthy of others' attention.

"Me?"

"You are the most beautiful woman here, and they are trying to figure out who you are and where you have been hiding. You are more radiant than any chandelier in this building."

Catriona's face reddened when she laughed. "You're sweet, but don't be ridiculous."

Soon, the concert was underway. It pleased him to watch her smile—mesmerized by the music. He reached for her hand. Glancing over, she smiled as she squeezed his fingers.

At intermission, they moved outside the Concert Hall for a glass of wine.

"Are you enjoying the concert?"

"Oh, my word, I am. The strings tug at your heart as the cello plays with its deep and moody sounds. The emotion is raw and the passion with which he plays touches my soul. I cannot wait for the second half of the performance."

The concert ended shortly thereafter with thunderous applause. As they pulled from the parking deck, he asked, "Where do we go from here?"

"I don't know. You're the one who has to work tomorrow."

"I told my secretary I would not be in until after lunch."

"You rearranged your schedule for me? How sweet."

"We could go back to my townhouse. I want to share something with you."

"Sounds intriguing. I'm in."

Not driving further than three blocks, Peter noticed the headlights of the same black sedan reflected in the rearview mirror. "Odd."

"What is?" she asked.

"I think someone is following us."

"Now?" Catriona turned to look over her shoulder, but he stopped her.

"Face forward. I don't want them to know I'm aware they are there."

"Should I call the police?"

"I don't think so. Let's see how this plays out."

"Are you sure, Peter?"

"It may be my imagination, but I'll turn at the next block."

Catriona fidgeted with her gloves. Peter turned the car at the next street corner, and the sedan continued straight on its original path.

"I'm not sure if I'm paranoid or not, but they seem to have gone."

"I'm so relieved. Does this happen often?"

"Not to my knowledge. I've been careful to pay closer attention to my surroundings since we were out with Scott and Lillian." He reached over and held her hand.

"Of course. How silly of me."

"Not at all. I'm sorry I caused you to worry."

Soon they arrived at his home. It was a beautiful townhouse not too far from Scott's. He pulled into the garage and closed the electronic door behind them. He never saw the sedan parked across the street with the engine running and lights off.

"Welcome to my home."

"It's beautiful."

She walked into the large living room where a baby grand was sitting in the corner along with two cellos placed behind it. The house was decorated with a mixture of antiques as well as modern touches. A Jackson Pollock painting hung above the fireplace mantle. She turned with eyes opened wide.

"Is this who I think it is?"

"Yes. It belonged to my incredible but eccentric grandmother. She was a collector of rare beauty and passed the trait down to me so I've been told. She loved everything pertaining to modern art. There's a Salvador Dali in the dining room."

"Oh my. She does sound eccentric. What is my surprise or do I have to wait?"

"It will wait, but first, would you like to make yourself more comfortable?"

"I didn't bring anything with me."

He smiled. "I think I might have a pair of sweats and a T-shirt you can borrow."

"No, but thank you."

"You can at least make yourself at home and remove your shoes and gloves."

"That's a lovely idea."

"May I get you something to drink?"

"Water, please."

"Coming right up, madam. Please, let me take your cape."

"Thank you."

He removed it from her shoulders and left the room. When he returned, he had removed his bowtie and had unbuttoned his shirt with a couple of buttons exposing the white tee beneath. He was standing in his sock feet, holding a glass of ice with a bottled water. His appearance caused her to giggle.

"Is something funny?" he asked as he poured her drink.

"Nothing. You do look comfortable. What did you want to show me?"

"This…" He pulled the old cello around for a better view.

"It's incredible."

He nodded in agreement. "It was my great-grandfather's. May I play for you?"

"Is this the infamous cello for sale, but not for sale?"

"It is." He twirled it around on its stand and laughed.

"I would love to hear you play." She sat on the sofa and removed her earrings, shoes, and gloves.

Taking the antique cello into his hands, he began to tune it with the help of the Steinway. "This old instrument's sound is untouchable and resonates like nothing compared to today's instruments, yet I have a hard time keeping it tuned. I don't trust leaving it with any repair shop."

"I wouldn't either. I cannot believe you tempted me with this at the auction."

His cheeks grew ruddy and she laughed at his embarrassment. "I apologize for lying to you. I was trying to keep your attention for as long as I could."

"No worries. You have my complete, undivided attention now."

"It is Italian from the late eighteen hundreds. The inlay and carving are impeccable, and if I recall, the woods are poplar and willow."

"Do you play the piano also?" Placing her glass on the coffee table, she walked over and sat on the piano's bench beside him. Her gown fell into gentle folds covering the floor beneath them.

"I do. Music lessons were never an option for me. You did it or nothing else."

She said, "I liked my lessons. Music has been one of my solaces, particularly during a tough time in my life. I find it calming. When I'm stressed, I either play the cello or ride horses."

She became silent watching him as he tightened each peg. His eyes were closed as he leaned forward listening to the sound of each string until the tune was perfect.

"Are you ready to hear this?"

"I am, sir."

He stood and pulled a chair next to the piano to face her. "This is a piece I wrote one summer while staying with my grandparents. I've added in a mixture of classical along with more honest notes I have found in melodies native to the Virginia Appalachian area. I think you'll like it... at least I hope you do. No one but my grandmother has heard it."

"I feel honored, and I promise I won't critique you... I'll keep an open mind." She winked.

Leaning the cello against his shoulder and taking the bow in hand, he began moving it with gentle sweeps across the old bridge as his fingers moved to form the chords at the neck.

She closed her eyes.

The instrument's tonality was remarkable. He played it as soft as silk and then he pushed it to reveal its rich, deeper sound. The mastery in which he played the score was awe-inspiring. The chords were full and complicated with their progression of depth and context, yet light and poetic.

He looked up and saw her crying. He stopped playing and pulled her toward him. Wiping the tears from her face, he said, "Allow me to make love to you." He leaned in and kissed her beneath her chin.

"I can't," she whispered. She stretched her neck back as he continued to kiss her.

He whispered in her ear. "Why not?"

"The timing…"

Surprised, he met her eyes. "Timing? The timing could not be more perfect. This weekend and the concert have been more than I could have hoped. I cannot remember being so consumed with anyone. I want you, Catriona. I thought you wanted me too… how did I misread you?"

"It has been wonderful spending time with you."

"Then come with me." He stood, lifting her to her feet. He kissed her deeply as she leaned into his grasp. Holding her hand, Peter led her across the hallway into his bedroom in total silence, except for the soft rustling from the fabric of her gown. He started unzipping the thick material and kissed the back of her neck. She stiffened, then shuttered beneath his hands. She turned to face him. He could not help but notice the panicked look in her eyes.

She said, "I must go."

"Why?"

"I'm sorry. It's not you; I promise. It's me."

"What did I do wrong?"

"Nothing. Nothing at all." She straightened her gown. "Please… hook my dress. Please."

"You are a walking contradiction, Catriona. One minute you are fine, and the next minute, you're not. I apologize if I have offended you. We can go about this a different way."

"You have not offended me. I'm the one who should be apologizing. I thought I wanted this, I truly did, but I feel sick and my stomach hurts." She trembled.

"Stay here tonight. I have a guestroom."

She shook her head no. "I cannot stop shaking. Is it cold in here?

"Do you want me to take you home?"

"I do."

"You really want me to take you home?" he asked in disbelief.

"Yes, I really do."

"It's two o'clock in the morning… but fine." He noticed her skin damp to the touch as he hooked the clasp at the top of the dress. She walked into the living room to find her shoes and earrings. He stared at the floor in disbelief as he tied his shoelaces.

"Where did you hang my cape?" She continued to look away avoiding eye contact.

"It's in the guestroom. Please stay."

Catriona shook her head and her lower lip quivered. He could see how upset she had become.

"Catriona, it's fine. I'll get it."

When he returned, they did not speak as he escorted her to the car. After driving several minutes, he contained his concern no longer and glanced at her. "You must tell me what's wrong."

Her voice trembled. "I'm not sure. I was fine, but when you kissed the back of my neck, I felt frightened. Oh, Peter, you know so little about me, and maybe we should keep it that way. I have demons not even I understand."

"Just because you are unwell at the end of this evening is no reason to stop seeing you, and there is no reason to be afraid. Is there another reason?"

"No. Will you forgive me?" she asked.

"There's nothing to forgive. I enjoy your company."

"Please do not allow my behavior to affect your relationship with Scott and this case. Maybe dating is a bad idea."

"It's a good idea, and nothing will affect my working relationship with Scott."

As they talked, the same sedan pulled out behind them. The driver did not turn on his headlights until they hit the major thoroughfare. The car followed as they parked in front of Scott's home. The unseen headlights turned off as the car pulled into a space across the street.

"Will you allow me to escort you to the door at least?"

"Yes. Thank you."

He circled the car to open her door and glanced over his shoulder. He noticed someone sitting in the sedan, but said nothing as he hurried her toward the townhome's entrance.

"Good night, Peter."

"Good night. I'll call you tomorrow." He looked over his shoulder a second time.

"I'm going back to Grace Meade tomorrow."

"So soon?" He turned back toward her.

"I think it's for the best."

"I'll call you tomorrow. Good night." He leaned in and kissed her on the forehead. She opened the door and closed it behind her.

Skipping every other step to the sidewalk, he bolted toward the parked car. As the car lunged forward, its squealing tires smoked as it sped past him. He thought he recognized Chad Parks in the passenger seat.

He screamed at the tail-lights as they disappeared, "What do you want, asshole?"

In his haste, he saw only the last two letters of the Virginia license plate. Walking back toward his car, he tried to recall if it were his frat brother or just his imagination after seeing him earlier in the evening. He searched for his keys when the door behind him opened and Catriona stepped outside.

"Peter?"

"Yes?" He could not see her face as her silhouette was dark with the foyer light radiating behind her.

"Are you okay?"

"Yes, I'm fine. Why do you ask?"

"I thought I heard someone yell. Was it you?"

"No. I took a walk for a moment to breathe in the cool night air. No reason to worry."

"Oh." She bit her lower lip.

"You need to go back inside. I hope you sleep well."

"Wait." She descended the steps toward him. "We did not part on good terms, I'm afraid, and I want to make this right. Please know I had a wonderful evening. The concert was everything I had hoped and the dinner was excellent. The highlight of the entire evening was your music… it was a beautiful piece, and I loved every note. Please know I never meant to offend… I'm not a tease. Do you believe me?" Her voice fell as she bit her lower lip, but her eyes held his attention.

"I do and you have not offended me." He smiled as her worried face displayed a guilty conscience.

"I can't believe you chose law over a music career."

"When you have something shoved at you long enough, you can find yourself running toward it or in the opposite direction when given the chance. At least that's how it is for me." Peter surprised himself by his bluntness.

"I do hope you will stay in touch."

Peter climbed the steps, stopping at the one beneath her bringing them almost eye-to-eye. "We'll see. What about tomorrow?"

He took her face in his hands and she bent down kissing him on the lips. He was taken in by her sweet demeanor and found wanting her all the more.

"Please do," she whispered.

"I'll make the time."

She turned to go inside, but he grabbed her hand.

"Catriona…?"

She turned, interrupting him mid-sentence. "I can't invite you to stay. This is new to me. Will you give me time… please?"

Peter nodded. "No worries. It will be your decision next time but know this, I won't refuse you."

"Good night, Peter. Be careful driving home."

"I will. Go inside. It's freezing out here."

She nodded and closed the door behind her.

Returning to his car, Peter sat for a moment staring at the road ahead.

What the hell just happened? She could be the key to furthering my success, there is no denying it. She has more than enough money, the family name, thoughtful, smart… and desirable too. Okay, so maybe she is a little prudish, but nothing we can't work out later. Every effort needs to be made to take full advantage of this opportunity. She will make the perfect politician's wife.

He realized he should show more compassion if she were to become Mrs. Peter Tramwell, and with it, a wedding gift of a law partnership along with the McKenna dynasty and the millions attached with her. He could not remember wanting anything more. As he pulled from the curb, the corners of his mouth turned upward forming an expression previous targets had fallen victim—he knew what needed to be done.

***

She walked through the French doors onto the enclosed terrace and closed her eyes as she remembered Peter's song. The sound of the cello had transported her to the mountains taking in the dip of each valley, hill, and peak as the music lifted into a crescendo pinnacle and then fell into a deep chasm. The music pulled at her emotions like the ebb and flow of an ocean tide with each cascading over her like an unexpected wave crashing against a jagged bluff, engulfing her body and soul. Music was her kryptonite and could weaken her into total submission. The sensation was savior and consoler. She could not think; everything inside of her yearning, wanting him, and building to the same crescendo as his music had taken her. The tune repeated itself within her mind and the same passion arose within her the same as when he pulled her to him. His touch and song were intoxicating.

Opening her eyes, she walked back into the living room, locking the doors behind her. The floral bouquet stared back at her. She took a rose from the vase and breathed in its sweet fragrance. Twirling it between her fingers, she wondered why a simple kiss could cause her to be repulsed and possibly want to vomit at any moment. Closing her eyes again, she remembered the touch of his kiss. With no warning, her stomach tightened. She dropped the flower as she covered her mouth, running toward the bathroom door.

CHAPTER 14

ARRIVING EARLY FOR their group session, Catriona bit her lip as she fidgeted with the crown on her watch. She noticed the second hand's pain-staking climb toward the top of the hour. Lillian took her daughter's hand as Dr. Pendergrass entered the room.

"I have read through Catriona's extensive psychiatric records and am surprised by the volume of information and procedures repeated from physician to physician. With your permission, we received her medical records from the time she was first admitted into the ER, along with her physical rehabilitation records from her pediatricians and other specialists to date. It may appear extreme, but I did not want to continue on the same well-worn path without a fresh look at her total medical history; however, I agree with most of my colleagues' diagnoses."

Scott shifted in his chair. "And here I thought we had been wrong in our choice of physicians."

"No. In fact, quite the opposite. Most of her psychiatrists reached similar conclusions once they diagnosed her symptoms. Their detailed notes have made excellent references; however, I have a different theory."

"I thought you agreed with her doctors," Lillian said.

She continued, "I agree with most; however, I believe they missed the complete picture of multiple issues. The memory is a complicated animal; we are learning more each day and research is presenting new variables and outcomes with positive results. The better we understand the mind, the better treatment we can provide to our patients; however, each person presents their own set of issues as each is different and suffers from a variety of circumstances. There is no 'catch all' treatment. Catriona's previous doctors have treated many of her symptoms and have touched on different aspects of her condition, but none have treated her symptoms as a whole. Also, because she was a child when the incident occurred and she sustained multiple injuries, she has been treated more as an adult suffering from a head trauma instead of a much younger patient suffering from a severe traumatic experience. Her burns alone are proof enough. Catriona, I believe your memory loss is psychogenic amnesia or more precisely defined, situation-specific or dissociative amnesia, along with PTSD symptoms."

"I don't understand." Catriona frowned creating a deep furrow at the top of her nose.

"Let me explain. Amnesia is the temporary loss of recall memory resulting from experiencing psychological trauma. It can be voluntary or involuntary and can last for a few seconds or even years… as in your case. Disassociation is your mind's way of coping with overwhelming emotions at the age of nine, it could not handle. It overrode all memories of what was happening at the time as the body's way of self-preservation. You are suffering from a phenomenon that occurs from a traumatic childhood event, and it can be unrecognizable in children because they are still developing mentally and physically."

"Are you saying my body is refusing to remember what happened to me?"

"Yes, I am. Our long-term memory is divided into two types; explicit memory, which is consciously remembering facts and events, and implicit memory, which is the unconscious memory of skills learned through practice and repetition, such as playing an instrument or tying your shoes. In your case, it is the explicit memory or declarative memory affected. Within the explicit memory, your episodic memory chose not to work at the time. It is located within the hypo-campus area of the brain and the autobiographical events of remembering the times and places associated with emotions and contacts have been suppressed. However, your brain has chosen to suppress the events of the fire, and through no fault alone, has buried most of your childhood memories leading to the event as well."

"Will I regain my memory?"

"I believe you will. Call it what you want… repressed memory syndrome or psychogenic amnesia… all fall beneath the heading of retrograde amnesia, meaning your memories should return over time, and then again, maybe not all. Your oldest memories will come back first, then remembering events leading to the fire, and the fire itself. If it goes as expected, your memory will return."

"I have remembered more from my childhood this week, but what about the flashbacks and nightmares? Are they actual events pushing through to the surface?" Catriona leaned forward in her chair.

"That is where the PTSD steps in. You are re-experiencing the original trauma through the symptoms of what we know was an intolerable life situation. Sometimes, it results from being physically or sexually abused, but those reasons can be complex as well. In an adult situation, it can be substance abuse or a result of experiencing the effects of war similar to the same symptoms that result in PTSD. However, I am unaware of you having outbursts of rage or causing self-harm, but I do know your blackouts may result from extreme stress or incredible fear. I noticed your previous doctor had you undergo an MRI. He may have been looking for some type of degeneration in the right temporal and frontal cortexes of the brain, but your results were normal, and that is good news. After such a long period of suffering from dissociative amnesia, it is unusual, but good news all the same." The doctor smiled at the three staring back at her.

"That was years ago. Do I need more x-rays?"

"Not at this time. I am going to be forthright with you, Catriona. This condition is hard to treat, but I feel comfortable knowing I can help you. I want to begin a mindfulness-based therapy you can practice at home; we can go over the details. Also, I will need to evaluate if you are unaware of any adverse effects this may be having on your career, such as forgetting client names. You may have experienced sudden outbursts, reckless behavior, such as sexual aggressiveness that is not the norm for you, or abuse of alcohol or drugs, even as far as new thoughts of self-harm, etc. Also, all of us will be involved in helping you remember details; however, I will guide you as we do not want to cause further disassociation which can occur. As I said, this is complicated. Once we address ways to relieve your stress, it may help memories resurface as well. It is a beginning to discovering who you are. It may happen over small periods of time or all at once. Again, memories are strange animals, and we will be proactive in helping you."

"That sounds good." Catriona's shoulders dropped relieving the tension between her shoulder blades.

Dr. Pendergrass looked at her parents. "I have a question for the two of you."

"Please, ask us anything," Lillian said.

"Catriona is an unusual case as she appears to be functioning normally except for recent nightmares and blackouts. Also, she has proved herself academically and professionally. Mrs. McKenna, why do you think Catriona is the exception to the norm? She does not fit the standard mold of someone who has suffered similar circumstances and is unable to function in the real world."

"I am her mother, but not always. She is a fighter and the self-preservation instilled within her was there before she ever came to be mine. My role has been one of whole support and completing what her mother started in helping to further shape the beautiful girl who lives within every beat of my heart. We fought her depression along with the intensive physical rehabilitation she was enduring, but I think the horses and her music brought her out of it more than any medication or person. However, to give a more solid foundation to your question, I believe Scott can better answer your question as his perspective is more holistic regarding her childhood."

Scott said, "I agree, doctor. This is complicated. Catriona is my first cousin by bloodline, but she is my daughter in every other aspect of the word. Our family roots are buried deep in the Appalachian hills and mountains of Virginia and Tennessee. We come from strong stock as the old-timers would have put it. Our grandparents' example of overcoming incredible odds of survival is undeniably relevant to our successes. My time in the military was hell, and I won't discuss those details today, yet I survived. I have weathered the storm and am stronger because of the experience, but also because of the role models I witnessed as a child. Catriona is part of the same family history. She is blessed beyond measure to have belonged to those resilient men and women who shaped her past. Her grandmothers on both sides of the family, her mother, and Lillian have each had their own positive and powerful influence. As far as I'm concerned, she is mighty. Considering who Catriona has become after all the pain she has endured is mind-numbing to me. We have been close to discovering the missing pieces of memory, but they are hers alone to find. I want her to remember the women and men in her past... of remembering who she is. Without a doubt, I know her survival is because of subconscious memories of lessons learned. Whether or not you believe in a higher power, the faith they shared and we witnessed lived out before us daily as children is the reason she survived that night. God was watching over her. We believe He watches over us. Even in the pain and suffering caused by others, He is here, and I believe He has led us to you, and I will do anything to help her become whole again."

His words overwhelmed Catriona. Scott rarely spoke of God, if ever.

Dr. Pendergrass said, "There is one thing I must request of you, Mr. McKenna."

"Name it and done."

"Catriona needs to return to her original home."

"Is going back necessary?" His eyebrows furrowed into his brow.

Dr. Pendergrass nodded. "I understand she has not returned to the site of the fire. Am I correct?"

"Yes."

"Returning to her hometown may be the key to opening the door to more lost memories. It may help her remember by seeing the places you have only told her about."

Lillian asked, "When should we do this?"

"I would recommend as soon as your schedules permit. Something is triggering these emotions, and we want to allow her the opportunity to pursue them under supervision before they cause more physical damage through these unpredictable flashbacks and blackouts."

Scott glanced down, then shook his head before he replied. "I'll make arrangements immediately."

"Catriona, you have a sound foundation upon which to build. You will see results and I believe soon. Mr. and Mrs. McKenna, thank you for taking the time to meet with me today. Your input is invaluable as we proceed. For the second portion of this session, I would like to speak with Catriona alone. Please, would you excuse us?"

Catriona smiled at them. "I will see you both at home."

"Okay, darling, but call us when you head our way." Lillian hugged her.

They thanked Dr. Pendergrass as they left, and the office grew quiet again.

"Catriona, have you ever undergone hypnosis?"

"No, I haven't."

"Are you opposed to hypnosis?"

"No, I'm not. Should I be?"

"Not at all. It's safe, I assure you. Sometimes when a patient is close to recalling the past, hypnosis can help tap into those memories. Would you like to try it?"

"I'm not sure."

"We will begin with your early childhood. I will not put you through too much this first time. My hope is this method will help you when you return to your hometown."

"I'll try anything at this point."

"Good. Let's begin."

Dr. Pendergrass gently guided her through the steps. She asked questions and Catriona responded. Realizing her patient had been through enough, she said, "Catriona, you will remember everything you have told me today, as well as your emotions at the time. You are safe. Nothing will hurt you. You will awaken on the count of one. Three... two... one."

Catriona opened her eyes and the tears fell. Not only did she remember more details of her mom and dad, but she remembered their house and how happy she had been. It was almost too great to comprehend.

"I believe you are close to remembering everything. Your answers were quick and descriptive. You will experience much emotion over the next few days. I want you to go about your normal routine, but without warning, you may remember something new from your past. Have you had further blackouts?"

Catriona hesitated. She wondered if she should tell her about the incident at Peter's. She said, "No, I haven't."

"Good. The next few days may be difficult when you return to your old home and more memories make themselves known. If you need me, call. My card has my cell number if you need to use it." She flipped through Catriona's chart. "I see your prescriptions are up-to-date too. Are you taking them as prescribed?"

"Yes."

"Good. Do not miss any dosages. Well, Catriona, I believe we are finished with today's session. I look forward to hearing about your trip. Write everything you remember into a journal, and we will discuss it at your next appointment."

Catriona thanked her and made an appointment for the following week. Walking out to her car, she could not believe what had happened in such a short time. Relief and pent-up emotions overwhelmed her. She sat in her car and sobbed as the tears seemed to wash away a portion of the veil concealing her past. She could not wait to tell Scott and Lillian. She turned the key in the ignition, but the car did not start.

"Are you kidding me?"

She tried cranking the car again, but there was total silence except for a faint clicking noise coming from the engine. She noticed she had left the headlights on when arriving for her appointment. Looking both ways for signs of life, no one was in sight. She did not want to call her parents, and she did not want to walk back into the medical building. She also remembered her phone was in Scott's desk at home.

"Great." *I need a strong cup of tea.*

She walked to the café around the corner and called their mechanic.

"Yes, it's dead... No, I'm sure... Yes, I thought I had jumper cables, but I do not... Thank you. I am parked in front of the medical center's side entrance... No, I'm using the café's phone. Would you mind meeting me at the Bluebell Café on Campbellton Street... Thank you, again. Please do not call Scott. I don't want to disturb him... Thank you... Take your time, I haven't eaten. Will an hour work... Great! You are an angel. Goodbye, Mitch."

"Well, aren't you a welcomed surprise?"

She turned and Declan was standing in the doorway. She frowned.

"Wow. Not the welcome I had expected. Did someone die?"

"My car battery."

"Where are you parked? I didn't see your car outside."

"It's in the parking lot at the medical center, but I've called Mitch."

"Call him back. I have cables in my truck."

"Are you sure?"

"Definitely."

"Thank you, Declan. You always seem to rescue me." She used the phone again while Declan found a vacant booth next to the window. Catriona slid into the seat across from him.

"Were you able to reach him?"

"Yes. I think he was glad someone else could help."

"Are you hungry?"

"Starving," she said.

"You wouldn't know it to look at you."

Catriona's eyes grew large. "I beg your pardon, Mr. O'Connell?"

"That came out wrong. I meant it as a compliment."

She could see his embarrassment. "You need to work on refining those skill-sets. Knowing Samuel, I'm surprised he hasn't taught you better." She laughed.

"Ha! Not funny."

"Yes, it is."

Sitting upright in the booth and straightening his jacket, Declan said, "Let's try this again." He winked at her. "Miss McKenna, you are looking beautiful today. Are you free for lunch? It would be my greatest pleasure to have you join me in this fine dining establishment."

"Oh, stop it."

They both laughed. Her body relaxed when sitting near him. "Why are you in town? Does Lillian have you overwhelmed with chores after the crazy weekend?"

"Nothing major and the hard work paid off in the end… what an enormous success."

"Yes, it was. I am happy for Lillian… I am happy for all of us."

"Me too. By the way, you are a pretty good dancer. I didn't realize debutants knew how to line dance."

"You are mighty pretentious for a country boy, aren't you?" She grinned.

"Thank you for the compliment. I'm only teasing. I enjoyed dancing with you too; however, I didn't have much of a chance to tell you."

"No? That's odd. I didn't realize we had not talked afterward."

"Ouch."

"Oh, no… that came out wrong."

"Now who needs to work on her skill-sets?" Declan laughed out loud.

"Peter Tramwell was our guest, and I was fulfilling my duties as hostess. I'm afraid he had my attention for the rest of the evening."

"I noticed."

"What does that mean?" She frowned.

"Nothing. Forgive me. Seriously, it's none of my business. I noticed you were enjoying yourself… you were enjoying yourself, right?" He watched her as she pulled her hair behind her ear.

"He is kind. I returned to Washington with him on Sunday where we had a fabulous evening enjoying the symphony together and then…"

"Symphony, huh?"

She was relieved he had interrupted her as she had almost revealed too much. Changing the subject, she blurted out, "I play the cello. Did you know?"

"No, I didn't. A detail you left out when we were together last week. Will I have the good fortune of hearing you play sometime?"

"Maybe... someday." It surprised her how much she enjoyed teasing him. This unfamiliar territory made her nervous, yet she remained composed.

"How are you?" His eyes danced as he spoke.

He is too charming for his own good. "Good. In fact, I think I may be on the road to healing. I'm afraid I may become emotional if I go into too much detail, but I must share my news with someone."

"Well, I'm a someone." He grinned at his little comeback.

"Yes. Yes, you are, Mr. Someone. You may have to give me a moment. I'm not sure where to start."

"Just start. You are safe with me, remember?"

"I had another session today with my doctor. She thinks my memory loss is from a head injury, and an event I may have seen or experienced. She said I show symptoms of PTSD. Then she hypnotized me, and I remember a little more of my mom and dad. Not everything, mind you, but a few things. I remember how beautiful my mother was and how funny my dad could be. I can see our small white house with its garden... too much to take in." Covering her mouth with her napkin, she coughed. "Where is our server? I need a cup of tea."

"Here, let me see if they have something stronger. Miss?"

"No. I don't want anything stronger. Tea will be fine."

"You need something over here?" their server asked.

"May we have two cups of your strongest tea? Hot, please."

"Yes, sir. Are you ready to order your food?"

"Not yet, but thank you."

The server walked away rolling her eyes.

"Hypnosis? I don't think I've known anyone who has been hypnotized. Do you feel dizzy? Are you feeling anything at all… are there side effects?"

"I'm fine, and no, there are none. She told me I will experience many emotions over the next few days, and Scott and I are to travel to Sageville. Have you heard of it?"

"No, I can't say I have. I'm not too familiar with Virginia, not yet. Is it far from here?"

"It is in the southwest corner of Virginia… close to Tennessee and borders West Virginia."

"That's coal mining country."

"Yes, it is. My dad's family were coal miners."

"Another fact you didn't tell me."

The server returned with their tea. "Here you go."

"Thank you."

The server asked, "Have you decided what you want?"

They both ordered the blue plate special. She sauntered back to the kitchen.

"She loves her job, doesn't she?" He made a face causing Catriona to laugh at his sarcasm. "When do you leave?"

"As soon as Scott can prepare. He's under the wire at work. What an inconvenience I have become."

"Let me know when you go. I will be sending good thoughts your way."

"Thank you." She stared at him. *He has a great face.*

"What are you doing?" he asked. "Do I have something in my teeth?"

"No, I was thinking what a sweet thing for you to say; I'll let you know." She frowned. "Oh my, I thought of something."

"Do I need to take cover?" He pretended to duck.

"Don't be silly." She laughed at his attempts to be cute. "Seriously, if my car works as it should, then I could drive to Charlottesville tomorrow and check on a few things at the store. Scott can meet me there when his plans permit; however, I have a problem. I purchased a desk that was delivered to Grace Meade instead of my shop, and I need to hook a trailer to my car or have someone deliver it. Lillian would love to have it out of her way."

"I can deliver it on Thursday."

"No, but thank you. Do you know of a delivery company in town? I'm not asking you to be my delivery guy too."

"I'm not so sure. I was your dance instructor a few days ago and your mechanic today; I might as well be your delivery boy."

"You are definitely not funny." Her cheeks turned a pale pink.

"You know I am." He winked at her.

"No, you really are not funny, Mr. O'Connell. You think you are funny, but you are not." She laughed. "Okay, will you be my delivery guy too? Is it possible for you to take time off?"

"Our fate must float amongst the heavens, sweet lady, because Lillian has given me the rest of the week off once everything returns to normal. I should be finished by tomorrow afternoon. I can meet you at your shop on Thursday."

"It is over two hours away."

"So? I can be there by ten or eleven, easy."

"Declan. Declan. Declan. What am I going to do with you? You are a jewel."

"A jewel?" he scoffed.

"No... I officially dub you as my rescuer. First a horse ride, then the two-step, today's dead battery, and now furniture; how will I ever repay you?"

"Oh, I don't know. What about a tour of your Charlottesville?"

She thought for a moment and said, "That's a great idea. I will be your tour guide. I can show you my shop and my alma mater, and if we have time, we can see Monticello too. Do you think you can handle an afternoon with me?"

"The real question is can you handle an afternoon with moi?"

"Moi?" Catriona laughed again. "Yes, I certainly can."

"Alright then. I can leave here before seven and will be in town by nine Thursday morning. We should be finished by ten, and then you can give me the grand tour. Will that work?"

"Perfect. It's a date." She corrected herself. "Oops, sorry. Not an official date, but a 'friend' day."

He stared into her eyes and then smiled. "I would prefer we call it a friend's date."

"All right. Me too." She remembered his kiss and dropped her eyes.

"Are you okay?"

"Yes, I'm fine."

The server plopped their plates onto the table. "Your food's ready."

They both laughed as she walked away.

He said, "Let's say we eat and get your car moving. We have lots to do."

"Sounds good." She beamed at him.

"Will you pass the pepper?" he asked.

"Sure thing."

Neither realized, but the other was equally excited about the possibilities. Peter never crossed her mind.

CHAPTER 15

CATRIONA FLIPPED HER jacket's collar to block out the cold as her every breath impersonated a chain-smoker each time she exhaled. She blew into the air as if she had returned to her childhood. It was her first morning surrounded by an early fall in the mountains, and she was thankful to have slept in her own bed the night before.

A natural entrepreneur, she owned The Feather Quill, a rare book, fine papers, and stationery store containing the unexpected by way of gifts featuring remarkable craftwork by Virginia-native artisans. Although a young businesswoman, her reputation was growing throughout Virginia and the D.C. metropolitan area as the "go-to" girl for the glorious bride-to-be of discerning taste. The store offered a one-of-a-kind gift registry, but also personally designed invitations to set a wedding apart from the ordinary. The store's available fine papers heightened the look of the embossed creations through the use of typography and letterpress techniques of a bygone era, and not the print-your-own so popular today. The most sought-after customization was her water-color and hand-scripted calligraphy—Catriona's forte. A new venture had fallen into place as a stable influx of other businesses came to depend upon her impeccable customer service for their specialty printing needs. New equipment was purchased and personnel hired to keep pace with the unexpected growth, almost doubling her income.

Situated near the pedestrian mall, The Feather Quill sat sandwiched between a coffee shop and chocolate boutique in the historic district. Besides her brides, patrons included town residents and tourists traveling the Blue Ridge Parkway, along with fans on game day.

During the past year, Tia Douglass and Catriona's friendship had grown. Tia had earned her spot as store manager. Not only one of the smartest women Catriona had the privilege of calling friend, but the most stylish too. She had a smooth confidence pulling one into her irresistible personality, including her latest admirer and new doctor in town, Dr. William Reid, who occupied much of her free time, and everyone understood why. Sweet and protective of her family and friends, along with her acute business savvy, Tia was a catch for any man.

Stepping into the warmth of the shop, Catriona found everything intact, as if she had never left. The aroma of fresh-brewed coffee filled the air to welcome customers and her day.

"Good morning, everyone. I come bearing gifts… Cookie's sour cream pound cake and cinnamon rolls. And to put your mind at ease, I declare it a law within these walls… calories do not count today."

Tia greeted her with a hug. "What a pleasant surprise! What are you doing here? I thought you were not coming back for weeks."

"Well, good morning to you too. I missed seeing your face every day."

"Welcome home. I'm sorry, but you surprised me. That's all. It is great to see you, but is everything okay?"

Catriona needed her more than ever. "No worries. I wanted to break this to you face-to-face and not over the phone."

"I knew it. You have that look when something's cooking inside that head of yours."

"Let's go into my office. I want to keep this private."

Catriona shut the door behind her. "I'm not returning for a while. Physical difficulties have made themselves known of late, and I plan to follow my doctor's orders by stepping away from as much stress as possible for the short term. Do you think you can handle the holidays without me? We will still close the shop for the week following Christmas through New Year's."

"I'm here in whatever capacity you need. Are you sure you are okay?"

"I will be. It is just like you to worry, but I'm taking everything in stride. I have tried to hide this from you, but the last few months have taken a toll on me mentally and physically with the expansion of the business. No appetite and the lack of sleep have not helped either. I promise once things become less hectic, we can talk in further detail. My mind is working overtime with growth opportunities, and now, there are plans in place to close on a property in Old Town Alexandria in a week or two."

"We're expanding? Why didn't you tell me?"

"It happened rather quickly, and the growth potential is limitless."

"Wow… that's exciting news. Let me grab a pen. I will add both items to our next conference call. How do you want to handle the custom invitations while you are away?"

"Oh, you can forward them via email, then we can make an appointment to FaceTime with the brides so everyone agrees with the product. I'm not disappearing; I can't, and I don't want to vanish completely. We may need to hire a second designer down the road, but we can consider that later too. However, I have full confidence in you, Tia. You are the one I need standing in the gap for me while I'm out."

"Thank you. I appreciate your confidence. As I have said many times, ask and I'm there."

"Please make sure everyone knows I'm fine, but I'm taking time off for an overdue vacation and needed time spent with family. Also, if they need to contact me for any reason, shoot an email. I will check my account every few days. If it's urgent, call. We are a great team and with the direction this business is heading, we will continue to be for a long time."

"It will be business as usual. Is there anything you want to review while you are here?"

"Yes, two things. Let's start with the most important."

"And that is?"

"If everything continues to progress in the direction I predict, I want to make you an offer. It will mean a larger commitment once Scott draws up the papers."

"What papers?"

"Miss Tia Douglass, my confidant... my friend... my incredible manager, I, Catriona Elizabeth Harrington-McKenna, owner of this company, am pleased to make you an offer you cannot refuse."

"What kind of offer?"

"I want to offer you a partnership on your one-year anniversary in February."

"What?"

"You have helped grow my company by leaps and bounds with the technical expertise and social media skills you possess. I could have learned, but the world is moving quicker than me with its social media logarithms changing daily. There are not enough hours in my day as it is. Everything involved with The Feather Quill will be divided equally; fifty-fifty. I need you, but in actuality, we need each other, and you, my dear friend, are unstoppable. For a while, I'll be acting in a silent partner role until I'm capable of operating at full capacity again. This deal is unusual in that you will not have to buy into the partnership. After my discussion with Scott, he agreed. With the remarkable way you have handled my company for the past weeks, and now, the forthcoming months ahead in my absence, your payment will be accredited as additional services rendered during this difficult time."

Tia placed her hands atop her head, then looked at Catriona in total disbelief. "This is crazy... are you sure?"

Catriona knew what Tia's answer would be before she asked. "Do you think you are up to the challenge? The offer is going once... twice... or do you need time to think about it? I will understand if you do." Catriona held out her hand to shake on the deal.

"A most definite yes! I'll think about it tomorrow!" Tia skipped the handshake and hugged Catriona so tight she could hardly breathe.

"We will talk details later, but as long as we commit to one another, then we will celebrate your successes along with my own."

Tia's eyes were wild with excitement. "Will I need an attorney?"

"I insist. Scott can recommend someone. I want you to have full confidence in me and our future together. Scott said he would have the paperwork finished by the end of the month so you and your attorney can review it as well. We will celebrate big on the day of our signing. Tia, you have given me such peace. I needed this today."

"You? Peace? I won't sleep for a week… no, a month. Is there anything else before my heart stops?"

"Nothing quite so dramatic." Catriona laughed out loud. "Make sure John continues to send everyone their paychecks while I'm gone. I don't want to lose anyone. He can reach me by phone. Oh, my word, I forgot to tell you the second reason I'm here. How silly of me. I purchased a desk for the shop to fill the blank wall next to the front door. A friend of mine is delivering it this morning, and then he wants a tour of the city."

"That's exciting. We need something by the door. Do you trust me to set the display for you?"

"Fifty-fifty. Remember? You are no longer a manager, but a soon-to-be partner."

Tia's eyes widened, and she tucked her chin in disbelief. "Wait a minute… did you say a tour to a 'him'? What him?"

"No one. Just a friend." Catriona pretended to look out of the windows into the shop disinterested.

"Uh-huh. Do tell."

With no emotion, she said, "He works for Lillian and Scott, and as a favor for making this delivery, I told him I would give him a tour of our town."

"Sounds like fun. Are you sure you understand the concept?"

Catriona grimaced because she knew Tia's words to be true. "I always appreciate your directness, but I will admit, I'm a little excited."

"My, my, my. Really?" Tia cocked her head and smiled an expression known only between them when there were secrets to keep.

"Stop. There may be nothing to this visit."

"I wondered why you dressed up today. By the way, your outfit is to die for. Did Sandra Harris make this one too?"

"Thank you. It is pretty, isn't it? The whole creation is hers."

"Go with this… are you ready?" Tia asked.

"I guess…"

Tia took the stapler into her hand and spoke into one end as if holding a microphone. "Next on the 'America's Next Top Model' catwalk, ladies and gentlemen, my new fifty-fifty partner is wearing the latest Harris creation in a full-length, pale blue, kimono-style dress with side slits opened to her hips, revealing a delicate Brussels lace slip you can see only when she moves."

Catriona laughed and then twirled. They both fell back into their chairs, laughing at the silliness seldom shared with the demands of their workload.

Catriona said, "We should laugh more often, but let's take a moment to think this through, shall we?"

"Uh-oh… here we go."

"Seriously. Sandra is talented, but our shop is not the right venue to show off her creativity. We could open another shop here in town focusing on fabric artisans. We could run the business and promotional side of her business and Sandra can design and sew to her heart's content. She has on more than one occasion hinted she wants to stop operating out of her home due to lack of space and privacy, but she doesn't want to deal with the daily operations of running a company. We could include the students in fashion design as her apprentices. We could offer space to other artisans like quilters, etc., and while we are at it, we could supply an assistant to answer the phones and make appointments. What do you think?"

"It sounds like fun. Do you want me to look for space?"

"Yes, but let's keep it between us. I will speak to Sandra, but I know she will love this idea."

"Noted."

The backdoor service bell interrupted them.

Catriona stood. "Oh my, he is right on time. Do I look okay?"

"Gorgeous. There is not a man within seeing distance who will not dream of you tonight."

"Oh, be serious."

"I'm always serious. You don't always see it through my great sense of humor." Tia laughed.

Catriona shook her head as she stepped out of the office. "Hey Stanley, would you give me a hand for a moment?"

"Sure thing."

When Catriona opened the delivery doors, Declan was combing his hair with his fingers as he looked into the rearview side mirror of his truck. When he turned, his appearance startled her. He was no longer in work clothes but had dressed for a fall day out on the town.

"Good morning," he said with a broad smile.

"Good morning to you too, sir. Wow, you are a surprise. Don't you look dapper? Nice sweater."

"Thanks... I clean up pretty good, don't I? I must say, Miss McKenna, you could stop time."

She noticed his green eyes danced in the sunlight and her cheeks darkened. "Thank you. Did you have trouble finding us?"

"Not at all. Your directions, along with my GPS, were spot on."

Catriona approached the back of the truck. "Stanley is here to help you. Do you think we need additional help?"

"No. I'm sure we can handle this small piece of furniture. Am I right, Stanley? By the way, nice to meet you." He shook his hand.

"You too. Looks pretty light to me."

They carried the desk through the rear doors into the shop.

"I want to place it on the wall next to the front door." She pointed them toward the front entrance and called out, "Make way."

Catriona watched Tia take a bite of cake just as she spotted Declan. Tia choked as he set the desk into place.

Catriona asked, "Are you okay?"

"I'm fine... seriously, fine." She cleared her throat. "Good morning, sir. Catriona, aren't you going to introduce me to your good-looking friend?" She smiled when approaching him.

Catriona shook her head and smiled. "Declan, allow me to introduce you to one of my dearest friends. She is currently my company's manager and soon-to-be partner. At the moment, she is overseeing the business while I'm away, and not surprisingly, she is thriving without me. May I present Miss Tia Douglass."

"It is my pleasure." He reached out to shake her hand.

Catriona continued, "And this is my friend, Declan O'Connell. He manages the Grace Meade estate and the equine business with Lillian."

"Declan, it is my pleasure. Funny, Catriona has not mentioned you before. How has that not happened?" Tia stared at her with a silly grin.

Catriona said, "We met a few weeks ago when I returned to Grace Meade. Isn't that right, Declan?"

"Yes, it is, but I feel I've known you longer." Declan winked at Catriona and grinned.

"Oh, I see." Tia's eyes gleamed.

Catriona laughed. "Come on. Let me give you the grand tour of my shop and introduce you to the greatest staff working anywhere."

"That would be great. I'm yours for the rest of the day, so you lead and I will follow."

"Really?" Tia asked, continuing to grin from ear to ear.

Catriona rolled her eyes. "Declan, you will learn to ignore her." Catriona's eyes glared her way. "Cookie's cake has gone to her head this morning. Let's go into my office." Catriona turned her face away from Declan and glanced at Tia; however, she almost laughed out loud as Tia blew kisses behind him. Catriona mouthed, "Stop, please."

Tia laughed as she shut the door behind them.

"The store is impressive."

"Oh, thanks. I am proud of it," she said.

"Is this where the magic happens?"

"I guess you could say it is. Follow me." Catriona led him out of the office and showed him the store, including the upstairs printing business and meeting her employees. When they returned to the front office, Tia was staging the writing desk.

"This looks great."

Tia said, "You can provide the finishing touches later. We should highlight a couple of antique books each month, along with the new specialty papers."

"That's a fabulous idea." Looking at Declan, she said, "We should be on our way as it's almost ten, and there is so much to see and do."

"I'm ready."

"Tia, I will call later," Catriona said.

"Declan. Now, don't be a stranger." Tia held out her hand to shake his.

He took her hand. "I won't, but that's up to your boss."

Catriona said, "You are not funny, Mr. O'Connell. Let's leave your truck parked in the back, and we'll take my car."

"Are you planning to be my chauffeur?"

"I am."

"As I said, you lead and I'll follow, but only for today. Goodbye, Tia."

Tia watched as the couple walked out into the sunshine.

Catriona stopped. "Oh, wait."

"What's wrong?"

"I forgot to tell Tia something. I'll be right back."

When Catriona walked back into the shop, Tia came out of the office and placed her hands on her hips. "Girl, what else is hiding at Grace Meade? He's gorgeous! And those eyes... sweet mercy. Now, that fine man is what I'm talking about. You go, girl."

"Please, stop. We agreed to remain friends."

"Friends? Have you lost your mind? You might lose him to this proud woman if you are not careful." Her laughter bounced off the rafters.

"No, I won't. You love William, and we both know it. Besides, I'm sort of seeing someone else."

"My Billy is something, isn't he? Wait... what? Two guys in a few weeks? I need to plan a vacation with you."

"We can talk later; however, I won't be back to the shop. I'm staying in town tonight, but are you sure we are good with my leaving?"

"Yes, and what I can see, so are you. Forget friends, honey. I wouldn't hesitate to go after that handsome man right there. You can tell he is smitten."

"He is not. I'll call you later."

"You had better. He is smitten."

Catriona laughed and hugged her again before meeting Declan outside.

"Everything okay?" he asked.

Yes, everything is perfect. Wrapping up unfinished business, that's all. I am sorry you had to wait."

"No problem. So where are we heading first?"

"Have you had breakfast?" she asked.

"Yes. Have you?"

"I have. Let's head to Monticello, my second favorite place on earth."

"Second?" He looked surprised.

"Grace Meade is first."

"Of course."

They walked toward the car and it could not have been a more perfect morning with the cool mountain breeze and the sun shining overhead.

"Why don't we ride with the top down? I can turn on the heater."

"I'm game, but I may be too tall to fit into this machine."

"Not at all. There is more room once you get inside. You can get in, can't you?"

He closed the door. "No problem."

They soon reached the long driveway to Monticello. A low fog greeted them like a stage's sheer scrim, allowing the audience to peer inside to a different place in time. The building's rotunda came into focus as if turning the lens of a camera as they inched through the parking area. With leaf tips of yellow, orange, and red overhead, the earth produced a rich aroma. A light dampness filled the air from the lifting mist as they crossed the lawn leading toward the East entrance. It was her favorite time on the historic grounds, which encompassed twenty-five hundred of the original five thousand acres of rolling hills and foliage.

"I cannot wait to show you everything," she said.

"Where should we go first?"

"The house. We can go behind the scenes and see the upstairs and the rotunda too. We will walk through the gardens and outbuildings later. After the sun shines through this creamy haze, it will be a glorious day."

"Okay, Miss Tour Guide, show me the way."

Catriona led them on an adventure back to the eighteenth century sharing many of the past President's quotes and ideas that helped form a nation. She talked of his skills as an architect, including his building designs on Virginia's campus and in D.C., as well as his personal faults. As they walked through the gardens, she held onto his arm as they strolled among the trees, vegetables, and flowering plants. They made a striking couple, and many visitors stopped to listen as she described Jefferson's design and experimentation with the grafting of plants continuing to flourish on the property. Declan remained awestruck by her obvious enthusiasm and excitement when speaking of this—her hallowed mountain grounds.

Catriona said, "I know the ideal place for lunch. Are you hungry?"

"Always."

"I have made reservations for one-thirty at Michie Tavern... it's been in operation since seventeen eighty-four. Can you believe it? You are going to love this place with their homemade biscuits, black-eyed peas, and fried chicken."

"Sounds perfect."

"Afterwards, we can take a long walk to see Virginia's campus, if you wish."

"I want to see it all."

"Really?"

"Yes, really." His smile reassured her.

After lunch, they entered the campus. They walked through campus, seeing the famous Lawn, touring many of the Neoclassical buildings, and stopped for a break in the outdoor amphitheater. Classes were in session and, although surrounded by students and administration, they were lost in their conversation.

"When is the next home game?" he asked.

"I'm not sure. Do you still want to go?"

"It would be fun. The last time we played Virginia was in the Sugar Bowl of ninety-one so I don't think we'll be meeting again on a football field anytime soon; however, I wouldn't mind seeing a game between Virginia and Virginia Tech."

"How did you know we played Tennessee?"

"I looked online in case you asked."

"But I didn't ask." She laughed at the thought of him going to so much trouble. "A game would be fun. I will check my calendar. Would you care for an ice cream now?"

"It's getting late. What about dinner instead?"

"Goodness, it's almost six o'clock. Let's walk downtown. There are tons of restaurants. How does that sound?"

"It sounds fantastic."

He helped her to her feet. As they strolled the brick street, he held her hand as if they had always walked in such a manner. She did not pull away. Soon, they entered her favorite restaurant where a local band was playing.

"I have an idea."

"Let's hear it," he said.

"Why don't we order take out and go to my house where it's not so loud?"

"That's fine with me. Are you sure you can stand my company a little longer?"

"Very much so. I want to know more about you." The increase in the music's volume caused her words to fall on deaf ears.

"What?" he asked.

"I want to know you better!"

He pointed at his ear. "Sorry, but I can't hear you!"

"What?"

They both laughed when they step toward the bar to order their food. Soon, the music turned to a slower pace.

"Catriona, would you give me the honor?" He nodded toward the dance floor.

"It would be my pleasure, sir."

He led her onto the crowded floor and taking her hand into his, he twirled her into his arms.

She smiled. "You have done this before."

"Possibly."

"Who taught you how to dance?"

"My mom. She insisted I learn. She said I would go far when trying to impress the ladies."

"Is that what you're trying to do? Impress a lady?"

"With everything within me."

"Well, Mr. O'Connell, I do believe it's working."

He laughed and twirled her again. He wrapped his arm around her waist, and she rested her head against his shoulder. Unrelinquished fears left her as he held her. When the song ended, he twirled her once more and she curtsied. They both laughed and walked back to the bar. They grabbed their take-out and exited to her car.

Declan climbed into the passenger seat. "How far away do you live because I need to be heading northward soon."

"Are you driving back tonight?"

"I had planned on it."

"I won't hear of it. You must stay with me." She then blushed. "I mean, not with me, but in my guest room. I insist."

"I'm not sure that's a good idea."

"I promise, I do not bite."

"Are you sure? Might be kind of fun..."

Catriona laughed hard. "Yes. You have nothing to fear."

"Now that I know I won't be bitten, here's the deal. Tomorrow morning, as payment for your hospitality, I will cook breakfast for you. I make a mean pancake."

"I like pancakes. I have syrup and I bought eggs and milk yesterday."

Declan said, "Well, that's a start. How about blueberries?"

"In the freezer. Will that work?"

"It should."

They drove to her small cottage. The outdoor carriage lights flanking both sides of the door illuminated the covered porch and swing. Declan was holding their takeout as she searched for her keys.

"Hurry, I can see my breath out here."

She laughed. "I'm trying." Finding the keys at last, her fingers ached from the cold while turning the lock. The wind blew harder, and she giggled watching Declan dance back and forth trying to stay warm.

"It's cold!" He laughed again with his teeth chattering.

Through the small foyer, he stepped inside the living room.

It was simple but sophisticated in its own way. The living room and fireplace were painted white, including the inviting kitchen visible from the front door. It was a twin to Samuel's cottage.

"I like your home... it suits you. I wasn't sure what to expect considering you live in one of the finest mansions in the state. It's welcoming and not stuffy, but Grace Meade is welcoming too. It makes me like you all the more."

"Thank you. I'm happy you like me." Catriona laughed. "Please, come in and make yourself at home while I fix our plates. Would you like something to drink? Wine, water, or tea?"

"Wine would be nice."

She carried the bags into the kitchen. "My fireplace has a gas starter. Will you build a fire? You can find the wood on the back porch."

"Sure."

Once Declan started the fire, she noticed he glanced at the artwork above the mantle.

"Is this your name sketched along the bottom of this painting?" he asked.

"It is."

"Wow. You painted this?"

"I did," she replied, not blinking an eye as she worked.

"You are good."

"Good at wasting paint, but thanks. You may take a tour of the house. It should take a whole three minutes to see everything. If you need to freshen up, the bathroom is at the end of the hall."

"Thanks, I believe I will."

When he returned, the stereo was playing vintage Norah Jones. Catriona had arranged place settings on the island. She transferred their food from the Styrofoam boxes to white stoneware dishes atop chargers, including hammered flatware, cloth napkins, lit candles, and crystal stemware to finish.

"Wow. This is unexpected."

"I hope you do not mind. One of my strict house rules is life is too short to eat off plastic, especially in my home. I prefer to eat my food from a plate and not rush through it. There is a lost art form in taking your time and relishing every bite. Here… take a seat."

Declan sat at the stool beside her. "Interesting. I can't say I've eaten burgers and fries by candlelight, so this is a first."

"I'm not a snob; there are so few pleasures existing in the monotony of the every day, and this is one of mine. Besides, why own a dishwasher if not for dirty dishes?"

"I've never given it much thought."

"Well, now you have," she said. "Okay, Mr. O'Connell. It's time to answer questions."

"Ask away. I am an open book."

"Who are you? You know way more about me than I do you. I am still embarrassed to have dominated our last conversation, so tell me about your family."

"We can start there. I have two older sisters, Shannon and Erin, and both are married. One lives in Atlanta and the other in Nashville. They each have one child and both are girls. They are gorgeous kids because they take after their Uncle Declan." He laughed taking several fries off his plate and dipping them into his ketchup before stuffing them into his mouth.

"How many can fit in there at one time, Uncle Declan?" She wiped the ketchup away from the side of his face with her napkin.

He laughed. "A few, and yes, Uncle Declan. I miss them, but I will travel home for Christmas."

"That's good. Do you gather at your parents' home?"

"We do."

She continued to ask questions, and he answered all without hesitation. Once they finished dinner, they moved into the living room. He sat on one end of the sofa, and she sat on the opposite corner with her legs curled beside her. He became quiet, staring into the flames dancing above the logs. She studied his face—rugged, but gentle too. His eyes were a deep emerald green revealing the Irish bloodline flowing within him.

"What's on your mind?"

"I have a confession," he said.

"And what would that be?"

"I am tossing this out there… just to see where it lands."

"Toss away," she said.

"Grandpops told me you were with Peter Tramwell in Washington. To be candid, I thought of nothing else while you were away. It's your decision with whom and how you spend your time, but I want more than a friendship… if it's not too late."

"What about Scott and Samuel?"

"What about them?"

"It's somewhat risky. Are you sure?"

"I am. I don't want to miss out on the opportunity of a lifetime." He then leaned in and kissed her. The same nervousness as before arose within her and she pulled back. He asked, "What's wrong?"

"While we are being transparent, I'm not sure where I am at the moment. I don't want to drag you into my drama."

"Try me."

"I have a request."

"Anything."

"Will you hold off a while longer?"

He looked surprised yet pleased. "I don't want to be too forward, but what's wrong with now?"

"A long-term relationship terrifies me. It always has. However, before I can commit to any relationship, I must work through some heavy issues, and I refuse to take anyone on this journey with me. In truth, I've been unfair by pretending to be okay when I am pulling you into my endless nightmare. I want to be normal first."

"No one is normal, Catriona, but I'll do whatever makes you comfortable. I apologize if I appeared pushy. The last thing you will receive from me is pressure."

"Well, it could be a long time. If something better comes along, don't wait for me."

"I am not going anywhere unless you ask me to leave."

She shook her head. "I've had a wonderful day and continuing this conversation may ruin it."

"Try me."

"There is much you do not know. I am not sure where to start." She took a large sip of her wine.

"You can start anywhere." The tone of his voice reassured her to share with no fear of being judged.

"This is awkward because only Scott and Lillian have seen my scars. I was in and out of hospitals for over three years because of multiple surgeries to rebuild my body from the burns I received. I am not what you think I am beneath this dress. Clothing can hide anything if styled with my imperfections in mind. My seamstress is a magician, but you need to know… I am not a whole person."

"I don't care about scars. What kind of man would I be if I worried about scars?"

"I am not sure I can function as a normal woman. Children may never come. I was too young to think about it then, but when you choose to be with me, it will not be easy. Before you decide you want the whole me, it could be more complicated than a girl with a screwed-up mind, but a body too." Her head dropped as the tears flowed. "I'm a mess."

Declan pulled her into his arms. "Your concerns are understandable, but you have nothing to worry about… at least not with me. Again, I'll wait and when you are ready."

"Thank you," she whispered.

"I appreciate your honesty, but I'm in too deep to turn back now."

She relaxed within his arms. She remained quiet, and they sat in silence watching the fire as the logs turned into small embers.

She sat upright. "What time is it? I'm not thinking. Scott will be here mid-morning. Oh, my word, I must sleep because I have much to do before our trip. Declan, I'm sorry."

"For what? I need to sleep too, but know this… I won't stop pursuing you. I want you to remember you deserve happiness despite any hurdles you need to overcome. Who knows? I can help you fight this battle, whatever it is. At least I'll try."

"You are too sweet, but I can't… not yet." She moved from the sofa and placed her glass in the sink. "I will make your bed ready."

"Have I scared you?"

"Not at all. Please forgive me because I misled us into thinking there could be more when I'm not ready."

"There is nothing to forgive. You come to me on your terms. You remembering your past is important, and now that I know more of your struggle, I understand all the more. Thank you for trusting me."

"It's been a good day. Thank you." She disappeared into the hallway. When she returned, she was wearing oversized boyfriend pajamas. "Follow me, please."

Declan put his glass in the sink and walked down the hallway.

"You can sleep in here, and towels are in the bathroom if you need to shower. There is a set of Scott's pajamas in the dresser. He left them when he and Lillian visited, but it has been a long time. Do you want to freshen them in the dryer? They are clean."

"No, I'm good. Thank you."

"There is an alarm clock available. What time did you want to wake?"

"I haven't given too much thought about tomorrow. I guess seven or seven-thirty?"

"Seven-thirty works. Good night, Declan."

"Good night… Catriona?"

"Yes?" She turned toward him.

He took her into his arms and kissed her with incredible tenderness causing her to shutter. "I will wait."

She said nothing. She walked into her room and leaned against the back of the door as it closed. *Sweet mercy. I don't know what I'm doing.* She heard him turn on the shower. The day had been almost too perfect. She did not realize anyone could be this happy and content—these new emotions frightened her. The thought of loving someone and having them return their love was incomprehensible. She had never allowed herself to think it possible before today. Could he be that understanding? As she considered the possibilities, she drifted off to sleep when another dream revealed itself.

Her mother whispered through the door. "Katydid? Katydid…"

"Yes?" She opened the closet door with great care so the hinges would not creak.

"Are you okay?" Katie Jo asked.

"Momma, can we leave? Please?"

"Sugar, he is down the hall. He doesn't know you are here. Under no circumstances must he find you."

"Please?"

"Shh. I hear him coming. You are to stay here… no matter what happens. Do you understand? You must stay hidden."

Catriona moaned aloud in her sleep. "… don't leave me."

He grinned. "I've spent some quality time with Sally and her sisters in my garage."

Katie Jo asked, "What do you mean?"

"They're sweet, but frightened little chickadees. When your daddy is the poorest man in town, it's easy to talk three little girls into doing anything you want when you've got a pocket full of quarters. Besides, I convinced 'em all I'd kill 'em if they told anyone."

Catriona moaned again in her sleep. "Sally?"

"Have you lost your mind? Sally is only nine and the youngest just turned five! You are a monster!"

He screamed, "You heard me. Lie on the bed!" He pointed the gun at her mother's face.

"I don't think so." Katie Jo dashed toward the open door. Grabbing her, he slapped her with the butt of the gun causing her to fall across the bed.

"You'll do whatever I tell you!"

"Don't hurt her…" Catriona murmured. She frowned while she slept.

Her mother stood in her slip facing him when he shoved her body face-first onto the bed. Removing his belt, he strapped her hands behind her back and then forced her to turn over.

"Please do not hurt me. I'll go wherever you ask, but not in here."

She moaned through the drug's effects as the high rushed through her body. His voice became more excited with each word.

"Yes, ma'am. You are feeling it! You are feeling it good! Come on, show me you can roar!"

Catriona screamed out, "Stop! No!"

Declan ran into the room and sat next to her on the bed. "Catriona, it's me… it's Declan."

She awoke crying with her body shaking in fear.

"You're having a bad dream." He then wrapped his arms around her.

She sobbed into his shoulder. "Oh, Declan. She was crying, and he had a gun."

"Who had a gun?"

"I don't know, but she was crying."

"Who was crying?"

"My mother."

"Lillian?"

"No, my mother, Katie Jo."

"It's okay. I'm here."

"He had a gun. I couldn't see his face, but he was hurting her. It was so real." She cried even harder.

"Shh…" He continued to hold her as she sobbed. Her body trembled. "Do you have medication to help you rest?"

She shook her head no. After a few moments, she whispered, "May I have a glass of water?"

"Sure. I'll be right back." He soon returned and handed the glass to her.

"I remembered there are sedatives in the medicine cabinet in the bathroom."

"I'll get them."

He returned, opening the bottle for her. After swallowing the pills, she dropped her head. "I am so embarrassed."

"Don't be." He tucked the blankets around her after she took another sip of water. "Better?"

"What does it mean? Do you think someone hurt her?"

"I don't know. You mentioned a gun. I thought the fire was an accident."

"It was."

"Maybe you should call your doctor tomorrow, but try to sleep. We will know more in the morning." He walked toward the door.

She whispered, "Please… don't go."

"What?" He turned toward her.

"Please. If I close my eyes, what will I see next?"

"Don't worry, I'll stay." He moved the chair toward the bed.

"Don't be ridiculous. You can't sleep there." She folded back the covers as she scooted across the bed. "Please, sleep here."

"Catriona, the temptation is too great… at least it is for me."

"I want you to hold me… nothing more. Please? Are you asking me to beg, Mr. O'Connell?"

He smiled. "I would never ask you to stoop so low, Miss McKenna." He climbed in next to her. "I'm not going anywhere. You're safe with me."

Wrapping his arm around the back of her neck and shoulders, he pulled her toward him. She rested in his arms and placed her arm across his stomach as she laid her head on his chest. His soft breathing calmed her as they slept in each other's arms.

# CHAPTER 16

WHEN THE ALARM sounded, she sensed him move trying not to awaken her. She opened her eyes. Rising on her elbow, she said, "Good morning."

"Good morning to you too."

"You do have the greenest eyes."

"That's what they tell me. How are you this morning?"

"Better, but drowsy. The medicine is still working."

She laid her head back on his chest. She could hear his heart beating as her head moved in unison with his chest rising and falling as he breathed in the room's cool air. Without moving, she said, "Thank you, Declan. Thank you for everything."

"You're welcome."

"I'm glad you're here."

"Me too."

They lay in silence. She found herself wanting him. Unable to bear the stillness any longer, she asked, "May I kiss you?"

With one arm wrapped around her, he raised her chin with his hand and kissed her, then more deeply. He rolled her back onto the bed, and reaching over his shoulder, she helped remove his T-shirt and tossed it onto the floor. Propped on his elbow, she traced the center of his chest with her finger while his body lay against her. He kissed her again. She pushed against him, rolling him over onto his back as she moved on top of him. Sitting on his stomach and leaning downward, her hair fell, draping around her face as it brushed his cheeks and she kissed him with a deep passion. Each hungered for the other. Her oversized pajamas were cumbersome, so she raised again, and swiping her hair from her face, she began to unbutton the loose top.

"What happened to waiting? Are you sure?"

"I think so; however, you should see the real me before we go further. Are you sure you can handle seeing me?"

"Here… let me help you." He unbuttoned her top starting at the bottom.

She grew anxious watching his fingers glide over the first button.

Similar to the sound of an unwelcomed fog horn, the doorbell echoed throughout the cottage.

"Who in the world?" She pulled her top down and looked over at the clock—it was eight o'clock. "I wasn't expecting Scott this early."

Panicked, they jumped out of bed. She pulled on her robe as Declan headed into the hallway. He stopped. Turning back, he kissed her, then whispered, "Don't forget where we left off."

She grinned and nodded, and he disappeared into the bathroom. The doorbell rang a second time.

"I'm coming… I'm coming!" Opening the front door, she found Tia staring back at her through the screen door.

"Good morning, Sunshine!"

"Good morning." Catriona bit her lip and glanced back over her shoulder toward the hallway.

"Aren't you going to invite me in, silly?"

"Sure. Come in." Catriona opened the door and tied her robe as they walked into the living room.

"Cute pajamas. Were you still in bed? That's not like you."

"It's been a long night." Catriona smoothed her hair back behind her ears to look somewhat presentable.

Declan appeared in the doorway dressed, but barefoot and hair disheveled. "Good morning, Tia."

Tia's face reflected every thought going through her mind. "Well, well. Good morning to you too, Declan. Did I interrupt anything important?"

Both responded with a simultaneous, "No." They blushed and Catriona looked away.

Tia laughed. "If you say so."

"Declan stayed in my guest room because it was too late to drive back last night."

"Oh, sure it was."

"It was. I overslept; that's all. Stop." Catriona frowned.

Declan said, "All is good. I promised Catriona as payment for allowing me to stay I would make pancakes this morning. Would you like to join us?"

Catriona motioned for Declan to smooth his hair in the front. Declan looked at his reflection in the microwave door and combed it through with his fingers.

"That sounds good. Thank you," Tia said.

"No, it doesn't. You were leaving. Right?"

"No, I wasn't."

"Yes, you were."

"No, I wasn't. After you left yesterday, I remembered several work-related items needing your attention. May we take a moment or two?"

Catriona nodded. "I'm sorry. Sure, we can. I'm not thinking this morning."

"Well, I can understand why you wouldn't be." Tia grinned and nodded toward Declan.

Declan said, "No worries, ladies. Point me to the flour and syrup, but first, I need to put on my shoes. Will you excuse me?"

Catriona moved toward the hallway with Declan. "Excuse me too, Tia."

"Sure thing."

Catriona followed Declan into the guest room. "I can't believe this. If this wasn't so funny, I'm sure I would be crying."

"It's all right." He grabbed her and they kissed in a full embrace. Stroking the hair away from her face, he said, "You are breath-taking, Miss McKenna."

"You're not so bad yourself, Mr. O'Connell."

"You must admit we have terrible timing."

"Or maybe it's a sign we should not be together."

"No, I'm positive it's only our timing," he said.

She smiled at him. "Don't forget your sweater." She walked back into the living room.

Tia whispered, "I am so sorry. If I had an inkling he was here, I would not have come; I swear on my grandmother's grave… God rest her soul."

"Don't be ridiculous. He's leaving this morning."

"Catriona, don't do this." Tia's voice dropped.

"He is. Scott will be here soon and we are driving south, but Declan is heading to Grace Meade."

"You need him."

"I love you, but you do not know who I need. I barely know him."

"Please don't shut him out. You close the door too soon, always. No, I take that back. You resist men once they have shown interest. Why?"

"What business did you need to discuss?"

"There. You are doing it again. Please… not this time."

"Again, talk only about the shop. Otherwise, butt out."

Tia whispered, "As your best friend, I need you to hear this. I love and respect you, but you are heading into a future of living alone. Forever… unless you decide life is worth sharing."

Declan interrupted them by banging the pots and pans, along with slamming the pantry door. They joined him as he set their places at the island's bar with dishes from the cabinet. Unexpectedly, the doorbell interrupted again.

Catriona closed her eyes, then shook her head. "Oh, my word! What is this, Grand Central Station?" Opening the door, she froze.

"Good morning, doll. Are we too early?" Scott asked.

"Good morning, Catriona," Peter said.

She looked as if caught in the headlights of an oncoming car.

"Catriona, may we come inside?" Scott asked. "It's cold out here."

"You have startled me… that's all. Come in and join the party."

"Party?"

"Come inside." She stepped back and waved them in with her hand as if introducing a stage act.

Tia met them in the living room.

"Good morning, Tia. How good to see you," Scott said as he reached for her hands and kissed her on the cheek.

"Thank you, Mr. McKenna. It is good to see you too. Who is your friend?"

"Tia, this is Peter Tramwell, my co-counsel on a current case."

Declan was drinking orange juice and choked when hearing Peter's name. His coughing grew worse.

"It is nice to meet you," she said.

Scott walked into the kitchen. "Declan? What are you doing here?" Scott turned and looked at Catriona who was shaking her head in disbelief.

"Declan delivered my desk to the shop yesterday, and I invited him to stay overnight."

"You did?" Peter looked at her in total surprise.

Declan asked, "Blueberry pancakes, anyone? There's plenty."

Tia laughed at the exasperated expression on Catriona's face.

"This is innocent, I promise." Catriona laughed out of nervousness. "It was too late for him to drive back so I invited him to stay in my guest room. He is leaving for Grace Meade after breakfast. Aren't you, Declan?"

"Yes, I am. Tia, would you like bacon?"

"Yes, please."

Scott said, "Well, I'm glad we made it in time for breakfast before you had to leave, but I did not realize you and Catriona were acquainted."

"Yes, we are, sir. Well acquainted," Declan said as he flipped a pancake on the grill.

"Oh?" Peter looked at Catriona again.

Catriona was shaking as she spoke. "Peter, this is Declan O'Connell. He helps Lillian with the equine business on our estate. Remember?"

"Oh. I remember you… from the dance. You and Catriona were the first on the dance floor." Peter then looked at her again.

"That was a… a… that dance was a…" Her words failed her. She watched Tia soaking in every detail.

Declan said, "I had asked Catriona for the first dance of the evening as an inside joke related to our future business partnership at Grace Meade. Isn't that right?"

She nodded in agreement and half-smiled while rolling her eyes.

"Oh, I see." Peter reached out and shook Declan's hand. "It's nice to meet you."

Catriona said, "Please, let's move to the dining table."

Tia helped arrange the dinnerware along with Declan's blueberry pancakes, applewood bacon, and freshly brewed coffee as they sat together. Peter sat by Catriona and clasped her hand in his. She dropped their hands beneath the table. Declan sat at the furthest end glaring at Peter and looking at Catriona with a confused expression speaking volumes. The conversation remained light, and once finished with their meal, kitchen clean-up was fast.

Declan stood to leave. "I had better be off. Nice meeting you, Peter, and seeing you again, Tia. Scott and Catriona, I pray you have safe travels and will see you back at Grace Meade."

Scott said, "Thanks for the breakfast… it was excellent. I'll let Cookie know you have untapped, hidden talents."

"Horses are more my style, but thank you all the same, sir."

"May I walk you out?" Catriona asked.

"Sure. Let me grab my jacket. I believe I left it in the bedroom. Goodbye, all."

When they walked outside, Catriona remembered his truck was at her shop. "Lovely. What do we do now?"

"Don't worry about it. Maybe I can catch a ride with Tia."

"That's a good idea. I am sorry."

"For what?"

"For all of this. I'm not reacting well," she said.

He pulled her from the view of the windows and kissed her again. "No reason to worry, sweet lady. Your secrets are locked away always. They are safe with me. Also, know I enjoy holding you even after the scariest moments of a dream. I can't leave without saying it was good they interrupted us because I'm not sure I could have stopped if we had gone a moment longer." He laughed. "I wish we had another day. May I ask you one thing?"

"Anything."

"Is Peter a serious contender?"

"I don't know. Why do you ask?"

"It was hard seeing his arm around the back of your chair. Believe it or not, I'm not the jealous type, but the more I see of you, the less I can imagine my future without you in it. I am falling hard here... leading me there or not. Our problem is we need to work on our timing." A sheepish grin crossed his face.

"Oh, Declan, I'm not playing games. I'm not sure I know how. He is important to Scott, so he will frequent Grace Meade's doors often, I imagine. I'm not sure how his presence affects me with Lillian and Scott's plans. He is a kind person, and I like him. I won't lie... he wants to be with me too." She was overwhelmed. "I can't do this."

"Well, no one can accuse you of not being direct."

"Direct, yes, but more confused. Before you arrived, I thought I was beginning a relationship with Peter, and you and I were only friends by mutual agreement. Remember? Mercy, why did you taste so good?"

"Thank you... I think." Declan looked more confused with each word.

"I am unsure where we go from here, but yesterday was incredible. I will never forget last night. You know more about me than anyone and spending another day together would be an easy decision for me too; however, in retrospect, maybe it's for the best. Blame it on the medication's side effects or my sinful nature as my granny would have put it, but I know I placed you in a vulnerable position this morning. Trust me... I'm out of my element with romantic relationships."

"Nothing happened, but we were close." He stepped in to kiss her again, but she stopped him.

"No. We cannot go there again."

"Ever?" He backed away from her.

"You have caused me to lose focus. Not your fault, but mine." Tears welled up in her eyes. *Keep it together, Catriona. Keep it together.* "First, I need to remember my past. My memory stands in the way of moving forward with anyone. Thank you for being honest with me as I have feelings for you too; however, please move on if you must. My memory returning could take another twenty years. The stress of dealing with you and Peter isn't helping either. Oh, my word, I'm all over the place."

Declan's eyes softened. He took her shoulders in his hands facing her. "I told you last night you will never feel pressure from me. Go out with Peter if you must. Take care of yourself first... get well. Remember to call your doctor today about that dream. Enjoy your time with Scott and explore Sageville for answers. I'll be waiting at Grace Meade should you need me. Again, I am not going anywhere unless you ask me to leave."

Tia walked onto the porch, closing the door behind her. "Pardon me."

Catriona moved away from Declan.

Tia said, "I realized Declan did not have a ride back to the shop. May I be of service? I said nothing to Scott nor Peter. I excused myself and they are none the wiser."

"Thank you. Yes, I would appreciate a ride." Declan looked back toward Catriona. "I'll be waiting."

She nodded. He reached out and squeezed her hand. She hugged him instead and then turned as he descended the steps toward Tia's car leaving the two women alone.

"I'll call you later, and we can go over your questions about the business. Thank you for everything." Catriona hugged her neck.

"I'm on your side, girl. Although, I'm unsure what is happening with you. That was one interesting breakfast. I want you to get well because we have tons of work regardless of those two gentlemen fighting over you."

"Work takes priority, but no one is fighting over me." She frowned knowing Tia had noticed.

"Then you are blind." Tia touched Catriona's cheek. "Remember, I am only a phone call away."

Catriona nodded. As they pulled out of the drive, she blew a kiss their way and waved. When Catriona returned, Peter was missing and Scott was in the kitchen.

"Interesting morning, sweetheart."

"Please, Scott, I don't need this. My night was unbearable."

"What do you mean?"

"Bad dreams again."

"I'm sorry. Is there anything I can do?"

"No, sir. Please know Declan is my friend… a dear friend. We slept in separate rooms, and then one of my nightmares hit hard. He took care of me."

"Sweet girl, you don't have to tell me. I know Declan is a good man. Lillian would never have hired him otherwise, and his grandfather… who adores you… has left him an outstanding example to follow. Now, I can better understand the glances at the table this morning."

"There were no glances."

"Darling, I don't know how to say this without hurting your feelings, but because you have never been in a deep relationship with anyone other than with your family, you cannot see what is happening around you."

"That's funny. Tia said the same thing."

Peter walked into the living room. "I hope I'm not interrupting."

Catriona replied, "Certainly not. More coffee?"

"No, but thank you." Peter stood next to her as if declaring possession.

Catriona poured herself a cup of hot tea. "Well, gentlemen, what is our game plan for today?"

"Scott and I rode together because I'm doing a little more research into our Mr. Thaddeus Franks."

"Please be careful… I don't like him."

"Thank you. Nothing is going to happen to either of us." Peter winked at her.

"I hope you don't mind, but we need to visit a couple of attorneys in town before heading to Sageville. Peter is planning to catch the train this afternoon."

"Please, gentlemen, do whatever is necessary and take your time. I need to pack. I cannot believe I'm still in my robe. Do you want to grab lunch or want me to prepare something here?"

"No, doll. We are eating in town... a scheduled business luncheon."

She said, "Good. That works for me. I need to change the linens and prepare my flower beds for winter. Digging in the dirt will help clear my mind before we leave."

"Is everything all right?" Peter asked.

"Nothing I can't handle, but thank you for asking." She sat next to him.

Scott said, "Excuse me, but I need to make myself presentable after pancakes and syrup."

"Washcloths are in the closet."

"Yes, I remember." Scott stepped out of the room.

Peter asked, "Is Declan a good friend?"

Surprised by his forwardness, she said, "Yes, he is."

"Anything I should know about?"

"I don't think so."

"No offense, but you are still in your robe. It's obvious you haven't combed your hair... not that it looks bad. You also appear to be comfortable wearing your robe around him."

"You are kidding me, right?"

"No, I'm not."

She pushed her chair away from the island. "Let me 'set the record straight' as you attorneys might say. It's none of your business, but Declan and I are friends. I do not appreciate this line of questioning; he helped me... that is all."

"I do not share women I am dating with others, Catriona; he is beneath you. He stared at you throughout breakfast so any foregone conclusion would be you two are close. After the cold treatment I received from you following the concert, it surprised me to find him here."

"Cold treatment? What do you mean? You told me you understood…"

Peter shrugged his shoulders.

She scoffed. "Fine. Conclude all you want. Yes, I enjoy Declan's company."

"Are you angry with me?"

"Yes, I am." She stopped mid-sentence and laughed. "Did he really stare at me throughout breakfast?"

Peter nodded.

"Are we having our first quarrel?" She laughed again.

"You have the oddest sense of humor."

"No, just a realistic one." She didn't smile as she took a long sip of tea.

"I apologize. This is not my normal behavior. I'm not afraid of a challenge… if there is one."

"Please don't. There is no reason to challenge anyone. My life is too complicated with my business responsibilities and a few other issues to consider a serious relationship with anyone. Maybe later."

Scott stepped back into the kitchen unnoticed and asked, "Is there a problem in here?"

Peter turned toward the door to leave.

"No, sir. Everything is fine," she said.

Scott said, "I noticed my pajama bottoms in the bathroom and my T-shirt on the floor in your bedroom. Did I leave those here?"

"Yes. I gave them to Declan to wear."

Peter turned toward her as a frown crossed his brow.

"Oh?" Scott raised his eyebrows.

"Oh what? Good grief. Why am I on the witness stand this morning? Listen to me… the both of you. This is my house. I can do whatever I want, with whomever I want, at any time I want. I could not let Declan sleep in his street clothes. Testosterone has taken over today. This entire situation has turned into insanity."

"Hey. I understand. Lillian would have done the same thing. No reason to be so sensitive, darling. You did not sleep well, did you?"

"No, sir. Thank you for realizing I was only being hospitable."

Peter remained silent.

Scott said, "We had better get started. They scheduled our meeting for eleven-thirty so I should be back around two. Will you be ready?"

"Yes, I will." She turned toward Peter. "I assume Scott will drop you off at the station this afternoon?"

"Yes. Maybe you and I can meet again in Washington soon."

"We'll see."

Scott said, "Peter, I forgot to ask. Lillian and I host a tent for my firm at the annual International Gold Cup Races. Why don't you join us?"

"Thank you. I have never attended the classic, but only if Catriona approves."

Keeping Scott at bay, she said, "You cannot miss it once your name goes on the invitation list. Besides, you would hurt Lillian's feelings… it's a great event. I don't know of anyone who would not enjoy it. You should go."

"I accept your invitation. Thank you."

Scott said, "Great. I'll make sure Lillian knows. Catriona, I'll meet you here later."

"Yes, sir."

She followed them out onto the porch as Scott walked to his truck. Peter stopped short of the bottom step and stepped back toward her. He reached for her hand.

"Forgive me. I was out-of-line. Seeing another man in your kitchen when I thought there was no other confused me. I assumed I was the only one interested in you. Anyone would have known otherwise. I must appear arrogant and conceited… nothing could be further from the truth. We have never spoken words of a commitment between us, and I have no say so in anything you do. I have acted a fool."

"There is nothing to forgive, Peter. In my defense, I did not know you were coming... not that it mattered. I'm not sure where our relationship is heading. I want what is best for all of us."

"Me too. May I escort you to the races or am I overstepping my boundaries?"

Pausing, she remembered Declan's words. She needed to know if Peter was the one. She nodded. "Yes, I would enjoy your company. We can talk early next week and make plans closer to time."

Peter smiled as he let out a sigh of relief. "I look forward to hearing from you. I hope you have a great time with your father this weekend. Why are you going?"

"Oh, no reason in particular." She had shared nothing of her problems or past with Peter. She certainly had not discussed her medical condition with him. "Catching up on old memories, I hope. No big deal."

"Enjoy yourself."

"Thank you. Will you do me a favor?"

"Anything."

"Watch out for Scott with that crazy Franks man. Okay?"

"I will." He turned over her hand and kissed her palm. "I am glad we ended on a positive note. I'll see you soon."

She closed her fingers as he waved goodbye from the car.

The day's hours had flown as she readied her home and garden for the next few weeks away. Scott returned early afternoon.

"How was your meeting?"

Scott rubbed his forehead with his fingers. "Good and not so good. A miner agreed to meet with us this morning. His wife drove him to Charlottesville because he was incapable, and for the first time, I saw the nitty-gritty of what this case involves. The poor man is only thirty-nine years old and is dying. He cannot breathe because his lungs are no longer functioning fully. It was terrible to witness. I cannot imagine his pain."

"Oh, Scott."

"I know. We have to beat Franks. We have to for that young man's family. He has little ones still at home and no income."

"You will. I know you will."

"Thank you, doll. Enough of that today. I need to focus on you and our journey. Are you ready for Sageville?"

Catriona replied, "I am, but I must admit I'm a little scared."

"It's okay, sweetie. So am I."

# CHAPTER 17

Her Momma's People

WHEN FACING UNBEATABLE challenges, the human spirit never fails to rise, revealing some heroes of magnificent proportions who deserve recognition on grandiose, pomp, and circumstance occasions for all to see. But there are also the quiet heroes of our everyday lives. Despite the misfortunes bestowed upon them through no fault of their own, they overcome with great tenacity and rise above with a joyful spirit unnoticed until much later. This was the world of Joseph and Nora Maureen Gallagher-Dunne, Katie Jo's parents.

Theirs was a large Protestant Irish family of the Cumberland Presbyterian faith. They lived on a farm in the same valley as Sageville, located somewhere between Belfast and Paint Lick, near the base of the Clinch Mountain range.

Born early in the last century, their simple way of life remained the same throughout the years. More gentle souls had never lived. They had six daughters and a son, and between the seven were born twenty-one grandchildren. Her grandparents were in their eighties when Catriona was added to the list of grandchildren, the youngest of them all. Like her mother, the next generation's children were closer in age than her cousins who were much older.

Katie Jo accredited the appreciation of family to living in Appalachia, where every Sunday, twenty to twenty-five Dunne family members would travel each from their own church to her parents' home for lunch. She never understood how Grandmother Dunne could afford to feed so many. They were of little means and material things, but never short on love and laughter in their home.

After Sunday lunch, Catriona played with her cousins' children as the grown-ups sat on the porch and discussed their week with one another. Her grandfather whittled as the shavings showered around the runners of his rocker, and the women chattered on about their week.

Catriona adored her family, but Grandmother Dunne was her most valued gem. Her grandmother was an understated, petite woman who wore an apron every day. With snowy tresses flowing past her waistline, she would weave the white strands into one continuous, flawless braid and encircle her head, placing the final hairpin in place. Catriona thought her grandmother looked as glorious as a queen wearing a crown.

Nora Maureen was a quiet spirit who radiated strength and perseverance from deep within. Katie Jo told Catriona her grandmother had lived a life similar to Cinderella before the Prince presented her lost shoe.

"It's true," Katie Jo said. "When your grandmother was a child, her stepmother treated her with little regard; she would not allow her to go to school on certain days because they expected her to do the family's laundry. She permitted her own children to continue their studies while she made your grandmother stay home; however, my mother showed no resentment. Little did my momma realize, but her stepmother was a warm-up of who was to come."

Nora's mother-in-law, Searcy Dunne, was hard and selfish—a mean woman with a black soul. She controlled all of her children, but none more than her eldest son. When Joseph married, Searcy demanded to live with the couple. She never allowed Nora to reign as queen of her own home, and Nora fell under the scrutiny of Searcy as her domineering overseer. Day in and day out, she did nothing right in the old woman's eyes. Her emotional, domestic abuse came from her mother-in-law and not her husband, although he was verbally abused as well. He never recognized it having been born into it.

There was a time when the couple's state of affairs had grown financially daunting, and Nora's brother-in-law and wife were in a much stronger monetary position to afford to have Searcy move in with them for a while. Despite the hardship of an extra mouth to feed, Searcy refused to leave and continued her demands with no added contributions to help make ends meet. The young family scarcely survived. Being a self-sacrificing person, Nora almost perished because there was not enough food to feed her children. For months and with no one's knowledge, she would go days without eating to nourish her starving family. Nora became ill to the point of death, and by the grace of God, her daughters nursed her back to health through prayer and vigilant care. When Searcy died in her late nineties, she had lived with her son and daughter-in-law for the first forty years of their marriage, yet Nora wept at her grave. Could it have been grief or relief? No one knew for sure.

Katie Jo said, "Can you imagine living forty years with someone so selfish and hateful? My mother was like the children of Israel who wandered in the desert, yet Momma had done nothing to warrant such an imprisoned, lifelong sentence. If that doesn't make you strong, child, nothing will."

Neither stepmother nor mother-in-law was successful in breaking Grandmother Dunne's spirit. She became sweeter over time. In the Holy Book, it speaks of the meek, not in a worldly definition of one who is weak, but in the example of Moses, David, Daniel, Esther, and Mary, the mother of Jesus. Whereas, they showed courage to live a life of endurance and strength, no matter what circumstances befell them. For Katie Jo, Grandmother Dunne was the epitome of those heroes mentioned in the scriptures.

Katie Jo told Catriona, "You have the same blood flowing within you, baby girl. When you think all is lost and you cannot go on, I want you to remember your grandmother and draw from her strength. When your Grandmother Dunne passes over into the great beyond, she will be awarded her heavenly crown containing brilliant jewels for all she has endured, yet she will continue to give with a cheerful heart. Joyfully and humbly, she will lay her diadem at the Master's feet… big jewels, Katydid. Big."

Music was a constant in their household. Looming high over the small living room, sat the old pump organ brought in by wagon into the valley over one hundred years before. Watching her grandmother's tiny frame pull at the knobs and bounce on the short stool as her feet pumped air into the old thing, she would sing hymns, but Catriona preferred a secular favorite, 'My Bonnie Lies Over the Ocean,' because it caused for greater entertainment.

Her grandmother was a wonderful cook and won the county fair each year with her canned pear preserves; a secret recipe handed down by her momma who had died when Nora Maureen was a child. She passed onto Catriona her love of flowers and fine needlework craftsmanship. Although Nora Maureen was a humble and soft-spoken person, she could have boasted to her quilting circle friends that hers were the tiniest of the other stitches, but she would never have thought to do so, much less mentioned it. Upon her granddaughter's ninth birthday, Grandmother Dunne surprised Catriona with a special quilt for her to cherish forever.

Longevity was a proven trait in the Dunne family's ancestral genes. Well into their late nineties, her grandparents never slowed in their gait of getting things done. Married for over seventy years, they had continued with good health and sharpness of mind. However, on one occasion, both shared the same hospital room. Granddaddy Joseph assigned Catriona a few chores while they were away.

One was to gather eggs in her grandmother's absence, but he instructed her to take Grandmother Dunne's walking cane should the new rooster try to attack. He warned he was of the flogging kind, and to "push him out of the way" if he approached her. As Catriona walked toward the barn, she was not holding the walking cane in its correct position. Instead, she was holding it like a golf wedge, swinging it back and forth striking the weeds along the fence row as she made her way toward the opened heavy doors flanking each side of the barn's entrance.

Just as her grandfather had predicted, the cocky rooster charged out of the barn and ran toward her at an incredible speed with his head low and his wings bowed by his sides. Without warning, the bird flew into the air with its sharp spurs turned upward toward Catriona's face. Being surprised, she swung the cane with both arms and with more force than she thought capable. The crook of the cane hit the rooster's neck at the perfect angle and beheaded the poor bird in midair much to Catriona's shock and horror. She screamed as the rooster ran around the barnyard without its head. As if hearing the bell in the starter gates at a horserace, all the hens scattered out of the barn. They charged the crazed feathered body and pecked the headless wonder to no one's understanding. Catriona screamed, but dashed into the barn and gathered the eggs with little regard to the mayhem a few feet away. When she crept back into the barnyard, the chickens were continuing their endless determination of destroying the lifeless body of red and black feathers. Catriona ran crying into the house with the filled basket forgetting the bloody cane still clutched in her hand. After calming her, Katie Jo took her daughter back to the hospital to face Joseph.

As Catriona launched into her story, she cried. When finished telling every morbid detail, both of her grandparents laughed much to her surprise.

Granddaddy Joseph said, "I'm sorry you had to suffer such a terrible fright, child, but I cannot remember a funnier story. He might have been a prized rooster, but too mean for sure. No need to worry about it any further."

Her grandmother consoled. "Don't worry none, Katydid. I hated that rooster. He had cut me many times on my lower legs. I'm just happy you weren't hurt. It's never wrong to protect yourself, honey. He will fry up good for Sunday dinner."

Although Joseph and Nora were blessed with a lengthy lifespan, it was to their family's inconsolable disbelief when Sunday never came. Nora died the same evening. It was then Catriona thought her grandmother's passing would be her deepest grief, but weeks later, Granddaddy Joseph added to her sorrow as he followed his precious wife into eternity.

Funerals had become commonplace for one too young to comprehend.

She wondered why death was shadowing her—was he determined to be her friend?

CHAPTER 18

THE TRUCK SAT at the stop sign with its engine idling. No other car was in sight, but they did not move.

Scott reached for her hand. "How are you, Katydid?"

"Butterflies are dancing the tango in my stomach, but I think I'm fine. Are you ready?"

"I think so."

Catriona squeezed his fingers. Surprised, it was clammy to the touch. "Are you sure?"

"No, if I'm being honest. I believe my butterflies are tap dancing on top of yours."

He pressed his foot on the accelerator and drove past the city welcome sign of Sageville. It was early evening in the small town. The once beautiful, thriving community appeared in the long shadows of the day to be more of a ghost town except for a few buildings—the post office, a small grocery store, Ella's Café, and a few churches, including the First Baptist Church. Most had fallen into disrepair. Scott mentioned he could not believe the changes from years of neglect due to lack of prosperity.

As Catriona looked from the truck window, she scoped every building; however, nothing appeared familiar. The schoolyard, mown recently with a broken blade, revealed chopped leaves in fine rows and uneven cut blades of brown grass. Two young girls were swinging on the playground equipment, oblivious to the worries of the outside world. One could describe them as innocence personified, and Catriona smiled when they waved as she passed.

Scott said, "I believe we should drive over to your parents' place; however, nothing is there. The property still belongs to you, but I had the burned rubble cleared and only the foundation remains. I have continued to pay the taxes, yet I've done nothing more. Seeing it may or may not help you remember."

"It's okay. I want to see it."

He made another turn and the large trees loomed over the street as if soldiers standing at attention guarding their way.

"I remember this. Our house should be around the next corner." Her heart raced.

As Scott pulled into the old driveway, the vines covering most of the property were acting as the new owner and welcomed Catriona home. There were no obvious signs of a house ever existing. He pushed the gearshift into park and removed the keys. Leaning forward and crossing his arms atop the steering wheel, he paused to catch his breath before moving to open the door for Catriona. She was standing outside the truck before he could reach her.

"Do you recognize anything?"

Catriona shook her head. It was not as she had imagined. She moved, but Scott stopped her.

"Wait. We may need these." Scott stepped to the rear of the truck and pulled out two pairs of high rubber boots and thick gardening gloves. Without hesitation, they removed their shoes and slipped on the boots in silence.

She resumed her hike over the broken asphalt driveway where weeds and roots had made their home between the cracks. In the back of the property, the invasive kudzu, originating from Japan and covering the Southern hemisphere of the country, swallowed an outbuilding and barn, except for the roof gables peeking through to the unexpected guests below. The jungle included shrubby privet and a little wisteria with its faded blooms grasping the last trace of fall's dimming sunlight. Catriona heeded every step through the overgrowth, pushing back the briars and brambles and pulling at the high weeds as she inched closer toward the structures with little progress. Soon cockleburs and stick tights covered her trousers. Scott made his way back to the truck to grab the clippers.

Catriona looked over the small field and remembered her daddy's garden now replaced with three large trees and grasses reaching more than waist-high. She recognized the wild rose bushes inhabiting the fence row still mixed in with the surrounding overgrowth. She thought she heard her father call her name; however, when she turned, it was Scott.

"Catriona? Did you hear me?"

"Yes?"

"Are you okay?"

"Yes. I thought I could hear their voices. I can see Daddy standing next to the garden fence. He would tell me, 'Honey, you walk behind me, and when the plow's blade cuts into the side of the row, the potatoes will pop to the surface. You can gather the potatoes, but stay behind me because I do not want ole Jack stepping on you.'"

She looked at Scott. "Did you know we had a mule?"

Scott shook his head.

She smiled, but her eyes revealed a sadness all the same. "Daddy would ask our guests if they knew the name of our mule and most did not. He would laugh and say, 'Then you don't know Jack.'" She chuckled. "He thought he was funny, and I remember they thought he was too. They always laughed at least." She sensed a release unexplained. "Please, may I have the clippers?"

"I'll do it, honey. We can stop if needed."

She pulled the cuttings to the side as he whacked a path into the forest of brush before them. Soon, one side of the small outbuilding appeared. They uncovered the only window, and Catriona cupped her hands against the glass, shading her face as she peered inside. The once blue walls were faded white because of the destruction of time.

"I can see my toy refrigerator... it's still there." Her mind raced back to a time where she remembered feeding Miss Callie in her high chair. "I remember," she whispered, but this time she was no longer dizzy. Her mind revealed images of her mother singing and playing with her in her tiny playhouse and she wept, "I remember her..."

Scott wrapped his arm around her shoulders and she buried her face into his jacket crying for losses; loss of time, loss of childhood, loss of memories, loss of a mother and father, and loss of self. He allowed her to cry. As he held her, tears fell in unison.

"Let's take a break, honey. We will come back tomorrow at first light. It's growing darker by the minute, and we need daylight to get through this brush without getting hurt."

Regaining her composure, she replied, "All right. I guess I can wait another day. I've made progress in a short time, don't you think?"

He nodded.

"Do you think the café we passed is open?"

"I don't know, but we can try. If not, we can eat at the B and B."

They walked arm-in-arm down their haphazard path to the truck and headed back into the central part of town. Once inside the diner, a woman in her mid-sixties greeted them at the door.

"Sit anywhere you like. Can I get y'all some coke or coffee?"

"Two cokes, please. Where are your restrooms?" Scott asked.

"Down the hallway."

"Thanks. We need to clean up a bit."

She replied, "No hurry, hun. We ain't going nowhere."

The pair made their way to the public restrooms to remove the afternoon's grime. Catriona removed her jacket and pulled away the remaining stick tights attached. Looking in the mirror, she removed the scarf and untied her ponytail. As she brushed her hair to rid any remaining cockleburs, she decided to leave her hair down, falling below her shoulders. She tied the scarf around her neck and added more blush and a touch of red lipstick. Straightening her white oversized blouse, she unbuttoned and tied the tails into a knot at her waist. Thinking she did not look too bad following their adventure, she walked back into the dining room and made her way toward their table. She ran her fingers across the top of the bench before sliding into the booth next to a large picture window. Catriona smiled. There was a familiarity about the place as if she had sat in the same booth before.

Although old, the eatery was clean. The diner's interior resembled a vintage movie set with its diamond-patterned and glittered linoleum floor stained yellow from wax buildup. The green and cream Naugahyde upholstered seats appeared to be original to each of the ten or more booths illuminated by a single 1970s-era, knobby globe held by a black chain—each table's ball of sunshine to brighten the contents below.

Tall swivel stools were mounted in a row in front of the long counter. Seated atop, several people were busy with small talk and reading the local newspaper. Some had stopped in for a cup of joe on their way to who-knows-where. Years ago, someone had nailed a lighted menu board advertising RC Cola above the grill. It showed its age, having turned dark yellow from the heat, yet it still worked.

Her eyes followed a wall of dark wood paneling where several items hung: an outdated calendar provided as free advertising by a local insurance company with its pages curled on the corners, a few faded pictures of coal miners in their work clothes standing on the rails or deep inside the mine itself, and last, a framed newspaper clipping whose headline read in large letters:

CAVE IN! MANY DEAD!

It looked to be the same paper as the one she had spotted in Suzanne's shop in Old Town Alexandria. As she inspected closer, she did not see the server approach the booth with her tray.

"Are you ready to order, hun?"

When Catriona turned, the server stared in disbelief. "Katie Jo, is it really you?" The woman looked as if she had seen a ghost.

Catriona looked surprised as well. "No ma'am. You are mistaken. I'm not Katie Jo."

"Of course, you're not. Please forgive me, but you sure look a lot like somebody I used to know a long time ago. I swear, it's... it's like... it's silly. You can't be her. It's impossible. You will have to excuse these old eyes."

"Do I look like Katie Jo?"

"Well, yeah, but again, I'm sorry. She was a dear friend, and this was her and Bill's favorite booth. I'm a confused woman with a poor memory... don't be payin' me no attention, sweetie."

Catriona interrupted. "Do you mean my mother, Katie Jo Harrington?"

"Your mother?" she asked in disbelief.

"Yes. My mother and father were Bill and Katie Jo Harrington."

"Well, honey, that can't be."

"What do you mean?"

"Bill and Katie Jo only had one girl and all of 'em died in a house fire. What must be... my word, how long has it been?"

Her words stunned Catriona into silence.

Scott interrupted, "May I help you?"

Neither of the women had seen him return to the table. Startled, the server tipped her tray, causing the soft drinks to spill with the red plastic glasses bouncing when hitting the hard floor.

"Heavens to Betsy! I'm so sorry! Please, let me get a towel and a mop. Did any of it get on y'all?"

Catriona shook her head.

"Excuse me. I'll bring more drinks." The waitress almost tripped. She disappeared into the back where the fry cook was leaning through the pass-through window to see the cause for the loud commotion.

"What is she talking about, Scott?"

"I don't know. What did she say?" Scott slid into the seat opposite her.

"She called me 'Katie Jo' and when I told her who I was, she said I had died. Why would she think I had died?"

"We need to go. I knew this was a mistake... I knew it. I'll explain everything outside. We must leave. Now."

"But Scott..."

He bolted from the booth and threw a ten-dollar bill onto the table. Grabbing her by the elbow, they hurried from the café and into the truck. She glanced back over her shoulder as they drove away.

***

Back inside the café, the server yelled through the order window, "Well, I never! Did you see her, Thornwell?"

He shook his head.

"Did any of y'all see her? Does anybody remember Bill and Katie Jo Harrington?"

Thornwell said, "I remember all of 'em. The Harringtons were some of the best bunch of people you'd ever want to know, I tell you. They'd do anythin' for anybody. If I remember right, their family moved on a long time ago. My goodness, it must be more than twenty-five years or more since the mines closed. That's when most of 'em left here. Sorry, but I didn't see her."

Harvey Rexford moved to the front counter. "Erline, why don't you tell us what happened."

"She's claiming to be Katie Jo's daughter. Well, she can't be. The entire family died in that gosh-awful fire. Remember? I think I'm goin' to call the police."

All the patrons whispered among themselves as she dialed the phone. The café was abuzz, except for one man who sat in the corner staring into his coffee cup.

She approached his table. "Daub, didn't you used to live close by to the family? Did you see her?"

He whispered, "No. No, I didn't see her."

She replied in a low voice, "Hey." She touched him on the arm. "I was real sorry to hear about your momma, son. She was a kind woman despite it all."

He nodded his head.

"You okay, hun? The funeral is tomorrow, ain't it?"

He looked into her face with dead eyes. "I'll catch up with you in a day or two. It's gettin' late."

"That's probably a good idea. You sure don't need no more trouble, do you? Get on home and I'll fill you in next time I see you. I won't tell Sheriff Walters about you bein' in here."

"Thanks."

She realized he was in no pain.

"You need to lay off the blow, hun. Do you need a ride?"

"Mind your own business for once, Erline." The man stood. He walked toward the door and into the night air.

She shook her head and began clearing the table where he sat. Because of her cousin's troubles, she had a soft spot for men who were making a go again after re-entry into society. Unfortunately, Daub had grown into the likeness of his daddy and everyone knew his father had treated his mother like the dirt beneath his fingernails. Now that both parents were dead, she hoped he would move on from Sageville and start anew elsewhere.

***

Back in the privacy of her room at the inn, Catriona was pacing to keep from hitting something.

"Catriona. You are becoming hysterical. I need you to calm down before they ask us to leave. I'm your father."

She stopped cold and looked at him in total bewilderment. "No. Bill Harrington is my father, or is he? Who am I, Scott?"

He dry-wiped his face with both hands as he pleaded with her. "Don't do this. This was not how this was supposed to have played out."

"Played out? Played out… really? I'm not part of one of your courtroom dramas. I'm not the prosecution. I'm not even the blasted defendant! Supposedly, I am your daughter, but who are you? You and Lillian were my foundation… the only two people in my world who I trusted with blind faith. Do Samuel and Cookie know?"

"No. Only me and Lillian, and law enforcement, of course."

"When I think about the lies and deception... it's incomprehensible to me. If you cannot talk without your lawyer BS, then let's pretend you're on the witness stand. I want the truth, the whole truth, and nothing but the truth, so help you God."

"I'll start at the beginning, but you must know Lillian and I love you more than life itself. We would do anything for you and have acted in your best interest always. We certainly never wanted to deceive or hurt you. The only choice we made changed your and our world forever."

"Is there someone other than you who can explain this to me? And Lillian. How could she? Is there anyone who isn't lying with every word that comes out of their mouths? I don't believe either of you loves me."

"You don't mean that, honey. If you want to blame anyone, then blame me alone. I convinced Lillian it was the only way to protect you, so we allowed everyone in Sageville to think you died along with your parents in the fire. Your mother and father had given us guardianship, and it was easy to have you disappear as we lived six hours away. No one knew me as our family never lived here; I visited my grandparents in the summers only. Bill's family had moved to different areas of the country after the mines closed. The sheriff at the time was a good family friend, and he believed the fire was not an accident but the result of something more sinister."

"What happened?"

"A few nights before the fire, Bill had taken a shortcut on his way home through a back road. A few men who had been drinking down along the riverbank stepped out into the road when his car approached. Who knows for what reason? Your dad stopped his car and confronted two of them. He asked them to move when threats were made. Bill gunned the car, causing one of them to jump out of the way, but not before hitting the second man with the front bumper throwing him into the brush. It was never his intention to hit anyone. He wanted to scare them, that's all. However, when Bill stopped the car to see if he had injured anyone, gunshots were fired, so he sped away. Bill drove straight to the sheriff's office, but when the officers returned, they found no one at the scene. The only signs of any confrontation were a few empty beer cans, and spots of blood on Bill's bumper along with a single bullet hole in the back windshield of his car. The sheriff believed these men sought revenge and targeted your parents' house. Your father had no clue who they were. Since the closing of the mines, dangerous groups were running drugs into the area, along with a few meth labs, and the police thought Bill had come across one of these groups. Rumors later confirmed mafia ties to the drugs. It was the only logical explanation. The sheriff, Lillian, and I, along with the VBI and FBI, knew the only way to keep you safe would be to declare you dead as well. I called in a few favors and the agencies leaked the false arson report and death certificates to the papers. We were unsure the culprits who had killed Bill and Katie Jo had any knowledge of you being in the house, but there is a strong possibility you saw something or specifically, someone, who could be identified. We could not take the chance of them looking for you; however, because of your memory loss, we had no other choice. Other than loving you, there was a second reason for changing your name to McKenna… so no one could find you. We never thought keeping you from your parents' home or Sageville would hinder you from remembering what happened. Not one doctor before Pendergrass had ever told us bringing you back here would help jog your memory. Our hope was you would remember at a doctor's visit far away from here. You must believe me."

Catriona stared in silence. She could not wrap her head around his words.

"Have I lost you, honey? Please speak to me."

"What do you want me to say?" Her voice hovered the same as dry air parches with little relief from choking.

"I'm not sure. I cannot imagine what you are thinking, but believe me, we meant no harm."

"I need fresh air."

"May I go with you?"

"No. I need you to stay away from me."

"It's no longer safe for us to be here."

"I saw a swing on the front porch, so for mercy's sake, do not follow me."

"Please, Catriona."

"Please what, Scott? Lies and more lies, and now this? I need to get out of here." She slammed the door as she ran downstairs into the lobby. Before walking onto the porch, she interrupted the clerk at the check-in desk.

"Chigger, may I stay out on the porch for a while or are you locking the house soon?"

"Stay as long as you like. You are my only guests tonight, but I won't be lockin' the doors until ten. You may want a cup of hot chocolate and a blanket. It's gettin' chilly out there. May I bring 'em to you?"

"Yes, that would be nice. Thank you. Wait… do you have hot tea instead?"

"I do. Is everythin' okay, Miss McKenna?"

Her voice cracked. "It will be. Would you add a little whiskey… with some honey?"

"Yes, we have both."

"On second thought, just bring the whiskey and a shot glass."

"Yes, ma'am."

Catriona opened the screen door and closed her eyes as she sat on the swing. Scott's words flooded her mind. She could not believe what had happened. She mumbled aloud, "Murder? I'm a witness? What?"

Everything she thought she knew was a half-truth. *How could they have kept this from me?* She opened her eyes and stared out into the darkness, except where the street light touched the edge of the lawn. *Oh, my word. Did I see my parents die? Surely, I did not see them die!* She dropped her head into her palms.

Through the hedges at the end of the porch, a man wearing a ball cap shielding his face from the porch light watched as she pushed the swing with her feet. He stepped forward when the screened door opened unexpectedly, and he stepped back into the shadows unseen.

"I'm sorry, Miss McKenna, but I couldn't find a shot glass."

"Thank you, Chigger. You can leave the bottle. The blanket is a good idea too, and you were right… it is chilly."

Knowing she was upset, he kept his voice low. "You are welcome. I'll check on you in a bit."

"Thank you. You are most kind."

He walked back inside but held the handle on the screen door until it closed without making a sound. She stood and covered her shoulders with the plaid throw, then crossed her legs beneath her when climbing back into the swing. It swayed slow under its own accord. She turned up the bottle and swallowed a big gulp. The liquid burned the back of her throat, causing her to cough. She closed her eyes hoping the evening had been another bad dream.

"Katydid?"

"Yes?" Catriona opened her eyes. A man stood before her with his face shaded.

"It's really you, ain't it? I'd recognize those baby blues anywhere."

Her eyes narrowed. "Do I know you?"

The front door opened, and the man jumped from the porch and ran into the street.

"Wait!" She bolted, spilling the bottle as Chigger ran onto the porch.

"Miss McKenna, are you okay?"

"Yes, I'm fine. Who was that?"

"I don't know. I don't remember ever havin' seen him around here before."

Unexpectedly, a police car slowed and pulled into the driveway. Chigger met him on the sidewalk.

"Good evening, Sheriff. I can't believe you're here. An unknown man has approached one of my guests on the porch and he just up and ran away. It beats all I've ever seen."

"Did you recognize him?"

"No, sir. I didn't, but she did." He pointed at Catriona.

The sheriff looked at the young woman coming toward him and asked, "What direction did he run?"

"Toward the gas station. He was a white man wearing a ball cap. It could have been black or navy with a red logo... maybe. He ran so fast."

The sheriff returned to his car and radioed the desk officer. "Hey, Tom. This is Sheriff Walters. Ready to copy."

"Come in, Sheriff."

"I have a possible Priority Three in progress, but at this time presents no significant threat. I need a patrol car to drive through the neighborhood by Chigger Walden's place on North Walnut Street and around by Jimmy's Gas Station. Be on the lookout for a possible suspect, a white male wearing a dark baseball cap. That's all. Stand by."

"Copy that, Sheriff."

Chigger, still startled, asked her again, "Miss McKenna, are you sure you're okay?"

"Miss McKenna?" The sheriff walked back toward the sidewalk.

"Yes, sir. I'm Catriona McKenna."

"I don't believe I've had the pleasure. I'm Sheriff Marcus Walters. I received a phone call from Erline over at the café. She told me a pretty remarkable tale about a young woman with black hair. Since this is the closest place to stay near town, I thought I would start here first. Do you know anything about it?"

"Yes, I do. May I collect my father? He can explain everything to you."

"I'll get him." Chigger stopped chewing his fingernails and stepped back into the lobby. When Scott appeared on the porch, Catriona was in the street with a police officer pointing toward the gas station.

"Did you get a good look at his face?" the sheriff asked.

"No." Catriona pulled the throw tighter around her shoulders.

"What has happened?" Scott asked as he approached them. Catriona told him about the stranger and his worried look turned into one of deep concern.

"Sheriff Walters, I'm not sure how you knew to find us here, but, please, come inside. I should have contacted your office before arriving in town. My name is Scott McKenna, an attorney from Washington,

D.C., and I see you have already met my daughter." He reached to shake his hand. "I need you to contact someone for me before we can begin. Does Sheriff Blake Royster live in town? I think he retired a few years ago."

"He lives about five or six miles from here, but it's too late to disturb him."

"It's only eight-thirty, and if you tell him it's me, he will come. He will confirm my story."

All of them walked inside as the sheriff dialed the number on his cell phone.

***

Chigger offered the four of them the inn's dining room, which provided complete privacy. Sitting around the large table, Sheriff Walters poured another cup of coffee and shook his head.

"That's some story, Blake. How did you get permission to cover up, or should I say, fake Miss McKenna's death so I do not arrest the both of you for fraud?"

"We didn't commit fraud. We didn't even lie to the newspapers. Higher-up law enforcement made that decision. If the local newspaper reported false facts provided by the coroner and the fire investigator, blame the VBI and FBI. No one knew of their involvement in the case. It was an unusual circumstance. Here we had a child who may have witnessed two murders… they wanted to keep her safe too. Scott and Lillian adopted her. They claimed no insurance papers on her behalf, only on her parents, whereby, Scott followed protocol. The McKennas were her legal guardians, according to the written wishes of her parents. They broke no laws, and since the family had a private funeral and burial service several hours north of here in their family's cemetery, there was no reason to use a fake tombstone to record her death. In plain terms, she was in a safe place, out of harm's way, getting the best medical care possible, and most importantly, no longer here. A great number of relatives on both sides of the family used to live around here but had moved before the fire, and the family members who attended the service at Grace Meade knew of only two deaths. It was easy, and it hurt no one."

"No one... except me," she said.

Sheriff Royster rebuked her. "I'm not sorry, Katydid. It was the only way to protect you. You must understand I loved your parents as much as anyone, and under the circumstances, Scott and I put you into protective custody, although it was our own little definition of protective custody. Everyone was acting in your best interest."

"Can you tell me what happened or how the fire started?" she asked.

"I'm not sure you should hear this."

"Please. Maybe it will help me remember."

Blake looked over at Scott, and he nodded for Blake to continue.

"We know there were multiple origins of fire throughout the house, and that is the reason it was impossible to put out. It consumed the frame house in a matter of minutes. It was unbelievable how fast it burned. They doused the room where we found your mom and dad heavier than the other areas with the same liquid. It was coal oil according to the investigator's report. A neighbor saw the smoke and called the fire department as the roof caved in. Two firemen pulled you to safety after finding you lying unconscious near what looked like a closet with only a couple of studs holding part of the beam that pinned you. It was a miracle they rescued you, much less you surviving. I know it may not seem like it now, but you are lucky or blessed, depending on how you look at it. For me... only God saved you that night."

Catriona's hands were out of view beneath the table. Her legs shook as her hand stroked the material of her trousers, tracing the burn scars on her upper legs. Her face turned paler with every word Blake spoke.

Scott interrupted, "Let's stop there... we can continue tomorrow. Katydid, honey, do you need to take a break?"

Emotionless, she said, "I'm fine. You can't stop, Mr. Royster. I need to know. I don't want to wait any longer and I think twenty years is long enough. Don't you, Scott?"

He dropped his eyes.

Blake continued, "The fire burned so hot and with such intensity, there was nothing anyone could do to rescue the bodies. However, the pathologist's report showed no carbon monoxide in their blood."

She asked, "Is that important?"

"It proves they died before the fire ever started. The fire appears to have been a cover-up to the murders. At first, some believed it a murder-suicide because of their injuries, but Bill would never hurt Katie Jo. Besides… the angle of the entry wounds could not have been self-inflicted. An odd thing too… some groceries were still in the back of Katie Jo's car. Someone interrupted her. But who and why?" His voice cracked. "My dear friends are dead, and there is nothing more I can prove or disprove. Scott pulled strings in Washington, and the FBI could not prove any attachment to those phantom men. It still boils my blood. I know they killed your parents, but I can't prove it. I have combed every piece of evidence, and there is nothing to go on. It remains an open case, and it still haunts me to this day. You, Katydid… you are the answer. If you can tell me anything about what you remember, it could be the key to this horrible ordeal."

She bit her lip. "I'm sorry. I remember so little as the fire is a complete blur, except in my dreams. My nightmares show my mother is crying, and last night, I saw a gun too. I can't remember the details. There are flashes of memory, someone's face… maybe, but nothing concrete. I want to help, I truly do."

"Well, now that you are here, we should get together tomorrow. What are your plans?" Sheriff Walters asked.

Catriona said, "My doctor thinks I might remember more of my past if I see the place where the fire occurred. She thought experiencing it first-hand would jog old memories and help me remember more of my parents. However, she is unaware of what has happened tonight or my nightmare last night. I'm having difficulty understanding it myself. I recalled some memories when we visited the property today. They were clear but overwhelming. I feel more pressure to remember everything. What if I never remember?" Tears welled up in the corners of her eyes.

Blake said, "I tell you what. Don't you worry your pretty little head about it. I will meet you both out there tomorrow." Trying to lighten the mood, he said, "I don't know to what extent you remember your parents, but would you like to know why they called you 'Katydid?'"

Catriona had never considered there would be someone besides Scott who could tell her about her parents. "No. Do you?"

"People would ask how you came to have the nickname, and your parents would end in a debate every time as if they had rehearsed a play over and over. Bill would argue, 'She reminds me of the summer insect that hums its song, pitching it up and down as it vibrates from the treetops on the long, smoldering summer evenings in July. It's a peaceful sound that settles upon your soul, and you know all is well with your world.'" He chuckled. "Some in town accredited him to be a poet with the way he could weave a story, but then your mother would correct him. She would say, 'No, Bill. It's because she's always humming when she plays.' However, in reality, everyone knew the true answer. You were and still are the spitting image of your mother... Katie Jo's mini-me. I cannot get over how much you favor your mother, sweet girl. She was something... one of the most beautiful souls I have ever known. I loved her." He sighed. "You know what's funny? No one could understand how Bill got her to marry him... not even Bill. They were something, those two."

Both he and Scott laughed. Catriona only smiled. Her mind was reeling from too much information.

Blake said, "Katydid, I would consider it a privilege to sit and talk to you sometime about your parents. It's the least I can do for them and you."

"Thank you. I would like that very much."

Sheriff Walters said, "I will meet you in the morning as well. I wonder if the man you saw tonight might have information."

"What man?" Blake asked.

Catriona said, "A man appeared on the porch when I was sitting on the swing. My eyes were closed when I heard someone call me Katydid. I opened them expecting Scott, but it wasn't. How did he walk toward me without making a sound? He also said he recognized my eyes. When I asked if I knew him, Chigger interrupted when he opened the door. Then he jumped off the porch and ran down the street. Mr. Royster, no one calls me 'Katydid' except my family and… you."

"How old was he and did you see his face?"

"Definitely older than me, but not by much… late thirties, maybe? I don't know. I'm not helping, am I?"

"You are fine. I wonder how he heard you were here."

Sheriff Walters said, "It must have been through Erline. She called me from the diner, and when I arrived, everyone was talking about the Harrington couple. Tongues will be a-wagging all night for sure."

"Do you think she's safe?" Scott asked.

"Are any of us… really?" Blake answered.

"That's not good."

"I agree with you, Mr. McKenna, especially after what you have told me tonight. Did you think it could have been someone other than those men who killed her parents?" Sheriff Walters asked.

Blake answered, "No, I didn't. Everyone in town loved those two. Katie Jo was well known for her generosity to anyone who needed help. The only connection to any conflict was their encounter with those men."

"How did you know about the other men?"

"Bill told me. He wouldn't lie. Hell, a bullet through the windshield was proof enough for me." He paused, then he pointed his finger at Walters. "Hey, you wait one cotton minute. What are you suggesting? I did my job, Marcus. Bill didn't make up that story, and he certainly didn't kill Katie Jo… evidence proved that. There are hundreds of cold cases across this state, and this one is mine. I'm not afraid of a different perspective, and I welcome all the input I can find but don't attack me here. It's too late and I'm too tired."

"Well, I still think it could involve tonight's unexpected visitor."

"Ok, you're the sheriff now. I get it. Maybe you are right, but where do we go from here? Everyone in town has a ball cap, and Catriona only knows he is a white male and his age possibly… and even that is iffy. One thing we do know is he can run pretty damn fast. It's not much to go on if anything at all."

Sheriff Walters said, "I agree, Blake, but two clues are better than no clues at all. A lead is a lead, no matter how small."

"I'm with you. I am." Blake turned toward Scott. "What time are we meeting?"

"Give us about an hour for Katydid's sake to see if she can remember anything before your arrival. This will be difficult for her."

"Do not answer for me, Scott. I am in the room. I want to go… for me, but I also want to know what happened to my parents. Is eight o'clock a good time?"

All agreed.

Scott said, "Oh, and bring your clippers and a weed-eater. It's pretty tough over there."

Everyone said their goodnights, and Catriona climbed the stairs toward her room.

"Katydid?"

She turned. Scott was standing at the foot of the stairs.

"I'm sorry you had to hear about your parents in such an abrupt manner. I never planned for you to know. Lillian and I thought it would cause more harm than good. I also never considered someone recognizing you in this town after so long, especially as an adult. You must believe me when I say you are your mother's daughter in every way… your charm, your beautiful spirit, your walk, the way you dress, and that gorgeous face of yours. I have placed you in harm's way, and I don't know what I'll do if someone hurts you. If we cannot get back to where we were earlier this afternoon… as father and daughter, I don't know if I'll survive. I apologize with everything within me. Do you think you can forgive me for the pain and betrayal?"

She stared at him as if all life had left her, then without uttering a sound, she turned and walked away.

CHAPTER 19

WHEN THE PRISON van arrived, the men piled out and into single file onto the broken driveway. They stood wide-eyed overlooking the property when the last one chimed what all were thinking.

"What the hell, Dep?"

"Hey! Watch your language, Percy. We're in mixed company."

Glancing over, Percy saw her. "Sorry, ma'am. I didn't see you standin' there."

Catriona nodded as she proceeded up the driveway. She motioned to the deputy. "There's water over here."

He smiled at her. "Thanks." The deputy called out to anyone within hearing distance, "We need to clear this brush as soon as possible. Be sure to grab a pair of gloves so we can pull the weeds and vines from the structures. You may need to shed your jackets as it looks like it may be a warm one today." The officer's instructions continued to echo across the property as Catriona approached Scott and Blake unseen.

Scott asked, "Who are these people, Blake?"

Blake leaned against the truck. "Looks like Sheriff Walters has pulled prisoners from the roadwork detail. I have to hand it to him… he's a smart one. They'll get this job done much quicker than if we work alone."

"What about Katydid?"

"What about her?" Blake asked.

"How safe is she? She will be uncomfortable with so many strangers, especially knowing her body reacts without notice. She's been known to pass out from stressful situations."

Catriona answered, her words hitting him in the back. "I won't be fainting, Scott. I'm stronger than you think now knowing the truth."

She brushed by him, grabbing a pair of clippers as she passed the tailgate.

Startled, Scott turned toward her. "Honey, I'm sorry. I didn't mean…"

She ignored him and turned toward the group who were fighting the foreboding vines.

He said, "You are in as much danger now as you were back then… maybe even more so. Am I wrong, Blake?"

Blake scoffed a heavy snort. "Quit being a father and get to work. Katydid, we did what was right and you know it, but we need answers. The sooner you remember, the sooner you will be back at Grace Meade away from whoever wants to hurt you."

"Yes, sir. That is my plan."

"Come on." Blake patted Scott on the shoulder as he grabbed the last pair of gloves as the three headed toward the shed.

Chigger had dropped Catriona off at the site along with bottles of water as he could not help in the clean-up because of new guests arriving at the inn. All appreciated his hospitality as the work was hard and the day's heat index continued to climb with the sun.

Within a few hours, the buildings came into view. Layers of weathered paint curled away from the old boards as if searching for sunlight under the darkness of shade.

Sheriff Walters said, "Ron, I need you to drive the men back for lunch. I'm sure they're hungry. In fact, let them shower and clean up before they eat."

"Yes, sir."

"Men, please follow Deputy Roberson and step to it."

"Thank you, gentlemen," Catriona smiled as each one passed. "Please grab a water on your way out. There's plenty. We would have been here past nightfall without your help. I so appreciate your hard work."

Percy answered, "You're welcome, ma'am." A few others smiled and nodded their heads as they crawled into the van. They were covered in sweat from the unusual heat on what should have been a cool day.

Blake asked, "Well, what do you think, Katydid?"

"I don't know. Maybe I need to do this alone. Sheriff Walters can drive me back to the inn once I'm finished." She turned toward him. "May I ride with you, sir?"

"Why don't you ride with me?" Scott asked as a frown formed across his brow.

"I would prefer to ride with Sheriff Walters. He can protect me if needed, and besides, Chigger said he would have a late lunch waiting when we returned. We should not be too long."

Blake could not help but laugh. "Sure thing, Katydid. Let's go, Scott, and leave her be. She is so much like Katie Jo… it's downright scary."

"You will stay with her?" Scott asked Marcus as he turned toward the truck.

"Sure. Going it alone might provide more answers without the distractions of too many voices," Marcus said.

"I could not agree more." Catriona walked toward the outbuildings.

When they pulled out of the drive, she noticed the familiar look of frustration as Scott's lips formed a straight line when he gritted his teeth. She didn't care. She was angry and wanted to guard her words before speaking again. It was not her way of punishing him, although it may have appeared as such. She did not want to talk, chalking it up to quiet reasoning.

"Well, Miss McKenna, where do we start?"

"In the smaller building… it was where I played as a girl."

"Let me go in first. There may be a raccoon or possum held up in there, and the roof doesn't appear to be stable either."

"Thank you."

He kicked in the door and raised the flashlight to brighten the little shed's interior although the sun was beaming outside. It was dirty and water stained from the leaky roof, and the linoleum was broken in chips, revealing the crumbled concrete floor beneath. Both stepped inside.

"There's not much in here," he said.

"Oh, but there is, Sheriff. There is."

She walked to where a café curtain covered the lower window pane. Yellowed from age with a few spots of mildew and old spiderwebs between the folds, she turned over the hem. There were the stitches made from her mother's sewing machine continuing to hold tight. Closing her eyes, she could see her mother's figure as she hung them.

"Katydid, this will be your special place where you can play and bring your cousins and your friends. You can decorate it however you wish. When you're hanging curtains, be sure to gather them across the rod with your fingers like this so they hang evenly spaced and do not bunch up in a wad."

A shallow smile formed across Catriona's lips as she remembered.

"Everything okay?"

She opened her eyes. "Yes. Everything is fine."

She stared at the vacant wall in front of her as she imagined her dolls in their bed. Dirt and vermin droppings covered the old toy kitchen, but closing her eyes again, she saw herself feeding her doll when it was new.

"Miss Callie, eat your oatmeal. They look like leaves, but if you squint really hard, you can make believe it's your breakfast."

She glanced at the sheriff. "I can see my favorite doll. I played in here all the time. It was my sanctuary where nothing could touch me." She then remembered an unfamiliar voice and turned toward the door.

"Are you okay, Miss McKenna?"

"Shh… did you hear him?" She turned and looked back at the sheriff.

"Hear who?" He looked concerned.

She held her finger to her lips. "Shh…"

Closing her eyes again, the voice became clearer.

"Whatcha doing there, Catriona?"

"Playing."

"Playing what?"

"Oh, nothing. Miss Callie is hungry."

"You're too old to be playing with dolls, aren't you?"

"No. I love my dolls. You leave me alone."

"Are you here by yourself?"

"Yes. Momma went to Smalley's for milk and some groceries. Daddy's at work."

"I got a new bike. You wanna see it?"

"Sure."

He was much older than she, a junior in high school. She walked outside where a boy's shiny red bicycle made for speed stood facing her.

"I'm saving up for a car so I can leave this stupid old town one day, but this will work for now."

Catriona frowned. "What's wrong with this town?"

"None of your damn business."

"You shouldn't say bad words."

"I'll say whatever I damn well want to, you stupid girl."

"There's no need to get all mad about it, and I'm not stupid." She frowned again. "I think I'm going to play inside."

"You can't... you didn't tell me what you think about my bike."

"It's real nice. Who gave it to you?"

He stood proudly as he pushed back the kickstand. "My maw. Today is my seventeenth birthday. Do you want to ride?"

"Sure!"

"Get on, and I'll stand in front of you. You can wrap your arms around my waist or hold on to the back of the seat." She followed his instructions. "Keep your legs stretched out so your feet don't get stuck in the spokes."

"What about my dress?"

"Just pull it above your knees."

"Don't go on the road. My momma wouldn't like that."

"How am I supposed to ride? Stay in the yard? You really are stupid or something. Besides, we have to ride on the street so I can take you to my house. We can play in my garage."

"No. We can stay in my driveway. I'm not supposed to go anywhere. You need to stop... let me off."

"Fine... get off then." He jerked the bike sideways, almost causing her to fall.

"There's no reason to get mad about it." She threw her leg over the seat, revealing her panties underneath, and stormed into the playhouse. She wondered why he had bothered to come over. He had never wanted to play before, and the other kids had said he was not right in the head. She talked aloud while placing her doll in the small high chair. "I'm not stupid. Boys are stupid. Don't you agree, Miss Callie? That boy is especially stupid."

"I'm not stupid."

She turned. He appeared to loom over her with lines burrowed into his brow.

"Do you want to play a grown-up game?" He asked in a manner contradicting his expression.

"I guess."

"Turn around and I'll show you how to play."

"Okay."

She did as he said. Without warning, he grabbed her shoulder from behind and tried to unzip her dress. He yanked her backward as he kissed her hard on the back of the neck.

"What are you doing? Stop!" She tried to pull away, but he held her tight. Possessed, he licked the side of her face and the back of her neck. She screamed and twisted out of his grip as she ran toward the door. He tackled her and shoved her face down onto the floor, and with his knee on her back, he ripped her green dress as he tried to unzip it.

"Stop! You're hurting me!" She screamed, trying to kick him off as she squirmed back and forth across the floor.

"Shut up!"

He panted as he threw himself on top of her, groping for her panties beneath her dress, and pulled them downward. He pushed his hand between her legs, and she twisted and kicked, causing him to scratch her. She shrieked out in pain. Using all of his body weight, he pressed her harder onto the floor. She lost her breath. He then grabbed his zipper, exposing himself. He let out an excited gasp as he was hard from the electricity flowing through him. Wildly, he kissed the back of her neck again and said, "All I wanted was to take you on a bike ride. None of this would'a happened if you'd done what I told you. Who's stupid now? It's all your fault. Don't ever forget... this is your fault."

She tried twisting from under his weight, but he let out a grunt as he pushed himself between her legs.

She screamed, "No!"

Jerking hard, she threw her elbow back, catching him squarely in the jaw, causing him to yell in pain.

Undetected, Katie Jo pulled into the driveway and slammed the car door as she stepped to the trunk to retrieve her groceries.

When they heard the door, he continued to hold her down and covered Catriona's mouth to silence her screams. Through his heavy panting, he whispered into her ear with a tone as smooth as satin as she struggled to breathe. "This is your fault. You tell anybody about this, and I swear I'll kill you... and them. You can count on it."

He laughed and licked her cheek. "Yessiree-bob, you stupid girl. I'll kill you. In fact, it might be kinda fun."

Shoving her head against the floor with his hand as he stood, he zipped his pants, ran outside, and grabbed his bike. He pushed it to the opposite side of the house from Katie Jo's sight and sped down the street, never looking back once.

Crying, Catriona pulled her panties into place and ran into the house. Through the tears, her shaking hands appeared to take over as they reached for a clean dress from the closet. She ran into the bathroom and slammed the door before her mother reached the kitchen back door. Removing her underwear and dress, there was blood on the white cotton material. She gasped. She grabbed the hand mirror from the counter and looked between her legs. The scratches high up on her inner thighs were deep and continued to bleed. She heard her mom walk into the kitchen.

"Katydid, are you in here, honey?"

She swallowed hard to gain control of her voice. She cried out, "Yes, ma'am. I'm in the bathroom... don't come in here!"

Turning on the faucet, Catriona drowned an old washcloth beneath the stream of water and squeezed out the moisture over her scraped hands. She took the warm *cloth and pressed gingerly against the bloody cuts between her legs. She moaned through the tears. Her thinking became jumbled. He had hurt her, but at least he had not penetrated her. Still, she thought it an odd thought all the same. Dabbing cotton swabs with alcohol, she cried out silent screams as she doctored the raw skin burning with every touch. Her hands continued to shake as she searched in the cabinet drawer for an adhesive bandage to cover her wounds. Changing into another dress, she hoped her mother would not remember what she had worn earlier in the day, and then she heard her mother's footsteps approach the bathroom door.*

"You okay? You sound funny, sweetheart."

Fighting back the tears, she hoped her mother would not be suspicious. "I'm fine, Momma. I don't feel good, that's all."

"Do you need some Pepto?"

Catriona whimpered.

Her mother wiggled the handle. "Katydid? Open the door."

"No, ma'am. I'm okay." She then vomited into the commode.

"I'll find the Pepto."

"No ma'am. I feel fine. Please don't."

"You don't sound fine. Place a cold wet cloth on the back of your neck. It should help. Let me know if you need anything."

She heard Katie Jo walk back toward the kitchen. Glancing into the mirror above the sink for the first time, Catriona's jaw dropped when looking at her reflection. Tears welled and flowed down her cheeks as she pushed the disheveled hair behind her ears, but she did not move. As she continued to stare at the stranger looking back at her, she moved her fingers to the back of her neck where he had kissed her. She vomited again into the commode.

Her mother's voice called once more through the door. "Katydid, are you still vomiting? What have you eaten today?"

Catriona wiped her mouth with the back of her hand. "I'm fine, Momma. Really. Please go away."

"I am worried, darling."

"I'm better. Truly, I am."

"All right, but call me if you need me."

Catriona heard her walk away. She washed the dirt from her face and brushed her hair back into the neat ponytail her mom had tied that morning. Her cheek was showing signs of a bruise. She neatly folded the clothing into a plastic garbage liner from the bathroom's trash bin and hid the package under her dress. With no sounds made, she opened the bathroom door, and without being seen, tip-toed to the front door and onto the porch. The screen door slammed behind her as she ran toward the barn.

Her mother called out, "How many times have I told you not to slam the door, Katydid?"

Catriona ran as fast as one of her bunnies into the barn. Her thighs were throbbing from the pain. Taking a shovel, she buried the bundle beneath the rabbit cages. She promised herself she would tell no one, and she didn't. In the following weeks, when she and her mother drove past the house where the red bicycle stood, her stomach would hurt. He terrified her.

One day, Katie Jo's great nephew was riding along in the car when he looked back toward Catriona sitting in the backseat. "You need to steer clear of the boy who lives in that brown house."

Katie Jo asked, "Why, Johnny Ray?"

"I see little girls playing around the house sometimes. It don't seem right. Only yesterday, I asked one of 'em what was so interesting in that nasty old garage, and she said they were doing something secret."

"What kind of secret?"

"She told me that boy would give her a quarter to rub herself against him and kiss him on his naked privates, but she wasn't to tell nobody."

"She said what?" Katie Jo stared at him.

"Aunt Katie Jo, that's what she said, I swear!"

She adjusted the rearview mirror to look at Catriona in the backseat. "Did you know about this? And don't lie."

"Yes, ma'am." Catriona shook with fear.

"Have you ever played in his garage?"

"No, ma'am." Catriona turned pale and her stomach ached.

"Katydid, are you telling me the truth?"

"Yes, ma'am." She choked, fighting back the tears until she could contain them no longer. Catriona's quiet tears turned into sobs.

Katie Jo sped toward their house and pulled into the driveway. She jumped out and opened the rear car door, moving into the back seat next to her daughter.

Taking Catriona's face into her hands, she asked, "What did he do to you, honey? You can tell me."

"No, ma'am. I can't." She cried even harder.

"Sweetheart, you're not in trouble. Please tell me the truth. Did he take you into his garage?"

Through the tears, Catriona said, "I'm not lying, Momma. He did not take me into his garage."

Katie Jo's face relaxed as she sighed with relief and dropped her hands, but then Catriona whispered, "He hurt me in my playhouse."

"Oh, please, God… no," Katie Jo gasped. She wrapped her arms around her daughter. "What happened?"

Johnny Ray stared from the front seat as Catriona told them everything while crying between sentences. When she finished, her mother stiffened. "Johnny Ray, take Catriona into the house. I need to visit someone."

"No, Momma! Please, no. He said he would kill me if I told anyone."

Katie Jo listened to Catriona's inaudible words through more sobs. Her face showed no emotion. "Johnny Ray, have you told anyone other than me about this?"

"No, ma'am."

Katie Jo said, "We cannot tell anyone, not yet… especially Bill. He will kill him, and then I'll be visiting him in a jail cell on death row. I need to think this through, but promise me you will say nothing until I give you permission."

"I promise on a whole stack of Bibles!" he said. He could not stop staring at Catriona.

"Both of you, listen… and I want you to listen good. This is my responsibility. I don't want either of you involved. Do you understand?"

"Yes, ma'am," Johnny Ray answered.

When Catriona reopened her eyes, she and Sheriff Walters were inside the old playhouse. Reaching for him, she slid down the wall to the floor for her legs could no longer support her.

Sheriff Walters knelt beside her. "Miss McKenna, what's wrong? Did you remember something?"

She trembled but nodded. Barely forming the words to speak, she asked in a whisper, "Do you have a shovel?"

"I think so. Why?"

"Do you think we can get into the barn or is it too dangerous?"

"We can try, but I should help you to the car instead. We can come back later when you are feeling better."

She shook her head. "No, I will be fine. I need to gather my thoughts." A knot formed in her throat as she continued to sit on the floor.

"I'll be back in a flash."

She nodded as she wiped her sleeve across her forehead. She then forced herself to stand and moved outside toward the barn.

Marcus called out, "You need to stay behind me."

She stopped short of the barn's entrance. Handing her the shovel, he slid open what was left of the old door. It fell backward and exploded onto the ground, tossing grime and dirt left untouched for years into the air. As the sun's rays poured through the holes in the rusted tin roof and past the rafters, she thought they resembled smoking theater spotlights cast upon a stage. As soon as the dust settled and they could see their way through the warm, musty haze, Marcus followed her to several old stilt rabbit cages standing next to the horse feed troughs. The aggressive vines had grown through the old rotten boards of the barn, inching their way around the cage legs and through the wiring as they formed a canopy over the top and ground below. Pushing over the last cage, she pulled away the vines and cleared the dirt floor with her foot.

She pointed. "Dig here... beneath the kudzu."

He frowned, then pushed the shovel into the hard soil. The sheriff's digging took on the shape of a shallow grave when a dirty plastic knot revealed itself in the disturbed earth. He stopped cold in his tracks.

"Miss McKenna? What is this... a small body?"

"No, sir. It should be a dress... a torn green dress and a pair of blood-stained underwear." She fell to her knees. "I can't believe it, but it must be true..." Her voice trailed into silence as tears ran down her face once more.

"What's true?" He lifted the bag, shaking away the remaining dirt.

Looking at him in astonishment, she said, "I think I know who killed my parents."

***

Sitting at the inn's table, Blake's face grew pale as he examined the bag. "I risked my reputation and career on assuming those two men were the killers. How could it be anyone in my town… much less a predator in a teenager's body?"

Catriona showed little-to-no reaction, yet Scott appeared to be an emotional wreck. In complete silence, Scott watched and listened to every word. His thoughts were spinning as he tried to comprehend what had happened to her as a child.

"Why would Katie Jo have left you alone?" he asked.

Blake said, "It was common to leave doors unlocked back then and children playing in their yards with little concern for their safety as everyone watched out for each other. There was no one to fear… or so we thought."

Marcus began questioning her. "Do you have any idea what his name is? What did he look like?"

"I don't remember his name. He was tall, but then again, I was only nine… everyone was tall. He wore red high-top tennis shoes that matched his bike. I can picture everything except his face. I wasn't sure it could be even remotely true because I couldn't trust my memory… that is… until we found the dress. There is no question. It must be true."

"Do you remember where his house or garage might be? Any details at all?"

"I don't. What I do remember is he assaulted me. He almost raped me! Those poor girls…"

The three men sat in silence while Blake untied the bag. He poured the clothing onto the table. The underwear showed several spots of brown bloodstains.

He said, "I was so prejudiced in my reasoning. What shoddy police work… I'm ashamed. I was a better officer than this."

Scott said, "You were too close to the victims. We both were."

Catriona could not swallow from the queasiness rising in her throat. "Please excuse me." She ran toward the restroom and vomited into the commode. Looking into the mirror, she splashed her face with water, then dried off with a paper towel. When she returned, she lifted the small dress where she could see the zipper. It was ripped from the seam.

Marcus asked, "How are you?"

"Better. Thank you." She sat hugging the dress against her chest.

He continued. "You mentioned there was a cousin… Johnny Ray. He was in the car with you. Will he corroborate your story?"

Scott interrupted. "Catriona would not know, but John died at the hands of a hit-and-run driver shortly thereafter… he was only sixteen."

No one spoke as the room appeared to grow darker with each passing gruesome second.

Chigger entered the room and asked, "May I get you anything?"

Marcus answered, "No, but thank you. We're finished… at least for a while. We have monopolized your dining room. I hope we have not caused too much inconvenience for you or your guests, Chigger. You have gone above and beyond."

"Not at all. In fact, no one is here at the moment. To be frank, this is the most interesting thing to have happened to me. Stay as long as you need."

Marcus asked, "Miss McKenna, would you like to take a drive?"

"Where?"

"Around town. I want to drive you past several houses to see if you recognize the garage. Would you be willing to try?"

"Sure."

Blake asked, "May we tag along? Scott and I can sit in the back seat and remain quiet. We will not utter a word."

"Blake, I need you talking for once. You were the town sheriff, so you may recall who lived near them and who had a teenage son."

"I can try. Hey… I may have old phone books in my attic from the same time period. You know there are some positives to being a packrat, although my Becky would strongly disagree."

The men laughed, but Catriona sat with a blank stare.

"You ready?" Marcus asked.

"Yes, I am." She followed the men out to the patrol car.

The quick tour around town proved to be a waste of time, as neither she nor Blake remembered anything. However, it was a start.

CHAPTER 20

A HANDWRITTEN NOTE lay on the floor. Opening the door, he looked down the hallway yet saw no one and stepped back inside the room.

The note read:

> *I did not wake you, as I wanted to go to the worship service this morning at my father's family church. Chigger has agreed to drive me. Please do not follow. I have my phone and will call the inn when finished. I'm sure you will want to return to Grace Meade today, so I will not be long. This is important to me, and we have much to discuss.*
> *Your daughter, Katydid*

Scott sighed. He could not contain his concern, as she appeared to have no regard for her own safety. He showered, dressed, and headed downstairs for brunch. Marcus and Blake were waiting for him at the table.

"Is Catriona here?" Marcus asked.

"No, she's gone to church. Why?"

"I have a few more questions for her. They will wait, but we have good news too."

"I would welcome some good news." Scott poured a cup of coffee from the old buffet and sat next to Blake.

Blake handed him a small booklet. "Last night, after I got home, I crawled through my attic and found this old phonebook. As I was going through the pages... there's only about twenty of them... a few names popped off the sheet at me. Several of those names were families who had children, including teenagers, who lived close to Bill and Katie Jo. I also highlighted those with street addresses surrounding the area. It appears nine families fall into that category. Also, I remembered one family with four daughters younger than Catriona who may have been the children visiting the garage."

"I'm not sure if this is good. Damn! What did that pervert do to those girls?"

Blake scratched his chin. "He was seventeen, according to Catriona. I would not call him a kid… more like a young psychopath, and he certainly is not a kid any longer. The statute of limitations ran out long ago to hold him accountable for sexual molestation, but thankfully, a murder charge is forever."

Marcus took a sip from his cup. "We need a name."

"It's more than what we've had to go on in the past. We're not sure these families have remained in the area, but Marcus has allowed me to head up a special task force to check any databases that might link to the names in this book. If I can locate one of those four girls, then possibly, they could provide us with a name."

Scott sat back in his chair glancing at the phone book in front of him. "That is good news. Why did you want to see Catriona?"

Marcus said, "I want to review the names with her to see if she remembers anyone."

"Makes sense."

Blake pulled at his ear. "I have an idea. If we could contact the high school for a few yearbooks around the same time, maybe she will recognize a face."

Scott couldn't believe his words. "Good grief. Are we planning to use a yearbook as a way to view mugshots? What is wrong with that picture? Our visit here has turned into a bigger nightmare than I could have imagined, and we are planning to leave for home this afternoon."

"So soon?" Blake shifted in his chair.

"I have pressing business with a high-profile case and I must get back to Washington. However, I want to catch this perve as soon as we can, but I also do not want Catriona in harm's way either. I'm uncomfortable with her remaining behind, but it's her decision. We can figure out plans once she returns from church. What time is it?"

Marcus stood. "It's a little before noon. I'll head to the church to spend as much time with her as possible. This man is not only a pervert but a murder suspect as well."

Blake nodded in agreement. "Let's hope we're on the right path. If he isn't the one, then we will be starting at ground zero for a third time."

"Don't worry, Scott, I have a gut feeling her unexpected visitor is tied in some way." Marcus patted him on the shoulder.

"What a bloody nightmare." Scott shook his head. "I appreciate you both willing to discover what happened to Katie Jo and Bill... and Katydid. Heaven protect me because I don't know what I'll do until that man is hung by his balls."

Blake grinned. "No worries... I'll be there to tie the rope."

***

Catriona slipped in unnoticed and sat on the back pew of the small church. Its simple stained-glass windows and hand-hewn pews were as pretty as the day they were first carried in over one hundred years before. She thought it strange to be back in the building, but as she glanced around, everything became more familiar.

"Please stand and turn to page one hundred and thirty-two in your hymnals as we sing all four verses of 'There is Power in the Blood.' Men, when we get to the chorus, I want you to double up on the powers. Instead of singing, 'Power'... 'Power'..., it will be, 'Power! Power! Power! Power!' Does everyone understand?"

As they nodded in agreement, the small congregation of sixteen stood and sang with a mighty voice.

Catriona held the hymnal as memories flooded in when looking around the small auditorium. She closed her eyes, and she was a child sitting next to her mother and father. Her family was active in a multitude of roles, including the role of a choir member. Everyone at the First Baptist Church sang regardless of talent. She remembered as a child hearing the music minister say, *"As far as God is concerned, he hears the hearts of those singing, and if you're blessed to have a voice to go along with it, well then, that makes it even more pleasing for the rest of us."*

It was sound theology and a good thing too because Mr. Clive, who was close to ninety-three years of age and one of the sweetest men to grace the church doors, sang loudest and the most off-key. He filled her heart as he praised God with every fiber within him, never giving thought to others within hearing distance.

Her mother had said, *"He's as close to the Father as anyone could ever hope to be."*

One mother, Mrs. Davis, would sit her children on the front pew while she sang from the choir loft, and if they misbehaved, she had the power to correct them with a single look. Everyone knew what would follow if her children didn't *"straighten up and fly right."*

Catriona sat following the first hymn as the congregation continued their singing. Soon the pastor stood to speak, but her mind was elsewhere.

White tin tiles separated by beams of the same color covered the ceiling and were placed in a pattern of sections stamped with smaller squares inside. She knew the exact number. During week-long revivals held each year when sermons were lengthy, she would lie facing upward on the pew with her head resting on her mother's lap and count each one. She smiled.

The floor was higher in the vestibule, and the floor slanted downward like a theatre toward the altar. She recalled the sound made when someone dropped a pencil or coin onto the wooden floor as it rolled to the front of the church before stopping at the bottom. Quiet giggles from old and young alike would disrupt the pastor's lofty words much to his chagrin.

Mr. Bernie Richards, a dedicated servant and deacon, would fall asleep each service. When nudged one Sunday morning because of his snoring, he stood and spoke aloud, thinking they had called upon him to pray—and in the middle of the sermon. She remembered her sides hurt from holding in the laughter. There was nothing funnier than trying to restrain a laugh in church, but Katydid knew she would face the wrath of her mother had she uttered a sound.

The church had no air conditioning and they would raise the lower half of the stained-glass windows to invite in the fresh air during the hot months of July and August. Paper fans with their stick handles would move the air quicker than the bulletins. Other than the occasional dirt dauber bouncing around the ceiling like a drunkard in a crowded bar, you could always hear the yelps of the mischievous child over the preacher when someone was *"taken outside"* for misbehaving. The shouts floating through the windows sounded more like someone filled with the Holy Spirit rather than a butt-whipping. The pastor's words became louder with each whelp as both voices would echo off the ceiling, rising into a swelling pinnacle for all to hear. Once the wailing ended (more for show than from pain), the pastor would ask, *"Do I hear a hallelujah?"* and the congregation would return a hearty, *"Amen."*

Catriona stared at the clock hanging behind the pulpit and smiled as the minister continued speaking. She recalled each fall, a homecoming service was scheduled—a call for all members, including previous members who had moved away, to return home. A guest speaker provided the sermon followed by a potluck dinner served on the grounds. As the clock's hands moved closer toward the noon hour, everyone would pray silently for the visiting pastor's sermon to end. For the children, their attention span was non-existent knowing what was to follow the service.

The men would carry the tables from the small fellowship hall and place them under the big shade trees lining the property. Cooks of every age would spread the tablecloths and their prized dishes prepared from the harvest of their gardens. Everyone would stand in line waiting their turn to fill their plate from each cook's kitchen. No one left hungry. Most thought Jesus had performed another miracle of feeding the multitudes because there was always more than enough food to carry home to enjoy later. Following the feast, a guest soloist or group would perform a special concert back in the sanctuary to top off the day's events.

The church held two services on Sunday; however, on Homecoming Sunday, the evening's events and services were canceled. It was the only time Catriona could skip worship service as Katie Jo made sure they were in attendance each time the door was opened. Catriona had taken many naps on a pew waiting for her mother to finish her church responsibilities, and Katie Jo provided her time with a cheerful heart of service to the Lord.

Distracted in her thoughts, Catriona could not believe when the invitational song "Just As I Am" played. She had not heard a word of the sermon. Following the closing prayer, each attendee invited her to return the following Sunday as they departed.

The church emptied quickly as most had lunch waiting for them at home. She wasn't ready to leave—not yet. The walls resonated with memories—wonderful memories. It had been a lovely dream, but this one would not fade; this dream was tangible. Her hand glided across the top of the pew in front of her. She grew excited at the possibilities of knowing who she was and where she came from, but questions filled her mind. She sat basking in the sanctuary's silence. The pastor, who had been outside shaking hands with his departing parishioners, interrupted her thoughts.

"Good morning or should I say, 'good afternoon.'"

"Good afternoon." Catriona stood to shake his hand.

"I didn't want to interrupt, but our congregation is small. It's easy to notice when someone is visiting. I'm the pastor, Joshua Boyd, but most call me Preacher. Welcome. And who do I have the privilege of meeting on this beautiful Lord's Day?"

"Oh, forgive me. I'm Catriona McKenna."

"Have you moved here or are you passing through?"

"The shortest answer to your question is I used to live here and I am passing through. I wanted to see my family's old home church again."

"What family?"

"Oh, they left this area a long time ago… you wouldn't know them."

"You are probably right. My wife and I moved here a couple of years ago. Please… be seated."

She moved back to her seat, and he sat on the next pew turning to face her.

He said, "Reminiscing can be fun… if that is what you are doing, but you seem troubled. May I help you?"

Catriona's eyes widened as her brows lifted high beneath her dark hair. "Hmm. My story is too long, Preacher, but I have a question."

"Please ask."

"Why do good people suffer at the hands of the wicked?" Catriona showed no emotion.

"Oh, that's a loaded question. What causes you to ask?"

"Well…" she paused, then brushed her hair behind her ear with her hand.

He noticed her hesitation. "I'll try to answer, but I'm afraid it may take a series of sermons to answer fully, but… go ahead. I have all afternoon and my lunch can wait."

"My parents died in a house fire that may not have been an accident."

"May God have mercy… I'm sorry for your loss. Did this happen recently?"

She could see the genuine concern reflected from the deep burrows in his brow.

"No, but I was injured in the fire too and have continued to struggle with its lasting effects." She blinked back the tears.

The pastor reached over the pew and touched her hand.

She continued, "I then discovered this weekend they may have been murdered, and somehow, this town has been under the misguided truth that I died in the fire too. My adoptive family has kept this from me, and I'm furious." Continuing to speak through the tears, she held nothing back. "Why did my parents have to die? Why was I left with scaring to remind me every day? Why is it okay for the people I trusted more than anyone in the world to lie to me? Where is God in all of this?"

He allowed her to finish before saying anything. The tone in her voice rose with each word as she continued.

"I'm angry at my parents... I mean, my adoptive parents... my doctors... the police... the person or persons who did this to me and changed my world forever, but more importantly, I'm angry because I cannot remember. I can't remember and it's eating me alive. Is He truly a merciful God?" She sobbed as if a dam had burst.

He stood and came to her side. Sitting on the pew, he wrapped his arm around her shoulder, and she dropped her head against him and wept. He allowed her to cry for a long time, releasing all the pent-up emotions building over the decades. He handed her a tissue from the box sitting at the end of the pew.

Taking the tissue, she wiped her face. "Thank you."

"You are welcome."

She looked at the cross hanging beneath the clock and asked, "Where is God in all of this? I was only a kid. Now I'm an adult, and I still can't wrap my head around any of it. I'm so angry." She wiped her eyes.

"Miss McKenna, my heart is breaking for you. You should be angry... a justified anger. Even Jesus was angry at the sellers on the temple steps. However, you have a great deal of information to process, but let me see if I can help. You asked, 'Where is God in all of this?' He is right here. He is beside you and has been beside you each step of this horrible journey."

"Doesn't feel like it. I pray sometimes, but what am I praying to... some being that allows horrible things to happen to His people?"

"Are you a Christian?"

"I think so, but I cannot prove that I am. God hasn't been a vital part of my life for a long time. I haven't attended church as often as I should, I guess, nor have I done anything to show Him I am... but does it matter?"

"I needed to know where to begin. As Christians, we believe God sent His son, Jesus, to die on the cross for the sins of all mankind. Not as a group, but for each person. God loves each of us so much that all you must do to become one of his children is admit you are born a sinner, an imperfect person seeking a perfect God, and you must believe Jesus came to earth as a man… born the baby of a virgin… lived a sinless life, and he died with the pouring out of his blood as total payment for all of your sins… cleansing you pure again. We worship the living God. He rose from the dead on the third day so we can have eternal life. One day, He will return to this earth to take us, His believers, home to live with him. He is the King of all kings, Lord of all lords, and the Prince of Peace. Because we believe, we are God's children. Each is a prince or princess in the eyes of God, the Father. You are no longer guilty but are free to have a personal relationship with Him. And because you follow Him… believe in His son, God makes a covenant promise to you… one that can never be broken… you will live with Him for all of eternity. Do you believe?"

"I do."

"So, if God loves us so much that He would sacrifice His only Son so you too could live with Him in eternity, then rest assured, He has not left us alone to walk through this life without help. As believers, He also sent His Spirit to live within you. He is here in this little church in the middle of nowhere, USA, and anywhere you are, He, the Holy Spirit, is as well."

"But why the suffering? Why did my parents die? Why is wickedness a part of this world?"

"In the Old Testament, God gave Moses the Ten Commandments to guide the people, and with that came a yearly animal sacrifice of the most perfect lamb from each herd. With the spilling of its blood, the people's sins were forgiven. And each year afterward, there was the ritual of sacrificing a flawless and guiltless lamb. However, one day, God sent his Son as the most perfect lamb… the ultimate sacrifice for all of mankind's sins, but only for those who call upon Him and ask for forgiveness for the wrongs they have done and receive Christ as their personal savior will true forgiveness come. God allows us to choose. He created us with the freedom of choice. He doesn't rule with an iron fist like some abusive parent and demands we love Him. It's our choice. However, in that choice comes the selection of choosing good or choosing evil. We are born with a sinful nature, and with that nature comes evil. Not until every knee bows when the Lord returns, will this world be rid of the evilness of mankind."

"So where is the comfort?"

"God is with you. He loves you. He is the Great Physician... Jehovah Rapha. There is no wound nor scar He hasn't seen nor He cannot heal. If it is for His greater purpose, He may choose to heal or not, but He is the perfect parent with your best interests at the center of His heart. Every decision He makes leads us to Him. We, in our finite minds, cannot understand the infinite mind of God. That is where faith comes in. We are to have faith and no matter what is happening in our lives at the moment, He will see us through if we call upon Him. He will give you strength when there is no strength. Miss McKenna, He will help you through this, I promise. You only have to believe."

"I want to believe, but the pain is too great." Tears continued to roll down her cheeks.

"Then place it on Him. He has big shoulders and He can carry it for you... Come ye, who are heavy burdened, and He will give you rest. There is one additional thing you must do to heal completely."

"What is that? Please tell me."

"It will take time, but you must forgive others who have wronged you to find peace. God is peace."

"Why?" The tears stopped as the anger re-emerged within her.

"As believers, God has forgiven us of our sins, and as such, we are to forgive others."

"I'm not sure I understand what that means."

"Think of it in this way... if God can forgive me for the things I've done, then who am I not to forgive others for the sins they have committed against me? Am I bigger than God? Am I superior to God?

I think we both would answer we are not. He is the one and only holy God in three persons. Forgiving others frees us to love wholly again. It frees our minds from the burdens of hate, resentment, and unforgiveness, otherwise, destroying us if we choose to hang on to those heavy choices. Do not allow anyone to have that kind of power over you by not forgiving them."

"Pray for me, Preacher, because I have too much anger and hurt. I'm not sure I can do this."

"Are you angry with God?"

"I'm angry with everyone." She then sighed. "Preacher, thank you, but I must go. I should never have said anything, not because of you or your words, but because I don't want to make changes. I guess you could say I'm happy in my anger, and why shouldn't I be?"

"Miss McKenna, God understands your feelings."

"Then tell God the forgiving is all in His court because how can I forgive? To be more transparent, anger is the only emotion keeping me alive at the moment. Memories are a gift from God and when we lose them to where we no longer know who we are or anything from our past, I do not know if I want or can continue this life God has allowed me to live. On the surface, I look fine, but beneath this façade, my heart hurts, and I am tired of dealing with my body as it is. I do not know who I am anymore. I thought I had a grip on my reality as I know it, but not even close. If only you could see the hell burning inside my head… I want my parents. I am re-living their loss again, and I am tired of carrying the pain. The discoveries made known to me over the past two days are incomprehensible, much less throwing God into the soup. I wanted to see the church, that's all. Thank you for trying to help me, but I'm a lost cause, Preacher. Let me deal with God on a different day."

"Forgiveness can be difficult to do on one's own, especially under your special circumstances where there has been violence shown toward you and your loved ones. I highly recommend you seek counseling because this will take time. With God, all things are possible. At this moment, we can lay it at the altar… at His feet forever.

He will deal with those who have sought to hurt us in His time, but we must let it go if we are to allow Him to heal our hearts and minds."

"One day, maybe, I would like to forgive. Your advice is appreciated and I will take everything you have said to heart; however, I will need a long time."

"Miss McKenna, I appreciate your honesty… most do not share so freely."

She scoffed. "Credit it to years of sitting on a psychiatrist's couch. I would not wish this hell on anyone."

Preacher pleaded, "I do not know God's plan for you. Maybe He has allowed you to walk through this darkness to show you how great His love is. You will need Him to get through the days and months ahead. I will pray He makes His plan known to you soon. He has saved you for a greater purpose, but no one fully understands the mind of God. He wouldn't be God, would He? I can pray right here, right now. There is no greater power than conversing with God."

"Someone needs to pray for me because I can't."

"Will you allow me to pray for you?"

She nodded without a word. He reached for her hands and they bowed their heads.

***

When the patrol car pulled in front of the church, there were no other cars in the parking lot, but the front door was open. The sheriff walked inside and heard a voice. Preacher was praying. Not wanting to disturb, he stepped back out onto the small church's steps. Shortly thereafter, the pastor and Catriona walked outside.

"Good afternoon, Sheriff. Are you waiting for me?" Preacher asked.

"No, sir. I'm here for Catriona."

"Did Scott send you?" she asked.

"No, I sent myself."

"Oh?"

"I need to go over some new information regarding a few names you may remember. Would you mind riding with me as we talk?"

"Not at all." She turned back to the pastor. "Thank you, Preacher. I will think on your words… truly."

"I'm glad. Here… take this bulletin. My contact information is listed, including my email. We may live in the sticks, but we have the Internet to help us connect to the outside world. Reach out to me anytime."

"You have been kind. Thank you." Catriona walked down the steps toward the police car.

Preacher said, "Sheriff, you're welcome to come to any services when you're not working. I hope you know you can call me any time as well."

"Thank you, Preacher. I'll try. You have a nice day."

***

Pastor Boyd waved as they pulled away. He stepped back into the church and locked the front door behind him. When he walked into the sanctuary, a man was sitting on the front pew. Startled, the pastor crept down the aisle for he did not know how the man had entered the church.

Without turning toward Preacher, the man said, "Sweet little prayer there, preacher man."

"Sir?"

"Do you really believe all that hogwash about a lovin' father?"

"I do."

"Then you didn't know mine."

"The God of Heaven is the perfect father. He will show you what true love is if that is what you seek. Earthly fathers are only human, and we all fail, but God does not. He is the truth, the way, and the life."

"Is that what you tell your sheep? That's basic brainwashin' to fill the minds of your small-minded church-goers. But hey… you need to earn a buck, but I'm too smart for your nonsense and any god who calls himself my father. My father was an ass of great proportion, and if I didn't like his truth, he'd beat it into me… and my maw. You could say I am filled with the man's truth."

"I am sorry you have suffered at the hands of your father. No child should experience such horror. Would you like to join me for lunch… my treat? We can discuss it further or not."

"No lunch."

"Then how may I help you?"

The man stood. He was wearing a ball cap pulled where the brim shadowed his eyes. The man appeared to be in his late thirties and of medium height and weight. He fidgeted with his hands and Joshua recognized he was high on something… just what, he didn't know.

"Yeah… you can help me. That woman who was in here… was her name, Katydid Harrington?"

"Why do you ask?"

"No offense, preacher man, but that's my business."

"Well, sir, the people who attend my church are my business. I have their trust."

He frowned. "What do you mean… trust? Another 'truth' you're selling?"

"They know they can confide in me, so they tell me things… private things… and at other times, the not-so-private things. I do not share those conversations as they are between me, them, and God."

"Tell me somethin', preacher man. Were some of her private things secrets?"

"Sir, as I told you, I will not say, but may I help you in another way? If you need counseling or something else, I can guide you. Will you allow me to help you?"

The man's jawline tightened. "I don't need no counselin'." He slurred his words when he spoke. "The only way you can help me is to tell me if she is Katydid Harrington. She's an old friend of mine and I thought I recognized her, but I ain't one hundred percent sure." His hand shook as he wiped the back of his finger beneath the base of his nose.

"I'm sorry, but no, that is not her name. The young woman's name is Catriona."

"Do you think I'm stupid?"

"No, I do not. Sir… please, take one of our bulletins. Listed are services available to help you, including my name and phone number."

The pastor turned his back toward the man to pull one from the paper stack when a forceful, intense pain landed between his shoulder blades, causing him to fall forward, knocking him against the altar table. When he looked down at his chest, red liquid seeped through the fibers of his cotton shirt beneath his tie. He turned, looking back at his attacker, and the man stabbed him again. With as much force as possible, the stranger drove the knife deep into the center of the pastor's chest.

As Joshua sank to the floor, he looked into the man's expressionless eyes and heard him say, "Thank you, preacher man. You can take her secrets with you straight to heaven… or hell… don't matter none to me, and when you get there, tell'em that Daub Tackett sent you with his kindest regards."

Pulling the knife from the pastor's chest, he wiped it clean against the reverend's clothing, then stepped back. The minister collapsed to the floor, and the blood soaked into the carpet in front of the church's altar.

Daub saw the offering plate with the day's collections. Using only his elbow, he knocked the plate, along with its few bills and coins, to the floor. He tucked the money along with his knife inside his jacket and exited through the rear church door.

CHAPTER 21

ALL THREE DOGS greeted Scott and Catriona at the front door with tails wagging and little yelps of happiness. They were encircling everyone's feet, including Lillian's. She planted a big kiss on Scott's lips.

"Thank goodness, you are home. We have missed you." She called out, "Cookie, they're home! Calm down, you darling beasts. Okay, you two, I want to know everything. Was it a productive trip?"

Scott looked at Catriona. They had left her car in Charlottesville so she could study the yearbooks Blake had provided on the trip home.

He said, "I guess you could say so, but it's late. Let's talk tomorrow. Believe it or not, I must drive into the city first thing in the morning."

"May I take a moment of your time before you leave?" Catriona asked.

His face reflected strain as he smiled at her. "Yes, I would welcome a moment."

"Love, what's up?"

"Lillian, please."

Cookie walked into the foyer. "Scott, you have a phone call from a Mr. Blake Royster. He said it could not wait until morning."

"Thank you, Cookie. I'll take it in my study."

"May I sit in?"

"Not this time, Katydid." He walked away with Patches following close behind.

Lillian said, "Come into the kitchen. I want to hear about your trip."

"I'll make tea." Cookie walked ahead as Samson and Delilah continued their dance down the hallway leading into the heart of the house.

Catriona sat at the island with slumped shoulders. "I'm exhausted, but I know you won't sleep unless we do this."

"I have been worried sick knowing you were involved in who-knows-what. Please share a few things, at least."

Cookie sat next to them at the island.

"The short-and-sweet version is I'm remembering my childhood and I'm overwhelmed. Some good, and some... not-so-good."

"Oh, darling, I hate you feel trapped on this crazy ride."

"I'm glad we went; however, in all honesty, it was too much at one time. If I sleep, it will be a miracle."

"Why?"

"First, and forgive my bluntness, you and Scott lied to me about my past. How could you, Lillian, after all of this time?"

"Oh, darling, you know?"

"Yes, and that isn't the half of it. My emotions are everywhere. I'm angry... sad, frightened, confused, and the list goes on and on."

"We did what was necessary to protect you; however, we should have been forthcoming after you were old enough to understand, and for that alone, I do apologize."

Scott sauntered into the kitchen with his head down—his eyes sunken.

Lillian asked, "What's wrong?"

"Catriona, I have upsetting news."

"More?"

"First Baptist in Sageville was robbed and their pastor attacked."

"Is he okay?" Her heartbeat quickened.

"Blake confirmed the attack happened sometime between one and two-thirty this afternoon. When the pastor did not arrive home for lunch, his wife returned to the church. She found him on the sanctuary floor where he had been stabbed in the chest and back. The doctors were surprised he was still breathing when he arrived at the ER. He is in ICU in a medically-induced coma, and it doesn't look good."

Lillian gasped. "Who would do such a thing?"

"Is it because of me?" Catriona covered her mouth with her hands.

Lillian asked, "Why would it be because of you?"

Catriona did not answer.

Lillian turned toward her husband with worried eyes. "Scott?"

Scott sat beside Catriona. "No. They believe it's coincidental because whoever attacked him also took money from the offering plate. Blake thought we should know... just in case."

Catriona's voice trembled. "Just in case? It was him, wasn't it?"

Lillian slammed her fist on the marble countertop as a straight line formed across her lips. "Will someone please tell me what is going on?"

"Of course, honey, I'm sorry."

Scott told Lillian and Cookie everything about their trip, including the mysterious man who had approached Catriona on the porch. Catriona then shared her memory of the attack in the playhouse, finding the dress, and lastly, the church service, including her conversation with Preacher Boyd. She touched Lillian on the sleeve.

"We must do something for Preacher. He was so kind and helpful. It's my fault he stayed late."

"I don't know what we can do."

"Can we fly him to Fairfax or take care of his medical expenses? Their church is struggling financially, it appeared, and he has so little. I have to do something."

"Sweetheart, I doubt they can move him in his current condition, but I'll check in the morning with the hospital. We can certainly help with his medical expenses. Please do not worry."

Scott said, "Ladies, I need to leave before the crack of dawn. It's past midnight. If I don't sleep, Peter will be on his own. I will return tomorrow afternoon once I'm finished."

Lillian smiled, although a sad one all the same. "We'll be fine, darling; you go on to bed... good night."

Scott kissed her and then touched Catriona's hand. "I'm sorry, Katydid. We should have told you about Bill and Katie Jo. I accept full responsibility for what has happened."

Catriona, in her state of concern for Preacher, realized how desperately she needed her parents.

"How can I not forgive you?"

She hugged them both as forgiveness was freely given.

Through tears, Scott's voice trembled as he spoke. "When I return, I will answer any questions regarding your parents or our family."

Catriona nodded. He stroked her face with the back of his hand and left the room.

"I'll run you a hot bath." Cookie made it to the door when Catriona stopped her.

"No, Cookie. Thank you. You are sweet, but I'm not sure I want to soak. I think I'll take a quick shower and grab something to help me sleep."

Cookie asked, "Where is your luggage?"

"I'll get it in the morning."

"Alrighty then."

Lillian said, "Why don't you sleep in, and I'll call the doctor for you. If I can arrange an appointment for tomorrow afternoon, would you go?"

"Yes. The sooner, the better." She left the room with an expression of deep sadness Lillian had not seen since she first came to Grace Meade.

Cookie said, "Lillian, she'll be fine. She is where we can watch over her. I'll call Samuel in the morning... he can run any needed errands. He will do anything for her."

"I know. Oh my, Cookie. Sexual assault? She was a baby. This is too much for any of us." Lillian found it difficult to breathe between the soft sobs. "My sweet baby girl."

Cookie came to her side and wrapped her arm around Lillian's shoulders.

"We will work through it together for her."

"Maybe in the morning, I'll call this Sheriff Walters. What if Scott is held up for a few days? I need answers too."

"All of us need to go to bed because who knows what tomorrow will bring?"

"You're right. It looks as if we are in for another tough time with our girl."

Cookie said, "Yes, we are, but we made it through the first time. Be positive. We are better prepared, and maybe this time, she will reach the other side without too much trouble. She is stronger and older, but we are too. Dr. Pendergrass has worked miracles thus far... we will pray toward that end."

"Oh, my. Re-living the grief process of losing her parents and the emotional struggles of the hospital stays and surgeries... it pains me to watch her. I'm not sure, but it may be tougher for her this go-around with this new information. We could be in for another nightmare as she remembers everything. Inform Samuel and Declan for me, will you? We all need to be watchful."

"Yes, I will. We've got this, Lillian... no more worries."

Lillian hugged her. "We are blessed to have you in our lives, Cookie. Blessed indeed."

***

Scott frowned as he spoke into the receiver. "Peter, I'm sorry, but she is refusing to take anyone's calls... no, it has nothing to do with you. Again, she's not well; however, she did go for a ride this morning... I will let her know you've called again. Please know our invitation stands for the Gold Cup races. I hope to see you on Saturday... yes, she has agreed to attend, at least for now... you are most welcome. See you there."

Lillian walked into Scott's study as he placed the receiver back into its holder.

"Who was on the phone?"

"Peter, again."

"Oh, my. What are we going to do, Scott? This was so much easier when she was younger. She is becoming more of a recluse every day, and I'm not sure the best way to handle this."

"I agree. Maybe we should have our own private session with Dr. Pendergrass."

"I think so too. I'll call her." Lillian grabbed a post-it note to write a reminder.

"Are we ready for this coming weekend?"

"We are. I have completed all the tent and food decisions. Declan and Samuel are planning to meet us on site with Black Bart. I believe we might win this one. Wouldn't that be something? This will be an excellent distraction for Katydid. I plan to buy her a new hat. Surely, she will change her mind about shopping. It would be a fun outing and a pleasant change of pace and place."

"I wonder how Tia is holding up?" Scott rubbed his brow.

"Catriona tells me she's doing an impressive job."

"Do you believe she has called her?"

"Love, she has not lost interest in her business. Maybe she should go home and dive headfirst into her work."

He shook his head. "Pendergrass is here. Katydid says she enjoys their sessions and is not ready to return to Charlottesville. I think I'll call Tia."

"We need to be careful… there are boundaries. Let's at least send Tia flowers and tell her how much we appreciate her."

"Your suggestion is a better idea. Include in the card if she needs to reach us, she may do so. Give her my office number too."

Lillian smiled. "I will. Maybe I can convince Catriona to check on the new business property. I believe construction crews are beginning work this week."

"Good idea. Why don't you two drive over early on Tuesday and then on Wednesday, go shopping? Mix a little pleasure with business."

"I agree. Are you leaving this afternoon?"

"I am. Tomorrow's schedule is packed. I'm ready for this case to be over."

"How much longer?"

"We go to court in less than three weeks. We need to be ready for anything."

Lillian moved across the room and wrapped her arms around his neck as she sat on his lap. "My intelligent husband, I love you. If anyone is ready, it will be you."

"Thank you for your vote of confidence, because I'm not comfortable. Thaddeus Franks has been an impossible opponent, but I keep seeing the faces of those dying miners."

"Oh, darling. I wish at times you would not become so emotionally entangled in each case. I can see how it wears on you."

"What kind of attorney would I be if I didn't? Black-lung disease is making a horrific comeback. It's growing at a greater rate of speed and afflicting at a much younger age. The numbers are staggering. You would think in the Twenty-First Century, we could do better."

"Why is this happening?"

"The modern equipment used to move the earth faster stirs up finer and more hazardous dust than fifty years ago. The miners and their families are in terrible shape physically, emotionally, and the money is non-existent for the sick. The governing regulations need to be revisited. I cannot let them down."

"You won't, love."

"I can't. In Sageville, Bill's family suffered horribly from the disease years ago. It's unbelievable that we continue to battle the same issues crippling men today."

"Well, I'm on your side."

Scott kissed her. "Why don't you come back with me tonight? It's been a while since we've been alone. How long will it take you to pack?"

"I wish I could, but I have commitments tomorrow." She kissed him on his forehead.

Cookie interrupted at the door. "Dinner is ready. Scott, do you want to eat here or do you want your dinner to go?"

"I'll eat here, but then I'll probably leave within the next couple of hours."

"I'll pack an extra plate to take with you."

"Thanks, Cookie."

Lillian stood. "I miss you terribly when you're gone, but you know that... yes?"

"I do." Scott kissed her again. "You are my life, Lillian."

They walked hand-in-hand into the dining room where Catriona was sitting.

"Good afternoon, darling," Lillian said.

"Hello. I'm sorry to be such a burden."

Scott said, "No negative thoughts. You are anything but a burden."

Catriona's lips formed the shape of a half-smile, but her eyes were dead.

Lillian said, "Sweetie, we were thinking you could join us in the city on Tuesday. We can go shopping and look in on the new property. How does that sound?"

"Sure. Whatever you want." Catriona did not look up from her plate.

Lillian frowned. "Do you think Tia would want to join us?"

"It's short notice, but I can ask. It depends on her workload."

"I thought it would allow the two of you to catch up and see the property together. When did you talk last?"

Catriona mumbled as she answered. "I don't remember, but I'll call after we finish eating. Will three women in the townhouse be too much?"

"Never. It would be good to see her," Scott said.

Lillian and Scott continued their conversation; however, Lillian could not help but notice Catriona playing with her food throughout dinner without uttering another word.

Interrupting, Catriona said, "On second thought, I don't think I'm up to traveling."

"Catriona..."

"No, I'm sure, Scott. I don't want to go. Sorry." She left the table without goodbyes or excuses and withdrew to her room.

Lillian said, "What will I do without you here, darling? We need to head off this depression before it takes her away for good. I'm worried."

"Call Dr. Pendergrass as soon as her office opens tomorrow morning."

Lillian agreed. "That is exactly what I'll do."

***

The days had been difficult since her return from Sageville. At first, Catriona had visited her doctor's office every other day but retreated within as she recalled more of her childhood. She wanted to feel nothing; however, guilt poured over everything. The medication kept her mind dull—her preferred state of being. The sadness consumed her to the point of not eating nor waking until mid-afternoon. Her mind begged for solidarity. No one knew, but she had not kept her past two doctor's appointments.

"What a great day! I wasn't expecting so many people," Peter said.

Catriona drank another mint julep. "Last year, there were over thirty-five thousand in attendance. This is an enormous deal for The Plains area."

"I'm happy you decided to attend. Beautiful hat, by the way."

"Thank you. It's my latest gift from Lillian. Every year, she hopes I'll enter the hat competition, but I never do. It's not me, but I enjoy watching. I think I need another drink." She waved down a server. "Make that two, if you don't mind."

"Yes, ma'am."

"What is you?" Peter asked.

"Right now, these drinks. Have you had one? They are so tasty." She drank it without a second thought. She sat the empty silver cup next to the other two.

"Yes, they are good."

"You asked, 'What is me?' I'm not sure, but we are not here for me. You see... this day is full of contests and races. The hats and the tailgating are judged, and I enjoy watching the terrier and pony races." She drank the last drink as fast as the previous ones. "The Steeplechase horseracing here is a wonderful Virginia tradition, especially for our family. I cannot imagine being anywhere else this time of year."

"Well, since this is my first visit, where's the best place to watch?"

"Right here on Members Hill… do you think Lillian would host a party any other way?" She sighed. "Do you see my purse anywhere?"

"Yes, it's beside me."

"Would you be so kind as to hand me the green bottle? I think I'm coming down with a headache."

"Sure." He pulled the bottle from her bag.

She took several pills and swallowed them down with Peter's drink.

"Do you want another?" Peter laughed.

"Yes, please." She continued the charade so he would not notice her misery. "Lillian and Scott have been Great Meadow Foundation Life members as long as I can remember, and they always host a platinum tent for their guests… around two hundred and fifty business associates… give or take a few. Lillian is about helping others no matter how big or small and by being life members, they help support the preservation of open space and free community access to Great Meadow."

"Where do others watch the races?"

Catriona called out to a passing server, "Sir? May I have another drink and will you take these cups away?"

"Yes, ma'am." He handed her another. She drank it without taking a breath.

Peter watched with some surprise at her veracity. He said, "You might want to slow down a bit, it's still early."

"Early, schmerly. It's okay. Grab one and relax a little."

"I'm good for now. You did not answer my question. Do most watch from here?"

"Oh, forgive me. Usually, the young professionals from Washington head toward the North Rail spots, and the locals and those more family-oriented are on the South Rail. Are you planning to place any bets?"

"Sure. Why not?"

"Come. I'll go with you. Lillian has a horse in one event today. The biggest event is the International Gold Cup Timber Stakes. Our horse is a five-year-old named, Black Bart. His odds are not great, but not bad either… about eight to one. The race is almost three- and one-half miles over twenty-three timber fences. They are solid jumps and they do not yield. That is why timber racing is harder than hurdle races. Lillian is hoping he performs well, but between us, I don't think she's expecting a win. However, you didn't hear it from me."

"All bets on Black Bart then."

"Excellent answer, Mr. Tramwell." She toasted him and gulped down her last julep.

***

Lillian watched as they walked away. She had not noticed Catriona's unusual behavior and was pleased she appeared to be having fun. The race could not have come at a better time.

Scott slipped behind her and whispered in her ear. "Who are you spying on?"

"Those two." She nodded toward Peter and Catriona.

"Good-looking couple. He's been patient with her."

"Yes, he has. Do you think he understands what is happening to her?"

"As far as I know, he's only aware of her depression, but I'm not sure he understands to what depth."

"Do any of us?"

"Not until you're in the thick of it. You make an excellent point." Scott kissed her on the cheek. "Lovely party, my beautiful lady."

"Thank you. You know I got my party sense from my mother and my horse sense from my daddy. I wish they were here."

"Me too. Sweet memories."

"Do you like my hat?"

"It's the best one I've seen all season."

"You are a smooth-talking devil, aren't you, Mr. McKenna?" She laughed.

"Why do you think you married me?" He returned the laughter as Declan and Samuel walked into the tent. "Good morning, gentlemen. How is our horse?"

"He's good and ready to run," Samuel said.

"Declan, do you think we have a chance?" Lillian asked.

"I do. I think he'll be a surprise for many today."

"I hope so. Please get something to eat and drink since the race is not until four. I want to introduce you to a few people too. Samuel, will you join us as we make the rounds?"

"Would love to. Let me say I'm always reminded of your parents when we're here."

"Oh, Samuel, thank you for saying so." Lillian beamed.

"Did Catriona come today?" Declan asked.

Lillian smiled. "Yes, she did. She and Peter walked toward the betting area only moments ago. He is an excellent distraction for her. They make a good-looking couple too, and it makes me happy to see her with someone who loves her."

Declan faked a smile.

Lillian asked, "Is something wrong?"

"No. Just checking to see how she's holding up. I haven't seen her at the stables. Funny, I keep missing her when she is there."

"She is probably avoiding you like she is the rest of us. Nothing to worry about as long as we keep a careful watch. Come, let's meet our guests."

"It will be my pleasure."

***

Catriona had consumed too many Mint Juleps in too short of a time—far from her normal one or two for the day. Peter enjoyed watching her pretend to be sober. He leaned his shoulder against the betting booth as she placed their bets.

"Race five. Ten dollars to win on the number four horse. Black Beauty is my horse… wait, Black Beauty?" She laughed. "No, that's not right… Black Bart. Yes, that's it. Black Bart."

Peter whispered, "Catriona, you are incredible."

"Please don't," she said, half-smiling. The alcohol mixed with the pills caused her to struggle to focus.

The teller asked, "You don't want to bet?"

"Yes, I do," she answered. "I apologize. He interrupted me." She frowned at Peter.

He whispered in her ear beneath her broad-brimmed hat. "You are beautiful."

She laughed again. "Please, stop."

"Madam, do you want to place a wager or not? There is a long line waiting," the teller said.

"I am sorry. Yes, I want to continue with my bet." She frowned again at Peter and he laughed.

The teller passed the ticket beneath the glass. "Are there others?"

"No, that is all." Catriona smiled.

Peter answered through the window. "Race five. Five hundred dollars to win on number four horse, Black Bart."

"Yes, sir," came the reply.

"What are you doing?" Catriona asked.

"Trying to get your attention."

"You have my attention. You don't have to spend money, Mr. Tramwell."

"Do I really have your attention?"

"Yes, you do."

The teller interrupted. "Sir, are there other bets you want to place?"

"No, thank you."

Peter placed the ticket inside his jacket pocket and, taking her arm, they moved out of the line back into the flow of the crowd. "Where to, my lady-in-waiting?"

"Peter, you can be funny." She stumbled, almost falling as she laughed.

"In what way?" They sauntered through the crowd back toward Member's Hill.

"I don't know. I'm not used to someone like you."

"Is that good or bad?"

"Both," she said. She giggled as she leaned against him, thinking she might fall. "You are sweet. I'm working through some things… not sure I'm worth the trouble."

He pulled her toward the back fencing away from the crowd. "You are worth more than any trouble you can throw my way." He kissed her passionately without considering who might see.

Catriona knew she was vulnerable and if he wanted to take advantage, she would let him. She had grown tired, and no longer cared about anything.

"Catriona, honey, is that you?"

Catriona raised her head. Declan and Samuel were staring at her.

Samuel frowned. "Lillian is looking for you. She wasn't sure where you had wandered off to…"

"I'm sorry, Samuel. I didn't realize I was being followed. Did she send you to find me? If she did, then I don't appreciate her butting into my business."

"You wait one minute, missy. You know better," Samuel said. "Do you need help walking back?"

"You do not have to worry about Catriona. I have the situation under control, sir," Peter said.

"It looks like it," Samuel said with a smirk.

"That's right, Samuel. He's taking good care of me."

Declan remained silent. She refused to look in his direction. "I'm fine. I need to sit, that's all. Peter, will you help me?"

"Of course."

Samuel grabbed his arm. "Mr. Tramwell, I don't like you."

Catriona snapped back. "Samuel! You are out-of-line. Peter has been the perfect gentleman. You should apologize."

"A perfect gentleman would not be kissing you in public as if you were alone in a back alley somewhere, Catriona. It would devastate your parents."

"My parents are dead or didn't anyone tell you?"

"That's enough. You're drunk." Samuel's face grew taut.

She had never known him to be angry with her before.

"Grandpops, Catriona knows what is and isn't appropriate." Declan pulled at Samuel's arm.

Catriona frowned. "Declan, you stay out of this. Peter, take me back to our table. I feel sick."

"Excuse us, gentlemen." Peter took her arm and guided her back to the tent.

***

Late in the day, the tent erupted into cheers as Black Bart won his race.

"Congratulations, Lillian!" Declan shook her hand.

She hugged him. "We did it, Declan. We did it… I can't believe it!"

"Black Bart and Jacques did the job of winning. I could not be prouder," Samuel said. "Good work, Grandson!"

Everyone walked toward the winner's circle when Declan asked, "Where is Catriona?"

Scott answered, "She became ill, and Peter volunteered to drive her home. He gave me their bets before the race and headed back a couple of hours ago. I'm afraid she will be disappointed when she discovers we won. Why do you ask?"

"No reason. I wanted to join her in celebrating our win."

The photographer said, "Please, everyone, look this way."

Declan frowned as the shutter closed. His mind was elsewhere. He had underestimated Peter, and it would be hours before they would be back at Grace Meade. Like Samuel, he did not trust Peter and had not considered Catriona's current state of mind. However, a little competition did not frighten him either. He recognized she was in a dark place; the true reason for acting out of character—inexcusable or not.

CHAPTER 22

PETER PULLED HIS car to the front entrance of Grace Meade and turned off the ignition. Catriona was sleeping. When he stroked the side of her face, she opened her eyes and smiled.

"Did I fall asleep?"

"Yes. Are you feeling better?" he asked.

"Maybe."

He leaned in and kissed her. Sitting back, he said, "Catriona, you are beautiful."

"Thank you, but please stop."

"Never."

"Even now?"

"Especially now. I like you being vulnerable and needing me. It allows me the opportunity to take care of you. Stay seated." He walked around to her side of the car. She tried to stand, but he caught her. "Be careful. I said I would help you."

"I'm not used to someone helping me. Am I drunk? Yes? I know I should be embarrassed, but I don't think I am." She laughed at her odd sense of humor.

"How many juleps have you had?"

"Six or seven… ten… I don't know."

"Ten?"

She was giggling as if a teenager had robbed the family's liquor cabinet. "I wasn't counting."

"You should never have had the first one with the meds you are taking."

"Oh, stop. Nothing to worry about… nothing at all." Fumbling for her keys, she opened the door and tripped into the foyer. "Oh, my word!"

Peter caught her before she fell. "Catriona, this is no longer funny."

"Yes, it is… loosen up, will you?" Samson and Delilah ran into the foyer, greeting her with licks and wagging bobbed tails. "Hello, my babies."

"Let's get some food inside of you." He led her into the kitchen and propped her against a barstool. "Sit." All three dogs sat on command.

Catriona burst with laughter. "Look… they are sitting!"

"Not them. You. Please sit before you fall."

"Kiss me, Peter."

He kissed her as he pressed her body against the island.

She pushed back. "Don't."

"What do you want, Catriona? One minute you want to be kissed and the next minute not. What is wrong with you?"

"Kiss me again."

"You need food. Here… let me help you." He sighed as he helped her onto the stool. She pulled him to her. "Stop, Catriona. I'm not doing this."

"Do you want me or not?"

"I do."

"Then walk me upstairs. You can do whatever."

"No."

"Are you making me beg?"

"You are drunk. In the morning, you won't remember this conversation took place. Let's eat and then we can think about the rest of the evening. What is your preference?" He opened the refrigerator door and peered inside.

"Do the dogs have food in their bowls?"

"Yes, and water too. The dogs are fine."

"Where's Cookie?" she asked.

"She is at the races. Don't you remember?"

Laying her face on the countertop, she said, "Now, there's a word for you… remember. What if I don't want to remember? I'm tired of trying to remember."

He closed the door. "What are you talking about?"

She raised her head and scoffed, "Never mind. You wouldn't understand… no one does." She closed her eyes and rubbed her temple with her fingertips. "Eggs. I want eggs… and sausage."

"Eggs and sausage. That's easy." He opened the cabinet beneath the stovetop range to search for a skillet. "Here we are."

She sat silently watching him cook. When the aroma of butter and eggs filled the air, she laid her head back on the counter. "I don't feel so good."

He turned off the eye and walked around to her side. "Lean against me." He lifted her to her feet. Helping her into the foyer, they stumbled.

"Oops. Why can't you walk straight?" she asked.

"Because you drank too much, my lady."

"Noooo… not me. I don't drink." She leaned against him harder.

"You have today. Too many drinks make a girl swagger."

"Swagger?" She laughed as she stumbled toward the stairs. "Who says, 'swagger'?"

He caught her so to miss the staircase. "Let's get you to bed."

"Bed?"

"Yes. You need to sleep. I'll carry you or we won't make it to the landing."

"Carry me to my room? Have you planned to ravage me with mad lovemaking, my liege?"

"Will you remember tomorrow if I do?"

"Yes… maybe."

"No, you won't. You need to sleep."

"You played your cello for me. Remember? You're the handsome, Peter Tramwell, and I am supposed to like you…" She poked her finger into his chest. "… a bunch."

"I like you too."

"Are you waiting for me to make a pass?"

"No more teasing, Catriona. Not this time."

She mumbled something before passing out. He scooped her into his arms and carried her upstairs. The hall light flooded the darkness of the bedroom, and he removed her shoes and turned back the duvet.

She moaned, "I'm sick."

He grabbed the small garbage can from the bedside and she vomited. She fell back against the pillow. Gathering a cold washcloth from her bathroom, he placed it across her temple.

"Peter?"

"Yes?"

"It's dark in here."

"Yes, it is. Do you need a light?"

"No. I'm sorry."

"For what?"

"Maybe I should leave and never come back. I'm lost..." Her eyes closed.

"Catriona, wake up. What are you talking about?"

Her eyelids moved at a snail's pace when she tried re-opening her eyes. "Peter, is that you?"

"Yes, it's me."

"May I ask you something?"

"Anything."

"Do you think you could... make love to me?"

He sat next to her. "Is that what you want?"

"Scott and Lillian want me to love someone... maybe. I don't know... isn't everyone supposed to love someone?" She closed her eyes as she struggled to stay awake.

He stroked her hair and smiled when she opened her eyes again.

"Peter? I don't feel good."

"I know, but I will take care of you."

"You will?"

"Close your eyes and sleep. I love you."

"You do?"

"Yes."

"Promise?"

"I promise."

She fell into a deep slumber. Peter kissed her on the cheek. He walked into the bathroom, turned on the faucet, and splashed his face with water. *This is too easy.*

Cookie was busy in the kitchen when Peter walked in.

"Good evening, Cookie."

"Good evening. Did you and Catriona eat?" She placed the skillet with its half-cooked egg into the sink.

"No. I started to cook, but she became ill. I carried her to bed."

"You did? Poor thing. Do I need to check on her?"

"Maybe later. I'm leaving shortly."

"You will do no such thing," she said. "The blue bedroom is ready to go. There is an extra set of pajamas in the armoire and an extra shaving kit in the bathroom. You make yourself at home. Lillian and Scott will insist you stay."

"Thank you, Cookie."

"Are you hungry? I can cook something. Would you like toast or a bagel?"

"A bagel sounds good."

Scott, Lillian, Samuel, and Declan poured into the kitchen from the garden, still in celebratory fashion. Samson and Delilah joined in with yelps and bouncing, while Patches greeted Scott with a wagging tail.

"What an incredible day," Scott said. "Lillian, you and this team of two, along with Jacques. You are unstoppable. You are winner's circle champions with ribbons and roses to boot."

"Thank you, darling. I have a talented team." She hugged them again for the fourth time.

"Now, now, Lillian. There is no reason for all of this mushy stuff," Samuel said, although everyone knew he was enjoying every moment.

"Thank you, Lillian. I think Jacques deserves…" Declan stopped speaking when eyeing Peter at the island.

Lillian turned. "Peter, forgive us. Where's Catriona? I must tell her we won. She will not believe it."

"Congratulations on your win. That's wonderful. I hate to say it, but Catriona isn't better. I put her to bed only moments ago. Hopefully, she'll sleep, but she will have a horrible hangover in the morning."

Lillian frowned. "Hangover? Scott, we need to call Dr. Pendergrass. She is becoming unhinged."

"It's race day. Let it go."

"You're right, of course... Peter, I hope you plan to stay with us."

"Yes. Cookie has given me my sleeping assignment. Don't worry about Catriona. I'll check on her before I retire for the evening. My bedroom is close to hers."

"Peter is staying in the blue bedroom," Cookie said. "Would anyone enjoy a late-night breakfast? You can call me Waffle House, Jr."

Samuel said, "I can't think of a better way to end this day."

Scott walked over to Peter and handed him an envelope. "I have your winnings... not too shabby of a day for you either."

Peter smiled as he took the money. He said, "You know, this day keeps getting better and better. Catriona and I had a wonderful day. I don't want to be too premature, but I also believe an announcement will be forthcoming soon. I don't want to spoil the surprise, so I will wait until Catriona is better."

"Ooooo... that sounds promising, doesn't it, Scott?" Lillian walked toward him, smiling from ear to ear.

Scott said, "Sure does. A partnership maybe?"

"You could say something along those lines," Peter said.

Samuel pulled Peter aside. "Declan explained I should be more aware of Catriona's state of mind. She is unwell, it seems. Still, that's no excuse for me acting so rude, but you have to forgive this old man just wanting to protect his girl. I still don't approve of your actions, but I also do not approve of mine."

"I understand, Samuel. A new start?"

"I think so."

Scott interrupted them. "Peter, I will be out of here in the morning. Would you like to join me at the office? Time is slipping away from us, and we need to discuss opening statements."

"Tomorrow is Sunday. Do you ever rest?" Peter asked.

Lillian said, "No, he doesn't, and that is why he wins the big cases."

Scott laughed. "Let's hope our team wins this one. Too many men are dying for no reason at the hands of Franks. His company is not following established guidelines, and who knows... maybe safer guidelines will be adopted across the industry following this case. It is time we addressed these issues before more become ill or die."

"Enough legal talk," Lillian said. "We are celebrating tonight, remember?"

"I agree, Lillian. This is definitely an evening worth celebrating," Peter said. He glanced toward Declan and was met with a cold stare. No words were spoken between them.

 CHAPTER 23

THE EARTH EXALTED its glorious colors on that Sunday morning in late October—the kind of day rewarded after the long, dog days of summer. The crisp air cleaned one's lungs and the sun's rays were peeking through the light fog rising from the fields beyond.

Lillian walked toward the stables where Black Bart was tied waiting to be loaded.

"Come on, you glorious winner. You certainly deserve a spa treatment today." She walked him to the rear of the trailer.

"Lillian, I'll take care of this for you. Let me grab a break-away strap out of the tack room."

"Thank you, Declan, but I've got it."

"Give me two seconds; I'll be right back." Declan disappeared into the stable.

Lillian whispered under her breath, "This is ridiculous. I have been loading horses for almost fifty years. Come on Black Bart, let's try out your new trailer."

Lillian walked the horse to the back and stepped inside. She waited for the thoroughbred to make his move. She knew if she relaxed, he would also. She coaxed him with soft whispers. "Come on, boy. You can do it."

"Good morning."

Lillian looked around toward the rear of the horse eyeing a man wearing a ballcap. "Yes, it is a good morning. Do I know you?"

"No ma'am. May I ask you a question?"

"Sure. Give me a second to finish loading this horse and I'll be right with you. Come on boy, you can do this."

Black Bart cocked his head back and forth and then stepped inside the trailer as Lillian eased backward inside. "Good boy... that wasn't so hard, was it?" As she petted his muzzle, she turned to tie the strap. Without warning, the horse bolted forward and pinned her between the trailer's side and his right shoulder. Multiple times, he lunged forward crushing her with each blow. She tried pushing back but had little strength against the twelve hundred pounds squeezing her every breath into lifelessness. As she crumpled to the floor, the horse stomped and his foot delivered the final blow to the side of her head. As quick as he had bolted, he became calm and backed himself out of the trailer.

***

Samuel walked toward the tack room from the office when Declan suddenly appeared carrying a break-away strap. "What's up, Grandson?"

"Grabbing a strap for Lillian."

Samuel frowned. "So, you're not going to church with me this morning?"

"No, sir. We will be leaving shortly to take Black Bart for his hydrotherapy massage. Lillian decided he needs a full immersion. She's concerned about his right leg after his win yesterday. You want to cover for me today?"

"Sure, I think I can handle it, but it will have to wait until after church. Who's on the schedule to work today?"

"Brad and a couple of others."

"Can Brad handle it until then?"

"For an hour or two, he can. Thanks."

Declan and Samuel walked outside toward the trailer. Black Bart was grazing by the fence alone. Declan looked around, but Lillian was nowhere to be seen.

Samuel said, "Is everything okay?"

"Did you see Lillian in the stables?"

"No."

"Will you grab Black Bart for me?"

"Sure."

Declan called out, "Lillian? Where are you?" He tossed the break-away to Samuel. "Hook this up, will you?"

"No problem." When Samuel changed out the rope, he reached down to examine the horse's right knee. He noticed the lower leg was covered in blood.

He heard Declan call out again.

"Lillian?"

Bending down to inspect Black Bart closer, Samuel did not find an injury. "Hey, Grandson, there's blood over here."

"Blood?"

"Yep... it's covering his hoof and leg."

Declan walked to the back of the trailer. When seeing Lillian lying on the floor in a pool of blood, he jumped inside. Kneeling next to her, he lifted her into his arms.

"Lillian? Can you hear me?" He wiped away her hair and saw her disfigured face. He screamed, "Oh, dear God... no... help! Anyone? Grandpops, help!"

Samuel dropped the reins and ran toward the trailer. Brad came running out of the barn and chased after Black Bart galloping toward the paddock. When Samuel turned the corner, he saw Declan holding Lillian with her head lying in his lap.

"She is not breathing and there's no pulse. Call an ambulance, Grandpops. Now!"

Samuel ran as fast as he could to the phone on the stable wall. His hands shook as he dialed the number.

"Yes, we've had an accident at the Grace Meade estate. We need medical care immediately! You might send the medical examiner and the police as well... please hurry!"

He then called the main house. "Cookie, is Scott still here?"

"No, he left about fifteen minutes ago heading back to the city. Why?"

"Lillian has been hurt. It doesn't look good. We have an ambulance on its way. I need you to call Scott, now!"

When Samuel ran back outside, he saw Catriona running out of the back door and into the garden toward them. He stopped her within hearing distance of the trailer. "Katydid, you don't want to see her. Stay with me."

"Why? What has happened? Lillian?"

"We're not sure, but it looks like your mother was hurt trailering the horse."

"I want to see her… let me go!"

Samuel held tight.

They could hear an ambulance and fire engine approaching the house. Cookie ran out of the front door directing them toward the stables.

Samuel and Catriona could hear Declan talking inside the trailer.

"Lillian, hold on. You're going to be fine. Just hold on."

The first responders jumped out of the ambulance and headed into the trailer.

"Oh no, Samuel. No, no, no." She panicked as the tears fell. Her body shook.

"Shh, sweetie… shh." He wrapped his arms around her as she held him.

Scott's car appeared out of nowhere and screeched to a stop as he jumped from the car. Running toward the group of firemen, they asked him to step back as they moved the gurney to the back of the trailer.

"That is my wife! I need to see my wife!"

"Sir, please, let us help her."

Scott stood in disbelief. When he saw Samuel holding Catriona, he ran to them. "What happened?"

Samuel said, "We don't know. It appears she was trailering the horse, but I can't say for sure."

The firefighters asked everyone to step back toward the fire engine so not to be in view of the rear of the trailer to allow the medics to work. For several minutes, they heard voices inside the trailer and then watched a young man move the gurney closer. After what seemed like hours, a medic appeared from the rear of the trailer and asked Scott to come forward. When he stepped behind the trailer, someone had draped a white sheet over a figure atop the gurney.

The medical examiner reached out and touched Scott on the arm. "I'm sorry, but there is nothing more we can do. She was gone before we arrived. I can tell you she did not suffer. It appears death was immediate."

"What?" Scott lost his balance. "I'm sorry... what? No!" He bolted toward the covered sheet. Declan grabbed him around the chest and held him back.

The examiner turned toward the medics and said, "I need to call this." Looking at his watch, he said, "Time of death is seven forty-five a.m."

"No! I don't believe you!" Scott fought against Declan's grip.

"Scott, let them take her to the hospital. You don't want to see her like this, I promise. You don't want to see her... not like this!"

Scott stiffened. "Let go of me, Declan. Now."

Declan released him. As Scott walked toward the sheet, he pulled back the fabric revealing his wife's once beautiful face. She was unrecognizable. He let out a moan resembling that of an animal who was caught in a trap. He moved her face toward him and kissed her.

All struggled to hear the activity behind the trailer. Catriona cried out as Samuel continued to hold her. Cookie grabbed Samuel's arm and covered her mouth with the back of her hand as she sobbed softly.

The medical examiner touched Scott on the shoulder and whispered, "I cannot imagine your pain. I'm truly sorry."

Scott stood frozen staring at the man's face.

"Sir, you need to sit before you fall."

Scott whispered, "She is a donor."

"I'm sorry. I didn't understand you."

"She is an organ donor."

The examiner said, "Mr. McKenna, we cannot conduct a major organ donation under the circumstances, but we might save tissue."

"Yes... please. It's what she would have wanted."

The examiner turned and said, "Medic, timing is critical. We need to move her to the hospital now."

Sheriff Wells, a friend of the family, approached. "Scott, I can drive you to the hospital, if you prefer."

As the medics rolled the gurney toward the ambulance doors, Catriona screamed when she saw the sheet covering Lillian's body. "No! No! No! Scott?"

She broke Samuel's grasp and ran toward her father. She buried her face into his shoulder. Scott wrapped his arms around her but appeared to be in shock. The medic approached him after Lillian's body rolled into the back of the ambulance.

"Sir, I think you should ride with us. You may need medical attention yourself. I can give you something to help with the shock. In fact, I insist."

Scott nodded his head.

"We need to hurry, sir."

Samuel said, "Scott, we will follow you. I'll drive Catriona to the hospital."

"Thank you, Samuel." He hugged Catriona again, and then removed her arms from around his waist and followed the medic inside the ambulance. The doors closed and they drove away.

Samuel saw Peter running toward them. He said, "Katydid… look."

She raised her eyes and Samuel nodded his head toward the garden. When Catriona saw Peter, she ran into his arms.

Peter held her. "Darling, I heard the commotion from upstairs. What has happened? Are you okay?"

"It's my mother, Peter. She's… dead."

"Dead?" His eyes narrowed, then widened from the shock.

Her knees collapsed beneath her as he held her tight.

"Declan, we're heading to the hospital. Call me if you need me," Samuel said.

"Thank you, Grandpops. Catriona…" His voice cracked as he reached out to touch her arm. "I'm so sorry."

She looked at him with blank eyes as Peter helped her walk toward Samuel's truck.

Cookie was trying to keep her emotions intact. "Katydid, you will need your purse. I'll get it for you." She ran into the house.

"Sweetheart, where does Scott keep his wallet?" Samuel asked.

"In his briefcase."

Peter said, "I'll get it."

He helped her into the truck and then ran to where Scott's car door remained open. He grabbed the briefcase on the front floorboard. Peter jumped into Samuel's truck next to Catriona and wrapped his arm around her. She laid her head against his shoulder.

Samuel pulled to the front entrance of the main house as Cookie handed the purse through the window. "I'll be waiting here for you and Scott when you return, sweetheart. Please call me if I can do anything."

Catriona nodded her head.

"Samuel, you call me," Cookie said through her tears.

"I will." Samuel pulled away.

***

Declan shook his head as he stared at the ground. Tears flowed down his face without making a sound. One fireman approached him stating the police and the medical examiner would take pictures for their records.

Declan walked toward the trailer and looked inside.

"Sir, I'm sorry, but you need to step aside," the deputy said.

"I know. I don't know why, but I needed to see what could have caused the accident. Nothing makes sense."

"Please, sir. Allow us to do our job."

"Of course. I apologize."

The deputy asked Declan to inform the men to stay away from the trailer. His officers needed to cordon off the area to ensure nothing was touched.

Declan nodded. Brad and a few others were standing by the fence still holding on to Black Bart. As Declan approached them, his body shivered while trying to hold his emotions together.

"Gentlemen, there are no words. It appears Mrs. McKenna has sustained fatal injuries, and we need to stay clear of this area so the police and firemen can do their jobs." His voice cracked. "I'm sure there will be many people onsite for the rest of the day. Please be accommodating as possible. I will understand if you need to go home, but I ask you to wait until the police have released you. They may want to ask questions, but I'm unsure at this time. Brad, I need you to take Black Bart back to his stall but do not clean him… not yet. I'm not sure if they need evidence from him."

"Yes, sir."

Declan dropped his head. He felt ill.

"Sir, may I help you?" Charlie, a new-hire on the estate, stepped toward him.

"What?"

"I can drive you to your house so you can change clothes and take a shower."

Declan looked down. He was covered in Lillian's blood. His hands were stained red, and his shirt and jeans were saturated, as well as his boots.

"Thank you, Charlie, but I can drive myself. I need you here to meet the others who might be arriving. Let them know I'll be back shortly. Make sure no one goes near the trailer and do what they tell you to do."

"Yes, sir."

Approaching the firefighters, Declan asked if he could go shower and return. There was no disagreement under the circumstances. As he made his way toward his truck, he stopped and vomited next to the fence. He could not wrap his head around what had occurred—it was too surreal.

Sheriff Wells interrupted him. "How are you doing?"

Declan wiped his mouth with his sleeve. "I'm rattled."

"Understandable. May I ask you a question?"

"Anything."

"One of my men told me you wanted to look in the trailer again. Why?"

"None of this makes sense to me. Lillian was an expert around horses. She knew the dangers and would never have taken unexpected risks, especially when loading a horse. Also, Black Bart has never been anything but gentle and has been loaded innumerable times. He has never been afraid of a trailer. I do not know what happened, but given the size and power of that horse, if he became startled or frightened, his natural reaction would be to flee."

"Where were you?"

"In the tack room, grabbing a breakaway strap."

"Is that important?"

"It's an additional safety measure when trailering a horse… to prevent something like this from happening."

"I see. So… you found her?"

"I did, but not immediately. Lillian was missing and Black Bart had wandered down toward the fence. I thought it odd she would leave any horse unattended, much less Black Bart. He won the Gold Cup only yesterday. We were taking him this morning for water therapy for his legs. My grandfather noticed blood on the horse's leg and hoof. I then moved to the back of the trailer and saw her collapsed on the floor."

"That is the first time you saw her?"

"Yes."

"Was she breathing when you got to her?"

"I'm not sure, but I don't think so. She did not respond in any way. Her head, it was… it was…" His voice trembled.

"Take your time. I know this has been a horrible ordeal for all of you."

Declan swallowed hard. "The side of her face and skull were crushed. There appeared to be brain tissue exposed and blood was everywhere. There was no way to revive her by resuscitation."

"Thank you."

"Is that all?" Declan asked.

"For now, I believe so."

"Would it be okay if I go shower?"

"Sure."

"I'll be back as soon as possible."

"No problem. We will be here a while."

"Oh. I almost forgot. I asked one of the trainers to not wash the horse until you could inspect him. Brad can help you."

"Thank you. Go home and take your time. We must investigate any accident to make sure there is no foul play. I'm sure you understand."

"Of course, I do, but Sheriff?"

"Yes?"

"This family is like none I've ever known. This couldn't be anything but an accident because everyone has the greatest respect for them... especially Lillian."

"I know. The McKennas are good friends; however, we must look at every angle, including negligence. Thanks again, Mr..."

"I'm sorry. I'm Declan O'Connell, the equine manager on this estate."

"Thank you, Mr. O'Connell. By the way, does that security camera work?"

Declan looked toward the top of the stable entrance. "It does."

"When you return, do you mind sending me the tape?"

"I will, but you won't be able to see the back of the trailer."

"Send it to me regardless."

Declan nodded.

As he pulled his truck onto the drive, he could see another police car approaching the stables. Once inside his house, Declan removed his clothing and stuffed them, along with his boots, into a garbage bag. Stepping inside the shower, he allowed the hot water to run over him. With no warning, his knees buckled causing him to place his hands against the tile in front of him to steady his stance. Raising his face to the ceiling, he yelled in pain as his chest heaved heavy sobs. He was riddled with guilt.

This can't be real. Why didn't she wait? We weren't in a hurry.

He watched the water turn pink as it ran into the drain.

Negligence? I should have prevented this. Lillian… I'm sorry.

When he closed his eyes, he could see Catriona's blank face staring back at him. He cried allowing the water to muffle his sounds until he could cry no more.

***

By Monday afternoon, everyone in Virginia was aware of the accident. The evening broadcast in Washington reported the ghastly details and all were abuzz of the shocking news of Lillian Rose McKenna's death.

Cookie opened the newspaper the following morning. As she turned to the obituaries, Scott entered the kitchen with Patches following at his heels.

"Did they publish it today?"

"They did. Do you want to see it?"

"I do." He poured himself a cup of coffee and sat at the island. He carefully took the paper from her hands. The obit was printed as follows:

It is with great sadness the family of Mrs. Lillian Rose Pruett McKenna announces her passing from this life into eternal glory following a fatal accident on Sunday at the young age of 54 years. Lillian was a beautiful person with an even larger personality. A bright light snuffed out, but nowhere greater than the equestrian world as her love and knowledge of maintaining the highest of standards in horse breeding and training will be irreplaceable, and her absence forever and deeply felt. Lillian's heart was larger than most. She fought for others, especially in her efforts to raise money to feed the children who lived within the Commonwealth. Her family stated as her final act of love, she was an organ donor so when her earthly body could serve her no more, it could help others. She is preceded in death by her parents, Nathaniel and Charlotta Emerson Pruett. She will be lovingly remembered by her devoted husband of 29 years, Scott McKenna, and their adoring daughter, Catriona E. Harrington-McKenna.

The family will receive friends at their place of worship, the Holy Episcopal Church, on Saturday at noon until 2:00 p.m. when the Celebration of Life service will begin with Father Eugene Perkins officiating. Interment will follow at a private ceremony at the family cemetery on the Grace Meade estate in The Plains, Virginia. Those who so desire may make memorial donations to her charity, The Children's Hunger Relief Fund of Greater Virginia, a nonprofit organization, where 100% of donations go toward the purchase of food. Please contact the Madison Reed Funeral Home for further details.

Scott stared at each word.

"I should have asked them to write more, but how do you describe the most beautiful woman in the world in a few short lines when a Thesaurus filled with words cannot capture who she is... or was?"

"I know, darling. I cannot believe she isn't here."

Looking at Cookie, he responded with only sarcasm.

"And as simple as that... five little paragraphs printed in the newspaper and she is gone. At least they printed everything correctly. I guess I should be thankful for some things. The true irony is each of us is allotted fifteen minutes of fame at some point in our lives, but for most, it will be our name appearing in an obituary column for all to read."

She said nothing.

"Cookie, what do I do now?" Tears ran down his face.

She walked over and wrapped her arm around his shoulders as he sobbed. He stammered, "My heart... my heart is shattered."

"I do not know what to say, Scott, except... I love you."

"I'm finding it difficult to breathe. I don't know how to get out of bed knowing she is no longer here. In truth, I don't want to live in a world where she isn't breathing. Oh, God, please take away this pain! I don't think I can survive this." His lips trembled as the tears continued to cascade down his face.

"You have us. Catriona is here, and you both need each other... more than ever. We wouldn't survive losing you too. She deserves to have her father with her."

He wiped his face with his napkin. Her words made him aware he needed to be stronger. "Where is she?"

"She ate earlier and headed to the stables before you ever thought about rising this morning. She is hiding from the world on the back of a horse."

"Good. Let her hide all she wants. In fact, I may join her."

Cookie nodded. "She has not slept."

"Are you sure? The doctors at the ER gave us both something to help with the shock. It has been the only way I've been able to close my eyes."

"I'm not sure she has taken anything."

Scott frowned. "Do you think having the funeral on Saturday is too soon?"

"I do not."

"When we talked at the hospital, Catriona told me she did not want a funeral visitation and neither do I... not really."

"You do what is best for you and Catriona. Everyone will understand you wanting your privacy during this time. Do I need to prepare any additional rooms for this weekend?"

"No. I don't want anyone here... not now."

"If that is what you prefer. The church has called and some people want to bring food by the house. I told them it was greatly appreciated, but unnecessary."

"I don't want it... it's thoughtful, but as I said before, I don't want anyone here. Who has called?"

"Many from your office. Peter called to let you know he is handling the case and asked you not to worry. Tia has called as well. All are expressing their condolences. At least with the paper's notice, everyone will know the arrangements."

"I'll call Peter this afternoon... no, I had better do that now. I'll call Shirley and ask her to handle the office inquiries. As far as the house phone goes, let the recorder do its job. Change the message to say the caller can contact the funeral home for further information regarding

Saturday's arrangements. I will listen to all other messages this afternoon. Maybe Katydid would like to hear them too."

"I'll take care of it. The florist has placed wreaths on the front gates. You and Catriona need to think about what you want for the casket."

"Thank you, I will. Did you ask Tia to order a wreath for the front door of The Feather Quill? Tell her to have the charges sent to me."

"She took care of the wreath first thing Monday morning."

"She is a good one, isn't she? Catriona chose her partner wisely. Good."

Cookie said, "Why don't you take Maximillian out for a ride? It may clear your head a little."

"I think I will. Thanks, Cookie, for keeping it simple for me and Katydid. I love you."

"I love you too. I need to keep my mind busy so answering phone calls or helping you in any way is healing."

Scott nodded his head in agreement. "Best advice today. I need to keep my mind busy as well. Will you call Declan and ask him to get Max ready?"

"Sure, but before you go, the funeral director is coming by for clothing for Lillian and the pallbearers' names."

"I want the men who work on this estate. Lillian loved them as if they were her own family, and Declan and Samuel are to walk ahead of her casket leading it to the altar. Also, you will ride with Catriona and me in the family car and sit with us at the service."

Her voice trembled. "I will let everyone know."

"What time will he be here?"

"One o'clock."

"What time is it?"

"Eight-thirty."

"That will give us enough time. Okay, I'll make sure Katydid is with me to go over everything, including the clothing and the ceremony. Will you call Father Perkins to join us as well?"

"I will."

"You know, Cookie, I've changed my mind. Please prepare a room for Tia. I think Katydid would like the company, but check with her before you call."

"I will. Don't worry about anything because the next few days will be hard enough. The funeral home will send a crew to prepare the grave on Friday. Do you want me to ask Declan or Samuel to oversee everything for you?"

"Ask Samuel to join me. We will do it together."

"I'll confirm the arrangements and let him know."

Scott stared into his coffee mug. With every blink of his eyes, Lillian's face was all he could see. "You are right. I need to get busy or I'll go crazy. I'm not sure where to start."

When he stood, he hugged Cookie and wept bitterly. They cried together. She held him tight like a mother would console her broken son. After pulling himself together, he disappeared into his office.

With tears flowing, Cookie dialed the stable.

"Yes?" came the reply.

She choked as she spoke, "Declan…"

***

Folding the newspaper, Thaddeus Franks stared at Hank Stone sitting across from him. "Seriously? How does threatening someone turn into killing them?" He rubbed his face. "What kind of lunatic are you?"

"Mr. Franks, I did not realize the cattle prod would cause the horse to push against her. I never expected he would crush her."

"Did anyone see you?"

"Only her. It was easy to slip away unnoticed."

"This better not come back to haunt me or she won't be the only one dead."

"You won't have to worry. Besides, our co-existence benefits us both."

Thad threw an envelope across the desk toward him. "Ten thousand should cover it."

"I don't think so. This is the beginning of a long and beautiful friendship. May I call you, 'Thad?'"

"You are kidding me, right?"

"No, I'm not. This situation is going to cost more than ten grand."

"Fine."

He opened the safe. Counting the money, he said, "I should keep every penny considering the hell-storm raining down if anyone finds out what you have done." He slammed the safe's door shut. "Here. Get your scrawny ass out of here before I kill you myself... go!"

He said nothing, but stuffed the envelope into his upper coat pocket and walked out.

Pushing the intercom, Thad said, "Get my attorney on the phone, and don't bother me until you have him... do you understand?"

"Yes, sir," the woman's voice replied.

"I'm glad someone around here knows how to follow instructions!" He slammed the phone onto the receiver.

He plopped down and turned his chair toward the phone. It rang.

"Mr. Franks, Mr. Jameson is on line two."

"Thank you, Sealey... Hello? Jameson?... I need you to get over here immediately... what? ... I don't care if you're busy. I pay you to be here when I call day or night... I don't care! I'll give you an hour and bring your team with you or I'll sue!"

He slammed the phone again and rose from the desk. Walking over to the window and wiping his face with both hands, he stared into the distance and screamed, "Damnation!"

A man was sitting in the corner. "What have you gotten me into, Franks?"

Thad turned. "You need to sit there and stay quiet, Tramwell. You are in this as deep as I am."

"I didn't sign up for someone dying," Peter said.

"You scratch my back; I'll scratch yours... isn't that how the saying goes?"

"Listen. You came to me. Remember? You would provide monies for my campaign if I would help your company's case with the State. I have given you everything regarding our courtroom strategies, the black-lung patient list to help you with payoffs, as well as making sure you knew the time Scott's family would be at the restaurant in D.C. In fact, you almost blew it by calling me at the table after you stormed out, so don't blame me for anything you have screwed up."

"You are as guilty as me. At least, you will end up with that pretty daughter of his, not to mention his money. Knowing McKenna, he'll arrange his new son-in-law to be perfectly placed for Junior Senator."

"All was going according to plan until you killed Lillian. What happens now?"

"You let me handle everything else."

Peter said, "I want you to remove Chad Parks from your legal team."

"What has he done? He's nothing more than a grunt worker."

"He's an idiot. I know you have had me followed for weeks and he's bad at it. He cannot be trusted. His reputation of running his mouth has ruined me in the past. The last thing either of us needs is someone who can't keep his mouth shut."

"I needed to know you could be trusted, Tramwell."

"Really?"

"I underestimated you. Consider it done. Anything else I should know about?"

"No. I'll handle Scott," Peter said.

"Make sure you do."

CHAPTER 24

WHEN SCOTT AND Catriona exited the church, they were overwhelmed at the outpouring of love shown. The attendance had been large, and many could not enter with no available seats. At the last minute, the church left their doors and windows opened so the overflow of mourners could hear the service. The words from the pastor and the testimonies from close friends were heartfelt.

In memoriam, Catriona wore one of Lillian's favorite black derby hats, her leather gloves, and draped across her simple black dress, a long strand of pearls Lillian was seen wearing frequently—a gift from Lillian's father. Catriona knew they were only material things, but they made her feel as though Lillian was sitting beside her. The shock had proved to be almost too much. She was thankful for the sleep-aids, as well as Scott not pressuring her to speak at the service. Mere words were unnecessary for others to understand the love she had for Lillian. She was her mother, and that was enough. Lillian certainly would not have objected. She would save her words for the privacy of the graveside.

From the family limo, she watched Scott talking to Peter upon leaving the church and hoped he would not ride with them to the cemetery. She knew she wasn't in the best frame of mind, but Peter had become annoying as the week progressed—even more than normal. All the endless questions, phone calls, flowers, and overzealous concern had mutated into ad nauseam for her. His incessant consoling appeared to be insincere, and it repulsed her. He had been with her at the hospital and she was grateful—nothing more. On many calls, he stated he had something of importance to ask, but wanted to wait until they were together. He was suffocating her. "God, help me," she whispered.

Cookie disrupted her thoughts when opening the car door. "Katydid, honey, may I sit next to you?"

"Certainly." She moved to the center of the back seat.

"It was an incredible service. I know Lillian would have been pleased."

"I think she would have been overwhelmed. It was beautiful."

"I do too. Sweetheart, you know how I feel about you, and I cannot remember a time when I've been prouder. You have shown incredible grace and strength throughout this entire nightmare of the past week."

"Has it only been a week? It seems like a year has passed since last Sunday, but thank you. I am happy Dr. Pendergrass set her schedule aside for me. I needed her, and Scott needs me… at least to help him through to the new year."

"He does."

"I can be his support, as he has been for me. Something has happened over the past few days. Dr. Pendergrass thinks the shock has allowed me to remember more. A great-aunt once said she saw a holy fire burning within me, and I have chosen to believe her."

Cookie had seen Catriona prove time and time again to have an extraordinary inner strength throughout her battles of recovery, and now, Catriona was aware of her own strength too. "There is nothing like a strong woman, Catriona. Nothing. And nothing more attractive nor powerful."

"Lillian and my mother were powerful women, and their legacies live within me as well."

"Yes, they do." She smiled through tears as she held Catriona's hand.

Catriona brushed the back of Cookie's hand with her gloved fingers, and then laying her head against Cookie's shoulder, she wept in silence.

Scott climbed into the back seat. "Sweetheart, are you all right?"

She sat upright. "Yes, sir. Are you?" She wiped her eyes with her handkerchief.

"I'm trying. I hope you don't mind, but I have asked Peter to follow us to the cemetery. He will probably stay overnight, Cookie."

"I will make sure there's a place for him."

"Tia and William will stay an extra night also," Catriona said.

"That's good." He reached for her hand. "I am glad they could make plans to be here."

"Me too."

She would discuss her concerns about Peter at a later time. As they pulled away from the church, a man in the crowd wearing a dark ball cap caught her eye. She looked at Scott. "Did you see him?"

"Who?"

"Him...," She turned back, but he was gone. "I thought..."

"You thought what? Who was it?"

She shook her head. "That was weird... I guess it was no one. It's been such an emotional day. I guess my eyes are playing tricks."

"It has been a hard day and it will be even harder in a little while."

She placed her gloved hand in his. The dark bags beneath his eyes revealed his defeated heart. She whispered, "I love you, Dad."

He caught his breath. She had never addressed him by that name before. "I love you too, honey." Holding back more tears, he squeezed her hand. "I do love you, my Katydid."

They rode in silence as the car meandered its way through the countryside and turned in at the gate. The family cemetery at Grace Meade estate was a serene place of silence and solitude, sitting on a shaded knoll where the gentle breezes blew across the valley throughout all the seasons. Surrounded by a wrought-iron fence and a few shade trees, their shadows covered most of the graves. A magnolia tree with its shiny green leaves stood in one corner while Nandina bushes, heavy with clusters of crimson berries, poked through the black railing keeping vigil over deceased loved ones whose voices whispered into the memories of the living. Two large iron urns atop stone pillars posed as guardians gracing each side of the gate as one entered its hallowed ground where family members who had moved on to Glory lay until the return of Christ. Most were Lillian's ancestors, but four markers belonged to Catriona's parents and grandparents. There is an indescribable peace that descends upon each mourner when allowed to be alone in a space tended through the ages from generation to generation whereby one can reminisce of loved souls who have gone from this earth and on to another place and time. Now, their precious Lillian would lie next to her stillborn son.

Keeping with the traditions of the McKenna family's heritage, all followed the casket draped in the family's clan colors as an Irish bagpiper played, "Amazing Grace."

They lowered the casket into the vault as Father Perkins read the Scriptures promising of a coming day when they would see each other again at the feet of a risen Savior to those who believed. Catriona, who had been seated next to Scott, stood and spoke a beautiful tribute to the mother who loved her regardless of all circumstances and whose influence would always be prevalent throughout the remainder of her life. She then dropped a white rose atop the casket. Each in attendance took a handful and tossed a bit of dirt into the grave. Lastly, Tia closed the brief service with a haunting acapella rendition of "When They Ring Those Golden Bells," and Pastor Perkins closed in prayer. The family and some guests lingered for a few moments and walked back to the house so the funeral home could complete their final burial tasks. Cookie had contacted the church condolence committee earlier and planned for food to be delivered while they were at the service. It was customary for the members of the church to send food. Many had prepared their best "death dish" to accompany the ham biscuits. There were more than enough casseroles to feed the family and the staff for a few days, leaving Scott and Catriona astonished by the outpouring of kindness. It was what one did for a neighbor in times such as these.

***

The next morning, Peter joined Catriona and her guests in the dining room for breakfast when Scott walked in looking more exhausted than the day before.

Catriona said, "You look so tired, Dad. Did you rest?"

He managed a smile. "Not really, but I'll be okay with a nap this afternoon."

"Why don't you take it easy for a few days?"

"I can't. I need to prepare the office for court this coming Wednesday. The past few months have been building for this moment, and I need to put some last-minute touches on my opening statement."

Peter interrupted. "No... you don't. The partners and I decided to wait until after the funeral to tell you that opposing counsel contacted us and asked for a continuance due to the unforeseen circumstances of the last few days. We agreed to a postponement, and according to Judge Cornell's docket schedule, we appear three weeks from tomorrow."

Scott stared in silence as the room rested in an awkward hush.

"Dad, why don't we go for a ride this afternoon?"

Scott ignored Catriona's request. "A postponement? Who called?"

"One of Frank's attorneys," Peter said as he sat his cup of coffee on the table.

"That makes little sense. Why wouldn't they use this to their advantage?"

"We planned to ask for a continuance ourselves... regardless of their plans. They just beat us to it."

Again, Scott was silent.

"Dad, did you hear me? Would you like to go for a ride? Tia and William, do you want to join us? I think Peter is leaving sometime this morning."

Tia looked up from putting jam on her toasted muffin. "No, thank you. We are planning to leave within the next couple of hours to give you some peace and quiet after the last few days."

Scott dropped his head. "Pardon my rudeness, Tia. I realized after I went to bed last night, I had not taken the time to thank you."

"For what?"

"How will I ever thank you for agreeing to sing at my darling wife's funeral? You did a beautiful job, and I will never forget it. Please do not leave on my account. I invite you both to stay for as long as you want."

Tia smiled. "It was my honor to do so, and I thank you, Mr. McKenna, but the shop is calling my name. I need to get back to business, and my Billy needs to return to his patients."

"Of course, you do. I'm not thinking clearly. William, I'm glad we finally met. Next time, it will be under better circumstances, I hope."

William wiped his mouth with his napkin. "Same here. I look forward to visiting again."

Tia whispered to Catriona, "We need to discuss a few business-related items before I leave."

"Sure... what about now? We can finish our meeting in my room upstairs... away from the noise of the rest of the house."

"That would be perfect."

Catriona asked, "Gentlemen, will you please excuse us?"

Peter grabbed her hand. "Catriona, we need to talk this morning... alone."

"Sure. What time are you leaving?"

"Within the next couple of hours. I have an important appointment this afternoon."

"Why don't you, Dad, and William walk to the stables or watch television in the family room until we're finished? I promise we won't be long."

Tia and Catriona dismissed themselves from the room, but not before Catriona leaned down and kissed her father on the forehead as she passed. Scott smiled up at her.

Peter turned toward William and asked, "Excuse me, but do you mind if I talk with Scott for a few minutes alone?"

"No problem. I need to pack and load the car so we can leave."

"Scott, may I have a few moments after you have finished your breakfast?"

"We can talk now. My appetite is pretty much gone. Please excuse us, William."

Scott and Peter walked into his study. "Take a seat. What is so urgent? Is this more information about the case?"

Peter cleared his throat. "Sir, the timing of this could not be more ill-planned. I thought I would ask this question with Lillian present, yet here is where we find ourselves. Again, I apologize for the timing."

"Spit it out, man. What question?" Scott frowned.

"Sir, I know you are aware of my deep feelings for your daughter. My relationship with Catriona has grown into one of mutual love and respect over the past few weeks. With your permission, I want to ask for Catriona's hand in marriage. May I have your blessing?"

Scott looked somewhat stunned. "Is Katydid aware of your feelings?"

"Of course." Peter's eyes widened. "Why would you ask?"

"Oh, I don't know. I'm good at reading my daughter, and she has mentioned none of this to me… nor Lillian, that I'm aware. I would have thought this would have happened a little later in your relationship… if at all."

"We love each other. We have spent time with one another and understand her issues. Maybe she isn't comfortable discussing how deep our relationship has grown under the recent circumstances."

"Forgive my candidness, Peter, but you have caught me completely unaware. Help me understand. When you mentioned an announcement last week, you meant a wedding proposal? I thought the firm had presented the junior partnership papers I had drawn up recently."

"A partnership with The McKenna Law Firm?"

"Yes. You have proven to be a great asset and a trustworthy candidate."

"I am overwhelmed. Thank you, sir."

"We have time to discuss those plans later. At the moment, let's stay focused on the matter at hand. I am sure Catriona will be more surprised than me regarding your proposal. How well do you know of her current mental condition?"

"She has everything under control as far as I know."

"Really? She's in a dark place emotionally and has shown signs of self-destruction according to her psychiatrist. Are you aware?"

Peter's brows turned downward. He hesitated before replying. "I am, and Catriona is more than aware of my intentions. You would have no worries regarding her well-being. I would take excellent care of her and we would be happy."

"I know you have the means to take care of her, but Catriona has been battling demons her entire life, and now, within the nightmare we find ourselves, I could not agree more with your first statement. Your timing is definitely ill-planned."

"Yes, I understand with the loss of Lillian, this makes it more difficult. Catriona is everything I could want in a spouse. She is smart, loyal, sweet, and beautiful too. Our relationship is one of deep respect and admiration for one another."

"Have you discussed children?"

"I'm fine either way."

"That's good to know." Scott paused for a moment and thought how much Lillian would have loved knowing her daughter would marry a good man. He then allowed himself to agree. "Peter, I could not be more pleased. I'm sure Lillian would be as well. When are you planning to ask?"

"This morning."

"This morning?" Scott frowned again.

"Yes."

"Why the rush?"

"I'm hoping we can marry before the new year."

"Really? You do know you are marrying a Southern woman, right?"

"What does that mean?" Peter shifted in his chair.

"A wedding takes months to plan. I'm not sure it can be done in less than two."

"I'm sure we can and must."

"Must?"

"I know I said I am fine either way, but there may be a baby on the way."

"What?" Scott leaned back in his chair. "Catriona's pregnant?"

"There is that probability, sir."

"A baby? My precious Katydid. Why wouldn't she say?" Scott's eyes beamed with tears.

"We decided to wait. Besides, I'm planning to run for what will be Virginia's vacant state senatorial seat next year once we wrap up this case. I know a wedding will be difficult to arrange from the backseat of a campaign bus, so the sooner, the better."

"Senatorial race too? Is Catriona aware of these plans and with a baby on the way?"

"The baby has not been confirmed... not yet, and we have discussed politics several times." Peter could tell Scott was taken back by the surprised look on his face. *I have him in my pocket.*

"You are hitting me from all angles this morning. When did Catriona express an interest in politics? My word, I don't know my own daughter, do I?"

"Your friend, Senator Williams, is pushing me to run upon his retirement. He has not announced his plans formally, but I have his full endorsement, and with my newborn and soon-to-be beautiful wife standing next to me, how can I lose?"

"Wait... Nathan Williams? Retiring? Well, good for him; bad for us. He is a trusted friend. I guess I have been so caught up in the craziness of this case and my dear Lillian, I was unaware Katydid felt this way. I feel unattached suddenly."

"Sir, may I ask you not to say anything to Catriona about the baby? She will want to tell you herself."

"Of course... it should be her announcement." Scott looked at Peter in amazement. "Truth be told, Peter, I'm not sure how to respond. For the first time in my life, I'm without words. But yes, I give you and my daughter my blessing. I wish Lillian were here."

"Thank you. I do too. Your approval means more to me than you know."

"Do you have something special planned? Do you have a ring?"

"I have my mother's ring upstairs in my room. Before she passed, she gave it to me for my future bride."

"I see. We have all suffered great losses, haven't we?"

"Yes, and that is why I do not want to delay."

Scott came from around the back of his desk and offered his hand to Peter. "I guess there is not much more to say except I wish you all the best."

"Thank you, sir." They shook hands, and then Scott hugged him.

"Welcome to our family. I find myself feeling better. I was dreading the day after the funeral, but you have given me something to focus on besides myself... a baby. Thank you for telling me. I know Lillian would be happy. Let me know when you are planning to ask and I'll make sure Cookie has champagne ready. Where were you planning to propose... the gardens?"

"No. I want to ask in front of her family in the main foyer. I think she would like for all of you to be included."

"Are you sure?"

"I am." Scott thought of Lillian. He knew she should be here to orchestrate this impromptu event, but he also knew he needed to do this for Katydid. "The girls are upstairs, so let's gather everyone into the living room, and when you ask her, we will join you in the foyer. Cookie will be overjoyed."

"I'll get the ring."

"Right... right. You get the ring... that's a good idea. We will meet you in the living room in five minutes. We need to hurry, don't we?"

"Yes, we do, sir." Peter smiled. *One down, and one to go. Too easy.*

***

Upstairs in Catriona's room, Tia said, "The weirdest thing happened the other day at the shop. I thought of calling you, but with everything that has happened this week, I thought it better to wait."

"What thing?"

"I was sitting in the office when a man entered the shop. He did not look like our regular clientele. To be frank, the way he was creeping around and staring at me, I thought he was trying to steal merchandise. He tapped on the office glass, so I walked out to talk with him. He asked if you ran the place and then said you attended school together."

"That's impossible. I went to an all-girls school."

"I thought so and told him as much. He said you were friends from long ago, and then he made a crude slur toward me."

"What did he say?"

"Not worth repeating."

"I can't believe you didn't throw him out. You should have."

"If it had been anyone else... but you didn't see him. He gave me the creeps. I remember thinking he couldn't be your friend, but then the florist arrived to put the funeral wreath on the door. I left him for a moment, and Percy came downstairs to help him. Poor Percy. The man asked where he could reach you regarding the funeral arrangements, and I'm afraid Percy gave him the name of the church. Then the man left. He didn't leave a name. The whole thing seemed untoward."

"Odd. I wonder..."

"Wonder what?"

"Was he wearing a dark ball cap?"

"Yes, he was. Why?"

Peter knocked on the door as he passed. "Hey, girls, we are waiting downstairs for you."

Tia laughed. "We'll be right there."

Soon, Catriona and Tia descended the stairs when Peter and William appeared at the bottom of the landing. William spoke first.

"Tia, would you join me in the living room for a moment? Scott wants to ask you something before we leave."

"Sure." Tia looked at him with a weird expression as he was smiling ear-to-ear. "Are you okay?"

"I'm fine, sweetheart." He reached out and held her hand as they disappeared behind the double doors.

Peter was blocking the stairs so Catriona could not pass.

"Peter, what are you doing? Please step aside so I can join everyone."

"May we take a moment? I need to ask you something."

"What do you want?"

The living room double doors opened, and Scott, Cookie, Samuel, along with Tia and William, were facing her with champagne flutes in hand. Peter pulled the velvet box from his jacket and bent one knee to the floor. "Catriona…"

"Peter… wait."

"Catriona, will you marry me?"

"What?"

Scott and Cookie were the first with arms extended. Scott said, "I'm so happy for you, darling."

"You are?" Catriona's jaw dropped.

Again, Peter asked, "Catriona, what is your answer?"

Cookie blurted out, "She says 'yes', of course!"

Everyone laughed, except Catriona. Peter took her hand and placed the ring on her finger. It was a large vintage solitaire, and she half-smiled. She needed Lillian. She wanted to run, but seeing everyone's cheerful faces, especially her father, she said nothing.

Peter said, "I want to hear you say it."

Realizing she had no choice, she whispered a quiet, "Yes."

Peter kissed her and everyone shouted their congratulations.

"Someone, grab her a glass of champagne. As the father of the bride… oh, I like how that sounds. As the father of the bride, allow me the first toast. Please, everyone, raise your glasses. Katydid, my darling girl… your momma and daddy… that is, Katie Jo and Bill… and your mother of the heart, Lillian, would be the first to join me in wishing you and Peter the greatest happiness life can offer. Peter, take care of my treasure, my heart, my Katydid. I love you, sweet girl. Here's to you both. Drink up… cheers!"

Everyone hugged one another and clamored on about the ring as she played the part of the new blushing fiancée; however, she was shaking in disbelief.

"When is the big day?" Tia whispered in her ear. "I cannot believe you have not talked about Peter when I thought Declan was the one."

"I don't know the date. This was unexpected."

Tia stepped back and looked at her. "It was?"

Scott interrupted. "Katydid, my heart is full. I'm not sure I could have made it through the next few weeks with the holidays upon us, but now, I have something to look forward to helping you plan... and my checkbook is yours. You buy the biggest and prettiest dress your heart desires and whatever else you need. No need to ask in advance. You may have as many guests as you wish, and I will have a great number to invite as well... that is if it's okay with you?"

"Of course. Whatever you wish. I do ask you not to announce the engagement... not yet. This is a little much considering Mother's funeral was only yesterday."

Her words cut through him. Scott placed the champagne flute on the mantle and walked into the kitchen. She followed him, leaving everyone still congratulating Peter.

"Dad, I'm sorry. May we keep this quiet for now? Please?"

"I would have it no other way. For the record, I would never disrespect your mother with an announcement so soon. You should know better."

"Please forgive me. It's inexcusable." She hugged him tightly. He held her too.

Peter walked in with everyone tagging along behind him.

"I hope I'm not interrupting anything, but I need to head to the city."

"So soon?" Catriona looked even more surprised.

Cookie replied, "Aww... she is already talking like a new fiancée. Peter, I want you to take a few slices of my pound cake so you can eat some later this afternoon." Cookie had grabbed a knife and was cutting into the dessert before he could answer no.

"Thank you, Cookie." Peter smiled.

Samuel interrupted. "I hope you're going to save us a slice of cake."

Cookie laughed. "Sure. If you will, please go to the cellar and bring another bottle of champagne. We are going to need it."

Catriona reached over and held Peter's hand. She whispered, "May we talk alone for a minute?"

"Of course. Walk me to my car." Peter turned to everyone and said, "Thank you for the good wishes. I'm sorry to leave this great party, but I do have to leave."

Everyone cheered again and then remained chatting as the couple walked through the door.

Catriona walked into the hallway. "I wish we had discussed marriage before you proposed in front of everyone."

"We did. I know it may seem harsh with the events of this past week, but it was going to happen eventually."

"We have never discussed marriage."

"Yes, we have. Remember?"

"I don't remember."

"Yes, you do. It was the evening we returned from the races. I had to fight you off, but not before you begged me to marry you. What was I supposed to say? No? I told you I would marry you. You told me you loved me. We made big plans… a house, kids, adopting a pet or two. I certainly couldn't turn you down after our night together. You were perfection." He kissed her on the lips.

"I seriously do not remember."

"Catriona, you are hurting me deeply. We made love… you were wonderful. Please tell me you remember."

Catriona stared at him. "We did?"

"Yes, of course. We are getting married so no more discussion. Not today. If I had not made an appointment this afternoon with Senator Williams, I would take you to bed and we would make love the remainder of the day. You are a beautiful woman and I want you to be my bride. I could not be happier. Okay?"

She nodded her head in agreement.

He kissed her again. "I love you."

She looked down at her hand. "The ring is breathtaking."

"It was my mother's ring."

"It was?" She choked back tears. Things representing family were dear, especially now.

"Yes, it was. We can have it sized."

"No. It fits perfectly, and it is beautiful."

"It was meant to be on your finger. We're going to be fine. In fact, we will have a life to be envied. Trust me." He kissed her again.

"I've never concerned myself with what others envied. I only want to be happy, don't you?"

Scott walked through the front door carrying pound cake in its container. He beamed when he saw them together. "You two look better together each time I see you. I don't know how I could have missed the feelings so obvious between you. You have made me proud, and it will be good to have another man in the family." Scott handed him the container.

"Thank you, Scott. I appreciate you saying so." Peter shook his hand.

Catriona blinked back the tears when she saw the smile on her father's face. "Thank you, Dad."

Peter kissed her again on the cheek. "I have to go, my darling. I'll call you tonight."

"Okay… drive safely."

Peter waved as he pulled out of the drive. Catriona reached for Scott's hand and realized her decision had been made. She would do anything to take away her father's sadness, even if it meant marrying a man she did not love at the moment, but maybe she could learn to love him in time.

"Katydid, what's wrong?"

"Nothing. I was thinking, that's all. So, you want a big wedding, huh?"

He threw back his head and laughed. "If that is what you want, little girl. The world is yours."

"I never pictured having a big wedding... not really; I have never pictured myself ever getting married."

"Oh, honey. You were meant to be loved and loved deeply. I'm happy you have Peter."

"You know, I am thinking a big wedding is exactly what you and Peter will want." She laughed. "You better start making an invitation list while you're home this afternoon. Does Lillian keep her addresses on her computer?"

"She does. I'll find her laptop for you. By the way, she never knew, but I have always known her password."

"Have you really?"

"Well, you never know when an extra laptop might come in handy." He laughed again. "I will begin working on my list, but first, let's dive into a piece of pound cake waiting for us in the kitchen."

"Sounds good to me."

"Are you happy, Katydid?"

"You know, I think I am." The answer surprised her.

"Good. Well, there is no time like the present; we might as well start practicing for your big day."

"And how do we do that, kind sir?"

"Like this..." He extended his arm, and she smiled as she rested her hand on the bend of his elbow. They walked arm-in-arm into the kitchen and were greeted again with cheers as they reached for another flute of champagne.

***

Later in the afternoon, after everyone had parted ways, the house grew still, and she craved the quietness. She knew Scott would be resting as he was lost to a world of disbelief, although the engagement seemed to have lifted his spirits for a brief moment.

Samson and Delilah followed as she crossed the room to her favorite space in Lillian's office. Stepping out of her mules, she nestled into the familiar, overstuffed pillows propped against the window seat while continuing to hold a warm cup of tea to keep her company. Both dogs paced back-and-forth yearning to be held.

"You miss her too, don't you, sweet babies?"

The dogs whined until she lifted each to their rightful place. As they snuggled next to her, she took Lillian's shawl tossed to the side and wrapped it tightly around her shoulders as she pulled her knees toward her. Soon, she found her mind locked in the seat of an emotional roller coaster running out of control.

The last beam of sunlight poured through the blown glass of the old panes, casting a distorted, looming shadow of the window onto the floor below. She watched the illuminated dust particles float aimlessly through the air, appearing to be captured within the only light source flooding the room. She blew into the air, interrupting the poorly choreographed ballet while scattering the foreign bodies into the atmosphere. They appeared to vanish offstage into the shadows before landing unwelcomed onto a piece of furniture or anywhere dust rests once wisped into the darkness. If only she could disappear as quiet and unnoticed.

The clean aroma of Lillian's perfume lingered on the silk wrap, and Catriona breathed it in, yearning for her mother to step through her office door once more, yet realizing it would never happen. Quiet sobs could be heard as she buried her face in the soft fabric. Her head throbbed as she tried to understand the events of the last few days. How would she survive without her? Lillian had been her closest friend and confidant. Catriona thought her heart would burst from the crushing weight of her grief. As she wiped her eyes with the damp tissue wadded in her hand, the ring caught her eye.

She stretched out her left hand into the fading, natural bright light, then wiggled her fingers back and forth. She watched the diamond facets glisten as each cast its prism around the somber room as though reflected from a mirrored ball. She stopped and stared at the precious stone through tear-filled eyes, wondering if Peter was the answer to having a life of peace without pain and turmoil. Would God allow her to live such a life? *Does He allow anyone to live such a life?*

Viewing the gardens from her window above, she reasoned with herself. Maybe she had been too hasty in her evaluation of Peter the day before. Although he had been overbearing with gifts, there was no reason to doubt his genuine affection for her. Funny, it was then Declan crossed her mind. She reasoned her affections toward Declan had been nothing but physical, and now she would devote her life and love to Peter. Without warning, tears fell again as she longed to hear her mother's voice of reason. She looked at the beautiful setting on her finger. *Mother would know what to do.* Lillian always did.

Interrupting the stillness, a voice came through the intercom. "Catriona, you have a phone call, honey."

She placed the cup on the desk and wiped her eyes. "Who is it, Cookie? I'm too tired to talk."

"It's Peter… line two."

There was silence.

"Catriona?"

"Sorry… yes, I'll take it. Thank you." She had been so lost in her thoughts she had not heard the phone ring. She sat at Lillian's desk and reached for the receiver. Taking a deep breath and releasing the air through her lips, she regained her composure as she pressed the number two on the keypad. "Hello, Peter?"

"Hello, darling. Are you better?"

"The same… I guess. I'm unsure how to feel if I am being honest. I cannot process everything." She cried and wanted someone to hold her. An all-too-familiar dark chill filled her. Surprised, she said, "I wish you were here."

"I wish I were too. It's nice to hear you say so."

She was having difficulty speaking into the phone.

"Catriona? Sweetheart? What do you want? I feel helpless here with you there."

"Me too."

"I know. Why don't you join me? It might do you good to come here for a few days. In fact, you can move in, if you wish. I will make the necessary arrangements."

"What? No. No, I'm not ready, Peter. Thank you, but the day will be here soon enough. Dad needs me and he is more important than me moving out. I have my house too. Besides… I want to be here. Please do not rush me."

"I'm trying to take your mind off what is happening there. I miss you, already."

"You are sweet, but you will be here tomorrow night. Right?"

"Tuesday."

Silence echoed from her end of the phone line.

"You know… forget Tuesday. It's only seven o'clock. I can drive back tonight."

"Don't be silly, Peter. I miss her. Why did this happen? None of this makes sense." Her voice trembled.

"I know you want your mother. It's understandable. You have experienced a terrible shock, and there are no straightforward answers. Rest assured, darling, if I did not have to be here for Scott tomorrow, I would be with you. I do hope you know if given the choice, I would never leave you alone."

"Thank you. I needed to hear those words more than you know." She relaxed.

"I have exciting things to discuss, but they can wait."

"Please. I cannot handle anything further today."

"I understand. You should rest; however, we need to visit my father to announce our engagement. I have cleared my calendar for Wednesday."

"Of course. Wednesday works."

"He will love you as much as I do, and then we can announce our engagement to the world."

"Slow down. It will be Scott's decision. I'm not planning to do anything soon out of respect for my mother. The funeral was only yesterday."

"I'm excited… that's all. And don't worry, Cat. I'm only a phone call away if you need me. Text and I'll return your call immediately. It may take a moment to excuse myself from the meetings tomorrow, but it won't be an issue."

"Cat?" She smiled. "You called me, 'Cat.' No one has ever called me anything but Catriona or Katydid."

"Did I? Well, that's how you will be known to me… my sweet, Cat."

"We'll see." She laughed.

"No worries. If nothing else, I made you laugh at least. If I can keep you laughing, then I've done my job. Right?"

"I guess so…" Her voice dropped and guilt overwhelmed her again. "Is it okay to laugh, Peter? Is it really?"

"Of course, it is. We shall spend our lives laughing."

"You promise?"

"I promise to love you."

She did not reply.

Listening to the silence again, he sighed. "I need to go. Sleep well. I'll call tomorrow."

"You have lifted my spirits."

"I'm glad. Good night." The line went silent, then a dial tone buzzed in her ear.

"Later…" she whispered into the phone. Looking at the ring on her finger, she was more aware of what she had agreed to do. Hopefully, the engagement would be lengthy so she could get used to the idea, and maybe allow herself time to fall in love with the man she had promised to marry.

She turned slowly in Lillian's swivel chair as she looked around the office. Her heart was broken. She thought she might crumble knowing she would never hear her words of wisdom or her laughter again. She could not comprehend the magnitude of their loss. Lillian had been the heartbeat of their home.

The door opened, and Scott popped his head around the door. "Hey, doll. May I come in?"

"Sure, but please do not have anyone lurking in the hallway with you."

"No. Only me. You look natural sitting behind her desk."

"You can't mean it… not yet… I refuse to go there."

"Understood. Me either, that is, if you want the truth, and nothing, but the truth."

"I always want the truth. You know me."

"I do. What do you want to do this very moment?"

She replied, "It's too late to ride, but tomorrow, Angel and I want to be left alone. There has not been a moment of silence in days. I crave it."

"Sounds like a good idea, but depending on when you leave, it could be cold. Dress warm enough."

"I will."

"Are you sure you want to go alone?"

"Yes, sir. I have had no blackouts or flashbacks in a couple of weeks. You will not realize I'm gone. Promise."

"It's been a big day. I'm going to bed and attempt to sleep. We can talk more about your wedding tomorrow if you want."

"No… let's not. Peter will be here on Tuesday evening. We are going to see his father on Wednesday. We can talk afterward."

"This is really happening, isn't it?"

"It is." She looked at the ring on her finger.

"Are you happy?"

"I haven't given it much thought."

"Do not let Peter talk you into doing something you don't want."

"I won't."

"Good. When is your next doctor's appointment? I want you to stay on top of your treatments."

"I will and I'm remembering more each day." She struggled to keep her eyes opened and yawned. "I think I'm calling for an early evening too. My body is crashing for some much-needed rest."

"I know the feeling."

"I love you, Dad. I am so sorry."

He nodded his head. "Me too. We will be fine. We need to think about what she would want if the tables were turned. She would want us to grieve, but not wallow. That is my goal. I don't want to wallow.

Promise me we will work through this pain together because I cannot do this alone."

"I promise. Together… we'll take one second at a time." She hugged him as tears fell.

"Shh, don't cry. We are going to be okay."

"You think?"

"We have each other, don't we? Lillian would be mad if we continued to feel sorry for ourselves. I can hear her. 'Scott, straighten up! We don't have time for this foolishness!'"

"That is exactly what she would say." She smiled and held her father tighter. She knew she was safe in his arms.

"I need to apologize." She stepped back and looked into his warm blue eyes.

"For what?"

"For thinking only of myself. I have acted foolishly lately."

"If I had to apologize for each time I've felt sorry for myself these past days, I would be apologizing for a long time. Come on. Time for bed."

"I'll get the lights," she said.

"What would I do without you?"

Catriona smiled. "Let's not find out. Okay?"

CHAPTER 25

CATRIONA HURRIED TO dress into her riding gear. She knew Cookie would be scurrying about the kitchen, and she did not want to stop for breakfast. Creeping down the back staircase, she heard Cookie inside the pantry. Catriona glided through the door leading into the garden unseen. She rounded the stable doors and saw Declan standing with his back to her.

"Declan?" She walked toward him.

His shoulders jerked as he turned toward her. "You startled me."

She could see he had been crying. "Sorry. Everything, okay?"

"I'm fine. Having a tough go of it this morning; nothing I can't handle. I did not expect to see you this early."

She noticed his forced smile. "I forget everyone rises with the sun around here. I thought I would be the first one out this morning."

"No, not quite. All of us try to be here before seven; I showed around six today. I couldn't sleep, and besides, I enjoy the quietness of the stables."

"Me too. What are you doing at this moment?"

"I have finished going over the horse trailer for the umpteenth time. I understand a horse can bolt... that is why there are safety ropes. However, how a seasoned horse who has entered a trailer four hundred times could repeatedly bolt to where he would crush her..."

"He crushed her?" Her eyes opened from the shock.

"Forgive me. I'm not thinking." His voice cracked when he spoke. "You must know... Lillian... she..."

"You don't have to say anything." She reached her hand toward him and he grasped it. She squeezed his fingers hard.

"My behavior has been unprofessional. I am an employee of this estate, and yet, I cannot express how deeply her death has affected me. Truth be told, I'm re-evaluating my position here at Grace Meade."

"Don't be ridiculous; we are family and Lillian respected you. She certainly knew her horses and their behaviors, as well as the dangers, and she would never have allowed anyone to work alongside her who she did not trust... but you know that... right?"

"I do." He dropped his head. "However, I'm no longer the man Grace Meade needs in this position."

"Declan, you need to continue the work she started... no... the one her family started forever ago. Grace Meade needs you more than ever. I need you."

"Thank you."

She touched his face. "You do not know what it means to me knowing you cared. Grace Meade cannot move forward without you running the business. This family cannot take losing another person. Not now."

"I have decided to go."

"I won't allow you to leave. It's not permitted."

"Catriona... please. I'm not looking for sympathy or a compliment. God knows my thoughts on this. I cannot do my work without seeing her beautiful face." He took both of her hands in his.

Catriona smiled up at him. "You know, I thought I wanted to ride alone, but I've changed my mind. Will you join me? I think we could use the fresh air."

"No. I have errands to run in town. Maybe another time."

"Are you asking me to beg, Mr. O'Connell?" She smiled.

He returned the same. "I would never ask you to stoop so low, Miss McKenna." He dropped her hands. "I guess I can run errands this afternoon, but it will have to be a quick ride."

"Grace Meade comes first, as it should. I may stay out longer, but you riding with me for any amount of time would be welcomed."

"Give me a second." He walked toward his office and called out, "Hey, Charlie? Are you here?"

"Yes, sir."

"Will you help Catriona with Angel? We'll be riding for a short while."

"Sure thing, Declan."

Turning toward Catriona, he said, "Would you like a thermos of coffee?"

"No, I have water, but thank you."

"Let's meet by the gate."

She mounted Angel and rode out toward the opening leading into the fields when Samuel yelled from his truck. "Hey, where are you going so early?"

"Declan and I are headed out for a morning ride. Do you want to come with us?"

"No, sweet girl. These old limbs haven't been on the back of a horse since I can't say when. Besides, I dropped by to talk to Scott. Is he still here?"

"Yes. You can catch him at breakfast."

"I'll do that… have fun."

"I will." She turned toward the pasture as Declan rode beside her.

He asked, "Are you ready?"

"Ready as I'll ever be." As she caused Angel to bolt and charge out into the field ahead, she shouted back toward him, "Race you to the top of the knoll!"

Samuel laughed. "Looks like she's winning, Grandson."

"Not for long…" He popped the reins in pursuit of catching her.

***

Samuel shook his head as he walked toward the main house. He whispered as he watched the horses disappear. "Peter better return soon if he knows what's good for him. Those two have too much spark between'em. Yes, sir… too much spark."

"Who are you talking to, Samuel?" Cookie asked, standing in the doorway.

"Only the smartest man I know." He laughed as he opened the door. "Is Scott in?"

"He's at the table. Would you like a cup of coffee?"

"Sounds good."

"Good morning, Samuel. You need me?" Scott sat the newspaper next to him.

"I dropped in to see how you are doing. Thought you might like to talk a minute or two."

"I could be better, but I'm back to work this morning. Let's talk later. I need to make a phone call."

Samuel smiled. "Sounds good. Work helps the soul. Well, my good man, looks like I'm not needed here. I reckon I'll head to the house. If you don't mind, I think I'll take a cup of coffee with me."

Cookie laughed. "You make sure you return the cup this time."

The phone rang. It was Sheriff Wells.

"Scott, it's for you."

"Hello?... Yes, this is he... I didn't know you had a security tape... Declan? Yes. I trust him with my life. Why?... You have this all wrong. Declan is a good man. He is as honest as the day is long, but sure, I'll be happy to come by tomorrow. What time?... May I bring someone with me?... Great. I'll see you at ten. Goodbye." Scott put down the receiver.

Samuel asked, "What was that about?"

"I'm not sure, but there appears to be something on one of the security tapes regarding Lillian's accident. Would you like to go with me tomorrow?"

"Yeah. I'll go with you. Why was he asking about Declan?"

"He said he saw Declan on the tape. Does Declan own a ball cap?"

"I've never seen him wear one."

"Then there is nothing to worry about."

***

When Declan caught up with her, she was laughing.

"You move kind of slow for a man so young. Someone might get the impression you can't keep up."

"Did you insinuate I'm old?"

"I did." She laughed. It was the first time she had laughed without guilt since Lillian's accident.

"You cheated," he said.

"You are a sore loser."

"Whatever... but we know the truth, don't we? So where are we headed?"

She swiped her hair behind her ear. "I don't know. Why don't we let the horses decide?"

"Sounds good."

They rode in silence as the horses walked over the rolling knoll. Before reaching the woods, the mood turned dark.

Declan broke the silence. "The guilt is overwhelming."

"Please tell me what happened. The therapist once said if you talk about it, you can begin healing yourself from within."

"Meaning?"

"I have felt such guilt about my parents' deaths because I survived. Not remembering makes it even more disturbing. Regardless, the guilt of living remains. It has almost destroyed me. You should talk to someone."

"I guess, but that is where we differ. No offense, but I do remember. I did not have the break-away on him... solely my fault. The safety of this estate falls to me, and the people on this property are my responsibility."

"Sometimes unrelenting guilt of witnessing death through no fault of your own can be just as emotionally detrimental if not more so than someone who's killed with forethought. Trust me, I'm speaking from experience. Please tell me what happened."

"You are not ready. It's too raw."

"I need to know. Maybe I had not expected to hear so soon, but if it will help you, then maybe, in the long run, it will help me too."

Declan stopped his horse. "Why don't we allow the horses to graze? We need to stand for this conversation."

They dismounted and flipped their reins over the saddles. Declan told his story, leaving nothing to the imagination. When she cried out in pain, Declan wrapped his arms around her, and they wept together.

She whispered, "Please don't leave Grace Meade." Removing her gloves, she wiped away his tears with her hand. She liked the familiar grooves in his face. "None of us are thinking clearly, so please don't make any life-changing decisions."

It was then she remembered the ring on her finger. She dropped her arms and backed away, realizing where she was, and to whom she had made a promise.

Declan said, "I have never been dishonest with you, and I do not plan to start now. I need time away."

"Forgive me, Declan, but I must go."

"Why?"

"Nothing. I'll be fine. I just need to ride."

Bewildered, he said, "Sure. Give me a second to help you."

There were no words spoken as he helped set her feet in the stirrups. When he reached for her hand, the ring caught his eye.

"What is this?"

"Oh... that. We need to talk, Declan." Her face beamed with redness in her cheeks.

"Catriona?"

"Peter has asked me to marry him, and I've accepted."

He showed no emotion. "When?"

"It happened yesterday."

"Yesterday? I didn't know."

"I meant to tell you, but it happened rather quickly."

His lips closed and deep lines furrowed into his brow.

"Declan?" The muscles in her throat tightened.

"Give me a moment, will you?" He turned his face from her, but within the breath of an instant, everything changed. He looked back. "Forgive me. I guess I should offer my congratulations."

She recognized the fake smile as he reached out to shake her hand. She hesitated, but she shook it. "Thank you. I hope you will stay as long as possible. Please try… at least for a little while."

"I wish you every happiness."

"Thank you." They continued to stare at one another. She whispered, "Declan?"

"Yes?"

"Forget it…"

"No. Forget what?"

"Let's talk when I return," she said.

"My schedule is tight for the rest of the day, and I have errands tomorrow as well. I might have some free time tomorrow evening."

"No. Peter will be here. We have made plans."

"There is nothing further to say. If you are happy, then nothing else matters. When is the big day?"

"I don't know… too soon to ask." She choked back more tears.

"Are you sure you want to continue to ride? Maybe you should come back to the stables with me."

"No. I need the quietness." She hesitated but remained true. "Please don't worry about me. This is what I do… it's my therapy. I'm not sure when I'll return, but let Charlie know I'll be much later. In fact, I may stay out all day."

"Be careful."

"I will. You have been kind to tell me about Mother. Thank you for your honesty. I need time to process what has happened to her."

"I understand. One more thing…"

"Yes?"

"Before I leave, always know I loved Lillian too."

She nodded in agreement. "I know. Thank you for saying so."

He released her hand and backed away from Angel. "Goodbye, Catriona. Charlie will be at the stables when you return."

He mounted his horse and did not look back.

Looking down at her hand, Catriona removed the ring and placed it in her pant pocket. She wanted no further distractions today.

Snapping the reins, she took to a full gallop into the field beyond. The cold air rushed against her face, releasing the past days' strains. She wanted to cry out but was afraid Angel would be frightened. Instead, she forced a silent scream into the endless sky above and wept. She pushed the black beauty harder and harder until the horse was struggling to breathe under the guidance of her uncontrolled rider. The horse's nostrils flared steam with every grueling breath appearing more like a locomotive than an animal. Catriona reached the lake and stopped the horse only moments before they would have exploded into the frigid water.

"Whoa, girl! Whoa!"

Angel stopped, almost throwing Catriona from the saddle. The horse stood tall shaking her mane hard and flipping her tail as if she too were cleansed by the purification of the dropping temperature.

"Cold. Isn't it, girl?"

She snorted in response. Catriona patted her soft mane.

"Sorry, sweetie. I'm sorry. I have pushed you into my insanity, haven't I?" She reached out and patted her neck again. Angel shifted her weight from one leg to the other and swiped her tail back and forth over her back as if to straighten the tangles. Catriona allowed herself to laugh out loud.

"Okay. I understand, girl." She pushed her hair from her face. "Am I doing the right thing, Angel?"

The horse snorted again.

"Was that a yes or no?" The horse did not respond this time.

"Fine, don't answer me. I know… let's visit Samuel. He can help me find my way. I promise to take the ride slower this time."

Catriona meandered her way around the lake and proceeded toward the northern corner of the property. She had forgotten how pretty the land sloped upward toward the small spring house. She could see Samuel's house in the distance, calling her to take refuge within its walls. As she approached, she spotted Samuel's truck located near the house and not in the garage where he normally parked. She frowned, then jumped from her saddle and tied Angel to the antique hitching post beside the end of the porch.

"I won't be long. I'll call the main house and let them know we're here."

The horse nodded as if she understood every word. Catriona laughed as she patted her on the muzzle. Angel nickered low. As she turned toward the front door, she noticed it ajar. She looked around. Seeing no one, she called out, "Samuel?"

Angel threw back her head and released a loud snort.

***

Scott excused himself from the kitchen table and retreated to his office. He knew in his gut something appeared to be wrong with the court date postponement. Picking up the phone, he called Jamie Schwartz, one of the firm's partners, asking him to meet at Grace Meade.

When Jamie arrived, Scott discussed his concerns.

"You can't be serious, Scott."

"You heard me. I want to know why Thaddeus Frank's attorneys have asked for a continuance. If the circumstances were turned, our firm would be all over this."

"No, we would not. We would never lower ourselves to their level of suspected, unethical practices, and you know it. And guess what, it appears they may not be the asses we considered them to be. Your grief is talking. My word, Scott, you only buried Lillian a couple of days ago. We need you to be in the right mindset in three weeks."

"Is that our definite timeline?"

"Yes. We met in Judges Chambers on the Monday following Lillian's death. Everyone agreed it was the right thing to do under the circumstances."

"I'm telling you, Jamie, it feels wrong. They have a weak case. As my Grandmother Dunne used to say, 'Something stinks to the high heavens, and I want to know what's smelling!'" He threw the file he held in his hand across the room.

"Scott, calm down. I feel you are reading too much into this. Everyone is genuinely concerned about you, man. Lillian's death has shocked us all."

Scott stood from behind his desk. "I did not ask you to change the court date. I asked you to find out why it changed. Call your friend, Robert Proctor. He has the contacts so he would be my first choice."

"As your friend, I will do this; however, it's unnecessary."

"I'm not asking as a friend."

"Fine." Jamie shook his head.

"You can make the call from here. Oh, and one more thing, ask Robert to contact Della Wells in Judge Cooper's office. She might have the inside scoop."

"Will do."

"Let's keep this quiet… just between us. We need to sort this out immediately. Also, if Robert needs to hire another investigator, he has my permission."

"Of course."

"And Jamie…"

"What?"

"Forgive my temper. I appreciate you coming to update me on the status of this case. We could not discuss this in the office… surely, you can understand. I have been out of sorts the past few days. We cannot lose. I refuse to lose to this poor excuse of a human being."

"We will not lose. Everything is in our favor."

"One last thing. I appreciate everyone's concern. Thank you for being a good friend."

"No worries, man. It's the least I can do. I'll have an answer for you soon."

"After your call, please come to the kitchen. I have asked Cookie to prepare lunch for us. Not a word to anyone. Understand?"

"Sure thing."

Scott walked into the hallway and closed the door behind him. As he entered the kitchen, he could smell Cookie's homemade chicken and dumplings. "You know exactly what I needed today… comfort food."

"I thought so. It seemed appropriate on such a chilly day. Everything is ready when you are."

"Where is Katydid?" he asked.

"I haven't seen her, but sleeping in is her normal lately. The poor thing is exhausted and needs her rest so I have not bothered her today."

"I thought she was planning a ride early this morning. Funny… she must have changed her mind."

"I'll check on her later."

"I guess we should begin thinking about wedding guests."

"Now, that is a positive distraction we can sink ourselves into. Has Katydid said anything about a venue or caterer? I hope she knows I'll prepare whatever she wants."

"I won't hear of it. You are not working on her wedding day."

"But I want to do something," Cookie said.

"All right… let's think. I know. You choose the best caterer available, but that is all. She will need you by her side. I guess the food depends on Katydid's wishes. Will they want to hold the reception here or in the city?"

"Surely, she will have the wedding at Grace Meade. I cannot imagine anywhere else."

Jamie rubbed his chin as he walked into the kitchen.

"Are you okay?" Scott asked.

"Yes, I have taken care of everything as asked. We should have an answer within a day or two."

"Good. Why the look of concern?"

"I'm stumped."

"Why?"

Jamie walked toward the stovetop and lifted the pot lid. "Cookie, I cannot figure out what savory aroma is filling the house, but it will be delicious, I'm sure."

Cookie laughed. "Oh, Mr. Schwartz, you have never been short on flatteries. It's my chicken and dumplings."

Scott said, "And the best in Virginia, I might add."

She blushed. "Thank you."

The phone rang.

"I'll get it. You two be seated, but first, serve yourselves." Cookie reached for the phone. "Grace Meade Estate, how may I help you…" She frowned. "Scott?" She motioned for him to take the receiver.

"Who is it?"

"Sheriff Royster. He says it's urgent."

"I'll take it in my study. Jamie, this may take a moment. Please… go ahead without me. Hopefully, I would be long."

"Mr. Royster, he will be right with you."

Scott disappeared into his study. When Blake stopped to take a breath between sentences, Scott sank slowly into his chair. He could not believe Blake's words. "What do you mean, he's in this area?"

"A few people who were attending the funeral identified Daniel Tackett by the picture we had circulating across several news channels. He was there, Scott."

"What picture? It's been more than twenty years since anyone has seen him."

"After Catriona identified his yearbook picture, we typed his name into the State's database. We received a current picture from his prison records. Apparently, he has been in the penal system for the past fifteen years on drug charges and attempted armed robbery. Arson too. They released him a couple of months ago."

"That can't be right. Why such a short sentence?"

"The original sentence was twenty-five years… should have been longer considering the charges. At first, Tackett proved to be violent on the inside… a couple of squabbles, but none were deadly. Ironically, he has kept his nose clean over the past few years… a model prisoner, you could say. I spoke to a couple of guards who said they considered him to be highly dangerous. However, they said he had become proficient in playing the game, and no one touched him… he was smart and deadly."

"So how did he get out?"

"His mother had been diagnosed with terminal cancer and no one to care for her. He petitioned the court for a compassionate release, and unbelievably, was freed in August based on time served and exemplary behavior. I reckon the system no longer considered him a threat. He returned to Sageville and has been caring for her at home."

"Is he still in town?"

"Not at the moment… his mother is dead. We believe he is in The Plains."

"Here? Are you certain?"

"Yeah, I am. Preacher woke earlier today and identified him as the man who attacked him."

"He's awake? Oh, thank God. It will thrill Catriona to hear it."

"And something else… once we started asking people in Sageville about him, it turns out Erline at the café has been keeping his return a secret. She is nuttier than a fruitcake. I swear, if her lips are moving, then you can bet she's lying. When we identified him as Preacher's attacker and that he may have killed Bill and Katie Jo too, she sang louder than if she was the lead soloist in the town's Christmas Cantata. It's him, Scott. Daub Tackett."

"I don't believe it. Why would he be in The Plains if we have been so careful protecting Katydid's identity?"

"You are kidding me, right? Think, man! You and Catriona show up in town asking questions and tearing up the old home place, and there she is, looking like the carbon copy of her momma. What did you think would happen? People around here have not talked about anything since. You throw in the terrible news surrounding Lillian's death… God rest her soul… and with your pictures plastered across every newspaper and broadcast between here and Washington, of course, he knows not only who she is, but where she is. It wouldn't surprise me if he were the one who approached her on the porch."

"Why would he come here? For what purpose?"

"He must think she knows something."

"Like what? She remembers so little."

"He doesn't know that... hell, I don't know what the man is thinking, but he was at Lillian's service. People called us."

"Are you coming here?"

"I'm already on my way, but you will need to protect yourselves. Hire protection immediately... a couple of security guards might be the ticket. I'll call the police in The Plains and Fairfax to send a couple of their off-duty officers to stay on the property if you prefer. I have already contacted the VBI. I'm faxing his current picture over to you now."

Scott was dumbfounded.

"Scott, are you there?"

"Yes... yes, I'm here. You do whatever is necessary to protect her, Blake. You have my permission to send an army, if necessary."

"I hear that. I should be there by seven o'clock this evening. The police or the VBI should contact you within the hour. Is Catriona with you or in Charlottesville?"

"No, she's here. Thank goodness. I'll try to keep this from her."

"Good luck, but she needs to be prepared. Did you get the picture?"

The fax machine sitting on the credenza began vibrating a page through its printer.

"Yes. It's coming through. Thank you, Blake. Thank you."

"Expect someone within the hour... see you tonight."

"Sure. We will be ready."

When Scott disconnected the line, his mind was racing. He made a few copies of the picture and took them into the kitchen. When he walked in, he was as pale as Cookie had ever seen him.

"What has happened?"

He explained the situation to both and told Cookie to monitor the gates. "Only open for the police. I will take his picture down to the stables. The police may want to handle this differently, but the staff should know."

"What about Katydid? Should we disturb her?"

"Not yet. Let's allow her to rest. As soon as I make this known to her, I'm not sure what her reaction will be."

"You don't think he will hurt her, do you?"

"I'm not sure what he'll do."

Jamie rose from the table. "Cookie, thank you for the lunch. It was delicious. Scott, I think I should head back to the office. I will put the staff on high alert as well. Do you have a picture you can spare?"

"Sure. Thank you, Jamie. Call me as soon as you hear from Robert. Also, make sure building security is aware of what is happening. I'm unsure what this guy is capable of doing."

"I will. Don't worry about the office. Is there anything I can do to help here?"

"Nothing that I'm aware. Drive safely."

"I can see myself out."

Cookie asked, "What do I need to do?"

"Not anything. We will go about our business as usual and stay as calm as possible. It may take some time before they locate him, but I will not coward. As soon as the police have a more detailed plan, we can start from there. I should ask Declan to be here when they arrive. Also, prepare a couple of extra rooms… just in case. Sheriff Royster will be staying with us for a while and should arrive later tonight."

"Good. It will keep my mind occupied. As soon as I clean the kitchen, I'll head upstairs. Are you planning to eat?"

"In a minute, but first, I should call Declan. Will you hand me the phone?"

"Sure. Try extension twenty-nine."

Brad answered and said Declan had left to view a horse a couple of hours away and would not be back until late.

"Brad, I need you to gather everyone near the offices in the stable. I'm heading down now."

"Yes, sir."

Scott called Declan's cell.

"Hey, Scott. What's up?"

Scott told Declan about the conversation with Blake. "I'm glad Catriona is still upstairs. She's been sleeping in today."

"No, she isn't. I rode with her early this morning, and it's almost one o'clock. Haven't you seen her?"

"No, I haven't."

"I'm coming back." The line went dead.

Scott ran upstairs. Catriona's room was empty.

***

Catriona poked her head around Samuel's front door.

"Samuel? Samuel, are you here?" There was no reply. Catriona walked through the living room and into the kitchen. "Samuel?"

"He's a little busy, Katydid."

She turned. Standing in front of her was the same man she saw at the funeral service.

"Do I know you?"

"I'da thought so."

"You… you were at the funeral."

"Oh, I'da bet you a C-Note you'da recognized me long before then… just think."

"Sageville? It is you. You approached me at the inn when I was sitting on the porch."

"You do remember."

"Who are you and what do you want?"

"Don't you know?"

"No."

He studied her face. "I'm an old acquaintance, but I'da knowed you anywhere. You got your momma's eyes." He sniffed as he wiped his nose with the back of his hand.

"You knew my mother?"

"I did." He walked toward her. Catriona backed into the chair sitting at the table.

"What did you say your name was?"

"I didn't, but you can call me Daub."

Catriona remembered the picture in the yearbook. "Daub Tackett?"

"That's my name... don't wear it out."

"You killed my parents, didn't you?"

"Uh... maybe. You don't remember?" He rubbed his chin.

She shook her head. "Only bits and pieces."

He bent over, laughing louder than anyone she had heard before. "Damnation! Just my luck."

"What is?"

"I've been chasin' a stupid girl who remembers nothin'!"

"Where is Samuel?"

His tone changed. "I told you... he's busy."

"Busy doing what?"

"None of your business."

"Samuel?" she yelled out again. This time, she heard a moan coming from the back of the house. "What have you done?" She moved toward the hallway, but Daub blocked the entrance with his body.

"Nothin'. Sit." He nodded toward one of the kitchen chairs.

"I don't want to sit. Get out of my way."

"I said, 'Sit!'" He grabbed for her, but she surprised him by slamming him into the refrigerator, causing him to stumble to the floor. She darted through the hallway and into the single bedroom and found Samuel lying in a puddle of blood.

"Samuel!" She knelt beside him.

Suddenly, she was jerked backward as Daub grabbed her ponytail and dragged her toward the door. She yelled out in pain.

Daub screamed, "Shut up!"

"Let go!" She grabbed his left leg, causing him to fall. Kicking with all her strength, her heel struck the middle of his chest. He gasped and fell backward. She ran toward the door, but he was faster.

Grabbing her neck, he yelled, "I'm not tellin' you again, woman. Sit your ass down!" He threw her onto the bed, pinning her beneath his weight.

Samuel continued to moan, unaware of the physical altercation going on around him.

"Shut up, old man." Daub kicked him in the back.

Samuel fell silent.

Catriona escaped Daub's clutches and rolled off the opposite side of the bed. When she cleared the braided rug, he grabbed her as she pulled away with all the strength she had, but he hit her full force with a right uppercut to the chin. It was a knock-out blow, leaving her lifeless as the back of her head slammed hard against the bedpost.

# CHAPTER 26

Twenty Years Ago

KATIE JO SIGHED after fitting the nervous bride's wedding gown and listening to the normal drama of bridesmaids. Monies made were her only consolation following a trying afternoon of nonsense and lace. It was the last day of classes for Catriona. Before reaching Sageville Elementary to collect her, Katie Jo bought milkshakes as an early celebration and pulled in behind the long carpool line, waiting for Catriona to be dismissed.

Tap, tap, tap. She turned toward the noise. Daub Tackett was knocking on her passenger side window as he straddled his red bike balanced against her car door. She hesitated, but then rolled down the window.

"Good afternoon, Missus Harrington."

"What do you want, Daub?"

His eyes widened. "Wow... your eyes are beautiful."

Katie Jo reached for the window's lever.

"I apologize, ma'am. Would it be ok if I mowed your grass this summer? I'm workin' to buy a car in the fall."

"I'll talk to Bill about it. Why don't you come by the house after six?"

"I will... thank you."

He grinned a greasy smile and moved to the car parked behind her. She thought him an odd kid, but certainly not the sick predator described. Watching him through the rearview mirror, anger swelled within her. Her grip tightened on the steering wheel as a scheme came to mind. She knew his arrival could not be better timed. Once Bill arrived home, she would inform him about Catriona and the other girls, and then, together, they would call Blake before Daub arrived that evening. It was the ideal plan, but she had not considered her daughter's reaction. On their way home, Katie Jo told Catriona what she had planned to do.

"I don't want him to cut our grass, Momma! I don't want him to come near us. Please! He told me he would hurt you!"

"Katydid, calm down. This is the best-case scenario for everyone. He cannot hurt you or me with your daddy and Blake there to protect us. I'm trying to protect your daddy from going to jail because he'll kill him. Blake will arrest Daub before Bill can do anything, no matter how much I want to see that little twit suffer. This will work in everyone's best interest."

"What about his momma and daddy? What will they say? Will they hurt us?"

Katie Jo remained quiet. She had not thought of Mr. and Mrs. Tackett, but at this point, she had no choice. Protecting her daughter and the other children came first. She would deal with his parents' reactions later. She thought she should call Scott, her nephew who was an attorney, but she did not want to drag him into her drama yet. She would call after Daub's arrest.

"You must trust me, honey. Bill will be home before Daub arrives. Everyone will be safe. Okay?"

Catriona cried. "Please, Momma. Call Daub and tell him not to come."

"Katydid, you are overreacting." She glanced over and saw her daughter's frightened face. "I'll tell you what... instead, you stay in your room where you won't have to see him. I'll come for you once Blake has taken him to the police station. Do you like that idea?"

Catriona nodded her head in agreement as she sipped on her shake. She was too afraid to speak, but she knew her daddy would protect them. Katie Jo stopped to buy their weekly groceries at Smalley's so they could begin Saturday morning enjoying the first day of summer. As soon as Katie Jo pulled into her drive, Catriona ran to her room and closed the door. It was five o'clock.

Katie Jo stepped inside the kitchen with her bags in tow when the screen door closed behind her. She turned. Daub stood in the doorway.

"Daub, didn't your parents teach you to knock first? You startled me." This was not her plan.

"I thought I'd come on over. Did you talk to Mr. Harrington about your grass?"

"Not yet, but he should be home any minute. Would you help me with my groceries? I have several bags in the trunk of my car. I sure could use your help."

"I think I'll wait here."

"If you will not help me, then you should go home. I'll call when Bill gets here."

He cocked his head sideways and his lips formed into a smirk in one corner of his mouth. "Nah, I'll wait." He turned the ladder-back chair around and slammed the legs against the floor as he straddled it.

"You are being rude, son. Do what you're told and run along home. I'll call you; I promise."

He laughed. "Do what I'm told? You're funny. You have no right to tell me what to do. Come to think of it, little miss Katie Jo, I'm gonna tell you what to do. Why don't you pour me a glass of sweet tea? I'm thirsty."

Katie Jo stiffened and placed her hands on her hips. "Daub, this is my house; my rules. Go home."

He lunged forward, causing the chair to fall as he shoved her against the sink with his body. His lips were only inches from hers as he stared into her frightened eyes. His pupils were large. "I'm not goin' anywhere, pretty lady."

"Get off me!" she screamed and pushed him backward.

Daub caught himself before falling, and raised up, slapping her across the face with the back of his hand. Katie Jo cried out in pain. He yelled, "I'm tired of people telling me what to do! Do you hear me?"

Katie Jo pressed her hand against the side of her face. She wanted to run, but needed to warn Catriona somehow. She bit her lip as tears formed in her eyes. Regaining her composure and straightening her dress, she remarked calmly, "Daub, I'm sorry. I'm the one being rude. You are a guest, and I should have asked if you wanted a drink, seeing how hot you are. Sweet tea, you said?"

"That's more like it. Make sure it's extra sweet too." His eyes followed her to the refrigerator as she pulled out the dark pitcher. She walked to the cabinet and took out a glass. "Would you like some ice?"

"Dumb woman. Who drinks tea without ice? What a stupid question." He laughed, leaning with his back against the counter and crossing his arms in front of him. "Have you always been so dumb? My daddy would'a slapped my maw for askin' such a stupid question. I guess Bill doesn't know how to control his wife."

"I wasn't thinking, Daub. Forgive me." The throbbing pain radiating from the side of her head, along with the taste of blood, was almost more than she could bear, but she kept her wits about her for Catriona's safety.

"Missus Katie Jo Harrington apologizin' to me. Who'da thunk it? I bet that's a first for you, ain't it? You know what I think? I think you're a beautiful woman."

Katie Jo pushed her hair behind her ear. "Thank you. It's nice for you to say so." She handed him the glass, trying to remain steady, but her hand shook as he took it.

"Yes, ma'am. Beautiful." He gulped the tea, spilling it from the corners of his mouth as it ran down both sides of his chin. He wiped his lips with the back of his hand.

"Bill should be home shortly. Do you mind if I brush my hair and wash my face before he walks through the door? I need to freshen up. I'll be right back."

"Yeah. You should clean up a bit. Maw uses makeup to cover bruises sometimes. Your cheek is turnin' on you. If you'd behave, you wouldn't have to clean up. My dad always makes Maw and me wash our hands. One time when I was little, I forgot and he..." Daub stopped. Katie Jo did not move. As if searching his memories, he rubbed his forehead with both hands. "Well? What are you waitin' for? A telegram? Go clean your hands and face or you'll wish you had, but don't forget… I'm watchin' you."

Katie Jo walked through the hall and into the Jack and Jill bathroom, locking the door behind her. She turned on the faucet so Daub could hear the water running. She then crossed over into the small bedroom. Catriona was lying across the bed, facing the window. She was listening to her Discman with her headset covering her ears. It was obvious she had not heard the skirmish in the kitchen. Katie Jo startled her when tapping her on the shoulder.

Looking back toward her mother, Catriona asked, "What's wrong?" She could see the red mark on Katie Jo's face.

Her mother held her finger to her lips and whispered, "Shh… Katydid, you must be quiet. I need you to hide in the closet."

"Why?" she whispered back in the same tone.

"I do not want him to hear you."

Catriona became frightened. "Is Daub here? Where's Daddy?"

"Yes, but I need you to hide in the closet. Stay quiet, honey, and do not let him find you. No matter what you hear, close your eyes or cover your ears, but above all, stay hidden. Don't forget. He is growing more unstable with every word. I'll come back first chance, and when I do, you are to run as fast as you can to Martha's next door, but right now, you are to hide."

Catriona crawled over the bed and sat on the closet floor. Looking at her mother, she asked, "Are you sure you're okay?"

Katie Jo remained calm. "Yes, darling. He doesn't know you're here. We cannot let him find you. He's watching the hallway, so you cannot leave… not yet. Daddy will be here soon."

"Okay," she answered.

Katie Jo smiled at her precious girl before speaking and stroked her little face. "I'll come back for you; I promise. I love you, Katydid. Please do this for me."

"Yes, ma'am."

Katie Jo closed the bi-fold doors. She placed Catriona's belongings into the bedside table, straightened the bedspread, then turned off the water in the bathroom.

Catriona called out softly, "Momma?"

Katie Jo hurried back and spoke through the closed door. "Shh, darling. I need you to be quiet."

"Momma, have you called the police?"

"Not yet, but I will… not another word." She pressed her finger to her lips. "Shh."

Daub pushed opened the door. "Who are you talking to in here?"

"No one."

"Don't lie to me." He shoved her aside and looked around the room. He then walked into the bathroom.

"I'm not lying." She spoke with confidence, surprising even herself.

"Where's Catriona?" he asked when walking back into the bedroom.

"I told her she could play outside. It's the first day of summer tomorrow and she wanted to get a head start. She's probably walked over to Sally's house. I think I may let her stay over because the city is shooting fireworks tonight. If you will allow me, I could call her mother and ask if Catriona could stay."

"You didn't brush your hair."

"What?"

"You said you were going to brush your hair. You sure have been in here a long time."

"I had to use the toilet."

"I didn't hear it flush."

"Well, it did. Maybe, you didn't hear because the water was running. Old house, old pipes."

Maybe." He stared at her with a stony expression.

"May I fix my hair?"

"Good lord, you're slow. Do you make Bill wait like this? He isn't much of a man, is he? My daddy wouldn't put up with it. Hurry before I hav'ta knock some more sense into you." He nodded for her to go into the bathroom. Leaning against the doorframe, he watched her every move.

She pulled a brush from the bathroom cabinet and glided it through her raven hair.

"You need to tie it up."

"What?"

"I liked it when I seen you last week wearing your hair up."

She tied her hair into a ponytail and then added lipstick.

"Do you do this every day when Bill comes home?"

"Like your daddy, my father liked for us to look presentable at the table."

"I bet you never got hit by nobody."

"No. Never. Does your daddy hurt you and your mom?"

"Shut up."

"Well, does he?"

"I said shut the hell up!"

"Yes, I like to look nice for Bill after he's worked hard all day. Call me old-fashioned, but that is what I do."

Daub pictured her getting ready for her husband and became aroused by her words. He stared down at her shoes and worked his gaze to the top of her head and back again. "You sure are beautiful."

"Thank you. Let's go back to the kitchen."

"I don't want to go to the kitchen."

"Bill should be here any minute." No sooner had she finished uttering the words, the house telephone rang. "I need to get that."

"No. Let it ring."

"I need to answer the phone," she said, moving toward him.

"No, you don't." He blocked the door with his body as she tried to exit the room. He was taller than she and could easily hold her back.

She spoke firmly. "You let me out of this room, Daub."

He laughed. "Ooo, look at her strut. You are not going anywhere."

The phone continued to ring but clicked over to the answering machine. They heard the recording sound out. "You have reached the

Harrington's number. Please leave your message at the beep and we will call you back directly." (Beep).

Bill's voice echoed through the hall toward them. "Hey, sweetheart. I'm afraid I must drive over to Titus Town tonight and pick up a few parts we need first thing in the morning. I should be home before midnight. I'll call later. Give yourself a kiss and throw one in for Katydid. I'll see you in a few hours. Bye, darlin'." (Click.) The machine turned off.

A slow smile crossed Daub's lip. "Well, well, well." He sniffed and wiped his finger across the base of his nose.

"Daub, I am asking nicely. Please let me out of this room. Would you like for me to fix you something to eat?" She did not blink nor waiver.

"Sally Turner?"

"What?"

"You said you could call Sally's mother. Were you talking about Sally Turner?"

"Yes. She is Catriona's friend. Why is that important?"

He shared with her his agreement made with three little girls too young to understand.

"Have you lost your mind? Sally is only nine and the youngest just turned five. You're a monster!"

He slapped her harder than before, and she fell against the dresser. He yelled, "Forget it! There will be no phone calls today!"

She could see his reflection in the mirror and noticed he had something tucked into the back of his pants beneath his jean jacket.

Without considering the consequences, she asked, "Do you have a gun? Where did you get it?" Terror ran through her as she realized she had underestimated him. Bill's guns were locked away, but he kept one hidden in the nightstand.

"I stole it from my daddy's workshop. You never know what kind of white trash you might run into around here. I use it for all kinds of protection."

"From whom?"

"I just told you, idiot!" He shook his head and scoffed, "Man, I don't remember ever talking to someone so dumb. What are you, some special kind of stupid?"

"No, I'm not."

"Are you saying I'm stupid?"

"No. I would never call you stupid." Katie Jo could not think, but she had to move before he found Catriona. "Why don't we go into the living room?"

Taking the gun from his waist and waving it in her direction, he said, "I like it better in here. You know, ever since the day you interrupted me getting a taste of your little girl, I have dreamed of another chance. But now, I'm wondering what it'd be like to be with a real woman for once. Since your precious Katydid appears to be missing, I guess you'll have to do. Lie on the bed."

"I will do no such thing."

"You heard me. Lie down." He pointed the gun at her face.

"I don't think so." She made a dash toward the open door.

Grabbing her, he turned her around and hit her cheek with the butt of the gun. She fell against the bed. "You'll do what I tell you!"

Catriona gasped. He turned toward the closet, but Katie Jo grabbed his arm to distract him. "Tell me what you want and I'll do it."

He turned back toward her. "That's more like it." He started unbuckling his belt. "Take off your clothes. You're going to like this, I promise."

"You can't be serious."

"You heard me. Strip!" He pointed the gun at her face.

With cheek bleeding, Katie Jo stood and turned her back toward the closet doors. She removed her clothes. Standing in her slip before him, he shoved her face-down onto the bed. Pulling his belt from the loops, he climbed on top of her and strapped her hands behind her back. He stood and pulled her over to face him. She winced in pain.

Her voice quivered as she spoke. "Please, do not hurt me. I'll go anywhere in the house, but not in here. Please."

"Why?"

"This is Katydid's room, and I don't want to stay in here. We can go to my room. There's a king-size bed and I'll do whatever you ask." Katie Jo cried softly as she tried to get off the bed.

He climbed on top of her, pinning her deep into the mattress. Pulling a small plastic bag from his shirt pocket, he crammed the white powder into her mouth.

"Chew on that for a while and then we'll wait a second or two for the party to begin."

She choked as she tried to spit, but he grabbed a fistful of her hair and licked the powder from her face. He pressed his mouth hard against her lips and she bit him. He tasted blood and slapped her with the back of his hand.

"I've wondered how you'd taste... not as sweet as I thought. You flit around town all high and mighty protecting those nasty kids no one gives a crap about. But what about me? Did you ever think about me even once?"

She shook her head.

"From now on, you'll remember me and won't say a word if you want to keep your little girl alive. In fact, I think we should meet once a week. How about it, Katie Jo?"

He licked the side of her face and across her eyelid. Katie Jo's eyes rolled back into her head.

"You're feeling it, aren't-cha? Don't fight it. We'll wait until it releases the tiger inside."

She shook her head and moaned again.

He laughed. "Who knew I'd be enjoying the prettiest woman in Sageville? My daddy has been watching you for a long time, but I showed him, didn't I? Who is the idiot now, old man? Let's see if my dad or Bill will want you after I'm through with the sweet Katie Jo Harrington."

He sniffed the remaining powdery substance lingering on his fingertips while continuing to point the gun against her cheek.

"Let's go to your room." He pulled her to her feet and pushed her into the hallway. She hit her shoulder against the wall. "Show me the way, sweet lady."

Katie Jo struggled to stand as she moved toward her bedroom door.

Grabbing her elbow, he pushed her inside. She tripped over the small rug in front of the bed and fell to the floor. She hit her chin, causing her to bite her tongue. Blood poured from her mouth.

"Get up." He grabbed her by her ponytail and jerked her head backward. Katie Jo screamed out. Daub pulled her to her feet and threw her face-down again onto the bed. Using all of his weight, he pressed her into the mattress and held her as she tried to twist from his grip. He pushed the gun against the back of her head and whispered, "I dare you to budge. Move an inch and I'll blow your head all over this room."

Katie Jo stopped moving except for her body's uncontrollable shaking from fear or the drug. She grew hot and then nauseated. Riding on the coke's euphoric high, he raped her. She cried out in pain as he continued his vicious rage against her until her mind and body could handle no more. She blacked out. Daub flipped over beside her and laughed. "I'd love to see my old man's face when he realizes I had you first."

Crashing from the high he was riding, he grabbed a pillow and placed it under his head, and drifted off to sleep.

A couple of hours later, Katie Jo opened her eyes. She tried to swallow, but her mouth was dry. Her body riveted with pain. She could feel her heart racing and remembered the cocaine. She was too terrified to move. The room was dark, and she heard his light snoring. Daub was sleeping next to her. She became queasy and afraid if she did not move, she would vomit. Her hands remained tied behind her back and her shoulders ached from the strain. She tried rolling over, but Daub grabbed her.

"Oh no, you don't. We are only getting started."

"Please, don't. Please," she begged.

The attack started again as if he were a starved animal ravaging for more.

Bill opened the unlocked screen door and walked into the kitchen. "Katie Jo? Katydid? Where are you two?" The house was dark. Flipping on a switch, he called out again, "Katie Jo?"

A random firework exploded somewhere in the distance. Bill flipped on another light as he walked into the hallway and called out again, "Katydid? Where are you, honey?"

Katie Jo cried out, "Bill!"

Running into the bedroom, he saw the man attacking her. Grabbing the back of the intruder's white t-shirt, Bill pulled the man from the bed and threw his body against the full-length mirror, causing broken shards of glass to fall across the floor. Bill's eyes widened in surprise when he saw him—just a teenager. "Daub? Daub Tackett? I'll kill you!"

Daub dove for his pistol fallen onto the floor, but Bill kicked him in his side, flipping him closer to the bed. Katie Jo tried moving with her restrained arms, but the pain caused her to scream in agony. Bill ran toward her, but Daub grabbed the gun, cocked, and fired aimlessly in Bill's direction. The bullet hit in the center of his chest, killing him instantly.

Katie Jo screamed, "No!"

Daub jumped to his feet, startled to see Bill covered in blood. He staggered backward and fell against the dresser as he tried to focus. Katie Jo screamed and tried to roll over to touch the floor with her feet. Daub, in a stupor, turned, and fired two more rounds in her direction when the second bullet rendered its fatal wound. Death was immediate as she fell backward onto the bed with her blood soaking the sheets beneath her.

Daub was dazed. His body numb, but his heart raced faster than before. Electricity shot through him, causing immense pleasure in what had happened.

One might have credited the drug's roller-coaster effects, but a smarter man would have recognized the wickedness living within him.

A joyful yelp shattered the quietness. "Oh, yeah! I showed you, didn't I? I surely did! Woo-hoo! Who's stupid now?"

He ran into the hallway and paused in the doorway of Catriona's bedroom. She was not there. His adrenaline was pumping as sweat ran down his face. Wiping his brow with his sleeve, he realized what he must do and ran toward the Harrington's garage.

Daub grunted as he strained to carry the containers through the screened backdoor causing it to slam shut against the frame. He hummed as he poured coal oil over everything in the bedroom, working his way down the hallway and into the living room, then returning to the kitchen.

Finding the matches in the drawer by the kitchen sink, he smiled as he lit the first one, watching its tiny spark glow in the darkness. He flipped the match onto the bedroom's floor, causing a combustion of flames to erupt into the air.

Daub ran down the hall, igniting each room as the heat grew hotter and hotter. When passing Catriona's bedroom, he thought he heard a cough. He ran inside. Smoke had filled the room when a loud cough exploded from the closet.

He jerked opened the doors and his eyes popped open when seeing Catriona crouched in the corner. Daub reached for his gun, but had left it in the garage. She fought like a wild animal when he yanked her from the closet and then continued to beat her within inches of her life. He then shoved her broken body back into the closet, wrapping the doorknobs with a wire hanger. He jumped into the hallway, dodging the surrounding flames. Flying higher than before, he sang out, "Old man, old man, oh, don't you cry for me!"

Daub escaped through the front door and stopped to watch from the night shadows of the Harrington's barn. The house took on the appearance of Hell spewing fire and brimstone as neighbors ran toward the raging inferno. The city's fire alarm system bellowed far and wide, beckoning volunteer fire department members to gather.

Daub's body shook with excitement. There was nothing left to incriminate him with the gun in hand, and he walked home as though nothing had happened. Hooked on the thrill of the kill, he never experienced a more satisfying high. Opening the backdoor to his house, his father sat at the kitchen table.

"What the hell is all that racket? Those stupid firecrackers have probably set someone's field on fire. Did you see any smoke?"

"Nope, and don't care."

"Look at me when I'm talking to you, boy. Are you a special kind of stupid?"

Daub turned just as his father struck him with his fist, knocking Daub to the floor. Daub grabbed his nose as the blood seeped between his fingers. He stood facing his foe. He was taller than his father and Daub charged, shoving him into the refrigerator.

Pressing his forearm against his father's neck, he warned, "Don't you ever touch me again, old man. I'm not stupid, and next time, you'll be sorry."

For the first time, he saw fear in his father's eyes, and Daub's ego grew from the power he held over him. He continued to choke him until his dad buckled to the floor, clutching his throat.

Looking into his son's dark face, he whispered, "Get out. I mean it. Get out and don't you ever come back."

"No worries, Daddy-O." He walked toward the drawer where his dad kept his wallet. Grabbing all the bills inside, he threw the empty billfold into his father's face and took a set of keys held by a small hook by the phone.

He walked past and kicked his father's foot as he headed toward the back door. "Thanks for the truck. I'm outta here."

His father spewed the last words Daub would ever hear from his lips. "Good riddance. Why don't you take your ugly maw with you while you're at it, and then I'll be free from this noose for good."

Daub turned back and straddled his father lying on the floor and pointed the gun at his forehead. His father shielded his eyes with his elbow.

"You touch my maw again, and you're dead, old man. You won't even see me coming. Do you understand or are you too stupid… asshole?"

His dad nodded.

Daub walked out and slammed the door behind him. He was free to go wherever his heart desired. Backing the truck from the driveway, he drove past the Harrington's house. There were two ambulances, three police cars, and two fire trucks parked out front with people running from every direction to contain the fire. Fire hoses were shooting water into the air, trying to keep the flames from reaching the next house. It was then he saw a single firefighter carrying a limp body in his arms.

A police officer directing the traffic waved him on with his flashlight. Stopping his truck, Daub rolled down the window. "Excuse me, sir? What's happened?"

"Looks like fireworks may have caused a fire. At the moment, we are not sure. I need you to keep moving."

"Anybody hurt?"

"Looks like the entire family is dead. It's awful."

"God bless 'em."

"Yes. Keep moving, young man, and have a good night."

"Yes, sir." Daub cranked the window's handle and pulled onto the highway. He laughed until tears fell down his cheeks as he beat the steering wheel with the base of his palm. "What a great night!"

The old truck turned on the next street, heading to wherever the road would lead.

 CHAPTER 27

CATRIONA MOVED HER head, yet she thought she heard her mother calling.

"Wake up, Katydid. Remember me. Remember him… he's coming. Wake up!"

Catriona opened her eyes. "Momma?"

She recognized Samuel's bedroom. Her head pounded from the bump on the back of her head, and she could not move her arms. She looked up. A rope wrapped around her wrists was attached to the top of the headboard. She glanced around the room. Samuel remained on the floor unconscious.

"Samuel?"

As she became more aware, her body trembled with fright. She remembered everything now. She could hear the screams of her mother and knew his demented mind. Daub stood in the doorway, watching as if he were a cheetah waiting to pounce.

"He can't hear you," he said and started humming an old tune.

"Why did you hurt my mother?"

He clicked his tongue. "So… you do remember, huh?"

She nodded, finding it hard to focus.

"Well, why not? She was easy. Besides, she thought she was better'n me, but I showed her, didn't I? I showed'em both. She was the prettiest woman I'd ever seen, that is until now."

"Until now?"

"Surely, you're smarter'n her? Take a gander at you… you're more beautiful than Missus Katie Jo. Never thought it possible." He continued to hum his little song, then stopped. "Man! This is gonna be a fun afternoon."

"Why little girls? Why did any deserve the cruelty you showed them?"

"Cruelty?" He threw his head back as his laughter filled the air. "Sweetheart, I was anythin' but cruel. I paid for services rendered, and sometimes I didn't. I wonder what happened to those girls… do you know?"

"How could I?"

He tapped his finger against his temple and winked. "That's right. Your noggin' was broken."

"I remember your red bicycle and how you hurt me."

"Oh, I remember too. By the way, I lied about them girls. Found out from the gossip at Erline's Café that two of 'em got real bad reputations and ended up pregnant before they graduated from high school… pure white trash. They must've liked the sex. I guess they couldn't get enough once they had a taste of me. Teach'em young and they'll keep coming back for more. I think the youngest overdosed in her twenties. Shameful, really."

Catriona's stomach turned into knots. Not only had his abuse destroyed those children, but her as well. She wanted to run, but couldn't. She asked, "Where have you been hiding?"

"Have you missed me?" He licked the corner of his lip where the toothpick was hanging. "Why do you care where I've been?"

"Seems the right thing to ask. I'm not going anywhere tied to this bed." Her arms were aching.

His eyes danced. He sat next to her and stroked her hair behind her ear.

He whispered, "I've been in prison, darlin'." His finger traced her lips.

"For what?" Her lips tightened, repulsed by his touch.

"Arson, mostly. I enjoy burning things… oh, and armed robbery with a stupid possessions charge. Speaking of… would you like some? I think it might liven things up a bit." He pulled a straw and small paper envelope from his jean pocket. "You're gonna like this, I promise."

Rage burned within her. Voices from the women of her past filled her mind as she recalled their words.

"Katydid, The Holy Spirit will give you strength in times of trouble."

She said, "Daub, I don't need it. I may look like Katie Jo, but my mother taught me a few things without knowing. You won't need to force yourself on me. I saw and heard what happens when someone doesn't obey. I guess I am smart… like you."

"You have the same blood flowing within you, baby girl. When you think all is lost and you cannot go on, I want you to remember your grandmother and draw from her strength."

She gained more courage as she spoke. "The more I think about it, I want to remember our time together. It's obvious you've been thinking about me for weeks. Why don't you show me how a real man operates? I've never had the pleasure of knowing someone like you. You differ from the others."

"It's never wrong to protect yourself, honey."

He stared into her eyes as blue as crystal prisms. "I believe you're tellin' the truth, Katy-girl." He spit out the toothpick and tossed his ball cap toward the bottom of the bed. "You got experience, do you? Well, well. If this is how you want to play it, then I can play straight. It's a little more excitin' when you are flyin' high, but we have time." He clicked his tongue. "I know. We'll play it both ways." He unbuttoned his shirt. "You won't be forgettin' me anytime soon, I promise."

"If you will untie my hands, I could enjoy it more. Then the next go-around, you could tie me back… I won't object."

"Well, what about that? Miss high and mighty knows how to get down and dirty. Nice thought, but do you really think I'm stupid?" His eyes darkened and his voice deepened. "No. You will stay the way you are." He pulled on the ropes, causing her to cry out.

"No, Daub, you have misunderstood. You're right. I was thinking only of myself. If tied is the way you want it, then I'm okay, but I have one request."

"You don't get to make no requests."

"Please. Surely, you can show a little kindness before you hurt me? That is what you are planning... aren't you?"

"Sounds like a plan." He became more aroused the more she spoke. "You must be a mind-reader. I tell you what, Katy-girl... tell me what you want and I'll make sure it happens."

"Take off my blouse. You'll have to untie one of my hands to remove it, but you can tie me back as soon as it's off." *Help me, God.* "You know, I'm beginning to enjoy the idea of us."

The same greasy smile from his youth crossed his face. "Okay. If that is what you want, I can oblige." He threw his shirt onto the floor and straddled her as he untied one hand. When unbuttoning her blouse, she trembled in fear, but he thought it was for pleasure. "Oh, you do like this, don't you?"

She nodded in agreement. As he unbuttoned the silk top, the scarring across her entire torso revealed itself. He frowned as he looked over her body with a dull stare. "What happened to you... damn, girl."

Her charade ended. She screamed, "You did this to me!"

He slapped her, and she scratched him down the left side of his cheek with her freed hand.

"You bitch!" He pinned her arm down with his knee as she continued to struggle beneath him. She screamed in pain. Wiping his face with his hand, he saw the blood on his fingertips. Staring at the mangled body before him, he laughed. "You are so damn ugly! I wanted to play nice, but then you had to go and make it nasty. Too bad, Katy-girl." He traced his finger from her chin down to her stomach. "That fire did a fine job on you, didn't it? Even burned off your belly button. Does it hurt? I hope it hurts because when I'm finished today, you will be hopin' you died in that fire. Come to think of it… a little fire to complete the job would be the perfect way to finish off this day."

"Get off me!" She continued to flip back and forth like a marlin at the end of a taut line.

Pulling the gun from the back of his waistband, he pointed the barrel against her forehead. "I suggest you not move another muscle or there won't be nothin' left of your beautiful face. Do you understand?"

She froze as the tears rolled down her cheeks.

He glared at her chest. Rolled, tangled scarring replaced breasts and thick scarring covered her entire lower torso. The skin on her chest had been too thin for reconstructive surgery, and pink scars covered her arms, revealing tightened muscle tissue beneath. The fire had mutilated her body.

"You know, Katydid. Maybe we should put your clothes back on so I don't have to look at you. It's enough to give me second thoughts. I'd close my eyes, but I like to watch."

"I feel sorry for you."

He began to button her shirt. "Sorry for me?" He stopped and smirked. "Oh, do tell, my ugly doll. Do tell."

"You are a screw-up, aren't you? Did your mommy and daddy not love you?"

"Shut up."

"Did they smack you around? Abuse you sexually, maybe?"

"I said, 'Shut up.'"

"Oh, I know what upsets you the most. A big grown tough guy afraid of a simple little word. Did they call you… 'stupid?'"

He slapped her with a hard blow. When she turned back toward him, blood was pouring from the side of her mouth. He kissed her hard, then licked his lips and said, "You taste like your old dead momma."

She spat into his face, causing him to jerk backward. He wiped his cheek with the tail of her blouse. Her laughter shook the bed, but then she cried out when he pushed his elbow deep into her shoulder.

"What's so funny?"

Her words dripped from her lips like sludge from an old oil can. "You… you pathetic excuse of a man who can only bed a woman when she's tied to a headboard. Your momma must be real… proud."

Shoving the gun against her mouth, he yelled, "I'll see you in hell! Goodbye, Katy…"

In mid-sentence, Declan slammed his full body weight into the side of Daub, causing him to drop the gun, and knocked them both to the floor. Declan was pounding Daub's head so hard that Daub did not know who or what was on top of him.

Regaining his senses, Daub fought back with intensity and great strength. He flipped Declan over and punched his head like a boxing bag hanging from the ceiling.

Suddenly, the men heard the cocking of a gun's hammer. Daub's eyes widened in fear as he turned toward the sound and with the squeeze of the trigger, a bullet penetrated his skull, killing him instantly.

Declan scooted away as fast as possible. He saw Catriona lifted on her knees from atop the bed with a pistol in hand.

Unaware of her actions, she continued unloading each round into her attacker until the chambers emptied. Although no cartridges remained, she pulled the trigger nonstop, as if frozen in a trance. Click. Click. Click.

Struggling to stand, Declan moved toward her with hands outstretched toward the pistol.

"Catriona, you can stop… it's over. He can't hurt you anymore."

She stared with eyes wide-opened as tears streamed down her face. He lowered her arms and removed the gun from her hands. She was in shock. Declan grabbed a blanket from the base of the bed and covered her exposed body.

"You are safe."

Unable to speak, she nodded in agreement as her body continued its adrenaline rush of tremors.

"I need to check on Grandpops? May I?"

She nodded again.

He placed her on the edge of the bed as she continued to stare at the lifeless body covered in blood. Declan knelt beside his grandfather and felt for a pulse—it was weak, but beating all the same. Grabbing the phone next to the bed, he called for an ambulance and then relayed the news to Scott and the team who had gathered to search for the rapist and murderer.

Daub Tackett was dead—the nightmare finally over.

CHAPTER 28

CATRIONA ROLLED HER WHEELCHAIR toward Samuel's room. The overhead light above his bed dimly illuminated the room. She stopped in the doorway as she stared at the man who had guided her with his down-to-earth wisdom most of her life. The machine over his right shoulder revealed every beat of his heart. The green light appeared to be in perfect rhythm.

"Do you want to go inside?" the nurse asked.

"Yes. May I sit with him?"

"I'm sure he will not mind."

As the nurse rolled her to the bed, Samuel's eyelids opened, and he smiled. "Well, aren't you a sight for sore eyes? I wondered where you'd been hiding. How are you?"

"I think I'm better than you at the moment." Her voice cracked.

"Now, now. Let's have none of that."

"Samuel, I'm sorry you have suffered. I never dreamt of hurting anyone, least of all you."

"Katydid... don't you go worrying about me. You should know by now I'm too tough and old to die. I'm like a piece of old gristle no one can chew." He laughed out loud, then grimaced, grabbing his side. "Ouch, that hurt."

She smiled, "Obviously, you are better."

"I'll be out of here before you know it. I may even beat you home."

"I'm betting on it." She reached over and held his bruised hand. Leaning in, she kissed his knuckles.

"On second thought, if you are going to come every day and hold my hand, I might stay a little longer." He smiled at her with warm eyes.

"I need to ask you a few questions."

"Anything."

"Now that you are going to be okay, I need to talk to you about Declan."

"Has something happened? I thought he only had a few scrapes and bruises. Is there something worse?"

"Oh no. It's nothing like that. I guess I'm being selfish, but apparently, that's my nature lately."

"Katydid, ask. You've never been selfish a day in your life."

"Why didn't you tell Declan about my engagement?"

"Why? Because he needed to hear the news directly from you."

"I guess you're right." She bit her lower lip.

"What is it you want, Catriona?"

"I want Scott to be happy."

"I do swear, girl, if I didn't laugh, I'd be crying. That's got to be the most foolish thing I've heard you say. Scott will not be happy unless you're happy. You know him better than anyone."

She placed his hand back on the sheet and looked out of the window. They sat in silence. Samuel did not interrupt her. She spoke while staring into the lighted darkness. "I don't know what I want."

"Don't you want to be in love with the man you marry?"

Catriona turned toward him. "I can learn to love Peter. It would not be hard. Most women would jump at the opportunity to marry him."

"I'm sure they would, but for crying out loud, sweetie, that's not how this works."

"Why not? Why can't I marry someone who has goals and knows what they want out of life?"

"You can, but I've got news for you. There are lots of men who have their ducks in a row, but you need love first. All else will fall into place."

"I guess. Does it matter that I find him incredibly attractive?"

"Sure, it does, but I find Raquel Welch attractive, but it doesn't mean I want to marry her."

"I could do much worse."

"Yes, but you can do much better too. Why do you want to marry Peter besides the other things you've mentioned?"

"I'm approaching my thirties, Samuel. The truth of the matter is I'm afraid if Peter sees me… completely sees me…" she paused, but gaining the courage to continue, she said, "… he will not want someone who looks like I do."

"Hogwash! You need to tell him about the scars. Show him if you must, but without love, your scars might make a difference. But with love, no man is going to give two shakes of a lamb's tail about your physical appearance. Especially when understanding what you've lived through. Your body is only a shell."

She frowned. "Do you think anyone can look past this shell?" Her voice cracked.

"Darling, I understand your fears. Yes, most men are first drawn to an attractive woman physically. But the good ones… the good ones love you for who you are on the inside and not turned off by the physical disabilities you have. That is how love works. You don't want a fella who focuses on the surface, do you?"

"Peter says he loves me, so his word is good enough for me. However, he smothers me at times, and I find it overwhelming. I feel pressured to marry him." She then recalled her Granny Francis's words.

"Remember, child, you can't keep any animal or anything living closed or shut up. Whether it be in a jar, a bad courtship or a coal mine with black dust a-blowing, make sure the living has enough room to breathe."

"Darling, God did not make you to settle. Peter may appear to be a great guy, but is he the right fella? God has a special someone picked just for you, and I think we both know who that is, don't we?"

She stared into his old face. Dropping her eyes, she whispered, "Declan?"

"Yes, Declan. And I'm not saying this because he's my grandson. When you are together, it's obvious there is an emotional, as well as a physical connection. I've seen it first-hand. Do you love him?"

"I don't know… I'm unsure… maybe."

"Katydid, I know of no one finer than Declan O'Connell. He walks a high moral ground too. He's kind, compassionate, works harder than anyone I know, and he will always see your needs come before his own. He would never coax you into rushing into anything, especially a marriage. For me, Peter should be ashamed of himself for asking the day after your mother's funeral. We are still in mourning for goodness' sake and will for the rest of our days, yet life goes on; I know that. But right now, you are vulnerable, especially after this Daub Tackett fiasco. A true nightmare. There is a time to grieve. Allow yourself time, but do not wallow in self-pity. When ready, you move on with the living. If you ask me, and I know you didn't, but Peter's actions appear to be self-serving and unforgivable. Frankly, I have no words and you know I have plenty to say."

"That's an understatement." She smiled at him and reached for his hand again. They sat in silence for a few moments and then she said, "I love you, Samuel."

"I know you do, but you needed to hear the truth. You need to wait until you can figure out what you want. But I will say this… you and Declan share the same religious belief system. Katydid, that is the most important aspect of any relationship. The relationship you have with God comes first. You should be equally yoked as a couple. Does Peter share your same beliefs?"

"I don't know. The subject of religion has never come up." Her words made her stop cold. It was then she realized she had her answer. "Oh, Samuel, what do I do?"

"Be honest with yourself. Be honest with Peter and with Declan. You deserve happiness, but so do those two men. Do not take advantage of either of them by not doing so."

"I don't know if I can hurt Peter. He will hate me."

"It's better he knows the truth than to marry under false pretenses. It may take some time, but he will come to appreciate your honesty and move on if that is what you want."

"I hope you're right," she said. "This will not be easy."

"Doing the right thing is not always easy."

She nodded her head. "I guess I should go back to my room. Hush is the word, okay?"

"You can trust me, Katydid. I won't mention our conversation to anyone."

"Thank you."

As they finished their goodbyes, neither realized Peter was standing outside Samuel's hospital room door.

***

The next afternoon, the hospital released Catriona. She tried to reach Peter by cell phone, but he had not returned her calls. She was quiet as Scott drove her home.

"Katydid? What's up?"

"Sir?"

"Are you okay today?"

"Yes, I'm fine."

"A lot has happened in the last few days." Scott looked over at her.

"Yes, sir. Life-changing really."

"That's an understatement. When you are ready to talk about what happened at Samuel's, I'm here. Declan talked to the police."

She nodded her head. "Sheriff Blake knows everything. I gave my statement while at the hospital. I'm sure my next session with Dr. Pendergrass will be a long one too."

"I'll read the statement if you prefer."

"Yes. I would prefer you did."

"All right, sweetheart."

"Dad, I want to go home."

"That's where we are headed, honey."

"No. I want to move back home… for good."

"What are you saying?" Scott pulled the car onto the shoulder of the road and stopped.

She answered, "What's wrong? I thought you wanted me to move back. At least, you have always said as much."

"Are you sure this is what you want?"

"It is. I want to move home to Grace Meade."

"Is this out of guilt? I don't want you doing anything on my behalf. What about Peter?"

"I need to tell you something, but please do not be angry with me."

"I won't be angry."

"I do not love Peter. I only accepted his proposal because that is what everyone else wanted."

Scott stared for a few moments. He said, "Your happiness means the world to me; however, don't you understand I would never be happy if you are in a marriage without love? I apologize if I've led you into thinking my happiness is more important than your own. I could not live with myself knowing that was your reality."

"Oh, Dad. The timing has been all wrong. Peter is wonderful, but he isn't the one for me. I've always known he wasn't. I was afraid to allow someone so wonderful to pass me by, thinking no one else would ask. Pathetic, I know. I also realize Peter is assuming too much."

"That's odd. I've never thought of him as someone who assumes anything, especially in our profession."

"Assuming might not be the best word. I do not blame him entirely because I had a role in misleading him."

"What do you mean?"

"I remember leaving the Gold Cup races, but nothing else. Apparently, I said things I don't remember discussing with him, and things may have happened between us. I don't know."

"Have you told him any of this?"

"I am planning to tell him today. He should be waiting at Grace Meade." She paused and looked out of the passenger side window. "I don't want to keep making mistakes. I want a life worth living."

"Of course, you do and you will." Scott reached for her hand.

Tears formed in the corners of her eyes. "How many times can one person be given another chance? I know Peter isn't my future. I've spent my life running back to a past I could not remember; however, I know with complete confidence, Grace Meade is my future now."

Scott released a heavy sigh. "Honey, Peter told me about the baby. Are you sure you want to raise a child without him?"

Catriona's eyes widened. "Baby? What baby?"

"Peter said the two of you were possibly expecting."

"I don't think so... I mean... I think I would know." She frowned. "I can't be. The doctors told me I could never conceive without medical assistance. Remember?"

"I do. How could he have assumed otherwise?" Scott's eyes darted back and forth.

"I have no clue."

"That's odd. He told me the two of you had discussed it."

"No. We have not discussed children that I am aware. Oh, wait. He said we did, but I can't remember anything from that night."

Scott frowned. "In Washington... five or six weeks ago, right?"

"No. At Grace Meade, two weeks ago."

"None of this makes sense, honey. Why would Peter lie to me?"

"He wouldn't. He may have just thought it possible. I mean under normal circumstances, it could have happened."

"Maybe or maybe not."

"Dad, Peter is not a liar. He must have assumed it to be so and became carried away in the conversation. I am sure you were not the easiest man to ask for his daughter's hand in marriage."

Scott nodded. "You are probably right. What about 'The Feather Quill?'"

"What about it? You and I will work something out with Tia. I know she can handle it. We will need to hire more people for the new location too. I think it would be a good idea if the three of us could build a business plan to benefit us all."

"Wow. You have been busy, haven't you?"

"Four days lying in a hospital bed allows one time to think."

"I know a few consultants who can help. Are you sure?"

"If you think I would allow Lillian's life's work to go by the wayside, you would have to think again. Grace Meade is my heart... my home.

You know it is. Of course, I will keep seeing Dr. Pendergrass as long as needed."

Scott smiled. "To say I'm not happy would be a lie. I'm surprised… in a good way, but one more time, are you sure?"

"It is what I want. The fact you are a part of my decision makes it all the sweeter."

"Well, I'm speechless."

"One more thing. I want us to go to church regularly."

"Done." He reached over and hugged her. "Now what, boss lady?"

She laughed. "Homeward, James."

"Yes. We should not leave Peter waiting any longer. You're going to make this right?"

"I am. The sooner, the better. I owe everyone an apology for not being truthful with myself. I certainly owe him the biggest one of all."

"Peter will appreciate the truth. I admit I was afraid of what the campaign trail might do to you, but he will make an excellent politician. I hope his senatorial race will be a successful one."

"What senatorial race?" Catriona's eyes widened.

"You didn't know?"

She shook her head.

Scott's eyebrows turned downward, forming a deep furrow at the top of his nose. "He did lie to me. He said you had discussed it also."

"No."

"What is happening here? Peter was hoping for a big wedding before the year's end so the two of you could announce his candidacy in early January."

"Oh, my word. I have no desire to be a senator's wife. In fact, I have no desire to be in the limelight whatsoever. How am I supposed to plan a big wedding before January? Oh, and by the way, I'm not into big weddings."

Scott looked puzzled.

She let out a heavy sigh. "Oh, Dad. Peter and I do not know each other at all. What were we thinking? My heart breaks knowing his plans will be destroyed, but I can't marry him. I love someone else. Thank goodness no engagement announcement has been made."

"Thank goodness is right. He has fooled me... and you. Not many can make that claim, can they?"

"No, sir."

"His plans won't be destroyed... disrupted, maybe. He and I will be having a lengthy discussion as soon as you are finished with him. Trust me, darling. Peter will survive..." He stopped mid-sentence. "Wait... did you say you love someone else?"

"I do, but he doesn't know."

"Who doesn't know?"

"Declan."

Scott stared without blinking.

"Dad?"

"Declan?"

"Yes, sir. From the first time I met him in the stables, I think I knew. I feel safe with him, and he always seems to rescue me when I need rescuing most. He saved my life. He saved Samuel's life. He calms me."

"Declan?"

"Yes, sir. What is wrong with Declan? Is it because he works for you?"

"Why would you say such a thing? I am trying to understand how little I know about you." Scott rubbed his face. "How did this happen? Have we been living under the same roof for these past few weeks? Who else knows?"

"Samuel." She smiled.

"Samuel?"

"Yes. He asked me to search my true feelings. Samuel saw what I had known for a while. I wish I had been as honest with Peter as I have with Declan."

"Now, I understand the trip to Charlottesville."

"What does that mean?"

"The time Peter and I found you in Charlottesville when Declan stayed overnight. I knew something was odd about that trip."

She laughed. "It doesn't matter."

"We both appreciate Declan for what he has done for this family. I will be indebted for as long as I live for helping you at Samuel's. Are you sure this is love and not gratitude? You need to be sure."

"I've never been surer of anything in my life."

"Sweetheart, how do I say this? Declan is gone."

"When?"

"He turned in his notice a couple of days ago and asked me to remain quiet until he could tell his grandfather in his own words. He accepted a job in Kentucky and headed out this morning."

"Well, get him back."

"First things first, honey. I think another man is waiting for his fiancée. You need to talk to Peter before anything or anyone else."

"Yes, sir. You're right." Her voice dropped.

He patted her hand. "Everything will work out for the best. It always does, Katydid."

"Do you believe it will?"

"I do. God will make a way if it is His will."

Scott started the car again and continued home in silence.

Her chest hurt with every breath.

***

Peter paced in front of the large fireplace at Grace Meade. His brow reflected sweat beading across his forehead.

I need to wrap this thing with Catriona as quickly as possible before I see Scott. All of these months of hard work... it's falling apart. If she is not planning to marry me, how do I make this work? If Scott finds out that I have lied to him and about Franks, I'm dead; not only in my profession, but my future in the Senate will be over too. What am I going to do? I can't go to jail. Damn Franks!

He looked up at the large painting of Lillian hanging above the mantle. Her kind eyes met his, and he almost vomited. Speaking to the portrait as if she could answer, he said, "Forgive me. You were never part of my plan. I don't know what to do."

He heard Catriona call out. "Peter? Are you here?"

"In here, darling. I'm in here."

Peter met her in the foyer and saw Scott standing next to the car parked out front.

Scott's phone rang, and he answered. "Hey, Jamie. What's up?" Scott waved.

Peter greeted her with a kiss on the cheek.

She whispered, "We need to talk."

Taking a deep breath, Peter closed the front door behind her, then entered the living room. "Let me start. Please, Catriona... will you sit?"

"Only if you'll join me."

"I think I would prefer to stand."

"Okay, if you must." She sat across from him.

"I've been thinking about us."

"About us?"

"No, wait... please... let me finish and then you can say whatever you wish. I'm not sure where to start."

"That's easy. Start from the beginning."

"Oh, Cat." His voice cracked as he continued, "After much thought, I'm afraid I can't marry you."

Her eyebrows shot upward. "Why?"

"Hear me out. I've realized I have been unfair to us both. I have pushed you into marrying me with no consideration of giving you time to grieve for your mother, and I apologize. My intentions were good, but all the same, self-serving. I saw stardom and thought only of myself. Please forgive me."

"Peter, there is nothing to forgive."

"Let me continue. In my own way, I thought I loved you and made plans. I have failed you and myself. I know you don't love me. In all honesty, I need to respect myself enough to not trap someone into a marriage."

Catriona's eyes saddened. "Please do not make this easy for me. If only I had been honest when you asked. I led you into believing we were more than what we were. I'm sorry too."

Turning his back to Catriona, he looked up at Lillian's picture and swallowed hard. Sirens could be heard in the distance. Peter turned to face her. "I don't have much time. Just listen. I… I lied about us sleeping together. You were sick, that is all." His face grew pale as the sweat continued to bead across his temple.

"What?"

"You would have made the perfect Senator's wife. I needed Scott's backing, a partnership… a marriage."

"What are you saying, Peter?" Catriona held her breath as her ears started to ring.

"I acted in haste… got in with the wrong person."

Without warning, Scott burst into the room and grabbed Peter by the throat, throwing him to the floor. "You son-of-a-bitch!"

Peter was gasping to breathe.

"Dad! What are you doing? Stop!" Catriona jumped from the sofa.

"You killed her!" Scott screamed.

Peter was shaking his head as he struggled for air.

"Let him go!" Catriona pulled at her father's arms.

A police siren sounded closer than before.

Cookie ran into the room. "Scott! Stop! What in the world are you doing?"

"It was Peter and Thaddeus Franks. The sheriff has a video of a man stabbing the horse with a cattle prod. He killed Lillian!" The veins in Scott's temple were bursting with rage. Catriona and Cookie pulled him away. Scott stood over him with fists drawn when Catriona stepped between them.

"It was an accident. Right, Peter?" Catriona's shocked expression spoke volumes.

They heard the sirens pull in front of the house.

He lifted himself upright while clutching his throat. He coughed, trying to recover from the attack, shaking his head in denial. "It wasn't me."

Police officers ran into the living room.

Catriona asked, "What did you do?"

"I didn't kill her. It was Franks and his hired goon."

Scott pushed the women aside and tried to reach him again, but the officers stopped him as another grabbed Peter and pulled him to his feet.

Cookie said, "I don't believe it."

The officer interrupted. "It's true. Sir, are you Peter Tramwell?"

"Yes, I am." The officer handcuffed him. "I am arresting you as an accessory in the murder of Lillian Rose McKenna." The officer continued to read him his rights.

Scott said in disgust, "You will rot in jail before I'm finished with you."

Catriona's mouth gaped open as she watched them escort Peter into the foyer.

"Wait," she said.

"Yes?" The officer turned, as did Peter.

"I won't be needing this." She removed the ring from her finger and placed it in his suit jacket pocket.

"Goodbye, Cat. I am sorry."

Catriona slapped him across the face.

"Ma'am. You cannot touch him," the officer said.

Peter said, "It's okay." He looked at her with shameful remorse, then turned away.

The officer asked Scott, "Sir, are you in control of your emotions or do I need to restrain you longer?"

He replied as he straightened his jacket, "No. I'll be fine."

The officer allowed Scott and Cookie to follow.

***

Back inside, silence dripped from the rafters like thick syrup from a maple tree. Catriona shed no tears as the patrol car pulled away. Looking up at her mother's portrait, Catriona turned and ran from the room. She pushed the kitchen door open as she sprinted into the garden and ran up the hill toward the family cemetery to Lillian's grave. It was covered with now faded flowers. The wind was blowing through the trees, pulling at the last leaves still hanging on with what little strength their small stems could gather. It was quiet. The horses were grazing in the distant field below as the evening air was turning cooler.

She broke the solitude of silence with sobs. "He stole you from us, Mother. Stolen for the greed of money and power. He fooled us all... even you... stolen."

She wept for what seemed hours until she could cry no more. Tears from years of pain and losses. Tears that would continue for months and years to come. Tears of cleansing away the past and fears of the unknown future.

The afternoon expanded into evening's light. Long shadows cast from the western line of trees as the departing sun no longer provided warmth. She shivered in the cold.

Raising her head, she said, "Thank you, Mother, for watching over me these past years. I'm sorry I didn't tell you. The last few days have been terrifying, but the past is no longer hidden in the shadows. I'm no longer scared. It has taken twenty years, but I have come into my own. However, I did take my time, didn't I?" She sighed. "You must know I've decided to take care of Grace Meade for you. I'm not sacrificing anything for anyone either. The Feather Quill will continue, but my role will be as a silent partner only. Who knows? Maybe I'll sell the company to Tia. I cannot picture myself anywhere but here now."

She did not see him walking up the path toward her. He stopped within hearing distance, not wanting to disturb.

"Dad can keep doing what Dad does. I will take care of him, and I will be happy. That infamous McKenna intuition is more right, than wrong; isn't it? However, there's one thing missing. I should say one person missing who would make everything perfect." Catriona bit her lower lip. "It's Declan, Mother. I love Declan. In the beginning before he and I met, Dad said you trusted him and I would too. He's gone and I don't know how to get him back." She cried through her words. "You taught me how to run a business and I can run Grace Meade alone, but I don't want to manage it alone. Peter was a farce and a killer. I need Declan because he will make Grace Meade a better place. I need him for me too. Maybe Samuel will ask him to return home."

"Why ask Samuel when you can ask him directly to his face?"

She turned. Declan was standing inside the gate. At first, she thought he might be another mirage, but this time, the image didn't fade.

"Scott told me you left this morning."

"I did; however, when I stopped at the main intersection in town, I could not imagine driving into my future without this special girl at the center of it. I turned back to fight for her. Besides, I once said I would never leave unless she asked me."

"Really? You think I'm a special girl?"

"I do."

Her voice broke with emotion. "How were you going to fight for her?"

"Well, my plan had two parts. First, I would beg Scott for my job back, which I did, and he told me there was still a place for me here. He hired me on the spot only minutes ago."

"He did?"

"He did."

"So, what is the second part?"

"I planned to fight Peter."

"No, you were not." His answer made her laugh.

"Not physically, but fight for you in other ways. I told Scott I was going to try, but then he told me about Peter's arrest... what a nightmare. I guess I missed my chance, huh?"

"Maybe."

"Scott also said he saw you running in this direction a couple of hours ago."

"He did?"

Declan nodded. "So... do I?"

"So, do you what?"

"Do you think I have a fighting chance?"

"For what, Mr. O'Connell?"

"Of winning the heart of the woman who will run this estate."

She bit her bottom lip and pushed her hair behind her ear. "I don't know. The lady would need to interview you first."

"Interview me?" His eyes opened wide.

"Yes. I have had my fill of dishonest men. Are you an honest man?"

"I am." His lips curled into a smile.

"Are you a hard worker?"

"The hardest."

"Do you know anything about horses?"

"Everything."

"Would you take advantage of your boss?"

"Never... unless she asked me." He grinned.

Catriona ignored the remark and continued. "Do you love Grace Meade?"

"I do."

She hesitated, then bit her lower lip.

He asked, "Is there anything else?"

"Do you think you could... love me?"

"I do love you, Catriona."

"You do?" She dropped her head.

"I do. With every breath I take, I love you." He took a step toward her. "Please, I need to see your face."

She raised her tear-filled eyes to meet his.

"Catriona Elizabeth Harrington-McKenna, will you be mine forever?"

She could only nod her head in agreement as tears streamed down her face.

"Well, then. Don't stand there, Miss Estate Boss Lady. Come here."

She ran into his arms and buried her face into his chest. "Oh, Declan. I love you. I've always loved you. I don't want to live another moment without you."

He lifted her chin with his hand and looking into her blue eyes, he asked, "Do you want to live at Grace Meade... and with me... a Tennessee boy?" He laughed.

"Are you asking me to beg, Mr. O'Connell?"

"I would never ask you to stoop so low, Miss McKenna." He then kissed her deeply. Holding her close, he whispered, "You will always be safe with me."

# EPILOGUE

"HOW LONG HAVE you been married, Mommy?"

"Almost fifteen years," Catriona answered, handing the basket of flowers over to her.

"That's a long time."

"Yes, it is."

Interrupting her sister, the red-haired little girl kneeling next to Catriona screamed in delight, "Hey, Mommy! I see my name! I see my name two times!"

"Those are your grandmothers, Lily Kate."

"They have my name!" She ran toward the kitchen, searching for Cookie to share her discovery.

Catriona placed the flowers at each headstone and smiled, but it was a sad smile all the same. "I miss them."

She stood and turned. Declan smiled back at her.

"So do I. Grandpops would have loved that one for sure."

"He would have loved them all."

"No doubt." Declan laughed.

Catherine Rose, donning the Dunne family's blue eyes, moved to the bench next to the iron fence and continued her line of questioning. "Daddy, when did you know you loved Mommy?"

"Oh, that's easy, sweetheart. She was wearing powdered sugar on her chin."

Catriona said, "Ignore him. He fell in love with me the first moment he saw me. I believe you blushed."

"I've never blushed!" he replied, winking over at their interrogator.

Catriona laughed. "Yes, you have. When you introduced my beautiful Angel, you blushed when all I said were two words... thank you."

"Yes, your mother is right. I did blush." He winked at her again.

"How will I know when I find my husband?" Catherine asked.

He said, "You are a little young to be thinking about husbands, aren't you?"

"Daddy! I'm almost nine. It's never too early." She answered in the same spirit as her mother.

Catriona wiped her forehead with the back of her sleeve. "Let me share the same advice my momma, Katie Jo, shared with me when I was your age. She said, 'Honey, I want you to grow up to be a woman who is independent and free-spirited. I also want you to be the kind of woman who can survive on her own without a man, but when you find a guy who won't let you, then that's when you marry him.'"

"Is that right, Mrs. O'Connell?" Declan laughed again.

"That's right."

"Catherine, listen to your mother. She is a smart woman." He kissed his wife on the cheek.

A dark-haired boy appeared at the entrance, looking as black Irish as any in his family before him. "Hey, Dad, Grandpapa Scott said your horse is ready to go. Are you ready to ride?"

"Always. I'll meet you by the stalls in a few minutes."

"Okay. Don't take too long," he shouted as he ran back on the same well-worn path.

Declan reached for Catriona's hand. "You coming?"

"In a minute... you go ahead. You know how he hates to wait."

Declan watched his wife kneel next to another grave. "Are you okay?"

"I'm fine; I need a moment."

He nodded as he spoke to the little beauty sitting on the bench. "Come on, Catherine Rose, let's join your brother."

"Yes, sir." Catherine took Declan's hand as they walked out of the cemetery together, talking about whatever fathers and daughters discuss, both laughing and enjoying one another's company.

The cemetery grew quiet. Gentle breezes blew the voices upward from the valley as Catriona looked toward the stables. She could see her son and daughters gathering for the annual kickoff of the summer camps. She had made a promise long ago to help make the world a better place, and together, she and Declan had worked hard to do so. In her mother's memory, the Grace Meade estate transformed each summer to include programs for burn victims and children who suffered from PTSD. The program included riding lessons and building self-confidence for those who had lost their way.

Catriona spoke aloud as she walked in front of Lillian's headstone and began pulling the random weeds poking through the earth surrounding its granite base.

"Mother, I miss you still. You would be proud of your family. Dad loves the grands. He retired after the miners won the compensation coming to them, but he's probably already told you. I wish I could say Declan's life has been easy living with me, but it's been hard as we continued working to clean the fragmented remnants of a nine-year-old's mind. We have made it through the tough times... the miscarriages too, but God has blessed us with children. Finally, there are no more psychiatrists... and not for a while. I permitted myself to forgive those who did not deserve my forgiveness. I feel nothing but pity. Forgiveness has been my greatest release from the past. Our lives have plenty of dents, but we're happy and our lives are full." She paused and allowed the words to rush over her. Closing her eyes, an extraordinary peace descended as she released a sigh.

She placed the pulled weeds into her basket and moved over to her parents' graves. She continued her conversation as if they were sitting on the bench across from her. With great reverence, she asked, "Momma, how did I get so lucky?"

It was then Katie Jo's words came floating back in the whisper of a forgotten memory.

"My sweet Katydid, always be thankful for what the good Lord has given you."

"I am, Momma. I am."

She could not help but bow her head. She whispered, "Thank you."

Following Lillian's murder trial and remembering her family's Christian legacy and courageous examples shown throughout her lifetime, she surrendered everything fully to God. Preacher's words remained true. She could see God had given her a life of abundance and never failed her even when life had proved too difficult to remember. He walked beside her through the pain, the suffering, the sorrows, and the greatest of joys while holding her hand daily.

Turning away, she strolled out of the hallowed ground, but not before glancing back once more at the loved ones who were waiting for her on the other side of Glory. She smiled and closed the gate behind her.

A tiny voice came up the path to greet her. "Come on, Mommy! Come on!" Lily Kate had returned to gather her.

"I'm coming, Sugar… I'm coming."

The End

ACKNOWLEDGEMENTS

This journey began seven years ago, yet I did not walk this path alone.

Thank you, Butch, for loving me through this crazy dream we call life. You still make my heart skip a beat. Thank you for your tireless support and for keeping the laughter alive for forty years.

Thank you, Ethan, Lydia, Tyler, Eden, Kera, and Mike for simply being. You are my inspiration for rising to face the world each and every day. You are my heartbeat and endless encouragers.

Lydia, your incredible photography and graphic prowess are amazing. You understood my vision and designed my book's cover to reflect the story within.

Kera, I cannot thank you enough for helping me with my marketing needs. You are a rock star.

To my incredible friends: Vicki, Mark, and Richard, where do I begin? Thank you, Vicki, my confidant and proofreader. Without your willingness to act as a sounding board whenever I called, texted, or emailed, I would have given up long ago. I could not have made it without you. Thank you, Mark, for your endless words of encouragement through what appeared to be an unending task. You lifted me when I needed it most. Without both of you providing your invaluable perspectives and acting as my beta readers, this book would not have seen completion. Never have two given so much to a friend with no expectation of anything in return. Thank you, Richard, for the workday treks to the cafeteria and your ever-listening ear and excitement shared of what could be. I owe each of you my unfailing love and gratitude... how can I ever repay? I guess I should start with dinner.

Thank you to all of my friends and family members who have dropped hints, pushing me to take this unfathomable ride. Small words render BIG dreams. I am forever grateful.

Thank you especially to the women in my family who have served as unwavering mentors throughout my life through their examples of incredible strength, faith, love, endurance, and sharing their stories and talents with me. I am blessed beyond measure to have been reared and influenced by Southern women from the hills of Tennessee. Without you, I would not be who I am today: Edwina (my incredible mother), Nancy Maud, Fannie Jane, Neva, Dot, Edna, Iva, Jennie, Lizzie, Rosie, June, Odell, Anita, Mary Ruth, Josephine, Helen, Johnnie Ruth, Patsy, Joan, and Evelyn.

Thank you, Daddy, for training me under your unrealized tutelage the subtleties of weaving a good story.

Most importantly and with the highest degree of praise, I thank you, my heavenly Father, for loving me despite all of my shortcomings and unbelief. Without Jesus Christ, we are lost. May all who come behind me, find me faithful.

Stephanie

MEET THE AUTHOR

STEPHANIE G. SEWELL considers herself blessed beyond measure. Throughout her professional career of working in the corporate world nearly forty years, she has worked shoulder-to-shoulder with incredible mentors - many who have influenced her without their knowledge. Never satisfied with a stagnant life or unreached potential, she is constantly reinventing herself. Her latest ventures include learning the piano and creating a children's book series.

Most importantly, she is thankful to her heavenly father for His tender mercies and incredible blessings - her family is everything. She is proud of her Appalachian heritage and life's guidance of her family elders.

Currently, she lives in West Georgia with her talented husband where you will find them renovating their seventy-year-old home and four acres of gardens they lovingly call Oakstone.

Blessed with three beautiful children, their spouses/significant others, and one perfectly gorgeous granddaughter, their lifelong ambition is to celebrate life to its fullest, surrounded by family and friends, with faith in God as their anchor. She enters the world of writing with her debut novel, Beneath the Kudzu.

Connect with her at www.sgsewell.com and on social media @authorsgsewell.